The Rise of Serge and the Fall of Leo

By Jules Lucton

Published by Word on a Whim

www.wordonawhim.com

ISBN 978-1-909118-00-3

Acknowledgement

Thank you Julz for creating Serge.

1

Introducing Serge

A long-limbed young man sits on the floor cross-legged, gazing through the patio doors into the back garden. The sun's rays highlight the luscious waves of his golden hair and his blue eyes are as pure and clear as the summer sky. His skin is flawless; his features noble. He has perfect posture and well-defined muscles. He is beautiful.

The doorbell chimes without interrupting his meditation.

"Serge! *Serge!*"

His mother's voice is calling. Eventually he stands and walks out to the hallway with the poise and casual grace of an athlete.

"Oh, *there* you are! Dominic has come to see you again."

The handsome face contorts into a lopsided grin and he shakes the proffered hand too hard, for too long. "Allo Nobidic!"

Dominic examines his hand with a frown. "Let's try shortening it to '*Dom*' shall we?"

"Dom," Serge repeats gravely. "Arwee goin' out today, Nobidic?"

Serge has learning difficulties, and that's not to say he struggles with algebra or quadratic equations. Serge was born into a family of solicitors; 'Freeman & Freeman.' Serge's father, Alistaire, and his Uncle Theo who is Alistaire's older brother, are partners in the firm, and Serge's older brother Leo joined them as an employee after graduating from Oxford with a first class honours Law degree.

Alistaire is convinced that Serge would have joined the family firm had it not been for the incompetence that had surrounded his birth. In Alistaire's mind, there is no such thing as fate or misfortune. Any accident that happens is always *somebody's fault*.

Apart from a tendency to be self-absorbed and sometimes withdrawn, Serge was learning *without* difficulties up until the age of four when he was admitted into hospital for a routine operation to correct a squint. The squint was the fault of the medics who delivered him. Seemingly reluctant to become a member of this society, Serge had been dragged kicking and screaming into this world with some sort of sucker on the top of his head and forceps either side. Alistaire had decided *not* to take action against the negligence that had resulted in the squint, since the negligence – or rather the *squint*, could be corrected when Serge was four … and corrected it was; leaving his youngest child destined *not* to become a solicitor but a '*client*' or a '*service user*' – depending on which particular party of professionals was knocking on his door on this occasion.

This time Alistaire had decided to sue and finally found a firm of solicitors with no conflict of interest – that is no family connections, however tenuous, and had won what seemed back then to be a tidy sum to be invested in a trust to provide financial security for Serge, to fund any future care needs that might arise.

Evidence suggested that Serge had suffered hypoxia during his squint-fixing operation, causing damage to the hippocampus – the area of the brain used for laying down new memories. In other words, his oxygen supply had been temporarily cut off and no one had noticed.

Serge's mother, Judith, hands Serge's kit bag to Dominic.

"Flask?" says Serge, anxiously. "*Flask!*"

"Won't be a minute," says Judith apologetically to Dominic, and quickly returns with a green plastic flask. Serge's face lights up and then relaxes as he cradles the flask and strokes its smooth hard plastic.

"Tea, I does, likes my tea," he mutters and heads happily towards the car, whilst Judith confides discreetly; "I only put water in it. He thinks it's tea, but don't worry, it normally comes back unopened."

Dominic smiles reassuringly. "Don't *you* worry, Mrs Freeman, I'll look after him."

Judith stands waving in the doorway for quite some time whilst the car remains stationary. She lowers her arm to rest it, and peers anxiously through the passenger window. Serge is fastening his own seatbelt … in his own time. "See, dunnit look!"

"Well done, Serge!" Dominic sticks his arm through the window with a thumbs-up gesture to Judith, and she begins to wave again as they finally drive away. Serge's legs are long and relaxed and Dominic is uncomfortable about having to touch his knee each time he changes gear.

"Arwee goin' out today, arwee?" asks Serge, yet again, then suddenly notices the world rushing past him, realises he is in transit and clutches the dashboard. "Aye!"

"We're going to the Leisure Centre, Serge, to have a look at the gym. Your case manager, *Reggie*, would like us to enrol there … to become members and to follow a fitness programme." Her proper name was Regina, but Serge *insisted* on making the obvious gaffe, just as he did when he tried to say Dominic. It was uncanny - he had to be doing it on purpose – it only ever happened when the name could be made more … *interesting*. Perhaps … just maybe … Serge was an unusually intelligent being, with extraordinary capabilities, who had chosen to play some sort of game with the rest of the world. He glances sideways at Serge, whose stunning blue eyes are gazing obliquely at the sky, and is disturbed to find him so attractive. Dominic comes from a small place up north where any man who openly admires the good looks of another man is considered 'queer'.

Turning his thoughts to today's mission, he frowns at the idea of enrolling for a fitness programme. It is no more than a case of being seen to be doing. He used to enjoy running and wouldn't object to taking it up again. It would be far easier simply to tolerate Serge jogging alongside him rather than subscribing to a gym but no; Regina required a membership card and receipts to go in her *bloody* case file.

Dominic glances again at Serge, who is now watching the street scenes travelling past him. “Okay there, Bud?” That’s another thing – he is employed as Serge’s ‘Buddy’. What the hell will that look like on his CV? It will have to go down as ‘support worker’. Not that he should complain about the job title – it was good money for a holiday job – twice as much as your bog standard ‘care worker’ would get – and at least Serge could wipe his own backside.

Serge eventually responds. “Oim orwight fanks!” Serge likes to watch the people on the streets. “She’s got big tits ainer? An’ that one’s got knickers all up ‘er cwack. Arwee nearly there yet?”

“Not far now, Serge. Left here … round this corner … up this little road … and here we are!”

“Nice ‘ere, innit?” Serge pauses in the foyer, his eyes scanning the new environment and settling on a familiar emblem. “Toilet!” He lowers the elasticated waistband of his new jogging bottoms; extracts his ample manhood and holds it poised ready to go. Dominic ushers him swiftly through the doorway.

A nice lady introduces them to the sports and leisure facilities. “The swimming pool has been improved recently, with a gentle slope at the shallow end.” They pause to appreciate the pale blue ripples, just as the aqua-natal class comes to an end. Serge is open-mouthed as whale-like women emerge and Dominic glares at him – willing him to shut it without commenting, but this time Serge is absorbed and almost lured, not by the women but by the patterns on the water’s surface. Finally they coax him away and recommence the tour.

“Corr! Look at that!” bellows Serge. He points with one hand at a group of women performing bending exercises in leotards, whist involuntarily resting his other hand on his crotch. Heads are turned.

"I'm Serge's support worker," announces Dominic loudly, blessing the sea of faces with a polite smile.

"I'll show you the gents changing rooms," says the nice lady, steering them away from the aerobics class. "Of course, I've never been in there myself, but you two can feel free to have a look around."

Dominic obligingly puts his head around the door and says, "Very nice!" with unfortunate timing for the lone male occupant who stands naked in the middle of the room.

They make an appointment for an induction session and retreat to the car. Serge looks back but the building has disappeared from his view. "Nice place innit? And a nice laydee. But they got them daft bikes wot don't go nowhere …"

Serge's father, Alistaire has decided to sue again. Share values have plummeted; property prices have rocketed and the cost of care is increasing rapidly. The trust fund is unlikely to yield enough for Serge's future care needs if the time comes when his parents are unable to support him. This time Alistaire is suing the solicitors who originally sued the medics responsible for that ill-fated squint-fixing operation. He has hired neuropsychologists to perform tests to localise the specific area of the brain dysfunction, and these tests have strongly indicated that, in addition to hypoxia, Serge has suffered frontal lobe damage – the sort of damage that results from a blow to the front of the head.

Was Serge allowed to fall from the operating table? Was he dropped? Did heavy equipment hit his head? Alistaire makes it his mission to expose what happened that day to cause his son's behaviour thenceforth to be so utterly unveiled and spontaneous; sometimes delightful and sensitive, but more often excruciatingly inappropriate.

2

Serge and Franchesca

Serge has a sweetheart called Franchesca. She is a fellow 'service user' who attends the same Day Centre as Serge. Judith used to struggle to coax her son aboard the minibus when it arrived to collect him on a Wednesday morning. "I ain't goin' on there wiv all them lot," he would protest. "Nutters, ain't they?"

Then, one day, the doors of the bus had hissed and parted, and his anxious blue eyes had been met by Franchesca's clear, vacant gaze. Serge had stood transfixed, until Marj, the minibus escort, gently ushered him to the seat beside her. "Come on and sit here, Serge, next to Franchesca."

"Hello, Fwan … Fwan-fing," he had said, and her huge, dark eyes had lit up with the sweetest of smiles from beneath her thick, brown fringe of hair. Serge was enchanted. "You got nice eyes, ain't you?" She had lowered them, shyly. "An' you got a nice nose … and nice lips ..." She was still smiling. "An' you got nice teeth." Now he was admiring her well-developed chest. "An' you got nice tits an' all." He noticed that her waist was a bit pudgy, and her hips and thighs looked broader than he might have preferred, but decided it would be impolite to say so. Instead he reiterated; "You '*ave* got nice tits!"

Her down-turned eyes were concealed by thick lashes and her healthy, round cheeks were flushed, clashing with the pink tee-shirt she was wearing. Serge suddenly realised she was examining his flask. "Hey, cup of tea, does you? Serge'll share it with you. Even got yer own cup look. Thissuns got two cups on it."

Escort Marge intervened. "Please don't open that as we're going along, Serge, else you'll spill it. We'll all have a nice cup of tea when we get to the Centre."

"Wants coffee today, I does," Serge had replied.

Now it is summer, and student holiday time. Serge has Dominic as his full time 'Buddy' so he has not been to the Day Centre for the last two weeks. Sometimes, lately, a feeling has come down upon Serge … a feeling that is new to him – a feeling that he does not recognise.

Today, as he stands in the back room, looking through the patio doors to appreciate the different shades of green that blend together to form his back garden, Serge is beginning to identify the source of this new feeling. He steps out into the garden, kneels down in the grass, and begins to search for a four-leaved clover. In the past, this would have occupied him for hours. Today he has no patience with the project and sits back, cross-legged to watch the trees swaying in the gentle breeze. Ralph, the Irish Wolf Hound, sits beside him and licks his face. Serge drapes an arm over the dog's broad shoulders, leans against him and sighs.

Now the sound of his mother's voice is approaching and his heart begins to glow … but still he is incomplete. She is talking to that nice man who has been taking him out in the car these last few days ...

"I don't know what's the matter with him, Dominic. Normally he's such a happy soul … but suddenly he's lost his sparkle. Maybe you could find out what's troubling him?"

Dominic steps through the patio doors and sits cross-legged before Serge, mirroring his position. The grass is damp and he shifts uncomfortably and now Ralph ambles towards him, head lowered to investigate with his nose.

Serge frowns and says; "Whatyer sitting like that for, Nobidic?"

"That's a very good question, Serge." Dominic uncrosses his legs with some difficulty and limps over to a garden bench, frowning as the huge dog follows him, sniffing noisily.

"D .. D – *Dom*?"

Dominic leans forward excitedly. Serge is attempting to say his name *properly*, which smacks of intimacy and trust. "Yes, Serge?"

"Dom … When is Furzday?"

"Tomorrow."

"Tomowow. Like not *today*, but *tomowow*?"

"Yeah, you've got it!"

Serge is looking thoughtful, and resumes his hunt for the four-leaved clover. Finally he holds up a small bunch of clover leaves. "My sister Beatie says there's no such fing as a four-leaved clover. She said I was stupid spending all day looking for wun cos I'd never find wun. So now I've gone and made wun. Lucky innit? Make Serge's wish cum true, that will!" Serge gazes at the distant willow as it sways in the breeze.

"Serge," says Dominic softly. "What are you wishing for?"

"I dunno." Serge appears confused for a moment. "Now I remembers. It's in me flask."

"In your flask. In your tea flask?"

"Aw, yes pleez, if you're doing one. Two sugars today pleez. *Plea*-eze!"

Dominic sighs; steps back into the house, and finds his way to the kitchen, humming a little tune as he goes, so as not to take anyone by surprise.

Judith is sitting at the kitchen table with a flowery box of stationery and an address book. She stops writing and greets Dominic with a sweet, motherly smile.

"Sorry to interrupt, but Serge would like a cup of tea," he says apologetically. "I'll do it. Would you like one?"

"Yes, why not. I'll show you where everything is. I don't expect he's drunk the last one yet – he seems to like to have a cup of tea beside him for ... for emotional support – in the same way that some flask or other has to go everywhere with him."

"Ah, the flask! Was there anything in it the last time you emptied it?"

"Yes, warm water, the same as I always put in it, and he hasn't caught on yet."

"Is that all? Only he mentioned his flask, and I imagined he was giving me some sort of clue …"

"Oh?" The kettle clicks itself off and Judith makes the tea herself, automatically, thinking hard, her eyes wrinkling at the corners. "Well, there was a card … you know – a sort of business card – they have a variety of them at the Day Centre."

Dominic nods. "Hoists, electric beds, protective underwear …"

"Yes ... There was one in his flask – underneath the cup. Sometimes he hides things there. I didn't take much notice of what it was advertising. Now, what did I do with it?"

Judith shuffles a pile of junk mail, rifles through the bits of paper beside the telephone, then lifts the upper half of a ceramic hen. "That's the one!" she says brightly, then looks puzzled. "'Riding for Special Needs'. Is that what they used to call 'Riding for the Disabled'? It's difficult to keep up with the correct terminology. Serge has never shown much interest in horses." She shrugs her shoulders and puts the card on a tea tray with two mugs. "There you are, Dear. See if you can find out what it's all about. And here are some chocolate Hobnobs – his favourite. Do you like them too? There's a packet of plain digestives if you prefer … or ginger nuts."

"Chocolate Hobnobs are my favourite too, Mrs Freeman. Thank you."

"That's the wun!" says Serge, excitedly, when he sees the card.

"So, what about it then?" Dominic waits to be enlightened.

"Eh?"

Dominic picks up the card and holds it in front of Serge's face. "What does this mean to you?"

Serge turns his face away. "Noffin."

Dominic has forgotten that Serge cannot read. "Sorry Bud. This is a business card to advertise a place that does horse riding for the … for people with …"

Serge becomes animated. "Fwanny! Fwanny goes there on a Furzday. She goes there an' 'as a wide, an' then she 'elps 'em wiv the 'orses." Serge looks away into the distance and mutters, "*Likes* Fwanny, I does. Anyway …"

"Would you like to go to this horse place … these riding stables … tomorrow? I could make a phone call and see if it's okay for us to call in."

"Yes pleez," says Serge, excitedly. "Wants to see Fwanny, I does." Extracting five chocolate Hobnobs from the packet, he adds; "Not goin' on no futtin 'orse though. Not me … *not Serge*."

At the riding school, Serge spots Francheska immediately in her orange fleece. She is grooming the left buttock of a chestnut pony with repetitive strokes, her lower lip drooping as she sweeps the brush down and then raises it again. The pony's expression mirrors hers as he shifts his weight over to one hock, sighs heavily, and resumes his afternoon nap. Serge wants to go straight to Francheska but someone insists on showing them all around the stables. Finally, he is free to join her. Without interrupting the rhythm of her brushstrokes, she looks up and meets his gaze. A beam of pleasure transforms her face as she recognises him.

"Ello," says Serge, politely. She opens her mouth as if to respond, but closes it again, still smiling. Serge pats the pony's neck. "Nice 'orsey, innit? Ain't you goin' to brush 'is uvver bum cheek? You've been doin' that wun since we got 'ere. Gonna wear anuvver 'ole in 'is ar-"

"Serge, is this your friend, Francheska, who you were telling me about?" Dominic steps in swiftly, just as a bored looking girl with long fair hair and sun glasses closes the book she is reading, yawns, slides down off the fence, puts on a smile and says; "Have you finished grooming the pony now, Francheska?"

Francheska nods and offers her the brush, but she refrains from touching it.

"Put it back in the tray if you've finished with it." The pretty young woman is making an effort to sound encouraging whilst Dominic notices that her hands are soft and smooth with long, painted nails, and her training shoes are clean and white, apart from a layer of fresh dust from the stable-yard. She is not a stable girl.

"Hi, I'm Dominic … here, as Serge's …" Dominic struggles with his official term of 'Buddy'. "I'm Serge's friend." *Oh no, that sounds wrong.* "I mean he's my *mate* …"

She takes off her sunglasses and grins at him. "You're Serge's '*Buddy*', right?"

"That's the one!"

Her green eyes sparkle prettily. "I'm Sabrina … employed for the summer as Franchesca's 'Buddy'".

"Aw, that's nice, innit?" Serge is captivated as Dominic and Sabrina eye each other up. Franchesca observes the scene, wordless as always, still holding the body-brush she has finished with. Serge suddenly recalls the purpose of this visit and returns his attention to Franchesca. "Shall Serge put that away for you?" She hands him the brush and watches as he fixates in rearranging the contents of the grooming tray to allow sufficient space for the brush to fit in without it touching any of the others.

Finally, he is satisfied and stands up straight beside her. "There. Dunnit. Look!"

Franchesca shuffles sideways to be closer to him, lowers her eyes and says, "Fankoo" in a voice so soft that only Serge can hear.

3

Digging

Serge is at home in the back garden, watching the flowers growing. Derrick the gardener has planted some seedlings, telling Serge they will grow in *no time*. Derrick has just mown the lawn, which pleases Serge for there is no need to look for four-leaved clovers, since there is no longer any clover at all, anywhere.

He is vaguely aware of the sound of a car turning off the road, into the driveway, approaching his house. *Visitors*. Serge continues to watch the flowers growing.

A small but curvy young woman with cornflower-blue eyes and thick blonde hair steps through the back garden gate. Serge leaps to his feet excitedly. "Beatie!" He loves his sister. "Cuddle, Beatie." She greets him with a hug and he runs a large but gentle hand over the smooth hair that tumbles down over her shoulders.

Their mother joins them. "He hasn't seen you for a while, Darling. He misses you. We *all* do."

Ralph bounds over and forces the weight of his body against Beatrice's bare legs, nearly knocking her over, then stretches up his neck to try to lick her face. "Ralphie misses you too, Beatie," says Serge, but shoves the dog away as he sidles round behind his sister's short skirt. "Bugger off, Ralphie; Serge knows your game."

Beatrice has recently moved into her own flat in central London, only eighteen miles from the family home, but much of her time is spent away with Geoff, a short, bald multi-millionaire who has employed her as a personal assistant to sit looking gorgeous on his yacht as it bobs about in various harbours along the south coast. She ducks out of her brother's embrace but clasps both his hands in hers to hold his attention. "Serge."

"Yes, Beatie?"

"Serge, do you remember my friend Sally?"

"No."

"Yes, you do. Me and her used to go out on a Friday night and share a taxi back here. Then she'd watch TV with you on the Saturday morning. Curly dark hair … and you always liked the pretty silk scarves she wore."

"Oh yeah, I remember. Nice lady. She was nice to Serge. *Very* nice. Gave Serge one ... of 'er scarves."

"Did she now? Well, she was hoping you might give her a hand."

"Uh?" Serge looks doubtfully at his hands.

"Yes. She lives in a house with a patch of grass at the front that's big enough to park a car. She can't always get a parking space nearby, which makes it difficult if there's any amount of shopping to carry especially with little Sam running around – he's three now, and a bit of a handful. She's got permission from her landlord and has bought a load of gravel but being a *single mum* she can't afford to pay anyone to do the work. It's just a matter of digging out the turf and some of the soil and then spreading the gravel. But she needs someone big and strong to *do the digging*. And we both thought of *you*."

"Serge likes digging. Do it today, I will. Do it now. Come on, hurry up!"

"Just let me sort out some old clothes for you," says Judith. "Fill his flask would you, Beatrice, there's a Dear."

Indoors, Judith lowers her voice to speak to her daughter. "I could hear him in the bathroom chanting your phone number this morning. He knows it off by heart, and he also knows when you're at home hiding behind the answering machine. I *know* he's hard work on the phone, but he only phones *once a week ...*"

Beatrice nods guiltily. It is true that when she is genuinely unavailable, Serge's voice on the recorded message will say; 'Beatie gone out today', whereas if she is simply not in the mood for his phone call, he is more likely to say; 'Beatie don't want to talk to Serge today'. "How does he *know*, Mum?"

Judith shakes her head. "There are some things he just *knows*."

Beatrice is racing back to Sally's house in the little red Porsche her boss bought her as a *five years' service* gift. Serge is clutching his flask in one hand and clinging to the passenger seat with the other. "Arwee nearly there yet. A*r-wee*?"

"Not far now, Serge, nearly there," says Beatrice in the calm little *Serge voice* she has picked up from her mother. Suddenly noticing the stationary traffic ahead, she brakes violently - then accelerates sharply as it starts to move again.

"*Too scarewee*!" wails Serge.

"Am I really that bad?" Beatrice resolves to dedicate more attention to her driving style, as well as to her brother.

"Here we are now. This is Sally's street. You see how difficult it is to park? Perhaps we can get into this little space?"

"*No, Beatie, no!*"

"Urm ... perhaps you're right. We'll try and find a space further along."

Beatrice knocks on Sally's door. Sally opens it with her three-year-old son sitting on her hip. He is blond and beautiful with huge blue eyes.

"Aw, you're a nice lickle boy, ain't you?" says Serge.

The child closes his eyes and buries his face in his mother's neck. Beatrice is stricken to see that Sam is the image of Serge when he was a tot ... and closing his eyes when feeling shy had been one of Serge's little traits.

"Say hello," Sally coaxes her son, and Sam reaches out towards Serge, and says, "*Daddy!*"

"He calls every bloke 'Daddy'," says Sally but seems slightly flustered as she allows Serge to take the child in his arms. She hurries away to the kitchen. "I'll put the kettle on if you can watch them for a minute."

Serge strokes Sam's back briefly and then lowers him to the ground. "Are you goin' to 'elp Serge wiv the digging, *are you*?"

Sally returns from the kitchen and Beatrice frowns at her. "No wonder you were so keen to establish that Serge's disability was *acquired* and not *inherited*," she says angrily. "Serge! Mark out a space where Sam can dig so that you don't hit him with your big spade. No, not near the road – up here by the front window."

Sam clutches his little red bucket and seaside spade and waits whilst Serge marks out a small rectangular plot just in front of the window. He cuts away the turf from the top as easily as if slicing the crust off brie then jabs his spade around to loosen the soil beneath. "There now. You stay 'ere and do your digging. Keep away from Serge's big spade and keep away from that road. There's some cwazy drivers out there. *My bluddy sister* for wun!"

Serge steps over to the edge of the plot nearest the road and begins to dig in earnest whilst Sam proceeds with the excavation of his own territory, muttering "*bluddy sister*" as he works.

Sally and Beatrice watch from the front room. "Please don't be angry with me," says Sally. "I did feel guilty afterwards, although he seemed to enjoy it as much as I did. I was surprised to find he was *capable.* I knew him well enough to know that alcohol doesn't really agree with him but he was *up for it* - my God, he was! But then he probably didn't even remember the next morning what had happened." She smiles and blushes. "In the morning I snuck off whilst he was still out of it. Only I couldn't find my knickers – my little black lace Friday night variety. They must have been in the bed somewhere, but I was afraid of waking him if I went rummaging around too much, so I went off without them. I've often wondered whether he discovered them, or whether your Mum or one of the house keepers found them whilst doing the bed ..."

Beatrice looks out of the window to hide her smile. "Mum's never said anything about it to me ... but then she wouldn't. Just look at the two of them together – they look so natural." She turns back to face Sally. "You know my Mum and Dad are pretty well off. I'm sure they'd be delighted to help with their first grandchild. Mum would love to be a Grandma, but she'll be lucky if I come up with the goods for a while yet ... although I think Leo and Bridget are getting broody."

"Are they? You know, I never thought their marriage would last. They're both such strong characters."

"You're not the only one who thought that, but Leo appears to adore her so much that he just backs down all the time."

"Really?" Sally sounds disappointed.

"Yeah! You know Leo has a reputation for getting his teeth into something and not letting go? Like he's *never* lost a case he's worked on, he's like *so determined*?"

"Yes, I've heard how successful he is."

"Well, *she* gets on the phone wanting him to do something and he just drops everything, putting her first the whole time. I sometimes think she does it on purpose if she senses he has something important going on. Like she hates to think he's got his mind on something other than *her*."

"The *bitch!*" says Sally vehemently.

"Yeah, she is a bit," agrees Beatrice, wondering why Sally sounds so bothered. "Anyway, Mum and Dad would hate to think of you claiming benefits for *their grandson*. And it's not right, is it, to be claiming when the family can afford to pay?"

"No!"

"*No what?*"

"No. We're happy as we are, me and Sam." A short silence. "Don't look at me like that, Beatrice! I wanted a kid, okay? Sam is the best thing that ever happened to me, and I hope he might have a little brother or sister – now he's three it would be a good time to have another one – but there's no-one on the scene. So, as soon as Sam starts school I'll go back into teaching, and then I won't embarrass you any more by *claiming benefits*. Okay?"

"I don't know, Sally. I've always shared everything with my Mum. And I think she filters the news, like, and then passes some of it on to my Dad."

Sally looks alarmed. "You won't tell *anyone*, will you? *Especially* not your parents!"

Beatrice looks out again at Serge and Sam. "I guess not. It would only hurt them, wouldn't it? To know that they had a grandson but they weren't welcome to see him? What do you intend to tell Sam when he's older and asks about his father?"

"The same as I told the benefits office … that Sam is the result of a wild night out in Corfu and I don't even know his father's name. That's exactly what I intend to tell Sam."

Beatrice opens and then closes her mouth and finally storms out through the front door. "Come on Serge, we're going home."

"No Beatie. Serge is digging. Me and Sam ... doing *digging*, we are."

Serge has already shifted a third of the turf with five inches of topsoil and hasn't even begun to perspire.

"Get in the car. We're going home. Now!"

Serge is resolute. "*No* Beatie. Serge is *digging*. Bye-bye Beatie. *Bye*. Ta-la!"

Both his hands are firmly clutching the spade handle so she grasps his forearms and is surprised by the breadth of steely muscle. "Come home with me, now, Serge."

"No Beatie, Serge ain't finished digging yet."

Beatrice gives in and retreats to her car, telling him; "I'll come back later and take you home in time for tea." She blinks away hot tears as she accelerates away. She shouldn't have left her brother there, with just Sally and Sam, but he is so much bigger and stronger than her, and, much as he loves his sister, Serge is not used to having to take notice of anything she asks him to do.

Childhood memories flood her mind – scenes of her father wrestling to hold her little brother still when he was having one of his 'episodes'. The outburst usually only lasted about five minutes, but during that time Serge was like a thing possessed, with super-normal physical strength and the repercussions would last way beyond the event. When it was over he would seem tired and confused, with no memory that anything had occurred. Finally, the doctor had prescribed Serge's 'magic pills' and these frightening scenes had receded into haunting memories, but Beatrice still wonders what might have happened just now if she had tried to force him away from his digging.

Later she returns to take him home for tea and finds the parking space completed – but Serge is guarding it and refuses to let her park there. He shakes his head, muttering, "Not messing up my gravel," and she is forced to drive on and find a space down the road. As she walks back to Sally's house, Serge is on his hands and knees, picking around in the gravel with a finger and thumb. He smiles happily as she approaches.

"I can't believe you've done all this today!" she exclaims, her tone filled with praise. "*And* you've put all the old soil in the skip. Well done, Serge."

"Serge swept the path an' all."

"So … what on earth are you doing now?"

Serge is arranging bits of gravel in rows, starting from the front and working back towards the house. "Done that row all in grey. Thissuns brown, look."

Beatrice looks closely and can see a fine mosaic emerging from the gravel patch. She shakes her head in disbelief and eventually coaxes him back to her car by reminding him of the chicken pie that Mum is cooking for his tea and mentioning that Sally is about to ruin his artwork by driving her car all over it.

"Spect she will an' all, the bitch," he says abruptly, and gets in the car. "*Anyway …*"

The twitching curtain in Sally's upstairs window does not escape his notice and he winds down the window and waves goodbye.

"Did … have you fallen out with Sally?" asks Beatrice, thinking it strange that she hasn't shown her face to thank him.

"No."

A silence.

"Well, I expect you'll be ready for a nice hot bath after all that hard work." Beatrice pulls a face and opens the window a little further to let some fresh air in. "You did very well today, Serge."

"That Sally wanted Serge to 'ave a bath in 'er 'ouse … but I couldn't."

"Did she *really*? Why *couldn't* you?"

Serge tuts and rolls his eyes. "Because I didn't 'ave me dark blue towel, of course! And she only 'ad pinkuns … or light blue and then she told Serge that she'd already run the bath and it was a shame to waste the water and that lickle boy was asleep … so would I scrub 'er back …"

Beatrice waits for him to go on but he is captivated by the flashing yellow lights on a breakdown assistance vehicle. She prompts him. "And did you?"

"What?"

"Scrub her back?"

"No." He cranes his neck round to watch the yellow lights disappearing into the distance. "Didn't *scrub* it, cos that would've 'urt. So Serge just sort of *wiped* it a bit. But I didn't futt 'er."

"You didn't *what?*"

"That Sally. Serge ain't stupid. She just wanted a good futtin. But Serge didn't give 'er wun. Not today, fank you!"

Beatrice feels this is probably the time to drop the subject. It would be far too nosey to pursue it just for the sake of hearing the details. "Why not?" she hears herself ask.

Serge turns to his sister, surprised by her lack of understanding. "Well, it wouldn't be right, would it? Wun day, I'm goin' to futt Fwanchesca. Not just yet, cos Fwanny ain't weady for it. She might not even know wot *futtin* is."

His sister's face is very pink and she fixes her eyes on the road, for a change. Serge gazes into the distance and murmurs; "Wun day, Serge'll futt 'er."

4

Beautiful and Free(man)

Dominic and Sabrina have organised a picnic for Serge and Franchesca. Dominic has packed a flask of tea and some chocolate Hobnobs in his rucksack, then remembers his petty cash allowance and stops at a garage to buy an assortment of sandwiches and drinks from the chilled food cabinet.

Sabrina, as Franchesca's support worker, has no petty cash allowance but has made some cheese sandwiches and packed them in a cool-bag with a jar of value pickle and a six-pack of Savers crisps.

After a long and arduous quest, a small patch of the countryside has been discovered that is acceptable to both Serge and Franchesca. Dominic and Sabrina flop down on the grass, relieved and exhausted, wondering why this particular spot is in any way superior to the rest of the land that their respective charges have rejected.

"Wants a cup of tea *now*, I does," says Serge, and then rephrases his demand in a slower, more emphatic voice; "Serge *will* have a cup of tea *now*." As an afterthought, he adds, "Plea-eze!"

"It's my fault," Dominic apologises. "I've been teaching him positive affirmations."

"You've been teaching him *what*?"

Dominic twists off the various levels of flask and pours Serge's tea. "No-one else will want any of this – it will be far too sweet."

"Fwanny want a cup o' tea?" asks Serge.

"Cup o' tea, I does," squeaks Franchesca.

"I stand corrected," says Dominic.

"*Two* cups on that flask," Serge points out, and Dominic carefully hands the second cup of sweet tea to Franchesca. She takes it and moves closer to Serge, pressing her shoulder self-consciously against his. "Watch where ya futtin spilling it!" he bellows.

"So, what's with the positive affirmations?" asks Sabrina, when the hullabaloo has died down.

"Oh … I was trying to teach Serge some NLP techniques."

"NLP?"

"Neuro-linguistic programming." Sabrina looks blank so he frowns intelligently as he tries to recall the definition he has learnt. "NLP is constantly evolving …"

"You mean you can't say what it *is*?"

Dominic becomes a little flustered. "It's … it's a set of observation-based theories resulting from the examination of the structure of behaviour and communication – from the examination of all subjective experience …"

"*Really*? Sorry I asked." Sabrina smiles, feeling superior over Dominic. She asks herself yet again what it is about him that she finds so attractive. When she is alone he is all she can think of. Now that they are together, she wonders why.

"Okay … I was attempting to teach Serge how to use language with greater precision in order to achieve his goals. It didn't turn out as I'd expected – but hey, that's life." He smiles at her and she smiles back, remembering suddenly what it is that she likes about him. He shakes his head and looks away.

"What's up?"

"Nothing."

In a poor imitation of Serge, Sabrina affirms; "Sabwina wants to know what's up *now*!"

Dominic laughs. "It's just … every time I attempt to explain to anyone what it is that I'm studying, it just … basically, it sounds like *shite*. And it reminds me of my Dad …"

"Right, so your Dad's an NLP practitioner?"

Dominic laughs ironically. "Quite the reverse! My family, '*Up North*' … it's not *quite* a flat cap and a whippet, but Dad's worked for the same firm for thirty years and drinks at The Working Men's club every Friday whilst Mum goes to Bingo with Auntie Marj. And I think it embarrasses them when people ask what it is that I'm studying, '*Down South*' and they have to admit that they don't really know."

He returns his attention to Serge and Franchesca. Serge has made a daisy and buttercup chain but is struggling to join it to form a necklace.

"Hey, allow me," says Sabrina. Serge finally gives up and hands it over to her and she makes the necessary incision in the stalk; shoves the daisy head through, and passes it back to him.

He receives it with a happy smile and kneels up to put the necklace over Franchesca's head. She looks down at it resting on her chest and blushes delightedly.

"Oh, isn't that *sweet*," says Sabrina, and extracts her mobile phone to take a photograph. "Hey, that's cool. I'll download it and print a copy for Fran's Mum."

Serge is feeling left out. "Oi! *And me, Serge*. Serge likes 'is picture taken an' all …"

By the time Sabrina has outlined him in the viewfinder, Serge's attention has been captured by a group of young women riding past on mountain bikes. Regardless, Sabrina takes the photo and shows it to Dominic, brushing his hand lightly as she passes him the phone.

"You know, that's a *really good photo*," he says.

Sabrina re-examines the image. "You're right. Not only is he gorgeous, he's very photogenic. Hey, Serge, let's have another piccie!"

Serge grins at her obligingly and again she captures the moment. "No, that's no good." She frowns at her mobile phone. "You've got to catch him unawares, when his attention's on something else. That's the secret. Hey, Serge, look at that squirrel!" She waits whilst he locates the squirrel, then his mouth closes and he watches its activities with fascination. She takes his photograph and reviews it. "There you go again. *Skill*. How cool is that! Hey, I wonder … my summer project … could I use Serge for my summer project?"

"*Use* him?" Alarm bells are ringing with Dominic about what Serge's family, and Regina, his case manager might think. "What exactly *is* your summer project?"

"We were given a choice of titles we could interpret however we wanted. The one that appealed to me was 'Beautiful and Free'. *And here he is …*"

Sabrina is still gazing lovingly at Serge's photograph and Dominic becomes irritated. He employs some of the techniques he has learnt in an attempt to combat the feeling but they don't seem to work. They are, after all, techniques he has memorised from his reading, and none of his own making. He returns his attention to Sabrina. "So, what exactly are *you* studying?"

"Uh? Oh, sorry … Commercial Art and Photography." She puts away her phone to give Dominic her full attention. After all, she *is* talking about *herself* and he does seem interested. "What you were just saying – about disappointing your parents and letting them down by ..."

"Well, I wouldn't go so far as to say I'd *let them down*," Dominic interrupts tetchily but instantly regrets his snappy tone.

Sabrina frowns. "I'm sorry. I was about to say we had something in common." She turns away huffily. "All right, Franchesca? More sandwiches anyone? I expect Serge will go for seconds."

"Yes pleeze, Shagina, 'ollow legs, I got."

Dominic leans forward attentively. "So, what makes you feel that you let *your* folks down?"

"Well I only let my Mom down in a very *small* way by not becoming a *model.* That's what Mom did, you see. She was a professional model when she was a bit younger and she thought *I* had the makings of a model …" She pauses long enough for him to look her up and down and nod appreciatively then resumes; "She took me to her favourite photographer – a guy who'd done her a *wicked* portfolio … and she left me with him. He asked me if I *really wanted* to become a model. And I said *no.* He said it was just as he thought and it was impossible to get a good picture if the subject was uncomfortable or unwilling ..."

Dominic is anticipating some traumatic disclosure and is preparing to employ the counselling skills he has learned. He formulates his next sentence carefully and precisely. "What was it, Sabrina, that you were unwilling to do?"

"Well, it just made me realise that I didn't wish to become a model. *That's all.*"

Dominic leans back and folds his arms. "So, you simply decided to study Commercial Art and Photography, instead of becoming a model?"

"Yes, that's right. After a long talk with Lloyd – that was Mom's photographer – he helped me to realise that my interests *did* lie in graphic art, but the difference between me and my Mom was that I had an *eye* for a good picture – instead of merely *being* a good picture. I saw it as a step up from being a model but Mom saw it as a step down." After a pause, she adds; "In other words, I'm better use *behind* the camera than in front of it."

A whole thirty seconds' silence later, Dominic clears his throat nervously and delivers his chat-up line; "But you've still got a great body … behind … or in front of the camera."

"Yes, I know that, but my choice is to be *behind* it," she insists, and moves away to sit next to Franchesca to help her to make a dandelion crown for Serge. It looks magnificent balanced on the golden waves of his hair and Sabrina is obliged to take more photographs. She examines the results and gasps; "He simply *must* be the subject of my project. *Nothing* would compare … not after *this!*"

Serge, rising to the occasion, says; "Serge likes 'aving 'is picture taken." He juts out his chin slightly, points at a passing pigeon, and says; "Do anuvverwun, Shagina! There, that's a gudden, innih?"

Sabrina examines the captured image, then looks back at Serge and shakes her head slowly, in awe. "*Wow*, I don't believe this ..."

Dominic looks at the photo and has to agree that Serge looks great. "But if you want to include him in your project, you'll have to get clearance from his sister."

"From his *sister*?"

"Yes, his sister, Beatrice. According to Serge's mother, she's suddenly come over all protective of him. I met her the other day and she seemed to be checking me out … *What, exactly is your role with Serge?* She was all suspicious and standoffish to begin with … then she softened and started telling me some tale of how a friend of hers had taken advantage of Serge. I didn't get the full story – but there was something about a car parking space that he was digging, after the friend had stayed over … after a drunken night out."

"Right, well, I guess I should approach his sister. What's her name again?"

Serge has realised they are talking about him and his sister. "Beatie! Beatie, 'er name is, *my sister* …" He begins to chant a series of numbers, merging them together as he becomes more animated.

"Hey, that's a Central London number he's quoting," says Dominic.

"*Beatie's* futtin' number!" qualifies Serge. He rolls his eyes; "Keep up, will yer!"

"I'll phone her now!" Sabrina begins to punch the number into her mobile. "Or perhaps it would be better if you spoke to her, Serge? It would be difficult for me to explain who I am."

Serge frowns and peers at her curiously. "Who *are* you then?"

"I'm Sabrina, of course! I am a student, and I'd like *you*, Serge, to be the subject of my summer project." She thinks for a moment and adds; "And you *have* expressed an *interest* in being my subject. But for some reason, I have to get your sister's permission. So, since you're willing, maybe you would have a word with her?"

Serge nods, wisely. "You do the phoning and Serge'll do the talking." Eventually, he is able to repeat the number more slowly, and Sabrina succeeds in entering it into the phone.

"Shit, it's an answering machine."

"Beatie at work," pipes up Serge. "Mobile Beatie!" He begins to quote her mobile phone number. Incessantly.

"Blimey," says Dominic, burying his face in his hands. "I don't even know my *own* mobile number, never mind anyone else's!"

Sabrina rolls her eyes at him. "That's because all your contacts are stored in your phone, so you don't *need* to remember them. Say it again, Serge. If she answers I'll hand over to you …"

Beatrice is sitting in the elegant foyer of a hotel, waiting for Geoff, her boss, to finish his meeting with a financial advisor with whom he is discussing a potential investment. The mobile rings in her handbag, growing in volume until she presses the button and Serge's voice booms; "Ello Beatie!" Heads are turned as his voice resonates from the phone.

"Hello, Serge." Beatrice employs a hushed tone, hoping to influence her brother's decibels.

"Ello Beatie!" he shouts back.

Beatrice frowns. *And my mother wonders why I don't like talking to him on the phone.* "Are you okay, Serge? This isn't your usual telephone time."

A short silence. "W - what time is it, Beatie?"

"Half past two."

Serge turns to Sabrina, Dominic and Franchesca and informs them, "Half past two, it is ..."

"Shall I have a word?" asks Sabrina. Serge hands her the phone and Sabrina launches into an explanation about her summer project, ending with; "So I was hoping I could use Serge as the subject of my project." *Oops!*

"*Use* Serge?"

Damn, I used the Use word. "Well … he seems very willing."

"No, I'm sorry but I don't think so."

Serge takes the phone from Sabrina. "Beatie!"

"Yes Serge."

"Beatie. Serge *likes* 'aving 'is photo taken. Okay?"

"No, Serge, I don't think you should let her …"

"Beatie! Serge *wants* to be Sabwina's summer pwojection!"

"Let me think about it, Serge. I'll phone you back. Rather I'll call this number later and speak with whoever answers it."

"Shag*ina*'s phone!"

"Er, *right*. I'll call back later. Bye for now!"

Geoff returns from his meeting looking pleased with himself. "What's up with you?" he asks jovially. "I pay you to look drop-dead gorgeous and there you're sat with a face like a smacked arse!"

"Oh, it's my little brother," she sighs, and Geoff heads off to buy a small vodka for her, a large vodka for himself and a bottle of tonic to share.

Geoff has a deep interest in other people's families and their problems, for he has no family of his own, or, more accurately, no family member he is prepared to acknowledge. Geoff adores Beatrice and is happy to pay her a fortune to do little more than provide seat cover for his expensive car or boat … or like today, to accompany him in a taxi and wait around whilst he attends an important meeting. Geoff has tried dating agencies but has been disappointed; the experience teaching him that owning a beautiful house with the best interior design and kitchen appliances that money can buy is not enough for some women.

He sets down the drinks on the table and wishes he could smoke his cigar here like in the *good old days.* He decides it is time to bestow some attention on Beatrice – to do something she will appreciate. After all, when she finds a more interesting job and leaves him he wants to be remembered as a good and understanding employer. It is almost a pity that her parents are well off. He wouldn't have minded sponsoring her brother in some way – after all, a charitable donation would not only save him some tax but would make Beatrice feel ingratiated towards him.

Suddenly he realises this same Beatrice is earnestly relating some story and sits forward with his head tilted in order to appear to be honouring her with his undivided attention. As he listens to the tale of how some student has beguiled Serge into thinking he wants to be a super model, a smile of satisfaction spreads across his face. "I've got a brilliant idea, Bea; you're going to *love* this one."

Beatrice waits for it … she doesn't usually love Geoff's *brilliant ideas*. She knocks back the vodka in one inelegant gulp. "Go on then, what's the crack?"

"Well, Bea, you must have noticed I've lost a couple of pounds since becoming a member of that new health club?"

Beatrice *hasn't* noticed but she runs an eye over him - his short stature demanding only the subtlest of eye movements. He appears the same as ever but she nods to humour him and wonders what Geoff's alleged weight loss has to do with Sabrina's summer project. She smiles, encouraging him to continue.

"Thing is, Bea, having reduced an inch or two around the midriff, I need to revisit my tailor to get some new suits made." He swallows his drink and a barman immediately appears with another one. "Cheers," says Geoff. "*Blimey*, anyone would think they was spying on us. As I was saying, Bea … that brother of yours is the classic male model figure … and the trouble I find with my tailors – all of them – is the samples they have in the shop are ready made to fit fellas like your brother. So, I'm getting there Bea, cutting to the chase, I am … why don't you bring him along to one of my fitting sessions? This student type can bring her camera along and take photos of the perfect stud modelling my suits." Geoff smiles with satisfaction. "How does that sound, Bea?"

"Well … *yeah*, I guess so, if that's all right with you." Beatrice flashes her teeth as a smile at Geoff but frowns inwardly. Much as she loves her brother, she hadn't envisaged taking him to work with her.

True, she had felt very protective of him after Sally's revelation … but answering his weekly phone call and allowing him to talk for up to twenty minutes *max* is her idea of fulfilling her duties to her brother. At least that's how she feels at this moment ...

Geoff is pleased with his plan and is ready to leave the hotel but Beatrice needs to make a phone call first. She returns the last call received on her mobile from … what was her name … Serena?

Sabrina answers the call sounding far too young, fresh and happy for Beatrice's liking. "It's about this idea of my brother assisting with your summer project," says Beatrice, frostily. Sabrina starts to make enthusiastic exclamations and Beatrice holds the phone away from her ear. *Kids*. "Look, I'll discuss the matter with my parents, and I'll speak to Serge about it when he phones on Sunday – but … I guess, basically, it should be okay."

"Oh, thank you Beatie!" says Sabrina. "Serge *told* me you were wonderful."

Beatrice ends the call and rolls her eyes.

"*Now* what are you frowning at?" asks Geoff.

Beatrice switches on her most dazzling smile. "Nothing, Geoff. I'm looking forward to spending some *quality time* with my little brother."

5

Medipacs

Serge's mother, Judith taps gently on his bedroom door … then taps again.

"El – lo," he says, languidly.

She goes in and is relieved to find him playing on his Play Station – one of his favourite pastimes. "Hello, Darling, how are you feeling now?"

"Oim orwight." He continues to stare at the TV screen. Judith follows his gaze and sees the rear view of a cyber-woman in shorts, oscillating gently, with what sounds like monks singing softly in the background. It is a familiar scene and therefore comforting. She sits on the bed and places a hand on her son's forehead, as she has done on so many occasions over the last twenty-seven years.

"Beatrice phoned. She was worried because you always call her at the same time every Sunday … but today you didn't … and she mentioned a '*project*' that the two of you were going to talk about." She sweeps her hand over the thick golden waves of his hair, wondering if he even realised it was Sunday. "Do you know what day it is, Serge?"

"No."

"It's *Sun*day – the day you always phone Beatie."

"But … but we 'as Yorkshire pudding on a Sunday."

Judith inhales sharply – a cross between a laugh and a sob. "You *did* have Yorkshire pudding, Darling. I made an enormous one and you ploughed your way through *most* of it."

"Oh? Well, if it's Sunday, phone Beatie, innit?"

Judith smiles. "I told her you would return her call."

"Phone Beatie …" Serge begins to chant his sister's phone number as he makes his way downstairs. As he reaches the phone the chanting ceases. "Goin' to do the number for Serge? Plea-eze!"

Judith presses '#2' to call her daughter and hands the phone back to Serge when it starts to ring out.

"Okay?" asks Beatrice. "I thought there must be something wrong when you didn't phone at your usual time."

"Yeah …"

"Is there something wrong then?"

"Yeah … no … Oim orwight."

"Yeah? We were going to talk about this summer project that some friend of yours is doing?" Since moving to her own flat and broadening her circle of friends, Beatrice has adopted that style of speech where every statement sounds like a question, doing away with clarifying indicators such as 'weren't we' or 'isn't it'.

Serge yawns. "Futted up me Medipac, Beatie."

"They've changed your medication again?"

"Naw … futted it up, that's all."

"Mom there?"

Serge returns the phone to his mother and trudges back upstairs. "I'll bring you a cup of tea in a minute," she calls after him.

"*Tea*, I does," murmurs Serge, and returns to his room to find that Lara Croft, left unattended, has been defeated by the bats in the cave. "*Bugger*." He restarts the game and the monastic chanting recommences. Serge conquers the bats, wins a Medipac for Lara, then sits back to enjoy the peaceful cave scene. On days like this Serge prefers not to venture beyond this level. Consequently, he and Lara have spent many hours together in this little cave listening to the monks, whilst the latest Play Station given to him for Christmas by his brother Leo remains in its box, unused since Christmas Day.

Downstairs, his mother is still talking to Beatrice. "Yesterday evening, he heard the clock in the hallway strike nine just as he came out of the bathroom, so he went back in and took the pills from the bathroom cabinet. Alistaire was just on his way in there, didn't realise Serge was putting them *away* and gave him some more. Meanwhile, I'd nodded off on the sofa; woke up

with a jolt at twenty past nine and went and gave him *another* dose. I phoned Doctor Ramage – you know how *kind* he is - he said not to worry too much owing to the size of him. So, your brother's been rather sleepy and out of sorts today … and I feel *awful* about it."

"Mum, it's not your fault."

"Whose fault *is* it then?"

"Nobody's. It's just one of those things."

"Thank you, Darling ... " Judith's voice wobbles a little. "I only wish your father could see through your eyes now and again … "

"Dad's blaming *you?*"

"No, no … but you know what he's like – hell bent on blaming someone for everything. He's been so wrapped up with suing all and sundry to *'ensure that Serge is financially secure when his father is no longer around'* that the *silly man* might just as well not be around right now!"

"Mum, *don't* get upset. Dad's *always* been focussed on his work … it's just that in other cases he doesn't bring it home with him."

Judith swallows and takes a deep breath. "Sorry, Darling, yes, you're right. It's just been a funny sort of day and your father's incensed by some medical report that's just come through –"

"A *medical report*. You're saying Dad's *ill?*"

"No, no, it's yet another report about your brother's condition. It's no wonder the medical profession is so over worked."

Beatrice checks her watch and frowns. This phone call is starting to eat into her night out. "Listen, Mum, there's some student wanting to photograph Serge wearing designer clothes. Geoff's prepared to allow everyone to tag along on his next tailors' appointment. I'll phone back soon to arrange a date. *Love you! Bye!"*

Judith returns to the sitting room where her husband is frowning over some document. "Darling, I *do* wish you'd put that away!"

Alistaire removes his glasses and peers at his wife intently. "I suppose you realise they're trying to make out that he's simply *autistic*?"

"*Simply* autistic? That's a contradiction in terms! I'm going to put the kettle on … tea or coffee?"

"Don't give me '*tea or coffee*'!"

"Very well; do without!" Judith begins to retreat to the kitchen.

"Wait!"

She halts in the doorway whilst Ralph the Wolfhound, who hates raised voices, attempts to hide beneath a coffee table. The table tips over, propelling a cup and saucer against the fireplace where it shatters. The dog yelps with fear and Judith clutches the door frame as he attempts to bolt between her legs but finds her too short and eventually leans to the right.

Alistaire, practically oblivious, merely raises an eyebrow. "Just listen to this!" He lowers his voice and quotes; "Serge's autism is evidenced by his intense attachment to particular objects for no apparent purpose and his fascination with repeated sounds or occurrences and his *obinterest* with arranging things in patterns or lines." Alistaire glares at his wife. "*Obinterest*. You *know* what *that* means don't you?"

"Of cour-. Well, no, I don't … it's the first time I've ever heard the word."

"It *means* they called it an *obsession* in the first place but then attempted to tone it down to *interest* but were insufficiently competent to cover their tracks! What it said in the first place was; 'Serge has an *obsession* with arranging things in patterns or lines.'"

"Well, it's true, isn't it?"

Alistaire sighs. "Maybe, but it's *irrelevant!*"

"Are you saying that the *truth is irrelevant?*" Judith realises Serge is standing at the foot of the stairs, wringing his hands and shifting from one foot to the other. Ralph joins him, cringing and shaking whilst wagging the tip of his tail ingratiatingly.

"Tea, pleez, if ya doin' wun. Plea-eze!"

His mother strokes a stray curl back from his forehead. Serge unclasps his hands to mimic the caress on the fretful dog, stroking back the hair that veils his eyes.

"I'll go and put the kettle on," says Judith.

6

Justin Beaver

Dominic has been worrying about Serge's appointment in Central London; driving around the suburbs being sufficiently challenging for a driver of his inexperience. He is daunted by the prospect of locating Serge's sister's boss's tailors' shop and has been quietly blaming Sabrina for setting him up for this. Now, as he approaches the same traffic island for the fifth time, he wonders how come everyone else seems to know which lane they should be in when he *doesn't.*

"Aye, steady on Nobidic," says Serge, clutching at the dashboard as Dominic is forced into yet another sharp right hand turn.

"Sod you, Sabrina, and your *stupid* summer project!"

Serge shakes his head. "It ain't Shagina's fault that you don't know yer way around 'ere, so don't you go blaming 'er."

Dominic frowns at his reluctant passenger and his one-second loss of concentration is almost the abrupt end of their journey. *I didn't think you were capable of such rationale – isn't that why I'm here now having every one of my nerve ends stretched to breaking point by you?* He takes a deep breath and exhales a mantra; "Om mani padme hum …"

"Yeah, that's right, innit?" Serge responds brightly and begins to hum a monotonous melody.

Dominic looks at him sharply, but the handsome face is blank. "I can see the flipping building over there! You see that place with the big green sign? It's the one next to it … but how the hell you get there is beyond me!"

"Flipping building …" repeats Serge, and then tries it again with a different intonation; "*Flipp*ing *build*ing." He lowers his voice a couple of octaves and enunciates "*Flip*…ping *buil*…ding," so eerily that Dominic snaps at him; "For goodness sake, *shut up!*" He feels a pang of guilt as Serge falls silent.

They drive in circles a while longer until Dominic can bear it no longer. He pulls over and stops behind some illegally parked cars and switches off the ignition.

"I'm sorry, Serge, I didn't mean to shout."

"*Shouting*, that was …" Serge is disturbed – he doesn't like it when people shout.

"The thing is, Serge, I'm getting stressed out because I keep seeing the fu- the fli- the building we want … but it doesn't seem possible to drive anywhere *near* it!"

"Why don't we *walk* there? Both got feet, ainwee?"

"That's an idea. Only we can't leave the car *here*."

"Why not?" Serge points to the row of cars in front of them. "They have."

"Quite true. Perhaps they know something about the local traffic wardens that we don't. Serge, how do you feel about living dangerously for once and risking a parking ticket? Bearing in mind it'll be paid for out of petty cash if we get one"

"Yeah … Serge is 'aving 'is photos done today. Come on, *quick!*"

On foot, they reach the appointed tailors' shop within minutes. Dominic hesitates near the entrance, wondering whether Geoff and Beatrice have arrived yet and begins to formulate his introduction in case they haven't. Serge peers in through the window and, after a short pause, a smartly dressed man peers politely back at him.

"Bit posh, innit?" says Serge.

"That's the general idea. So, where the bloody hell's Sabrina?"

"Oi dunno."

"I'm here. Sorry we're late," says Sabrina coldly. "We had trouble finding somewhere to park."

Serge smiles at Franchesca and she lowers her head, shyly, until her eyes are concealed behind her thick fringe.

The polite man inside the shop is by now regarding the people huddled on the doorstep with suspicion. “Come on, we’d better make ourselves known.”

The polite man fixes his smile as they filter through the entrance. He surveys them individually and settles for the tall good-looking one. “Good morning, Sir. Welcome to ‘Braithewaite and Comfitt’. May I be of assistance?”

Serge shakes his head. “Oi don’t *fink* so.”

Dominic steps forward. “We’re here to meet Beatrice Freeman. I believe her boss, er … Geoff … has an appointment with you.”

“*That’s* my *sister’s* name,” Serge informs Dominic, whilst the polite man consults the desk diary and frowns; “Ah, yes. Mr Geoff Jeffries *was* due at ten o’clock.”

“Well, I’m here now, Chauncey! Didn’t realise you ran such a tight schedule.”

“Oh, good morning Mr Jeffries!” Chauncey, the polite man, turns slightly pink and shakes Geoff’s hand vigorously.

“Ello, Beatie!” Serge hugs his sister too hard, forcing her to employ her usual tactic of pressing her thumbs in the soft spot at the front of each shoulder.

“Aye!” He backs away and Beatrice quickly introduces him to Geoff. “Ello Mr Jeff-Jeff.”

Geoff shakes Serge’s hand warmly. “All right, mate? Just call me Geoff.”

“Oi did, diddun I?”

Geoff guffaws as if a hilarious joke has been made. “Tell you what, Chauncey can measure me up round the back whilst you youngsters have a scout around here for some suits for Serge to try on. I’ve okayed it with Mr Braithewaite for you to have the run of the place for this morning. Hey, speak of the devil ...”

Mr Braithewaite nods his approval at the charcoal grey suit with the silver waistcoat that Sabrina has selected and recommends a white shirt with a fine satin pin stripe. “These trousers are tailored for Mister Average. This gentleman will require a longer length." Serge is ushered to a fitting room and Dominic follows. "May I check your inside leg, Sir?"

"Oi, gerroff!"

Dominic steps in; "Serge, you hold the end of the tape measure in place. Mr Braithwaite needs to know how long your trousers are."

Dominic helps with his tie and cufflinks and the various unfamiliar buttons and buckles. He steps back to take in Serge's new image. "*Wow, just look at you!*"

Serge frowns at himself in the mirror, shrugs and asks; "Is Serge ready to 'ave 'is picture taken now?"

"You most certainly *are*."

Serge is greeted with a gasp of admiration and gazes around to see what all the fuss is about. Sabrina begins to photograph him, managing ten rapid shots before Serge realises what's happening and stares into the lens with a lopsided grin. She lowers the camera.

A small, dark-haired man, flamboyantly dressed, whom Serge does not recognise, is standing beside Sabrina. His eyes are watery and he is breathing deeply and slowly – hands clasped before him. He speaks softly, with a flowery inflexion; "Never *before* have I encountered *such beauty* in the human form …"

"Ello, what's your name?" asks Serge, clutching at the pink crushed silk shirt cuff that emerges from the sleeve of the man's suit.

"Justin Beaver." The little man proffers his hand, grimacing only mildly at Serge's enthusiastic grasp.

Dominic laughs politely, thinking he is joking.

"*Why* do you *laugh?*"

Dominic's ears turn red. "Urm, it's just that I thought you were Italian, and that doesn't sound much like an Italian name."

"Ah, but you see my *father's father* was English. Sadly, my father gave me my name, and then he died, so I never did know him."

Dominic, not knowing what to say next, is grateful that Geoff has rejoined them. "Your old man had a sense of humour, didn't he, Justin?" says Geoff.

Justin shrugs his shoulders. "Like I said, I did not know him."

"Well if he *did*, mate, it's bloody *skipped* a generation! Haw-haw-*haw!*" Geoff pats Justin's shoulder good-naturedly and turns his attention to Serge. "Doesn't our young man look fine and dandy now?"

Justin nods. "I am barely able to withdraw my eyes. I must draw him. *May* I?"

"Do what to him?" asks Dominic, stepping casually between him and Serge.

Serge tenses slightly, giving Sabrina some more good shots.

"Justin is a fashion designer," Geoff explains, "and right now he looks like a man inspired."

Justin walks around Dominic to get near Serge. "*May* I draw you, Sir?"

Serge steps back a couple of paces. "Do woh?"

"Look, I show you." Justin unzips his leather portfolio and extracts sketches of his latest fashion design ideas. "See, you allow me to draw you and …" he mops his brow and dabs his eyes on a handkerchief, "Such beauty as yours will compel me to create …"

After a short but respectful silence, Serge pipes up, "Ainyer got a camera then? Sabwina ull lend you wun."

"No-no-no! I need to take you home with me. Of course I will pay you."

Serge, out of his depth, retreats behind an impressively dressed tailors' dummy and mimics its posture. "Thanks, Serge …" murmurs Sabrina, clicking her camera furiously.

Justin waves his hands in the air and looks desperately from Dominic to Beatrice who look questioningly at each other. He darts a fleeting glance at Franchesca but looks swiftly away as she returns a sweet, pouting smile from beneath her heavy fringe.

"I will pay him, *well*," insists Justin.

"Pay him for *what?*" asks Beatrice, suspiciously.

"For his *time*, of *course!*" Justin looks nonplussed.

Geoff presents Beatrice with a sample of fabric – shoving it closer to her face when she does not appear immediately interested. She remembers who is paying her wages; "Hey, that's exactly your colour. It would suit your personality just *great*," she enthuses, remembering that it is her job to flatter Geoff and feign an interest in his affairs, just as it is Dominic's job to look after her brother. Dominic realises Beatrice is staring at him and looks back questioningly. "You're okay with my brother?" she asks. "You can handle him?"

He nods his head and the buzzwords come to him eventually. "It's all about *empowerment* and *enabling*, you see ..." *Good job I visited that website last night to gather material for the thesis.*

"*Right*, I see what you *mean*," says Beatrice and begins to study Justin's small, soft leather shoes, wondering how much he paid for them and whether he's ever considered hiring a PA, and, if so would he require female or male, and what would be the salary?

Dominic feels obliged to comment. "Urm, well ... if Mr Beaver wants to pay him the going rate as an artist's model, there's nothing to stop Serge earning a living, is there?"

"*Precisely,*" says Justin, with his hands in the prayer position. He inclines towards Dominic. "You are a good man. You know me well. Of course, I cannot draw him in *this* place. I must take him to one of my homes ... to my London flat. It is not far from here. *Please?*"

Dominic is uncertain. "I must check with Serge's parents, and with his case manager. But I expect it will be okay..."

"And of course you must come along with him ..." Justin is beginning to get the picture. He extracts a business card from the side pocket of his portfolio. "Here is my card. Please phone me, *any* time –"

Sabrina butts in. This is, after all, *her* event. "Haven't you got any other suits to try on, Serge?"

"*Oi* dunno."

Geoff pipes up, "Come on, Chauncey! Our man looks like a bloody undertaker. Let's have something a bit lighter if you've got it in his length."

"Yes, Mr Jeffries, I'll examine last summer's range, if the gentleman would like to follow me?" Dominic ushers Serge back to the fitting room, shaking his head as Chauncey adds, "And the gentleman's *friend*, of course."

Serge returns wearing a finely woven, ivory linen suit - the natural fabric moulding itself around his svelte contours.

There is an appreciative silence, broken by Geoff, who inhales deeply and says, "Whooo!"

Beatrice wipes away a tear and wishes her mother could see this.

Sabrina remembers her project, and raises her camera but Serge presents her lens with a protesting palm. "Just a minute, 'old it!"

There is a respectful silence.

Dominic clears his throat. "What's up Serge?"

Serge blinks and waits for the thought to cycle round again. This time he catches and retains it. "Cum 'ere Fwan!" Franchesca scurries to his side and hides her face shyly beneath his arm. Serge strokes her smooth thick hair. "Serge wants his picture taken wiv Fwanny."

"Shit!" breathes Sabrina, disappointedly.

Dominic moves close enough to speak into her ear. "Just take the photos. Fran'll get bored in a minute and move away."

Serge, by now, has coaxed Franchesca into mirroring his happy lopsided smile.

Sabrina grins at Dominic and says, "Where's your flask, Serge?" Her shutter clicks furiously as Serge blesses her with an expression of dignified consternation from every angle.

"Phew!" Sabrina lowers the camera and takes a deep breath. "Intense or what?" She reviews the photos, sharing them with

Dominic, and muttering under her breath ... "*Skill!* Just look at *him*. Shit! I'll never be able to edit Fran out of that one. Urm, I guess I could get away with elongating her and … and maybe superimpose a different head over the top … I could do a self-portrait! Then again, maybe I could get some mileage out of the contrast. You know – 'Beauty and the –'. No, that's no good … Fran's not *that* bad. How about someone old … some wrinkly old hag - my friend Yvonne's mother maybe ..."

"Shhhhh …" Dominic is appalled. He smiles encouragingly at Franchesca and she lowers her eyes, snuggles up to Serge, and smiles shyly at Sabrina.

Sabrina raises her camera again. "One for the road."

7

Model Serge

Dominic consults Serge's parents about the feasibility of him posing for Justin as a model. Alistaire, having always struggled with incentives and aspirations that differ from his own, is bemused by the proposition and mystified by Judith's display of pride and enthusiasm. He grants permission on the basis that having to sit still at someone else's request will be a good discipline for Serge, but tells Judith to ask Beatrice to verify Mr Beaver's credentials with Geoff.

"This Justin Beaver," says Beatrice to her boss. "My brother will be okay going round his flat? Mum and Dad said I'd to ask you."

Geoff spreads his scone thickly with butter, then remembers his diet and scrapes some off. "Justin only wants to *look at* your brother." He stirs his tea, considering the matter. "I've known him a long time, but never heard mention of a girlfriend, *or* a boyfriend. I guess his art is such a passion there's nothing left for sex. Do you think that's possible, for a geezer?"

Beatrice shrugs her shoulders. "I'm not a *geezer*, am I?" She extracts her mobile from her handbag and phones Judith. "Hi Mum, Geoff assures me that this fashion designer who's taken an interest in Serge is to be trusted …"

Dominic pauses to check Justin's directions, turns off the road and steps out to enter an access code in a panel on the wall. The barrier rises and Serge grips his car seat anxiously as they drive down a steep slope to the underground car park beneath the apartment block. Dominic smiles at the man in the Jaguar who is frowning suspiciously and, with more care than usual, parks his Metro in an allocated space beside Justin's Lamborghini Diablo.

Serge gets out of the Metro and stretches. "Smells of piss around 'ere."

"Yes ... you're right. There are thousands of pounds' worth of vehicles down here and security cameras everywhere but yet it smells no different from any other enclosed car park."

Dominic presses the buzzer and Serge takes a startled step back as Justin's voice responds loudly from the intercom. Serge does not like lifts and clutches Dominic's arm as they ascend – releasing it as the doors glide open and Justin is waiting to greet them. He smiles at Serge but stands immobile, fixated by his beauty. Serge returns a blank stare. Dominic fidgets, wanting to step out of the lift, and reports that they found the flat okay, thanks to Justin's helpful directions.

"I beg your pardon, forgive me! My flat is just here – *do* come in." Justin flings open the door and enters the flat whilst his guests halt abruptly in the doorway.

"Take your shoes off, Serge," says Dominic, removing his own and wondering where to put them. Justin's flat is vast and airy with an ivory carpet, sheepskin rugs and a white leather sofa. "Just as well we didn't bring Ralph."

"Ralphie wanted to come with us," Serge informs Justin.

"If Ralphie is your friend, then he is welcome here."

"Yes. Ralphie is my friend. Sometimes Ralphie sleeps with Serge."

"Really?"

"Yes. But 'e got fleas at the moment. Caught 'em off an edjog. So Mom won't let 'im." A white fury cushion on the sofa suddenly expands, revealing itself to be a Persian cat. "And 'e don't like cats."

Justin laughs. "Ah, I see! Now then … can I get you a drink or something?"

"Tea pleez! Tea I does. Nice man, innih? Ay, good cups … *careful* Serge."

Serge explores the flat, trying out the window seat, looking over the veranda, stroking the cat on the sofa whilst Justin stands in the middle of the room and sketches furiously on a large board that he rests on a barstool, revolving around it as his subject crosses from one side of the room to the other.

"Shall I try and make him sit still?" asks Dominic.

"No, no, no, I must capture his movement, his grace, you see?"

Justin has created a montage of Serge in action. Serge examines it with interest, pointing his finger at each sketch in turn; "Walking Serge, sitting Serge, cat-stroking Serge … dunno *what* Serge is doing on *that* one. Good drawer, ainyou? But Serge's jeans don't look like that."

"I draw you in a flowing fabric. I have such garments in my dressing room. Would you care to try them?"

"*More* dressing up?"

"I think you will like these creations. They are unlike the suits you experienced before … and you will inspire me to … to generate more."

"Orwight then, Justin. If it'll 'elp you to jenny-wait."

Justin dabs his eyes with a large white handkerchief as Serge emerges from the dressing room clad in purple silk. He recovers and begins to draw again, attempting to capture the flow of the silk with extravagant flourishes. He steps back and frowns. "And now I make him look like a clown. I need his photographer. The lady Sabrina - is she the only photographer you use?"

Serge nods gravely. "Yes, I don't use any uvvers."

"Can we contact her? Do not worry I will ask your P.A. Dominic, do you have a contact number for his photographer?"

"Urm … yes. I don't know if she has any other engagements today. I could phone her and ask …"

"Oh? Please, *please!*"

Dominic makes the call. "Sabrina? Are you free, Bri?" He risks a glance at Justin and finds he is being stared at … intently.

"Tell her I will pay twice her hourly rate, in addition to expenses, in addition to costs of prints et cetera!" He throws his hands in the air, and then allows them to flop helplessly to his sides. In a quieter voice he adds, "Tell her I need her here now, and I am sending a taxi. It is on its way. Now!"

"You still there? Justin says your taxi's on its way."

"Really? How does the taxi know where I am?"

"Good point! Where are you?"

"At Franchesca's house, just having a coffee and a chat with her Mom and her Nan. I've got my camera in the car boot. Never go anywhere without it. You reckon mine's good enough for what he wants?"

"It takes good pictures, doesn't it?"

"Good enough!"

"The taxi's on its way!"

One hour later, Sabrina arrives with Franchesca in tow. Justin frowns, wondering why Franchesca is here, but decides to let it drop and turns his attention to Sabrina who is rapidly capturing images of Serge wearing an introspective expression and the most sensuous deep purple silk.

"Must get a few shots of him looking drop-dead gorgeous - before he realises what's going on and starts to smile."

"Dear young lady, I recognise how precious is your time, and you must be rewarded accordingly. What rate do you charge for this service?"

"Err-right! … Would forty pounds be okay?" She wonders if forty pounds for the afternoon is pushing it.

"Your hourly rate for such talent? My dear, you sell yourself too small! Your time is worth so much more to me. And of course there are these photographs. I would like large prints please, and I must have the negatives. Expense is not an issue in this matter. He must be mine alone!"

"It's a digital camera. There *are* no negatives. I store them on my computer."

"Then I will buy your computer. How much you want for it?"

"I'm sorry but it's not for sale – I need it for my course work. I can give you a CD with the photos on – you can get as many copies as you want from that."

"But no-one else must have any *copies*."

"Then I'll delete them off my PC once I've saved them on the CD. Will *that* do?"

"I suppose it must ..." Justin shakes his head dubiously and picks up the phone. "Hugo? I require your immediate assistance. You must prepare a contract and bring it to me now!" He mops his brow and adds, in a calmer voice; "If you please."

Serge has turned his attention to Franchesca. Her mouth droops at the corners and her lower lip protrudes in a sulky expression. "Matter Fwan?" he asks, but she shakes her head and buries her chin in her chest.

"She wanted to go riding today," Sabrina explains. "But a couple of the ponies are coughing, so they're resting them, and the others were fully booked." She turns to Franchesca and says brightly; "But we've booked you in for the day after tomorrow, haven't we?" Franchesca, who has no concept of 'the day after tomorrow', continues to sulk.

"Never mind, Fwan." Serge rests his forehead against hers, and lowers his voice. "When Serge is a millionaire, Fwanny'll 'ave 'er own pony. She might even 'ave two … just in case one gets a cough. And she'll 'ave 'er own stables and 'er own field … Just you wait and see, Fwan."

Franchesca's face brightens with delight that quickly fades as she reassesses her immediate surroundings. "Want it *now*, I does."

Justin has removed himself from the gathering and is watching for his solicitor, Hugo Fluck, to arrive. Each time a taxi slows down at the junction beneath the window, he presses his face to the glass then steps back in disappointment as it follows the flow of traffic. *Make haste, Hugo, there is much that could be lost.* He turns from the window to check his prize and inhales deeply, attempting to control the emotions induced by the exquisite scene of Serge sprawling languorously on the sofa with the Persian cat. Sabrina sees his reaction and takes rapid-fire photos.

Hugo arrives and Justin ushers him discretely to the study and closes the door. Sometime later they emerge, Justin looking flushed and animated, clutching a document close to his chest. Hugo is a tall man with thin grey hair, a thick moustache and long bushy sideburns. He assesses the gathered company, frowning over his spectacles as if wondering why so many people are involved in Justin's latest enterprise. His eyes settle on Serge, and Serge stares back at him. Deciding Justin is too preoccupied for formalities, Hugo introduces himself. "Hugo Fluck," he says, without much emphasis on the 'H'.

Serge gets up off the sofa and backs away. "*You* go fu-"

"Serge!" Dominic smiles brightly. "The gentleman was telling you his name." He offers his hand to Hugo. "My name's Dominic. Pleased to meet you, Hugo. Serge, say hello to Mr err …"

"Fluck," says Fluck. "But you may call me Hugo."

Thank fluck for that. "Serge, say '*hello Hugo*'."

"*Hello Hugo*," says Serge, obediently.

Hugo runs his fingers lightly over his hair, checking his comb-over, as he habitually does in uneasy situations. He turns to Justin and lowers his voice to communicate the necessity of altering the contract to comply with the legal obligations when an *interested party* is a *mental deficient.*

Justin and Hugo return to the study for a hurried conference and amendment of the document. When they reappear, Hugo addresses Dominic. "Are you in charge of Serge?"

"Well, I'm his, urm … Buddy."

"His what?"

"His *support worker*."

"I see." There is a long and awkward interval whilst Hugo formulates his next sentence, one of those pregnant pauses that solicitors feel they have the right to impose. He glances around the flat, wishing again there were a few less people milling around. Franchesca is examining the cat to see if it is a boy or girl, and shrieks when Sabrina hurries to its rescue. Hugo waves his document in the air with a gesture of despair, and asks Dominic, "Would you join us in the study for a moment to discuss this?"

"Are you all right with these two for a minute, Bri?"

"Yeah, I guess so," replies Sabrina, wondering what is going on as Dominic goes off with Justin and Hugo.

Hugo Fluck comes straight to the point. "My client, Mr Beaver, is offering your … erm … *client*, Mr Freeman, what is in *my* opinion, a very generous contract. So enfat- … so fixa- … so *impressed* is my client with young Serge, that he is offering *seventy thousand pounds* as an initial payment for a modelling contract, and a generous retainer, on condition that Mr Freeman does no modelling work for any other fashion designer."

Justin clasps his hands against his heart. "So besotted am I, that I must have him to myself. The money is not the object."

Hugo's eye-roll is barely perceptible. "The terms of the contract are clearly stated in this document, but Serge must *sign* the contract. But, erm, owing to his, er-hurm … *mental condition*, we will require a second signature, or else someone to sign on his behalf." He raises his eyebrows hopefully at Dominic, who shakes his head.

"Serge's father is a solicitor. I expect he'll be keen to look over the document and do the necessary."

"Excellent. I'm sure his father will understand the generosity of Mr Beaver's offer of employment …"

Justin is glowing. "And now we must all go and dine together. There is a *bea-u*-tiful Italian restaurant on the Main Street."

"Serge loves Italian food," says Dominic. He returns to the living room and is relieved to find that nothing has happened. "Pizza? Pasta? How about it Serge?"

"*Pizza Shack*, yes *plea*-eze!"

"Pizza Shack? Pah! We go to Raphael's. Money is no object!"

Dominic lowers his voice, a technique he uses to make people listen. "Money is no object to Serge and Franchesca either, but they *like* the Pizza Shack, and I think it would be more … *appropriate*."

Justin tilts his head to one side, as if picturing the present company gathered round a table at Raphael's, and feels inclined to agree. "Pizza Shack, *eccellente*!"

Franchesca leans closer to Serge. "Three ponies, Fwanny wants."

8

Contracted Serge

Dominic does not normally see Serge at weekends, but is anxious to hand over to Serge's father the contract of employment that Justin and his solicitor, Hugo have prepared. Yesterday evening, Alistaire and Judith were enjoying a rare evening out and only Aunt Devina had been there to receive Serge – a lady so coldly polite that Dominic had declined to leave a message. Today, to his relief, Judith answers the door, wearing a pink apron dusted white with flour. She looks hot and flushed from the kitchen and Dominic is taken by surprise by a sudden pang of passion. He opens his mouth, closes it again, and his face colours to match hers. How come he'd never noticed until now quite how lovely she is?

"Are you all right, Dominic?" she asks kindly, and his armpits begin to perspire.

"Yes, yes, yes thank you ..."

"Then would you mind joining me in the kitchen for a moment - I've got something half baked." Dominic follows her to the kitchen where she bends over to check the contents of the oven. "Good, that seems to be rising nicely … Now, what can I do for you, Dominic?"

Swiftly averting his eyes as she straightens up and battling with thoughts he is ashamed of, he does not answer immediately. Judith fears the worst; "Oh, I *do* hope you haven't come to say you're finishing with Serge … Is it because of the names he called you for going home with his flask still in your car on Thursday? Really, I don't know where he picks up such words. I was hoping he would have forgotten about it by the time he saw you again."

"Urm, he never said anything to me about the flask. I thought I'd got away with that." Dominic puts Justin's contract on a flour-free space on the kitchen table. "*This* is the reason I came here …"

"What's this? Not bad news I hope …"

"No, not at all. I'm hoping it's *good* news."

Judith wipes her hands on her apron and frowns at the sea of words on the sheet of paper, trying to extract the relevant few. Being married to a solicitor, she has some familiarity with the format of legal documents, but remains in wonderment that this particular profession has denied the evolution of the English language for so long. Does it *account* for the fixed and stubborn nature of her husband, or is it some deliberate attempt on the part of solicitors to keep up their sleeves something that could otherwise be understood by many? She shakes her head and Dominic watches the soft hazel curls tumble around her slender neck. "You picked a good day to bring this here. Alistaire and Leo are in the study just now, having one of their *meetings*. Goodness knows why Leo can't come home for tea without having to arrange a *meeting*." She hesitates, then adds, "I think I *do* know why. Leo makes out it's business because his wife, Bridget, feels awkward coming here. It's such a shame ... Serge finds her very attractive, you see, and he's erm… not always very subtle with his *attention* to her …"

Dominic nods sympathetically, "Yes, I can imagine."

"And the poor girl doesn't seem to know how to take it. Beatrice's friends just laugh it off or else *go along* with it, but Bridget finds it embarrassing and offensive." She remembers the contract and picks it up with an air of briskness. "Anyway, Serge is the subject of this particular meeting … so let's go and add *this* to their agenda."

Dominic follows Judith from the kitchen to the study, lowering his eyes to the parquet floor and then raising them to the ceiling. The high walls of the hallway are decorated with tasteful works of art that Dominic makes a mental note to appreciate next time he is walking behind someone other than Judith.

She opens the oak panelled door of the study and walks in on an animated conversation between her husband Alistaire and their son Leo. Dominic hangs back in the doorway. Didn't his presence warrant knocking before entering? The men seem oblivious to the intrusion and carry on talking, about Serge.

Alistaire thumps his fist on the desk; "Agenesis of the corpus callosum was ruled out by a scan when he was *five*. What the devil are they talking about?"

"Clearly they didn't read his full case history. I'll make a note of that." Leo scribbles furiously, pressing too hard so the pencil lead snaps and flies across the room. Whilst marvelling over its trajectory, he notices his mother is in the room and there is a young man he does not recognise standing hesitantly in the doorway.

Dominic steps back in retreat from Leo's steely stare. He is fascinated by how similar he looks to Serge - but yet how different. Leo, like Serge, is fair and handsome with blue eyes, but Leo's eyes are a paler blue and piercingly intelligent. His expression betrays no emotion yet there is something resolute and uncompromising about the set of his jaw. Serge, on the other hand, has innocent deep blue eyes with full pink lips that look soft and warm. According to Sabrina, apart from having a fantastic body, Serge has an overall countenance of vulnerable beauty that will melt the heart of almost every woman, and quite a few men.

"Autosomal recessive trait and x-linked dominant trait were ruled out in the very same appointment for heavens' sake," declares Alistaire disdainfully.

"Alistaire," says Judith in a soothing tone that might be used to calm a fractious child. She inserts Justin's document between her husband's nose and his desk. "It seems that the fashion designer gentleman who wanted Serge to model for him is offering a contract of employment."

"A what?" Alistaire examines the paper before him and extracts the few significant words within a nanosecond. He removes his spectacles and rubs his eyes. "Good Lord."

"What is it, Dad?" asks Leo.
"Potentially, this man's prepared to pay Serge more than we're out to sue for."
"Pay him to do what? Let me see." Leo scans the paper and hands it back. "You're right," he says quietly.
"We must have a nudity clause written in," says Alistaire. "You know, decent photographs only. I'll write it in now."
Leo raises his eyebrows. "You're going to let him do this?"
"If he wants to. I've nothing *against* him earning a living. I simply didn't believe he was *capable*."
"I just hope it's not too much for him," says Judith worriedly.
"Too much? As far as I can see he's only got to pose for a few photos or sketches."
"But what if he can't keep still? I think we should have a 'to the best of his ability' clause written in as well."
"Good idea, Dear. And if *that* young man - come in, we don't often bite, if *you* would accompany Serge on these proposed 'studio sittings', then I think you should be entitled to some supplementary remuneration in return for you time."
"Well thank you, Mr Freeman!"
Judith hurries away in response to the heavy clunk of the front door closing. "Who was there, Serge? I never heard the doorbell."
"That's cos she knocked. *Quietly*."
"*Who* knocked?"
"Lady lost a tortoise. Asked if Serge had seen it. Said it was a thirty centimetre long tortoise, so Serge said No." He starts to retreat to the television room. "The one eating your lettuces isn't that long, so it couldn't be 'ers."
"Oh, *Serge*!" Judith opens the front door and dashes down the drive in her apron and slippers. "Excuse me! Hello there!"

Dominic feels it would be bad-mannered to leave without dropping in on Serge – especially after Mr Freeman's generous promise of extra cash in return for sitting around watching Sabrina taking photographs, or drinking proper coffee in

Justin's plush studio whilst a bit of sketching goes on. Just last night he'd had a phone call from his mate Rick who was struggling to hold down a job in an abattoir and had turned vegetarian. It had made him appreciate working with Serge.

Serge is watching a televised debate about euthanasia featuring terminally ill patients being interviewed alongside medical professionals. "That's a bit morbid, Serge. Isn't there anything else on?"

"Herr!" whispers Serge, with a finger across his lips. "That man's going to die soon. Serge wants to watch. Serge never seen that before …"

"Eh? He isn't going to die on this programme, Serge."

"How do you know? Seen it before av yer? Futtin repeats."

"No, they mean he's likely to die in a few months' time … not right now."

"Huh. That's how they as yer. Makes out it's goin to 'appen today so you watches it … and then they strings it out for a few more episodes." Serge flicks between channels and lands on 'Lady Chatterley's Lover' – the Sean Bean version. Just as Mellors grunts, fastens his flies and declares, "We kem off together that taam", Leo enters the room, frowns at the television, casts Dominic an intent look and perches on the setee arm beside his brother. "How are you doing, Serge?"

"Oim orwight."

"I've got something for you."

"Present for Serge?"

"Yeah." Leo hands Serge the latest Tomb Raider game.

Dominic observes a softening in Leo's voice and demeanour in response to Serge, making the brothers even more alike. Leo is about the same height as Serge but not so well built. His hair is short and smart; he has a pale complexion and fine bone-structure. Dominic, who has a round face, discreetly admires the contours of Leo's cheek bones and lower jaw.

"Mum said you like this game on PS1." It had been Judith's tactful way of telling Leo that the Christmas present he bought Serge was still in the box. "I've been told that the graphics on this version are much better and that Lara's hips sway when she walks and you can navigate up over the top and look down on her - and there's even a gym where you can take her for a workout."

"Can you navidown below and look up 'er twat?"

Leo covers his face with a hand then removes it and winks engagingly at Dominic, drawing him in. "I guess you could try it, but I don't imagine the game writers have invested much effort in that particular angle."

"Shame. Fwank'd like that!"

"Frank?"

Serge points to his crotch and says in a confidential tone, "Fwank", then puts the finger over his lips and whispers, "Herr!"

Leo grins, flashing his perfect teeth at Dominic. After some hesitation, then in a grave tone he says, "Listen Serge, about this contract, do you know what I'm talking about?"

"Yer … went to the Pizza Shack, we did. Much as you can eat for four pounds ninety-nine."

"Serge, do you want to be a model? Do you want to have your photograph taken to advertise those weird suits that Italian chap designs?"

"Yes Leo. Especially if Shagina is my phototaker, and Dominic and Fwanny can come and watch sometimes. Serge likes 'aving 'is photo done."

"In that case, we'd better go to the study and sign the contract. It's a very good offer." He turns to Dominic and asks politely. "Would you mind joining us, as an impartial witness?"

Back in the study there is an air of solemnity as Serge's father and brother read through the document one last time. "Shall I sign for you, Serge?" asks Leo.

"What sign is it, Leo?" asks Serge.

"Sign your name … you know, write your name here, on the contract, to say that you agree with and accept it."

"Serge can write his *own* name," says Serge, firmly, and picks up his father's fountain pen from the desk.

Judith looks astonished. "You can write your name? Since when?"

"Erm, we've been practising," says Dominic modestly.

"You have taught him to *write his name*? I tried to teach him for years. We gave up in the end."

Dominic glows with pride. "We break things down into small chunks, you see. First he learned to write 'Se' and then 'rge'."

Serge's mouth hangs open in concentration as he writes his name on the paper next to Leo's finger; 'SErge'. "There, dunnit look!"

"Well done, Serge," says Dominic. "As you can see, we're still working on linking the two sections together."

Leo signs his name beneath his father's and picks up his jacket. "Time I was off."

"Give Bridge one from me," says Serge.

"I will convey your regards to her," responds Leo.

"Oh, I'll put some fresh muffins in a bag for you to take home Leo, they're probably still warm."

"Pleaz can Serge 'ave a warm muffin?" Serge follows his mother to the kitchen.

"Yes, of course, Dear. Would *you* like one Dominic?"

"Urm, yes please!"

Alistaire, alone in his study at last, picks up the document and studies his younger son's signature with interest. 'SErge'.

9

Meet the Parent (and Grandparent)

Franchesca lives with her sixty year old mother and ninety year old grandmother. They share a housing association dormer bungalow on an estate sixteen miles from Serge's house. Franchesca has the upstairs bedroom, from which she can look out over the matrix of small plots of land that are the back gardens of her own street meeting with the back gardens of the next street. Over the years, Franchesca has enjoyed many hours observing the activities of her neighbours; mowing, pruning, digging, hanging out washing or attempting to play ball games, each within the constraints of the boundaries of their allocated territory.

As far as her mother and grandmother are concerned, other than the odd word, Franchesca does not speak and never has done, although they would describe her as being *happy in her own way*. One particularly odd word that has cropped up with increasing frequency over the past few days is "surge". When they mentioned this to Sabrina, the mystery was solved.

"Serge? He's this guy who goes to Fran's Day Centre sometimes, isn't he Fran?" Franchesca tucks her chin against her chest and closes her eyes tightly.

"Oh, she was saying his name!" Franchesca's mother bellows with laughter and it turns into a bronchitic cough. When sufficiently recovered, she shouts to the old lady in the armchair; "Serge is a chap's name, Mum!"

"Yrr what?"

"*Serge.* It's a man's name!"

"A man's name?" Franchesca's grandmother's eyes wander around the room and finally land on Sabrina. "'*Surge*' she kept saying. We looked up at the ceiling. Pat checked the bathroom overflow pipe, and checked Franchesca *down below*, didn't you Pat? We didn't know what she was on about …"

Pat asks, "What's he like then, this Serge?"

"He's gorgeous. I'd fancy him myself if he wasn't a – I mean if he was …"

"Oh, you mean he's like our Fran!" Franchesca's mother smiles. "I thought you was talking about someone that *worked* at the Centre. What does he reckon to Fran?"

Sabrina taps Franchesca's shoulder and she opens her eyes and blinks rapidly. "He thinks she's cute, doesn't he Fran?"

"Serge loves Fran," she responds, and turns slightly pink.

"Did you hear that, Mum? No, I don't expect you did. It's a pity we can't meet this Serge."

"Well … it could be arranged …"

Today, Serge is going out for tea at Franchesca's house. Dominic will be taking Serge, and Sabrina will be attending also; since it was *her idea*.

Judith is gathering together a few essentials to put in Serge's kit bag. His favourite tape measure is missing, so she substitutes it with the one from her sewing box and hopes he won't notice. "I got Derrick, our gardener, to cut some flowers for Mrs Cunliffe and her mother." Judith hands them to Dominic, along with Serge's flask. "Would Serge like to take a small bouquet for Franchesca, or is that going a bit far?"

"Well remembered Mom!" Serge heads for the back door. "Fwan don't need fallars cos Serge got 'er a tree."

"A *tree*?"

"Yer … Derwick put a lickelun in a pot. Serge was goin' to take an oak tree, cos Fwan likes collecting acorns, but Derwick said it was too big and to take this lickelun instead."

"Honestly! I wondered what had happened to that oak tree. It looked as if someone had taken an axe to the trunk … bark and wood chips everywhere!"

Dominic has some trouble locating Franchesca's house. A number of street signs are concealed by graffiti; others by groups of youths wearing hoodies and *up yours* expressions.

He decides it is time to buy a sat nav and claim it as an expense.

"Fwanny's house is the one with the big black mark outside it."

"What sort of black mark?"

"Oi dunno."

"Well, this is the street we were looking for …"

"Black mark – there it is look! Dunnit! Phew!"

"It looks as if a car's been burnt out here."

"Park on it Dom, park on it!" Serge leans out of the window. "Go forward, go forward. Now back a bit!"

"We're all right here, Serge." Dominic switches off the engine, but finally concedes and releases the handbrake to roll back a couple of inches. "Anything for an easy life."

Dominic and Serge gather together the bouquet of flowers, the flask and the sapling in the plant pot. By this time, Franchesca and her mother are standing in the doorway, with Sabrina behind, grinning over their shoulders. Franchesca is wearing a ruffle-collared dress with a full, pleated skirt in a pink and yellow floral fabric. Dominic advances with a friendly smile and an armful of flowers. Mrs Cunliffe returns a display of nicotine-stained teeth, stares into Dominic's eyes and says, "Hello Serge" loudly and slowly, then winks at Serge and says, "Thank you for bringing him."

Dominic opens his mouth and then closes it again. Sabrina giggles delightedly, "You've got them wrong, Pat. Serge is the good looking one! *This* is Dominic."

"Cheers, Bri," says Dominic.

"Oh, I'm *terribly* sorry," laughs Pat. "Pleased to meet you both! Let's go on in and put the kettle on, shall we?"

"Tea pleaz! *Tea* I does. Kettle on. Nice laydee, ainyer?"

"And you're not too bad yerself, sweetheart, if you don't mind me saying so."

Serge places a hand on her shoulder and looks into her eyes with a hypnotic gaze. "Serge don't mind you saying so."

Pat is spellbound by the bright blue charm of Serge's eyes and doesn't appear to notice that the kettle has clicked itself off.

"Kettle's boiled, Laydee. Two sugars pleez. Oh no! Not them cups an' saucers. Serge don't like them posh cups – rattles around too much and they don't hold nothing."

Pat laughs wheezily. "Franchesca's Nan thought we should make an effort and get her old tea set out. It's not often we get company ... and as you can see, they're thick with dust. So, if you prefer a mug then I think we'll all go along with that. This is Nan's mug, that one's mine, and that one's Fran's. Which one would you like?"

"Wun like Fwanny's, I does. What's to eat?"

"Well, I did some sandwiches earlier. I hope that's all right, only I wanted to meet *you*, not spend all the time you were here flapping about in the kitchen."

"Samwidges! Serge *loves* samwidges! Ave em now, can we? Go on, *ple-eaz*!"

"'Course we can, sweetheart! Here, grab a plate."

Dominic comes to Pat's rescue; "Hey, one at a time Serge, leave some for everyone else! Sorry, Mrs Cunliffe, he loves his grub – I don't know how he keeps his figure."

"Come on, Fwan - wanna see your bedroom!" Serge is already half way upstairs and Dominic sets off in pursuit.

"Sorry - I'd better keep up with him." Dominic ascends the short flight of stairs to Franchesca's bedroom and is not surprised to find it decorated in a chaos of conflicting colours and patterns with walls flanked by an army of cuddly toys. Serge is looking out of the window through a pair of binoculars, which he has successfully focussed on a neighbour who is pruning her dwarf roses. "Lady bending over ... with yellow gloves on."

"Don't do that Serge, it's rude."

"What's he doing?" asks Sabrina anxiously from the bottom of the stairs.

"It's okay, he's just looking at people with binoculars."

Sabrina comes up to join them. “Oh, Fran does that all the time ... just make sure the light isn’t behind him, and no-one can tell through the net curtains.”

“But he’s pointing them right into the opposite bedroom window now! Hey, Serge, you can’t do that – it’s just *wrong*.”

“Man dancing around playing a saxophone wiv ‘is todger bouncing up and down.”

“What?”

“Corr ... the missus is there now with a guitar... look at the tits on that!”

“Here Serge, let me see.” Dominic takes the binoculars from Serge and puts them to his own eyes. His jaw drops. “Bloody hell, Bri, take a look at that!”

Franchesca decides it is her turn to use the binoculars and pulls them away from Sabrina. She has no interest in the events in the opposite bedroom and directs them to the bird table in the garden, where a pigeon has just landed. “Birdie!”

Sabrina begins to hunt frantically around the bedroom, “There must be another pair of binoculars somewhere – she never just has *one* of *anything* …”

“Come on Fwan – I got you a tree. Let’s go plant it!”

Dominic grabs the discarded binoculars and adjusts the zoom. “Flipping heck!”

“Let me see, let me see!” says Sabrina.

Some moments later they are distracted by the sound of splintering wood and lower their gaze to the garden. “*Oh shit!*” says Dominic, and races down the stairs and out into the garden, with Sabrina in hot pursuit. “*Serge!* What the hell are you doing?”

Serge has pulled a fence post from its concrete base and is attempting to relocate it some distance back from the garden boundary with the panel still attached. “Cheers Dom, you come to give Serge a hand? It kind of split when I moved it, so I fink we’ll ‘ave to pull the posts out first and move it all in one go. So … if you can ‘old it ‘ere, I’ll come an’ pull that wun out.”

Franchesca's mother has joined them in the garden. "*Omigod*," she says, and lights a cigarette.

Franchesca is holding a plant pot with a sapling in it. Sabrina lowers it to the ground. "Put it down for a minute, Fran. What on earth are you two up to?"

Franchesca lowers her eyes, "Serge gave Fran a tree."

Serge explains, "Yeah, and Derwick said not to plant it too close to the house cos it might grow quite big, so Serge was just moving this fence to make more room for it ..."

The neighbours opposite have finished in the bedroom and come bursting out through their patio windows, red faced, dishevelled, wide eyed and open mouthed.

"Oh no, here's Mr Farnell," says Pat, and takes a long drag on the cigarette.

Dominic takes charge. "I'm terribly sorry about this, and I assure you that the damage will be put right as soon as we can possibly get it sorted. Serge, here, is a friend of Franchesca's, and I'm his *support worker*. Unfortunately I was … urm …distracted and there was a misunderstanding here …"

"Distracted? Misunderstanding? Go and phone the police, Brenda!" Mr Farnell is apoplectic.

Serge steps between them and gazes at Mr Farnell with huge sad eyes. "Serge wants to say sorry. *Sor*-wee! Serge just wanted to plant a tree for Fwan." He turns appealingly to Mrs Farnell. "Serge don't wanna go to jail."

Sabrina smiles at the Farnells. "Don't worry, his father's loaded. We'll have this fixed in no time."

"Well, I want a proper job done with a matching panel," says Mr Farnell. "And if you can't get a matching one, you can replace the whole fence."

"Cheers Mister! We'll get a new wun. And Fwanny can choose what colour we paint it!"

"Red and yellow," says Franchesca, and her mother looks delighted.

"You hear that, she's started saying colours now!"

The Farnells appear to have softened a little. "You can paint it what colour you like on your side, so long as we can't see it."

Serge blesses them with his most charming smile, and they can't help but smile back at him. "Nice man aren't you? And a nice lady." He turns away to go indoors, then adds, "Oh yeah, and you got a cracking saxophone Mister! Come on you lot …cup of tea I does!"

10

Copyrighted 'SErge'

Justin Beaver is pacing the floor of his apartment, making a path in the plush pile of the carpet as he switches from one window to another, impatiently awaiting a special delivery. The white Persian cat knows better than to rub against his legs today, and keeps its distance in the corner armchair; tail twitching tetchily each time he sweeps past. Finally the buzzer sounds and the cat leaps from the chair and into a bedroom as Justin dives for the door. He scribbles a hasty signature for the delivery, then kicks the door closed behind him and sets down the box on the large oval dining table, cursing himself for not having scissors ready at hand. The box is finally opened and Justin extracts the contents and folds back the layers of white tissue paper with trembling fingers to reveal a rich silk fabric in gun-metal grey. "My beauty," he whispers, and feels the smooth texture with his neck and face, then moves it swiftly away as his eyes fill with tears. He mops his face with a huge cotton handkerchief, then covers the table with the tissue paper, carefully unfolds the garments and arranges them on the table top. "My *own wonderful creation.*"
Justin is seized by an urgent desire to see the suit modelled by the figure that inspired it. He needs to see Serge wearing this suit. *Now.*

Dominic, incarcerated in his student digs, has just started work on his summer thesis which he has been putting off for ages. Pleased with himself for having written the first sentence, he decides he deserves another cup of coffee; swills his mug under the cold tap, adds some *value granules* and attempts to dissolve them with water from a flask that he stored earlier after being forced to boil too much in order to fill the kettle above the 'minimum' mark. The flask was lent to him by

Serge – a gesture that Dominic appreciated as a mark of trust and a huge development in their relationship. He returns to his desk and re-reads the opening sentence. 'Even when people share the same point of view they sometimes struggle to communicate with each other because they have different styles of speech, for example one might have an auditory style whilst the other has a kinaesthetic style.' *What a rubbish introduction!* He frowns, shakes his head and deletes it, to face a blank page yet again. *Shit.*

His mobile phone rings.

"Dominic, this is Justin. I need Serge here now."

"What on earth for?"

"The *suit* has arrived, and it is *beautiful*, but without him it is a mere shell. It is a peacock's tail feather without a peacock. It is a moonlit night without stars. It is a sea without waves ..."

"Justin! I get the picture, but I'm not working with Serge today. He might be busy doing something with his family." He hears a gasp and what sounds like a sob. "Justin, are you okay?" There is a pause whilst Justin composes himself.

"Get him here now, and I will pay you a hundred pounds bonus, on top of your hourly rate and your travelling expenses also."

"Well ..." Dominic has a strong sense of morality and is troubled by the idea of taking advantage of Justin's irrational passion. He looks at the coffee granules still floating in his mug. A hundred quid would boil a few kettles. "Leave it with me Justin. I'll see what I can do."

Serge is watching his 'Rainman' DVD yet again. Dominic knocks on his bedroom door and enters, accompanied by Judith, during a scene of a consultation with a psychiatrist. "What's three hundred and twelve times one hundred and twenty three?" asks the psychiatrist.

"Thirty eight thousand, three hundred and seventy-six," says Serge, before Dustin Hoffman has even opened his mouth.

“Four thousand three hundred and forty-three times one thousand two hundred and thirty-four?”

“Five three five nine two six two,” says Serge, and Dominic’s mouth falls open.

“Square root of two one three zero?”

“Four six point one five one nine two three zero four.”

“My God, he’s an autistic savant!” exclaims Dominic.

“No he isn’t,” says Judith, mildly. “He’s been watching that film over and over again these last few days. He has a good memory for numbers and he’s something of a mimic. He can reel off my mobile phone number when I don’t even know it myself.” Serge obligingly quotes his mother’s mobile phone number.

“Oh, and talking of him being a mimic,” Judith lowers her voice and looks serious. “Alistaire and I have noticed a few *obscenities* creeping into his vocabulary of late. I don’t suppose you’ve any idea where they’re coming from?”

“Urm ... I think that would be John at the Day Centre – he’s one of the ... urm ... *service users*. His Dad is a lovely guy but a bit of a rough diamond and John tends to mimic his Dad, so I guess it’s rubbing off on Serge.”

“Futtin dickedd is John,” says Serge, as if to confirm the theory.

“Serge, please don’t use such language!” says Judith, and then continues in a softer tone, “Now then. Dominic would like to take you to see Mr Beaver, the fashion designer. It seems there’s a suit he has designed and he needs you to try it on. Only Beatrice *did* say she might call in this afternoon, and you were out last time she visited.”

“I wonder if Beatrice might like to tag along with us to Justin’s?” Dominic suggests quickly, for fear that his generous financial reward might be in jeopardy. “Or perhaps she’d prefer to meet us there? I believe she lives closer to Justin’s place than to here.”

"Beatie come to Justin's – see Serge do 'is model! Mobile Beatie, Mom!" Serge begins to chant his sister's mobile phone number …

Dominic and Serge arrive at Justin's apartment to find an Aston Martin in the space where Dominic had parked his Metro on the previous visit. "I'll phone Justin and ask where we should park," says Dominic, and fishes out his phone to find nine missed calls from Justin. He returns the last call, half expecting a torrent of Italian abuse, and is relieved when it takes a few rings before Justin calmly answers.

"Hi Justin!" he says and then lowers his voice an octave. "It's me, Dominic, and I've got Serge with me. But there's nowhere to park."

"Of course there is, my friend, you simply drive around the pillar and there is an ocean of car parking spaces!"

"Oh. Sorry! Righteo, we'll be with you in a minute." They drive around the pillar and find an ocean of car parking spaces. "Hey, look at *this*! I have to say, Serge, Justin's excited tone earlier today had made me a little nervous about this visit. And now, here we are, and Justin sounds far more calm and amenable."

"Yeah, burrit *still* smells of piss in this car park ... dontit?"

"Well, now you come to mention it ..."

Dominic presses the buzzer and Serge takes a startled step back as Justin's voice responds loudly from the intercom. Serge still does not like lifts and clutches Dominic's arm as they ascend – releasing it hastily as the doors glide open and Justin greets them. Justin smiles at Serge but stands immobile, fixated once again by his beauty, whilst Serge returns a blank stare. Justin, satisfied that Serge is as beautiful as the image imprinted in his memory, attempts to draw attention to himself. "Tell me, do you see something different?"

Dominic looks past Justin and takes in the ivory carpet, sheepskin rugs and white leather sofa. "Urm .... No."

A man appears in the kitchen archway. He is elegantly dressed – in fact it could be one of Justin's designer suits he is wearing. His appearance is let down by his hair, which is long, thin and lank. It flops across his face whilst his scalp shines pinkly through. "Ah, I spy a visitor!" Dominic smiles and waves, pantomime style.

"I meant do you see anything different about *me*?"

Dominic looks Justin up and down then raises his eyebrows at the visitor. *Give us a clue.*

The visitor lifts a lock of hair and makes a scissor action with his fingers.

"Oh, you've had a hair cut, Justin! *Very* smart."

"Yes, today we are visited by one of London's top stylists!"

"Really?" Dominic looks over Justin's head and smiles again at the man still lurking near the kitchen. "I guess you're next for the chop then!"

The visitor throws back his head and laughs, revealing a set of large teeth that are somewhat crooked and not particularly white. He advances and shakes Dominic's hand, his eyes still twinkling with mirth. "Hey, I didn't come here for a hair cut – I'm the '*top stylist*' who just cut Justin's hair."

"Oh *heck*, I'm terribly sorry ..." Dominic turns his standard shade of red.

"Don't worry! I guess it's true what they say about painters and decorators having the worst houses. Now then, you must be Dominic, and this must be Serge. I've heard so much about you both. By the way, I'm Ivan."

"Pleased to meet you," says Dominic. *What a really nice guy.*

Whilst Dominic resolves to keep his trap shut in future, Justin is gazing in awe at Serge, who is gazing into space and stroking the smooth hard plastic of his thermos flask. Ivan begins to explain his presence. "Justin normally visits my salon, but I don't mind doing home visits occasionally, in special circumstances such as these."

Dominic smiles and nods understandingly, then furrows his brow, "What are today's special circumstances?"

"Well, you know, Serge coming here to model the new suit ... it means the world to Justin. He's also sent a taxi to collect Serge's personal photographer."

"*Personal photographer*? Oh, right, is Sabrina coming over? Blimey ... Serge's sister Beatrice is due here too. A full house again."

"Anyway, I'm here today to cut Serge's hair. Justin wants him to have a bit of a trim, prior to his photo shoot."

"Ah, okay. But I'd better give his Mom a ring first. Although I'm responsible for him right now, I still have to get his parents' permission for everything." Dominic extracts his mobile phone and selects 'Serge home'. After several rings, Judith answers, sounding husky and breathless. To Dominic it sounds as if she has just been interrupted in the middle of an energetic sex session. "*Hello?*" she says yet again, and Dominic pulls himself together. "Oh, hello Mrs Freeman, this is Dominic. There's no problem, I just need to ask your permission for Serge to have his hair cut."

"*His hair*?" says Judith after a long pause. "I didn't realise he was due a haircut. There's a lady who comes here regularly to do mine, and she always gives Serge a bit of a trim if he's in the right frame of mind."

"Oh, his hair isn't a problem but Justin has got his personal hair dresser round here to do Serge's hair before he models this suit and has his photo taken. If that's okay?" Judith is trying to take this in and does not respond immediately, which flusters Dominic, especially since he fears that the arousal she has evoked might be obvious to all. "Justin's hairdresser is a top London ... hairdresser ..."

"Really? Anyone I might have heard of?"

"His name's Ivan ..." Dominic looks round at Ivan for help.

"My surname is Ardonne. She may or may not have heard of me."

"Ivan Ardonne!" proclaims Dominic, and transforms from red-faced to violet.

"Oh!" gasps Judith, but when Dominic looks back to Ivan for help, there is only the back of his head and shoulders shaking helplessly with mirth. Judith recovers first. "Actually, I think I may have heard of him. It's the sort of name that *sticks*, isn't it! Anyway, so long as it's just a bit of a trim and a tidy-up – nothing too extreme, then that's fine." Judith clears her throat and hesitates before continuing, "Of course, it would be a good thing to put in your diary - you know - your work diary with Serge - to say that you took him to the barber's maybe. Dominic, I'm only mentioning this because Regina, his '*case manager*', was on to Alistaire this morning about it, and she is, of course, your employer ... technically speaking. And I want you to know that Alistaire and I are entirely happy with your work with Serge ... but for the sake of this ... *bloody court case* that has taken over my husband's life lately, then we *need* you to follow *Regina's Regime,* and that is to be *seen to be doing*. This involves keeping a diary, which might be used as evidence, to prove how fruitful Serge's life could be, given the support of people like *you*, which might prove expensive in future years. Because, lovely as you are, Dominic, and a wonderful influence on Serge ... we've only got you for another three weeks, and then you'll be moving on to the bigger and better things that you deserve ..." Her voice fails and Dominic hears a stifled sob. He walks over to the corner window – as far away as possible from the gathering company. Beatrice has just turned up and Serge is greeting her with noisy enthusiasm.

"Mrs Freeman ... *Judith* ... yes, I'm sorry, I have strayed away from my original purpose. On Monday I will go to the gym with Serge, and on Tuesday I will see how he feels about going for a run with me ... or just a bit of a jog perhaps ... I know I put *running* on my CV but that was when I lived up north, and I'm a bit out of condition now. And I will record these events in our diary. Regina *did* explain to me my role in securing the finance for Serge's future care ... I can only apologise if you feel that I've let you down."

"Oh no, of course we don't," gulps Judith, "and I'm sorry if I've given you that impression. I trust you *implicitly* with him, and you've no idea what that means to me. I'm so sorry ... you just caught me unawares – I never intended to *off load* on you like this – I just worry so much about what might happen to Serge when Alistaire and I are no longer around to take care of him ... and you have to realise that we're not out to sue the negligent authorities out of greed ... it's simply to protect our son ... Oh God, there's someone at the door now – never a minute's peace!"

"Hey, Judith! Mrs Freeman, you don't *have* to answer the door."

"Oh, I better had – it's probably the ironing lady. Yes, by all means get his hair cut, but no funny colours please! I'll speak to you later, Dear. *Bye!*"

The call ends and Dominic stands staring at his mobile.

"Is there a problem?" asks Ivan.

"What? Oh no, his Mom's okay with the hair cut so long as it's not weird or colourful. Hey, is that your real name, or were you joking?"

"Ivan Ardonne is indeed my *real* name. Don't worry about his hair – it was never our intention to do anything way out. Just a trim, that's all." Ivan hesitates, then adds, "And whilst I'm here, I could do something for you, if you wish?"

Dominic runs his fingers through his hair, self-consciously. "I've never been too much into hair and clothes and *image*. I guess it shows."

Ivan homes in, looming over the top of Dominic's head. "You see, when you are thinning on top you need a much shorter cut. There is no point trying to conceal the obvious."

"Now there's the pot calling the kettle black," says Dominic, and they both laugh.

Beatrice joins them with Serge standing very close behind her. "Hi Beatrice, I've cleared it with your Mum for Ivan to cut Serge's hair."

"You've spoken to her? How did she sound?"

"Urm ... she sounded stressed ... menopausal perhaps?"

"*Yeah!* ... Yeah. I turned up there last week and she was kicking a drawer because it got stuck. Completely out of character. I thought she was losing it. Menopausal? Yeah, good one. Nice explanation." Beatrice turns to Ivan. "You're a top Fleet Street stylist?"

Ivan bows his head modestly. "So, you've heard of me ..."

"No. I was *asking* you."

Serge puts his head over his sister's shoulder. "Beatie has an interrogative intonation. She was *asking* you."

Beatrice glares at Dominic. "He's heard *you* say that?"

"Yes, sorry!" Dominic grins, and her glare softens into a smile. "Hey ... you look like your Mum when you smile ..."

Ivan touches Serge's shoulder to get his attention. "Ready for a bit of a trim now, Serge?"

"Serge is ready," says Serge and follows Ivan to the kitchen where a stool has been positioned beneath a light.

"Don't worry, this won't take long and I'm not going to take much off."

"Serge ain worrit."

Justin strokes his chin thoughtfully as he watches the first few golden locks drift to the kitchen floor, then squats down and begins to gather them in the palm of his hand.

"*For fuck's sake!*" yells Ivan as he stumbles over him and narrowly misses sticking the scissors in Serge's head. "Sorry, mate. We'll do this at my salon next time."

Justin is tilting his hand at different angles beneath the light as if trying to verify the authenticity of a jewel he has found. "This hair is like silkenized gold – and now I know what we must do with it. . . . I say I *know* what we must do with it!"

Everyone is looking at him, waiting for him to explain.

"What must we do with it, Justin?" asks Dominic, when it becomes clear that no-one else is going to ask.

"We must use it to create the label!"

Everyone looks blank.

"You must know how important the label is on a designer suit? The label is the mark of its identity ... the mark of its authenticity. Each and every suit will bear the label, and the label will bear the name, and the name will simply be '*SErge'*, exactly as he writes it all by himself – you know, with the big 'SE' and the small 'rge', and the name will be embroidered in this beautiful golden silk."

"But he said he wasn't going to cut much off," says Beatrice. "Mum will be *so not happy* if he goes home with no hair."

"No, no-no-no, no," says Justin. "You misunderstand. *This* hair will provide the blueprint label. It will create the model label upon which all other labels will be ... modelled. Only the blueprint label will utilise the hair, and the others will be woven of embroidery silk, using the closest possible match of colour."

"Hey Serge, you're gonna be a designer label," says Sabrina, and snaps him with her camera. She checks the result in the viewer. "Oh, he opened his mouth as he looked up. I keep forgetting he needs a different technique from a normal person. Hey, Dom, I reckon Serge should copyright his name, you know, the way he writes it, like it's gonna be used on this label. We covered that last year, and now I always put 'Bri' with the little copyright symbol on all my photos. The software I use does it automatically."

"Copyright? That might be an idea." Dominic wishes Sabrina didn't feel the need to speak so loudly and feign a Californian twang when in the company of people she was trying to impress. It did not work.

Ivan has put away his scissors in the black leather man-bag he calls his *pouch*. He sidles up beside Sabrina and leans against the same kitchen unit. "Have you had many of your photos published?"

"Not so far, but I'm thinking ahead. Hey, I think you just switched on the oven."

"Oops," says Ivan and realigns all the dials, then stands awkwardly in front her and attempts to put hands in pockets that were not designed to accommodate anything bigger than a condom.

"Hey, would you like to be in my summer project?" asks Sabrina.

"What project is this?" asks Ivan.

"The title is *Beautiful and Free*."

"Well, I'd be happy to help ... and I'm 'free'. But no-one has *ever* called me *beautiful*."

"Yeah. Serge is the main subject, but I thought his beauty might be emphasised and maximised if I set him against a collage of ugly faces, just as a background, see? I asked Dominic if I could use his face, but for some reason he wasn't up for it. He would have been ideal, except that *he's* got *good* teeth, but I could have photo-shopped them yellow. In your case I could just use the image straight. You are just *ideal*."

Ivan throws back his head and laughs, his eyes dancing with amusement.

Dominic rolls his eyes and walks over to Beatrice. "I wonder if we should mention this Copyright idea to your Dad ... or perhaps that wouldn't be his area of expertise."

"Dad's expertise covers *all* areas. Friday afternoon ... he's probably on the golf course. I'll try his mobile."

"Oh, please don't disturb him. We can ask him about it some other time."

"Hi Dad, it's me, Beatrice."

"Hello Darling. Is everything all right?" Alistaire's voice, sounding convinced that something must be wrong since she is calling him during Friday afternoon golf can be heard clearly from Beatrice's mobile. Beatrice attempts to explain to him the idea of copyrighting Serge's name, written just the way Dominic has taught him to write it. "So, we thought you might like to register it, but give Justin free use of it for his suits and stuff, since using it as a label was his idea in the first place. That's if you think it's a good idea?" The phone is quiet for a moment except for the buffeting noise of wind from the golf course. "Dad?"

"Well, if I'm honest, Beatrice, that's one of the most ludicrous ideas I've heard for a long time, and believe me, I've heard a few. Are you coming over for dinner on Sunday? Leo and Bridget will be there, and you know how your mother enjoys having everyone together ... for some reason."

Beatrice looks at Dominic and sighs. "Okay, Dad. See you Sunday. Love you. Bye." She puts the phone back in her handbag then takes it out again. "I'll phone Leo." She beckons Dominic to follow her to a corner of the living room, and switches her mobile to loudspeaker mode.

"Hi Beatrice"

Leo's voice immediately makes Dominic feel nervous, and his armpits begin to perspire.

"Leo, you remember how Serge wrote his name – the way Dominic taught him to write it?"

"Yes."

"Well, Justin – he's the guy who's contracted Serge to model his designer suits - would like to use that capital 'SE' and lowercase 'rge' for the designer label, and we thought it would be good to get copyright for the label. Only it was Justin's idea, so we want him to use it for free."

"But you want me to draw up an agreement so that anyone apart from Justin has to obtain copyright for the use of that label henceforth. Yes. Good idea. I'll sort it." Beatrice beams at Dominic, and he sees the natural beauty that is veiled behind her expensive makeup. Leo goes on; "And then, when someone comes up with a 'SErge' deodorant or what have you, our brother will benefit from the sweet smell of other people's armpits."

Dominic is still surreptitiously sniffing his own armpits when Beatrice ends the call but he manages to turn it into an itch on his nose.

Beatrice is looking happy, "People who don't know Leo think he's insensitive, but he's as soft as anything if it's to do with Serge." Her face clouds as if her spirits are dampened by some memory from the past. "So am I, I guess. Which makes me really appreciate what you've done for my brother over these past few weeks." She glances across to the kitchen, where Sabrina is sharing her glass of champagne with Ivan, giggling and spilling it down his front as she tries to pour it in his mouth. "Those two are *flirting*. You and Sabrina. I thought you were an item?"

"Well ... so did I ..."

"Fancy a glass of champagne?"

"Best not, I'm driving your brother home, remember?"

"Yes, of course ..." Beatrice clears her throat. "Maybe some other time ... if you happen to be free. You've got my number." She kisses him lightly on the cheek and leaves quietly.

"*Bloody hell ...*" murmurs Dominic. He notices Serge is standing away from the group, stroking his plastic thermos flask and shifting from one foot to the other. "All right, Bud?" he asks.

"Serge as ad inuff now. Come on Dom, let's gowome."

"Okay Serge, home soon. Let's just put the suit on quick so Justin can see you wearing it and Sabrina can take some photos ... if she's not too busy over there ..."

Justin, Ivan and Sabrina gasp in unison as Serge emerges from Justin's dressing room wearing the grey silk suit.

Sabrina makes some adjustments to her camera. "Do you think you could get him to put that flask down for a few secs? Thanks." Sabrina works rapidly, knowing she only has a narrow time slot with Serge.

Justin is ecstatic. "See how he moves. See how he is enjoying the feeling of the fabric!"

"Yes, it is giving him an Ardonne," says Ivan, and Sabrina's camera shakes with her uncontrollable giggles. She reviews the last few shots. "Ooooooh yeah, you're right! I can't use those last two. Hey, but just look at his face – he's glowing! On second thoughts I *will* use those – I'll just have to crop them at belt level."

"I think it's time we were off," says Dominic, suddenly annoyed. "Come on, Serge; let's get your proper clothes back on."

Serge reappears from the dressing room in his jeans and tee-shirt. Dominic pauses to frown because Sabrina is taking photos of Ivan, who is posing against the white wall where Serge had been standing just a few minutes ago. As Justin approaches, he puts on a smile. "We're leaving now, Justin. Serge thrives on routine, and it's time he got back home to watch a bit of telly and so on. But thank you so much for this afternoon. I'm sure it was very rewarding for him and clearly he loved wearing the suit."

"Rewarding ... Yes, of course, well rewarded – I mean well *reminded*." Justin hurries away and returns with the envelope of money that he prepared in advance but then forgot about. He thrusts it into Dominic's apparently reluctant hand, saying, "Yes, yes-yes-yes, yes. You *must* accept this."

"Well ... if you insist." Dominic stuffs the envelope into his back pocket and stands awkwardly for a moment, feeling it inappropriate to rush off the minute he's been paid.

Serge comes to the rescue. "Oi faut we was going Nob ... Dom. *Simpsons* is on soon ..."

"Okay, Serge, we're just off. Say thank you to Justin for ... urm ... allowing you to wear his suit."

Serge grins lopsidedly at Justin. "Fank you Just for ... urm ... allowing Serge to wear his suit." Serge gives Justin a thumbs-up sign and simultaneously wiggles his wrist. "And Fwank enjoyed it too ..."

Dominic has almost made it through the door when Justin taps his shoulder. "I must buy a special gift for Serge. What should it be? Does he enjoy something gold? Or is platinum more suited to his colour?"

Dominic pauses to think. "You know Justin, I think what he would *really* like is a new flask. If I were you, I would choose the most colourful one I could find. A big plastic flask with a bright pattern." He presses the button to call the lift.

Justin frowns as he considers this. “Thank you, Dominic. I understand.” He waves as the lift doors close and chuckles at Serge’s departing words.

“New flask, I does. New flask for Serge. Cheers!”

11

Futt, futt, futt, futt, futt!

"Futt, futt, futt, futt, *futt!* Futt, futt, futt, futt, *futt!*"

Serge is sitting on a bench in his back garden. He is clutching to his chest a large plastic flask with a colourful diamond pattern. This flask is precious to Serge not because it was a gift from Justin Beaver but because he loves and is fixated with its colourful diamond pattern. Today, Serge is agitated, and he rocks back and forth as he cradles the flask and chants, "Futt, futt, futt, futt, *futt!* Futt, futt, futt, futt, *futt!*" Ralph is resting nearby, his huge shaggy head on his paws, his dark eyes watchful and anxious. He has learned to keep his distance on these occasions, but glances worriedly at his friend from time to time.

Dominic stops his Metro in the lane a little before the entrance to Serge's house. He is early and he has driven there on auto-pilot, immersed in the chaos of his mind. He closes his eyes for a moment, places his fingers on his temples and begins to chant a positive affirmation, which he soon ditches in favour of a calming mantra. When he opens his eyes again, the lady outside whose property he has parked has come out to check for weeds in the flower bed by her gate. Dominic restarts his car on the second attempt and drives off in a cloud of black smoke, turning into the Freeman residence almost immediately.

When someone finally answers the door it is Judith, looking pale and tired. Realising this is Dominic and not someone trying to talk her into changing gas and electricity supplier with a special bonus and reduction of monthly direct debit, she alters her expression so that the lines in her face curve upwards. "Hello Dominic, are you all right, Dear? You look ... erm ... tired."

"Yeah, I've been doing a lot of thinking about the future ... about *my* future ... about where I'm going with my career. Uh-hum. Sorry Mrs Freeman, I mean *Judith*, I came here to work with Serge, so I shouldn't start bending your ear. Only three more sessions to go, as it happens ... and then I've got a bit of decision making to do. You look tired as well. Is everything okay?"

"Yes, fine. Well, no actually, but we've been through worse. Serge is in the back garden having a bit of a wobbly – it's sometimes best to leave him to it for a while. Come on in the kitchen and tell me what's troubling you. I'll put the kettle on. Other people's problems are always far more interesting than one's own." She looks out of the kitchen window. Serge is still clutching the flask to his chest and agitating back and forth, muttering to himself. "There's no point making tea for him when he's like that. I'll do another one when he's finished."

Dominic stands beside her and looks out into the back garden. "What brought it on this time?"

"Oh, it's Alistaire and this damned court case …" Judith's hands shake, spilling tea leaves all around the pot.

"You sit down, I'll make the tea," says Dominic.

Judith sits down, fighting back the tears as she always does when she is tired and someone is kind. "In a nutshell, the solicitors acting on behalf of the insurance company that will have to pay out if Alistaire wins the case are maintaining that Serge has *autism* and is not brain damaged. We know he displays some characteristics of autism, but that doesn't mean he's *not* brain damaged. Alistaire wants Serge to have yet another assessment. It's not unusual for Serge to become a little agitated at the prospect of an appointment, but this time he just *flipped.* I've been trying to remember if anything unpleasant happened at his last assessment but I can't think of anything. What do you think, Dominic? Does he come across to you as autistic or brain damaged?"

Dominic hesitates. "It is something I've thought about, knowing there will be a court case soon. I gather that Regina's plan is to demonstrate that Serge can lead a full and active life with the support of a '*Buddy*', but the Buddy role needs to be funded, which is just one reason why Serge needs more compensation money."

"Yes, that's right. That's the idea, Dear. But what do you think in your own heart? I'm too close to be able to see properly now."

"I think he is brain damaged. I know he shows some characteristics of autism, but then *autism* is a catch-all term for a variety of behavioural symptoms. Sure, he likes routines and rituals and gets attached to things … such as flasks, but he has a great personality and I've witnessed him demonstrate sensitivity to other peoples feelings, which severely autistic people are not renowned for … in fact he's capable of being very kind and thoughtful."

Sensitivity ... kind ... thoughtful ... "Erm ... can you recall any examples of Serge demonstrating such behaviour? Gosh, sorry, I'm starting to sound like my husband now."

Dominic laughs, "That's okay - I can see why this might be important to the court case. I *can* think of a couple of examples ... there was the time we were playing crazy golf and someone mentioned there was a thunder storm approaching. Serge had seemed to be really enjoying the game, but he insisted we got back because Ralph would be scared if it thundered and he wasn't there to cuddle and reassure him. Urm ... and then there's the way he is with Franchesca." He hesitates, wondering how best to put this over to Serge's mother.

"*Go on*," urges Judith, leaning forward and looking at him intently.

"Well, he says he would like to marry Franchesca one day. He wants to buy her a pony of her own, and, well, he would like to make love to her ..." Dominic feels his cheeks burning, and ends hurriedly, "but not until she is ready."

"Did Serge actually say he would like to *make love* to Franchesca?"

"Well, those weren't his exact words."

"No, I didn't imagine they would be ..."

“But that was the *meaning*. And that’s what counts.”

“Yes, absolutely!”

“In fact I’d say it was significant that he *did* use his own words – albeit they were adapted from words he’s learned from John at the Day Centre – rather than something he’s picked up from watching TV.”

“Funny he should fall for someone like Franchesca. He’s always had an eye for the ladies. I’ve told you what he’s like with Leo’s wife, Bridget. She doesn’t know how to handle him, poor girl ... but then she *knows* what he’s like and yet she still wears such short skirts and low cut tops when she visits.” Judith shudders as she recalls last Sunday when Leo and Bridget came to dinner. Serge had become quite graphic about what he would like to do with Bridget and then Alistaire had exploded and sent him to room. Perhaps there was another Day Centre that Serge could attend … one where his pal John did not go …

“Serge is very protective of Franchesca,” says Dominic. “They do seem *right* together, and well,” Dominic chooses his words carefully, “Serge perhaps realises that it would be difficult for him to have a proper relationship with a woman like Bridget.”

“Maybe we should invite her round. Or perhaps it would be wrong to encourage the relationship when there’s no future. I mean, they couldn’t live together without supervision ...”

They both sit up with a start as Alistaire walks in with a laptop case and a folded Daily Telegraph and declares stridently, “And that’s why it’s important that we win this compensation case – which is why I want him to have this assessment!”

“Hello Dear, I never heard the door go,” says Judith, feigning brightness. “How did the meeting go?” She gets up and puts the kettle on. “Cup of coffee?”

“I’ll take Serge his cup of tea,” says Dominic, and wonders why Alistaire’s arrival has made him feel nervous.

Alistaire looks out into the back garden and frowns at the sight of Serge rocking back and forth, still clutching that *bloody flask.*

"Erm ... I hope you don't mind me asking, but what does this latest assessment entail?" asks Dominic bravely then lowers his eyes as Alistaire turns from the window with the frown still etched on his face.

"Very little," he replies curtly, and his tone prompts both Judith and Dominic to look at him questioningly. He sighs. "It's just a simple process of applying transcranial magnetic stimulus to ..." Alistaire hesitates and clears his throat, "to temporarily disable the frontal temporal lobe. That's assuming it's fully enabled at present, and, as you know, I have my doubts. Then we can see if he still remembers all the family's mobile phone numbers and so on ... and just generally test for altered brain function."

Judith continues to stare at her husband, eyes wide and mouth slightly open. Then she utters "No, Alistaire ..." and bursts into tears.

The kettle clicks off and Dominic quickly pours water on a tea bag, bashes it against the side of mug, throws in milk and sugar and hurries out to the back garden.

Ralph is happy to see him and trots over to meet him with a wagging tail, prancing with his front feet as if about to plant them on Dominic's shoulders. "No, this is hot!" says Dominic so Ralph buries his nose in his crotch instead with a loud snort. Dominic launches himself onto the bench beside Serge. "*Bloody animal* ... here's your cup of tea - or at least the two thirds that's left of it."

Serge stops rocking, puts his flask down by his feet and takes the mug, gazing at the contents. "That's not two thirds; it's three fifths, ha, ha, ha!"

Dominic shakes his head. "I just don't get it."

"Ha, ha, ha. Futt, futt, futt!"

"Don't use that word!" snaps Dominic, suddenly irritated. "You know your parents don't like you to use such language."

Serge lowers his voice and adopts a mysterious tone. "Futt is merely a word. It is the manifestation of sound energy, owig – owig - owiginating fwom the Dzogchen 'A' or Hindu 'Om' … from the ultimate sphere of transcendental reality … the dharmakaya according to Vajrayana Buddhism … ha, ha, ha!"

Dominic shivers suddenly and rubs the goose pimples on his arms. Tiredness from lying awake last night contemplating his future is making him feel chilly in the cool summer breeze. "Is that the sort of pretentious drivel you've heard me talking? Sometimes I amaze even myself with the rubbish I come out with." He rests his elbows on his knees and his head in his hands and closes his eyes for a moment then recoils from a warm cloud of fishy breath as Ralph's muzzle is planted heavily on his lap. Dominic tries to push him away, but he is a heavy dog and will not budge.

"Are you sad, Dom?" asks Serge.

"I suppose I am a bit," Dominic replies.

"Don't be sad, Dom. Ralphie don't like it."

"Really?" Dominic looks at the woeful expression on the dog's face, at the huge eyes, full of concern, gazing into his own, and feels that his heart is about to break.

Judith approaches with a jiffy bag in her hand and Dominic shuffles along the bench so she can sit between him and Serge. Her eye lashes are still wet with tears but she is glowing with the endorphin induced euphoria that tends follows an emotional outburst. She squeezes Serge's hand, "It's okay Serge. Dad and I have decided that this latest assessment will not be necessary after all."

"Woht?" says Serge, the intense angst of the previous hour apparently forgotten.

Judith moves swiftly on. "Look, the postman brought this for you." She hands him the jiffy bag.

"Letter for Serge!" Serge pulls it apart excitedly, scattering the contents in the grass around his feet.

Dominic gathers them up. "Hey look, Serge, you've got your own business cards!"

There is also a letter in the envelope that Serge gives to his mother, "Letter, Mom!"

"They're from Justin Beaver. Oh, how nice, he thought you might like your own business cards." Judith takes one of the cards for a closer look. It bears the 'SErge' logo, embossed in gold, with 'Serge Freeman' in a bold black font centred beneath it. In the bottom corner is the Justin Beaver website URL and the email address for Justin Beaver & Associates. Judith returns to the letter. "He says if we look on the internet, on the web address shown on the card, there are some photos of Serge modelling the new range of 'SErge' suits … and these suits are now available in shops on Savile Row!"

"Shall we go indoors and have a look on the internet?" asks Dominic hopefully. He is starting to feel chilly in the garden.

"*Do* let's," says Judith enthusiastically. "Come along Serge, let's go and see your photos on the internet."

Dominic huddles next to Judith as they wait for her PC to boot up. Her knees are very close to his knees, and her head is very close to his head, and he can smell the delicate scent of her hair shampoo, or styling mousse, or whatever it is ... There is a corner of his mind that wants this moment to last for ever, whilst the rest of it wishes the PC were not so excruciatingly slow. Serge mooches back and forth behind them, tracing his big toe around the swirly pattern of the Persian carpet. When finally the internet connection is established (which is in fact ten times faster than Dominic is used to on the dial-up in his digs) and Dominic has managed to type in the correct address for the Justin Beaver website (which isn't easy with Judith being so close), he and Judith gaze in awe at the slide show of photos of Serge modelling the full range of 'SErge' suits. All of the suits are cut to flatter his graceful, athletic physique, and all of the photographs have captured those moments when he is gazing obliquely at something outside of the picture – moments that exhibit his fine-boned facial structure and his thick golden waves of hair, recently tamed by a top stylist, to their best advantage.

"My God he is *beautiful*," whispers Dominic, and glances at Judith to find there is a fresh tear running down her cheek. He extends his hand towards her but then flounders and withdraws it again. "I guess you're not used to seeing Serge like that ..."

Judith is touched by his understanding. "That's precisely it." She sobs and sniffs delicately, then takes a tissue - previously used and dried - judging by its crunchiness, from her cardigan pocket and blows her nose with surprising volume.

Serge, startled by the noise, squats down beside her. "What's up, Mom?"

Judith takes his face in her hands and kisses the golden lock of hair that has fallen across his forehead. "Just look at you," she murmurs softly and nods towards the computer screen. "You've always been my little *special* boy ... but just look at you there! These photos are amazing. Do you know who took them, Dominic?"

"Yes, I know her," says Dominic. "Well, at least I *did* know her." He points to the bottom corner at the copyright symbol and 'Bri', then sighs sadly. It is a dramatic sigh, intended to be noticed by Judith.

"Oh, I *see*," she obliges. "Is that why you're not your usual happy self? Of course, Bri is short for Sa*bri*na. She's the young lady who's been looking after - I mean working with Franchesca during the summer."

Dominic lowers his eyes sadly, so Serge helps him out. "Yer, and Dom was shagging Shagina but now Shagina wants to futt Ivan's Ardonne. According to Fwanny."

"*Serge!* I *am* sorry, Dominic."

"Not at all, he summed it up rather nicely," says Dominic with a wry smile. "It's great to think of Serge and Franchesca gossiping between themselves about us – especially when Franchesca's mother thinks her daughter cannot speak!" His face clouds over. "Anyway ... maybe it's for the best that Sabrina and I have drifted apart. You see, I've decided to pack in my NLP course."

"Your...? Oh, you mean the course you're studying. To be honest, I don't entirely understand what it is ..."

"You're not the only one." Dominic laughs sardonically. "I remember trying to justify it to my Dad, when he wanted me to learn a proper trade – to be a plumber or an electrician. And now I'll have to go back to North Yorkshire and tell Dad he was right. Not that I want to be a plumber or an electrician. Or maybe I do ... it would be preferable to working on a factory production line. But I can't muster any enthusiasm for it ... or for *anything* right now ..."

"But do you have to go back *up north*?"

"Well ... I can't stay in student digs if I'm not a student. And I'm already in debt with a student loan. I have no choice but to move back in with my parents. And yes, I know I should think myself lucky that I have them to go back to, but frankly it's not much compensation right now."

"Oh, Dominic." Judith pats his shoulder gently and he fears he might burst into tears. "What do you *really want* in life, Dominic? What would make you happy?"

"I wish I *knew* ..." Dominic pulls himself together and adopts a cheerful tone. "How about you, Serge? What would make *you* happy?"

"Serge would like cwispy pancakes for lunch. Wiv oven chips. An' red sauce, pleez. Lurvley, that would!"

Dominic laughs. "You know what, Serge, sometimes I wish I had a mind like yours."

Serge pats Dominic's shoulder in the same spot where his mother just did but not so gently.

"Ouch!" says Dominic. "Steady on mate!"

"You almost sounded like a *Londoner* then!" exclaims Judith. "You can't *possibly* go back *up north*." Dominic reflects that Judith sometimes adopts an emphatic tone of voice – almost as if every other word is spoken in italics. "Do *you* like crispy pancakes, Dominic? Would that cheer *you* up *too*?"

"Well, I *did* come here to work with Serge, so it seems a bit of a *cheek* to have you cooking for me. However, I *am* partial to crispy pancakes and it's been *ages* since I had them." *Oops, it's catching.* "Listen, I've been thinking. How about we write off today in terms of doing something constructive with Serge? What if I come back tomorrow instead and take him for a ride out to Savile Row to see the shops selling his designer label suits? That would be a good one for Regina's diary ... and we could print these pictures off the internet to go in his scrap book. And I'll take a photo of him standing next to a cardboard cut-out of himself. That's if Serge hasn't got anything else planned for tomorrow, of course."

"Serge ain't got noffin planned," says Serge.

"Well, that sounds good to me - if *you* haven't got anything else planned for tomorrow," says Judith.

"I *would* have been working on my thesis. Only there's not much point now ..."

"Cheesy ones, Serge does. *Pleez.*"

Judith stands up, "Are cheesy pancakes okay for you, Dominic? Or there are some with minced beef filling if you would prefer."

"Cheesy sounds great. Thank you!"

Back in his bedsit, early afternoon, Dominic switches on the TV and channel-flips. Rubbish; adverts; adverts, more rubbish. He switches it off, puts on a CD and flops back on the bed, but the noise only irritates him, so he reverts to the background noise of other people's music, traffic and water travelling along pipes. He checks his mobile – no messages – and begins to compose a text message to Sabrina. It overflows into two messages, so he scrolls back and abbreviates it – but there is still so much he wants to say to her. *Sod it.* He quits the message and phones her instead – and wonders why his heart is thumping so ridiculously hard as it rings and rings ... probably at the bottom of her handbag somewhere. He pictures her frantically tipping the contents onto the floor to get to the ringing phone.

"Hi Dom," she answers finally, but her tone is cold, as if she has been deliberating for some time whether or not to take the call.

"Oh, hi there, Bri!" he responds with forced brightness. "Urm ... is it okay to talk?"

"Yeah, sure!" A pause. "Well, I've got a minute or two, was it something important?"

"Important? Well ... that's relative, isn't it? I mean, what's important to me might not be important to you ... in fact it very probably isn't ... Oh, but there is something that I'm sure will interest you."

"Yes?"

"Yes. If you look on the Justin Beaver website, there are some brilliant photos of Serge modelling the 'SErge' range of suits, and guess who took the photos?"

"I took them," she answers flatly, then unable to conceal the excitement in her tone she adds, "Actually, he paid me a fortune for them! Far more than I would have asked, but then he appears to be loaded and I think he's paranoid about being seen to be exploiting young people - or anyone for that matter. And guess what?"

"What?" he obliges.

"Justin's offered me a contract along the lines of the one he's given Serge. I am to work for him, photographing his designs. Naturally I will finish my course – I would be mad not to pick up my degree, even though I don't really need it now, but I can still work for him part time until I'm through with the finals. Isn't that all just *great*! Life has never felt so good – like everything's fallen into place for me. Anyway, that's enough about me. How's life treating you? Is everything okay?"

"Urm, yes ... fine ..." He hears something clinking in the background and senses that he does not have her full attention now that she has finished talking about herself. "Listen, Bri. Are you doing anything this evening? Do you fancy going out for a pub meal or something?"

"I can't tonight, I'm sorry, I've .... I've got a visitor."

"Oh. Anyone I know?"

"Well, yes ... it's Justin's hair stylist, Ivan. You *have* met."

"Yes, I did notice you seemed to be getting on with him quite well."

"Yeah ... He came round to give me a bit of a trim, and I asked him to stay for tea. Mom's still in Paris, so I can do as I like for a few more days, which is great." She stops but when Dominic does not fill the silence, carries on, "I would ask you to join us but we're treating ourselves to fillet steak and we've only got two steaks ..."

"Forget it, I wouldn't dream of playing gooseberry. Have a nice evening. Goodbye." Dominic ends the call and flops back on his bed. *Fuck, fuck, fuck!*

12

Hero Serge

Bright and early the next morning, Dominic turns up at Serge's house to take him on a trip to Savile Row. His heart sinks to find Serge with an unhappy face yet again and Judith looking tense and anxious. *Now what?*

"It's okay," says Judith, reading his expression. "His new flask, the one Justin gave him with the diamond pattern, has been temporarily misplaced. But he's going to use this nice green one, just for today until we find it. Aren't you Serge?"

"Futtin greenun. Want uvverun. *Uvverun*, I does ..." chunters Serge.

"And he's got a few business cards in his wallet, in case he makes any contacts there ... haven't you Serge. You'll have a *lovely* time!"

"You're welcome to come along with us, Mrs Freeman. I imagine Savile Row is more your scene than mine."

"You know, I'd *love* to Dominic, only I've got people coming here for a charity fund-raising meeting today. The vicar and his wife are attending, and you know how unpredictable Serge can be in his words and actions."

"Serge gorra semi on," announces Serge, fiddling with his crotch.

Dominic laughs at Judith's mortified expression and says "Yes, I know exactly what you mean! Come on Serge, let's get going!"

As Judith waves them off, Dominic congratulates himself on handling that little scene very well. Only a couple of weeks ago he would have had a beetroot face and soaking armpits if Serge had said anything of that nature whilst Judith was there ... He realises Serge is frowning at the green flask he is holding. "Hey Serge, why don't you put that in the back ... just shove it behind my rucksack so it won't roll around but you know where it is if you want it."

Serge flings the green plastic flask angrily over his shoulder and Dominic grips the steering wheel and clenches his teeth but manages not to close his eyes as it hits the rear window, lands on the parcel shelf, rolls off the back seat and wedges itself behind his rucksack. "Good shot!"

"Huh. Sum futter nicked Serge's gudden."

"There's nothing wrong with that green flask. He's your *Old Faithful*. That was the flask you always had when I first met you – and you couldn't have wished for a better flask at the time."

"Dom!"

"Yes?"

"Stop talking cwap."

"Okay. Fair enough ..."

They travel in silence in traffic that is busy but moving and seem to be making good progress until suddenly they encounter a stationary queue.

"Road works, I expect," says Dominic, but his passenger is sullen and withdrawn. After a few moments, people begin to alight from their vehicles, holding onto doors and standing on tiptoe to see if they can see what the holdup is. Dominic notices his temperature gauge creeping upwards and switches off the engine. Immediately the cars in front begin to move forward so he starts it up again and mouths a silent obscenity when the progress is but two car lengths. He takes a couple of deep breaths, rotates his shoulder blades and turns his head from side to side, frowning at the crunching noise that emanates from his neck. He gazes up the adjacent side street. "Blimey, I thought this was a decent area. Look at those windows boarded up and the rubbish outside. It's surprising what you notice in a traffic jam that you would normally drive straight past without seeing ..."

"Must be the wecession," says Serge, wisely. That was what everyone seemed to be saying these days.

The traffic begins to edge forward again. "There's nothing coming the other way so the road must be closed. It can't be road works or temporary traffic lights causing this. I hope it's not an accident." A police van, a police Land Rover and two saloon cars, all with flashing lights but no sirens glide quietly past them, using the lane that would normally be heaving with traffic leaving London.

"Ah, here we are," says Dominic as they draw near enough to see orange tape stretched across the road flapping in the breeze and a sign saying 'Police Incident'. "So, it's an *incident* not an *accident*."

"Wot's the difference?"

"Urm ... hopefully it means no-one's been hurt. Shall we put the radio on and see if they tell us anything about it?" Dominic begins to scan for a local radio station whilst Serge surveys the surroundings, taking in tattered net curtains behind cracked windows above boarded-up shops.

"Wuff ere innit? Must be the wecession ..."

A uniformed police officer is directing the traffic off the main road and up a side street. She is trying not to make eye contact with the drivers to discourage them from lowering their windows to ask what's going on.

As Dominic takes a left turn to follow the diversion Serge startles him by exclaiming loudly, "Aye, that's Serge's flask!"

"Where?"

"Up in that big building. Serge saw it in the window. Gone past it now. Go back Dom! Go back!"

"We can't go back - this is a one way street. There's nowhere to turn round. And it can't be *your* flask anyway, it's just one that looks the same."

"*Serge's flask ...*"

"Look Serge, if your flask doesn't turn up I'll find out from Justin where he got it from and get you another one. Okay?"

"Okay, Dom. But I think I'll go and check this one out anyway." Serge gets out of the car.

"Serge! SERGE! Get back in the car *now*! SERGE!" But Serge is walking purposefully back towards the main road.

Dominic gets out of the car lunges after him; then ducks back in the car to switch off the engine just as the traffic in front moves on again, leaving a gap in front of him. Horns begin to sound, and a police officer appears. "You can't stop here Sir, please get back in your vehicle and keep the traffic moving."

"But my passenger just got out and went off – he's disabled you see. I'm his Buddy – his *carer*."

"He can't be all that disabled if he's out of sight already. You'll just have to find somewhere to park and then come back on foot to meet him. I'm sorry, but you'll have to move on."

Sweating with anxiety, Dominic gets in his car and moves along to close the gap.

Serge is on a mission; concentration etched on his handsome features as he strides past a 'Police Incident' sign, steps over some orange tape and hesitates in front of a large rectangular sign that reads '*Authorised personnel only beyond this point.*' "In the way here," he mutters and drags the sign off the pavement and sets it on the road, steps back to reassess it and straightens it up a little. "Better," he says and resumes his pursuit of the flask which is now almost close enough for him to count the orange diamonds down the side. He looks around. Maybe there is a ladder somewhere he could borrow to climb up, break the window and grab the flask. It would have to be a long ladder though...

A man in a suit is hurrying towards him looking anxious. It is a crumpled, baggy suit, not like the nice ones that Serge has become accustomed to modelling. "You must be the negotiator." The man holds out his hand.

"*Must* I?" Serge shakes the man's hand solemnly then remembers his business cards and hands one to his new friend. "Serge," says Serge.

The man gives the card the briefest of glances and stuffs it in his pocket. "I'm Clive, as you know," he says. "You did well to get here so quick in this traffic without a police escort. Where did you leave your car?"

"Serge came with Dom, in Dom's car."

"Nice one Dom, whoever he is." A woman, young and pretty, approaches with a loudspeaker. "Would you like to try a loudspeaker first, from down here?" Clive asks Serge. "We've seen him at the window once or twice."

"Yes *pleez*." Serge takes it eagerly from the woman and speaks into it. "Hell-ooo! *Hell-ooooo*!" People glance at each other and shrug their shoulders. Serge hands it back to the woman with happy smile. "Nice laygee. They 'ad wun o' them at the Centre sports day, but they wouldn't let Serge av a go. What's your name?"

"Avril," she says with a besotted smile. She looks into the end of the loudspeaker and shakes her head. "This thing looks like it's been knocking around for years, no wonder it's no good to you."

Serge returns his attention to Clive, whose face is fixed in a quizzical expression; his mouth slightly open and one eyebrow raised. Clive clears his throat, "Anyway, are you up to speed?"

"Oi don't fink so ..." Serge is gazing up at the window where the flask is, as Clive consults his clipboard.

"Well you've obviously been briefed but so far as I can make out it's your typical domestic; firearm aside, of course. Divorced couple, massive row, *Gina*, the woman's name is - she's been using the boy to get back at him, saying he can't have him weekends anymore, so Paddy – that's your man – has kidnapped the lad, holding her at gunpoint whilst ordering the boy to get in a van he has borrowed that he is not insured to drive. This building is derelict and has been closed for some time. It gets used by squatters and druggies but we're pretty certain the only occupants right now are Paddy and the boy, Tommy."

Clive glances up from his clipboard and notices that Serge is gazing up at the window, where the butt of a gun can clearly be seen alongside what looks like a flask ... the sort of flask one might use for a hot drink if a long journey had been planned. "Is that a flask up there?"

"Flask ..." says Serge.

"Well, I'd see that as a good sign! Like you don't make up a flask if your intention is to end it all, do you? Oh, sorry mate, you must be wondering how the hell you're supposed to get up there."

"Serge was just wundring ow the 'ell to gerrup there. Gorra ladder av yer? A biggun?"

Clive wonders if they deliberately picked a negotiator from Northern Ireland so that Paddy might sense a kindred spirit and form an immediate bond of trust. He had always found the Scottish accent difficult to understand and Geordies could catch him out but Northern Ireland was impossible. "The entrance is round the back. Best I walk round there with you. I heard some talk of CO19 being called in."

A small crowd of official looking people with grave expressions has gathered a short distance from the entrance to the building, which is flanked by two police marksmen, poised on one knee either side of the entrance, watching the door along the barrel of a rifle. They lower their weapons as Clive and Serge approach. "This is Serge, the negotiator," says Clive. "He's just going in ... Good luck, mate!"

The gunmen scrutinise Serge, making a mental note not to shoot him.

"Cheers mate," says Serge to Clive as he enters the building. The door closes behind him with a clunk and it takes a few moments for Serge's eyes to adjust to the lack of daylight in the dingy hallway. A staircase materialises before him and Serge begins his ascent.

On the landing of the second flight of stairs he can hear the sound of an engine. *Funny place for a motorbike.* As he ascends the third flight the engine noise grows louder and there is a distinct smell of exhaust fumes. The fumes are drifting from an open door on the third floor landing. Encouraged by the door being open, Serge goes in to investigate and finds what appears to be a car engine, running by itself with no car surrounding it. A four-gang extension lead is plugged into it. Serge has seen these before, in fact there is one in his father's office at home, but this one is different in that the switch is red transparent plastic with a light behind it, a light that attracts Serge's finger to feel the shape of the switch and then of course to press it. The engine is still running but a wail of dismay from an adjoining room sends him back to the doorway.

"Dad! The telly's gone off Dad! I was just winning an' all!"

"Well, the generator's still going, so it is, it's ter be hoped we 'aven't blown der fuse." A door opens inwards from the adjoining room and a small man limps through. He frowns at the generator and quickly notices the four-gang is switched off. "Strange..." He switches it back on again inducing a cheer from the next room. "Yay! It's going again now Dad!"

The small man is about to rejoin his son when the exhaust from the generator makes Serge cough. The small man swings around, startled. "Holy Mother, who the feck are you?"

"Serge," says Serge and begins to cough again.

"Is that what it was, a power surge?" The small man frowns at the four-gang. "Well, I'll be damned, it says here der thing's surge protected." He shrugs his shoulders. "Dis must be some sort of trip switch."

"Dad! Who's that?"

"Oim not too sure, to be sure." The small man returns his attention to Serge. "Hey, you're not using are you? I don't want that going on around me boy."

"Oi don't fink so," says Serge.

"So what the feck are you doin' here?"

"Urm .... Oh yeah, Serge knows. Oi cum for me flask."

"You what?"

"Me *flask*! Serge saw it on the windowsill ..."

The small man narrows his eyes and stares intently at Serge, who returns a steady gaze. "Look, I don't wish ter offend but are you all right in der head?" Serge continues to gaze, benignly. “Are you ...” the correct term eludes him, “are you like one furlong short of a mile?”

“Well ...” says Serge. “Some people fink I was born like it and uvvers ... like me Dad ... finks I ‘ad a bang on the head.”

“Why does your Dad think that?”

“Because if ees wight Serge gets a load of money, but if ees wong it’s just Serge’s own fault for being stupid. Anyow – Serge came for ‘is flask. Pleez. Saw it in the window …”

“Yer really are a fruit cake, to be sure! What makes yer think that’s your feckin flask? Got one like it, eh?”

“Serge’s name on its bottom. Let’s go see. In there is it? Cum on!” Serge heads for the adjoining door to the next room.

“Hold it! Hold it!” The small man pushes past Serge and dives at the windowsill, reaching it first and grabbing the sawn-off shot gun he has left beside the flask.

Serge looks at it with interest. “My Dad’s got a gun like that. He keeps it in a special box and goes to a shooting club. He don’t shoot *real* pigeons though. And Serge ain’t allowed to touch it. Some futters broke the end off yours … that’s a shame. Can Serge av a go of yours? Won’t pull the trigger or nothing …”

“No you bloody can’t!” The small man is suddenly edgy now that the gun is in his hands. He thrusts the flask at Serge. “Just see if it’s got yer name on it why don’t yer!”

“*Flask!*” Serge seizes the flask and turns it upside down but there is no writing on the bottom. He unscrews the secret compartment where his sugar lumps are normally hidden but finds it empty. “*This* ain’t Serge’s flask!”

“I never said it was!” The small man’s face creases in amusement and he starts to laugh but it turns into a sob and he wipes away a tear.

“Aye, don’t be sad,” says Serge. “Serge don’t like people being unhappy. Serge’s flask’ll turn up. Everybody sez so. Nice man. What’s *your* name?”

"Paddy Smallman," he replies. "And this 'ere is me son, Tommy, so it is."

"That's a nice name ..."

"Hey Mister, you any good at COD?"

"Woht?"

"It's the latest COD, this is! Dad just got me it. I never played it before. Have you?"

Serge looks at the TV screen where an image of the butt of a machine gun vibrates as it fires and the screen becomes spattered with blood. "No. Mom don't like Serge playing shooting games."

"Neither does my Mam, but Dad don't mind! Good fun being with Dad."

"Does yer Dad like shooting games?" Serge glances round at Paddy, who is standing to one side of the window, pointing the butt of the sawn-off shotgun at the people gathered below.

"Yeah!"

"Pity someone broke the end off 'is gun …"

"Yeah," says Tommy. "It won't shoot very far like that."

"How come?" asks Paddy, turning the gun on himself to examine it.

"It'll just blast everything close range like that, and blow your brains out" explains Tommy, and demonstrates by shouting "Bang!" and rolling over on the floor, pretending to be dead.

"Don't do that, son," says Paddy, disturbed.

"Men outside the door av got long guns," says Serge.

"So there's gunmen guarding this place? How come they let you in here?"

"Oi dunno. Only popped in to get me flask. Guess they faut that was okay."

Tommy launches into a zombie act - awakening from the dead and holding the spare controller out to Serge. "Have a game Mister. Sit down here and we'll do split screen. I'll show you what to do."

Serge sits cross legged beside Tommy on the folded sleeping bag. "Just a quick'n then cos Serge better go 'ome soon."

Paddy returns his gun to its position the windowsill beside the flask. "Live around here do you?"

"Oi don't fink so," replies Serge.

"Live with your parents, do you?"

"Yer but Serge will buy 'is own house one day when he marries Fwanchesca."

"Are you engaged?"

"Oi don't fink so. Does you and Tommy live 'ere?"

"Well … we just moved in here today, like. I know it's not much, but it's a roof over our heads. I didn't really plan much beyond today...."

"Oh well. You gorra telly and a flask."

"A telly and a flask," Paddy repeats it slowly. "This time last week it seemed I had it all and now here I am with me poor laddie and a telly and a flask."

"Dad worked as a groom at a horse racing stables," explains Tommy. "He lived there see, just next to the stables so he could guard the horses. But they weren't making any money so they decided to get rid of half of the horses and got rid of my Dad as well. So now he hasn't got a job or nothing."

There is a short silence.

"Must be the wecession," says Serge, wisely. His game with Tommy ends conveniently a minute before the generator runs out of petrol. He looks round at Paddy, taking in his strong sinewy arms with faded tattoos beneath hair which appears to grow healthily from every visible area except his shaven head. His eyes look tired and wrinkly and his chin is dark with stubble. Serge thinks Paddy looks a bit of a hard nut and is surprised when he begins to shake … just like Ralph does when he senses a thunder storm.

"And me Mam's being a feckin bitch," adds Tommy in a low voice.

"Tommy I won't have yer speak of your Ma like dat," says Paddy sternly.

"Well that's what *you* called her."

"That's different!"

"You any good at looking after ponies?" asks Serge.

"Aye, to be sure …"

"My Dad used to be a jockey. But then a horse fell on him and crushed his leg and it never mended properly. There were bits of sharp bone all sticking out through the skin and –"

"Tommy, that's enough!"

"Fwanchesca wants a pony. Well, she wants *fwee* ponies. But she won't be no good at looking after em. She'll just brush the same bit over an' over an' over until she wears the fur off it."

Paddy laughs and shakes his head sadly. "Your girlfriend … Is she … urm … *special*?"

"Fwanny is *very* special to *Serge* …"

Nobody says anything for a while.

Serge stands up. "Anyow. Serge 'ad berrer be gerrin off. Dom ull be wundrin where Serge as got to."

"Dom?" says Paddy.

"Yeah ..."

"Who is Dom?" asks Tommy, on behalf of his father.

"Dom looks after Serge. And now he keeps pwetending to be 'appy when we all knows he ain't."

"Like me Dad?"

"Yeah ... but Dom ain't got a gun."

"If you're going now ..." begins Paddy, but his voice falters and he looks at the floor, blinking hard. "If yer going now, take Tommy." His voice is barely a whisper. "The police will take him back to his mother ..."

"Dad! I thought we were going to Ireland!"

Paddy shakes his head. "There's no way out of here for me now, Tommy."

"Yes there is," says Serge. "Serge knows the way - it's just down some stairs."

"You take Tommy. Go on now, *go* man!" Paddy covers his face with a shaking hand and Tommy runs and wraps his arms around him, pressing his head against his father's chest. "Tommy, yer know how much I love yer, don't yer, Son?"

Tommy nods. "Well there's times when love alone is not enough. You'll be better off without me. If I leave dis place I go to jail, and dat I would not survive. Your old Dad's a free spirit – okay, call it unreliable, like your Ma does. I've let yer down, Son, I know I have. Now you run along with your new friend."

"Come with us Dad," sobs Tommy.

Serge wishes Ralph were here. Ralph always knows what to do when people are unhappy.

"There's no point!" wails Paddy. He is openly bawling now with loud gulps and sobs; tears and watery snot falling copiously on his son's head. "They know about the gun and there's only one use left for it. Go away now the pair of you and let me end it all!"

"No Dad!" Tommy turns to Serge, looking for help. "Tell him Mister, else he'll blow his brains out. He'll soon get another job and somewhere to live ... There's plenty other horses needs grooming. *Tell* him!"

"Well ... Fwanchesca will need someone to look after all 'er ponies when she gets them. Will that do?"

"Yeah, my Dad will sleep in the stables with the ponies. He's not fussy."

Serge pulls a face. "Don't fink I'd like to sleep with ponies. Them at Fwan's riding school is always farting."

"Well, so's me Dad." Tommy chuckles and Paddy's sobs transform into uncontrollable laughter. He wipes Tommy's damp head with the end of his tee-shirt, drops a kiss on it and steers him gently away.

"That's better," says Serge. "Tell yer what, I'll give yer one of me cards." He withdraws a business card from his back pocket. "Mom said to bring them along in case I met anyone important."

"I don't imagine dis is what she had in mind," says Paddy, and giggles hysterically.

"Av you gorra pen to put Serge's phone number on the back?"

Tommy extracts a packet of felt tip pens from his backpack. "What colour do you want?"

"Red pleez. No – blue. No, *that* one," he points to the turquoise. Serge turns over the card and sticks out his tongue in concentration as he writes 'SErge'. He hands the card and the pen back to Tommy. "Now you write Serge's phone number on there. Justin didn't 'ave me phone number put on there in case we got nutters phoning up."

"Den yer best be a tad careful who yer give it out to," says Paddy and is seized by another fit of laughter and tears.

Serge repeats his phone number a few times to make sure Tommy has got it. "Can't you write then?" asks Tommy.

"No," replies Serge.

"Neither can me Dad," says Tommy. "He can't read either."

"Well he don't 'ave to read stories to Fwan's ponies, so that don't matter, do it?"

"Dad never went to school. His Ma was a traveller and he never stayed in one place long enough."

"My Mom used to go twavelling. But then she 'ad me and couldn't go nowhere. Sept to apologise, ha, ha, ha ..."

"Is that what she tells you? Is your Mam a -" Tommy lowers his voice, "feckin bitch?"

"No. But sometimes she gets fed up of been stuck at 'ome wiv Serge. Specially when 'er mate Viv is off to Barbados. Only she'd never say it to Serge cos it would make 'im sad to fink of it."

"But you heard her say it to someone else ..."

"Yeah ..."

"Pack yer things up now Tommy. You're going out with Serge."

"You *are* coming with us, aren't you Dad?"

"I guess so." Paddy shivers suddenly and rubs his arms. "But let's hurry up before I change me mind."

"Let Mr Serge hand the gun over to them, Dad. If you go out there with it they'll blast your head off."

Serge's eyes widen with enthusiasm. "Let Serge carry the gun, pleez!" He picks it up off the windowsill and Paddy ducks.

"Jesus, man, don't hold it like dat or you'll blast all our heads off! Here, just hold the end and let it point at der ground. And don't go marching out there with it. Bang on the door first and tell 'em yer handing it over. Understand?"

"Oi fink so …"

"Hey, I can't let yer do this, it's not right. Gimme back der gun."

"No." Serge holds the gun behind him, where Paddy can't see it.

"Don't let him have it Mister," says Tommy. "Take it down to them now, then come back and tell us what happens!"

Serge descends the stairs, holding the gun like Paddy showed him. He reaches the front door and knocks on it. To Serge it seems strange to be inside a building knocking on the door to go out instead of being outside and knocking to come in. Animated mutterings from behind the door are followed by a loud and clear demand, "Who's there?"

"Serge," says Serge, and when nobody says "Serge who?" he adds, "and I've got a gun!"

After a muffled conference, the loud and clear voice says, "Hello Serge. Would you like to hand the gun over to me?"

"Yes pleez."

"Okay, Serge. This is what I'd like you to do. Open the door, very slowly with the gun pointing towards the ground, and place it on the step outside. Do you understand?"

"Oi fink so …"

"Good. Come on then. Nice and slowly. No sudden movements."

Serge opens the heavy front door and peeps round it. The two police marksmen are poised ready to shoot, watching the door through the sights of their rifles.

"Ello," says Serge.

A voice echoes through a loudspeaker. "Place the gun on the doorstep."

Serge looks all around the gathering of people, trying to see where the voice was coming from. He catches sight of Clive and waves. "Serge, *put the gun down on the step*," the voice insists.

"Oh yer … sorry, Serge forgot." He puts the gun on the step and one of the marksmen shuffles forward to retrieve it.

Clive steps forward. "Nice work. Is the kid okay?"

"Tommy's 'appy."

"What's Smallman like?"

"He's quite a small man and 'is nose looks a bit squashed and-"

"What is his state of mind?"

"Uh?"

"Is he, erm, *happy*?"

"Well … first ee was 'appy. Then ee was very sad. Then ee was 'appy again cos ee's gonna look after Fwanchesca's ponies. But ee don't wanna go to jail. That'd make 'im sad." He frowns at the two police marksmen who have now lowered their guns. "And ee's coming out in a minute and I don't fink you should point your guns at him cos ee's scared enough already. Understand?" With that, Serge turns and goes back upstairs.

Tommy has packed his games in his bag and is ready to go. "Coming then?" asks Serge, and Tommy shouts "Yeah!" and leaps around the room.

Paddy is leaning against the doorway, his extreme pallor emphasising the dark shadows around his eyes. He starts to shake again and Serge watches for a moment then begins to run his hand down the back of Paddy's neck, repetitively, like he does to Ralph when he gets scared and shakes. It always works.

"Come on, let's go!" says Tommy and bounces out onto the landing. Paddy follows and Serge rests a steadying hand on his shoulder when he hesitates at the top of the stairs.

Serge opens the front door a fraction and looks out. The gunmen are still positioned either side of the doorway but appear more relaxed since taking possession of the sawn-off shotgun. Clive steps forward. "Okay, Serge, let's have Tommy out of there."

"Go on then, Tommy. Mind the step." Serge guides him gently through the doorway and Clive ushers him to a lady with a kind smile who is wearing a police uniform. Serge watches as she escorts him to a car, arm around his shoulders, and takes a back seat next to him. The car goes off with Tommy staring anxiously out of the back window, looking for his Dad.

A group of uniformed police officers moves forward towards the doorway and a voice over the loudspeaker startles everyone. "Patrick Smallman! Put your hands on your head and leave the building now. Keep your hands on your head and walk slowly with no sudden movements."

Paddy takes a deep breath and Serge pats his shoulder. "Don't worry …"

Paddy gives Serge a quick firm handshake. "Thanks." He puts his hands on his head and Serge pulls the door wide open and moves aside to let him through.

The uniformed officers swoop on him; one grasping his wrists as another applies the handcuffs and another conducts a body search.

Serge advances, suddenly overwhelmed with anger when Paddy stumbles as they propel him towards a police van. He hollers with rage, "Oi! No need for that, you futters! Paddy did as you asked!"

Paddy – his hands shackled behind him - thrashes a little and briefly shakes off his captors, taking them by surprise with that astonishing physical strength sometimes possessed by small men. "Steady boy, steady ... it's okay ... easy now." Paddy calms Serge with the voice he normally reserves for frightened race horses.

Serge watches quietly as Paddy is bundled into the back of the van. Suddenly Dominic arrives at his side, breathing heavily and sweating profusely as if he has just run a few miles. "Ello Dom," says Serge.

"Serge …" says Dominic when he can finally speak. "I thought I'd lost you. What on earth would I have told your mother? Please don't ever do that again …"

"Do what, Dom?"

Clive, standing a short distance away, is watching the scene with a puzzled expression when a tall slim young man with fair hair hurries towards him. "Hi, I'm Sean Freemantle, the negotiator." Clive shakes his hand, his expression deepening into a bewildered frown. "Sorry it's taken me so long to get here – it was impossible to get through the traffic without a police escort. Still, I'm here now if you'd like to bring me up to speed."

13

Fame and Fortune

Judith tips the remaining cup cakes into a tin and covers the assortment of sandwiches with cling film. Serge will no doubt have those as a snack before dinner. She wipes lipstick off the china tea cups and loads them in the dishwasher, wondering whether this evening might be a good time to broach the subject with Alistaire of the large charitable donation she has promised from 'Freeman and Freeman'. He has always grumbled that her idea of fundraising is to give away half of his profits and whilst that is an exaggeration it is true that she will never make a good fundraiser – it simply isn't in her nature to ask anyone for anything, thus she is always attracted to projects designed to help people to help themselves. She switches on the dishwasher and goes into the lounge where Ralph is busily snuffling up crumbs from the carpet. She ruffles the coarse hair on his back and he arches his spine and squirms with pleasure. "I was going to get the vacuum cleaner out, but let's just watch The News and see how it looks when you've finished."

She switches on the television, steps back, and becomes suspended in animation, still pointing the remote control with her arm outstretched and her bottom poised a short distance from the chair she was about to descend upon. "Oh Dear God," she says out loud as she watches the video footage of Serge emerging from some doorway and placing a gun on a doorstep. Next a child walks out - with Serge still there in the background - and then a small man appears with his hands on his head. The camera pans in to a reporter with a microphone who says, "When interviewed about this heroic deed, Serge played down his bravery - saying that he only went into the building to ... erm ... *to look for his flask.*"

The car pulling up in the drive outside is unmistakeably Dominic's owing to the rattle from the loose exhaust pipe.

Judith rushes to the front door to meet them and is relieved when Serge greets her in his usual style; "Any of them samwidges left? Serge is 'ungry. Ope they 'aven't eaten 'em all."

Dominic trails behind, dishevelled and exhausted, his thin dark hair sticking to his head with dried sweat. "I just saw *The News*," says Judith, the alarmed expression still on her face.

"I'm *so* sorry," says Dominic. "We got stuck in a traffic jam you see, and he saw a flask the same as the one he lost and he got out of the car and just *went*. There was no stopping him ..."

"Oh heavens, the phone's ringing now!" Judith hurries away as if her life depends on answering the phone.

"*Samwidges*, I does," calls Serge from the kitchen, and Dominic follows him in and removes the cling film from a plateful of assorted leftovers - some curling up at the edges - and hopes he won't get the blame if Serge gets food poisoning.

Judith answers the phone from Alistaire's study. "Judith, it's Theo," booms Theo's rich deep voice. Theo is Alistaire's elder brother, the senior Freeman of 'Freeman and Freeman'. "I don't know what my younger nephew has been up to today but the phones here haven't stopped ringing for the last hour. It seems he is something of a hero. It's all very vague at the moment but there's some tale about a hostage situation with a sawn-off shotgun involved. Leo is on the other line at the moment, negotiating with journalists who want to buy Serge's story. Is Serge home yet?"

"Yes, he just came home with Dominic. They set out on a trip to Savile Row, but – well, I've no idea what happened ..."

"Alistaire's on his way home now. I know you're ex-directory, but we wondered if the press had tracked you down."

"Not so far, thank goodness. Anyway Theo thanks *so* much for your call but I'd better go and see Serge. He'd literally just come through the door when the phone rang." She hangs up and heads for the kitchen where Serge is working his way through the pile of sandwiches, then hesitates in the hallway when she hears Dominic talking to someone at the front door.

"No, I'm sorry, I *can't* ask you in," he says firmly. "I'm only a visitor here myself, so it's not my place to do so. Goodbye." Dominic shuts the door and slides the bolt across.

"Thank you Dominic," says Judith and sits down at the kitchen table next to Serge.

"Tea, I does," says Serge and she automatically stands up again and puts the kettle on.

There is a thunderous knocking on the front door.

"Oh no ..." says Judith.

"I'll get rid of them!" Dominic returns boldly to the front door. "Go away and leave us alone!" he yells, with gallantry fuelled by his recurrent fantasy about protecting Judith. "Clear off or I'll call the police!"

After a short pause and a final ineffectual turning of the door handle, Alistaire clears his throat and says, "It's me ... Alistaire. I think someone must have bolted the door."

Dominic pulls back the bolt and flings open the door in panic. "I'm *so sorry* Mr Freeman; I thought you were the paparazzi."

Alistaire walks in, tall and glowering, shuts the door and on second thoughts bolts it again. "Did they follow you back here?" he asks with a frown.

"Urm ... I wasn't aware of it but I suppose they must have done." Dominic looks down at the floor, feeling that everything is his fault.

Alistaire walks past him, then hesitates and looks back, "Thank you for bringing him home safely. Of course I understand how difficult he can be."

Dominic leans back against the door and glows with pleasure at this acknowledgement from Alistaire. He is still congratulating himself when a sudden rap on the door sends him reeling away.

"Open up, it's Leo," demands a quiet, clear voice, and Dominic leaps into action to be left examining the flap of skin the bolt has lifted from his finger as Leo thanks him briefly and walks through to his father's study with his laptop PC, answering his mobile as he goes. "No, I'm sorry; a radio interview is out of the question. It wouldn't work – it has to be visual. No, no, it's not about the fee – it simply would not be a good interview; Serge would not make good radio." He ends the call and types his password into the laptop, telling his father, "Justin Beaver's secretary has been on the phone as well. There's an email account linked to his website and he's been inundated with enquiries about Serge. I told him to forward them to me for the time being. '*Luminaire*' want exclusive rights to Serge's story about today's hostage situation, but '*Good Innit*' have offered a hundred and fifty thousand more." Leo pauses to read an email. "And '*Fayme & Fo*' would like to do a feature on him also. I think we should sell the hostage story to the highest bidder, but make some sort of deal with all other interested parties, so the second highest bidder for the hostage story can have the story of Serge's rise to fame – and we could offer an exclusive photo-shoot to one of the many *homes and gardens* magazines. And then –"

"Leo, wait!" Alistaire paces up and down the office a few times rubbing the back of his neck and then stops and rests both hands on the desk. "Are you telling me Serge is suddenly in demand?"

"Well, *yes,* he is *in demand* - but it's not *sudden,* Dad. It's just that *you* haven't noticed – you've been too wrapped up in suing someone over his brain damage and meanwhile Serge has been earning himself a small fortune. At least it started off as a *small* fortune but right now I'm struggling to keep account of it. Bridget made me go shopping at the weekend and every department store had larger than life cardboard cut-outs of Serge. He's *everywhere!* And of course next weekend sees the launch of the new 'SErge' aftershave, so the 'Serge Mania' is likely to reach new heights."

"*Serge Mania*?" Alistaire shakes his head incredulously and drifts from the study to the kitchen, where he stands in the doorway and looks at Serge as if seeing him for the first time.

"Are you all right, Dear?" asks Judith, and Dominic, who has now joined Serge and Judith at the kitchen table, thinks it is a shame that she always seems slightly nervous of her own husband. “Shall I fetch a pot of tea into the study for you and Leo?”

Alistaire shakes his head.

“*Tea*, I does,” says Serge and pauses to belch loudly before stuffing the last sandwich into his mouth, folding the crusts to make it fit all in one go.

Alistaire shakes his head again. ‘*Serge Mania’* ... He retreats to his study.

Judith puts the kettle on again and then places a bacon sandwich in front of Dominic who hasn’t eaten all day. Noticing how drained he looks she pats his shoulder gently. “Let’s put a plaster on that finger else you’ll get salt in it,” she says, and a First Aid box appears as if by magic. “You’re not allergic to them, are you?” Dominic shakes his head and wishes he could rest for ever in the haven of Judith’s kitchen.

Serge shifts his weight on to his left buttock to break wind more easily and then announces, “Serge go see Leo now,” and leaves the room.

“Well, thank you for leaving us with *that*,” grumbles Dominic.

“I’ll bring your tea to the study,” says Judith. “I expect Leo would like some too.”

Leo is typing furiously on his PC.

“Ello Leo,” says Serge, and Leo sits back, visibly relaxing and softening.

“Serge!” Leo pats the chair next to him and Serge sits down. “Looks like you’re in demand. Lots of newspapers and magazines … all wanting to report everything about you. How do you feel about thousands of strangers looking at photos of you and reading about everything you do?”

“Serge don’t care.”

“They want to pay you well. Play your cards right - or perhaps let me play them for you, and you’ll be a rich man.”

"Serge would like that. Serge wants to be rich so he can marry Fwan an' live in a nice house wiv stables so she can 'ave fwee ponies and Paddy can come an' look after 'em."

"Ha! That rings a bell. Some reporter quoted something similar to me. So it's true then? That's your plan? I'm not sure where you'd stand with marriage - must look into it."

Judith pushes the door open with her foot and sets down a rattling tea tray on the desk. Alistaire rolls his eyes; *Judith and her bloody tea.*

"Thanks Mom, *lurvley* ... but ..." Serge hangs his head and looks up at his mother, an expression he has learnt from the dog.

"But *what*, Darling?" asks Judith.

"But Serge never *did* find 'is flask ..."

"Uh-hum," says Alistaire, and they all look at him. He opens the bottom drawer of the desk and slowly extracts Serge's flask – the one Justin gave him with the colourful diamond pattern. He places it on the desk, wordlessly, and Serge's face lights up with joy. Serge takes it gently in his huge hands then cradles it against his chest and rocks it back and forth.

"*Why*, Alistaire?" demands Judith. "*Why* did you hide it from him?"

"That's *precisely* why!" says Alistaire, indicating the way Serge is behaving with the flask. "It makes him look *autistic* ... this attachment that he has to a particular object for no good reason. So I took it and hid it." After a short silence he says, "I'm sorry Serge."

"That's all right Dad. You can borrow Serge's flask whenever you want. Serge don't mind ... so long as you keep the sugar separate wiv this one. But you'd better *ask* next time, pleez!"

14

Home?

Dominic is travelling up the M1, heading back to his northern roots. Rather he *was* travelling but then he reached the eternal roadworks near Chesterfield, and now he is stationary with the sun blazing down on his car, the windows wide open, the dashboard smelling of hot plastic and the temperature gauge creeping upwards. Seeing the queue of traffic ahead, curving northwards as far as he can see, he turns on the car heater and blowers to try to take some heat away from the engine. He begins to repeat a mantra – not out loud because of the open windows – but he is not in the mood and soon it starts to drive him slightly mad, so he stops and allows the thoughts to flood his mind.

He had said his normal casual goodbye to Serge, without mentioning that they were unlikely ever to meet again; arguing with his conscience that Serge was so much in the present moment that *goodbye forever* would only confuse him. Or maybe he was just too choked up to say very much after Judith presented him with a boxed pen set as a leaving present and thanked him emotionally for all he had done and wondered *what on earth* they were going to do without him.

And then there was Sabrina ... Dominic sighs. He had thought they were getting on really well ... but then she had met someone even more unattractive than himself. Ivan seemed like a really nice guy, but he was quite remarkable for his ugliness – apart from being almost twice her age. Was Bri going out of her way to demonstrate that looks don't matter, or did she like to be seen with ugly men to emphasise her own good looks? *Or perhaps I'm just over-analysing as usual...*

Finally he passes Sheffield, avoiding the lane that leads to Meadowhall's, and looks down in wonderment at the number of cars in the huge car park surrounding the shopping centre.

What on earth was the attraction? On impulse, he takes the next exit off the motorway and heads for the Howden Moors. He is in no hurry to return to his parents' home, but had even less desire to hang around this morning after returning his library books and handing in his keys. Friday ... Mum's bingo night and Dad's beer night, so maybe eight o'clock would be a good time to turn up at home. They will both be out and will come back later in a good mood, hopefully, and then it shouldn't be too long before they go to bed.

He parks the car and walks a short distance to a grassy slope where he sits beneath the shelter of a huge oak tree and allows himself a minute to take in his immediate surroundings; the variety of greens in the grass before him, the fluctuating patterns of light and shade as the branches sway above him, and the vivid sky, as blue as Serge's eyes, with just a few transparent clouds floating by. He takes the sausage rolls from his backpack; two remaining from a pack of four that went off at midnight according to the date on the packet. He sniffs them and decides to risk it, washing them down with a bottle of water - no flask today - then settles down to read for a while. The book is one he has read several times before, but he still finds comfort from dipping into it and being reassured that everything is okay *right now at this particular moment* and any past regrets or future fears are merely stories that his mind has created.

Leeds is always Dominic's benchmark for being almost home. This evening, the city has the added significance that he is most likely to gain employment somewhere out there ... Consequently he views it with new interest and an attitude of respect and hopefulness. Travelling northwards, leaving the city behind, the scenery becomes greener and less cultivated, the roads narrower and the architecture tall and grim with high buildings of blackened stone and tall rectangular windows. He hasn't been home to Ravensgrave since last Christmas, and although nothing has changed, as he enters the village he sees it objectively, as a first time visitor would see it – the main street affluent and imposing - not particularly welcoming. Turning off the main street and up towards home, the picture changes. The houses are crowded together; many of them run down with peeling paint on old wooden window frames and overgrown gardens enclosed by broken fences. Had Ravensgrave gone down hill suddenly, or had it been a gradual process that he had not noticed?

He turns into the cul-de-sac and drives up to the end to turn round. His Dad's Fiesta is in the driveway, but hopefully he has walked down to the Club. Dominic parks outside the house, half on the pavement as the road is narrow, and walks up the drive and tries the front door, key at the ready as he expects it to be locked but the door opens and he is greeted by his mother's delighted smile. It is the expression that she always wears when she has not seen him for a while, and it never fails to make him feel warm and happy – for the first half hour at least.

"I thought you'd be at the Bingo with Auntie Marj." He surveys the living room and finds it much the same as the last time he saw it; old fashioned, on the shabby side, with an assortment of rugs covering threadbare areas of carpet, but homely and immaculately clean.

"No Love, not tonight, what with you coming back an' all. Our Vera said she'd go along with Marj. Your Dad's gone downt Club. He *ummed* 'n *ahhed* about it for a bit, but I told him you wouldn't mind." She winks knowingly. "Anyhow, he said he wouldn't be late."

Dominic takes his bags up to his room and stops in the doorway. It has been redecorated. The walls are plain magnolia with a pink floral border a foot down from the ceiling. He can't remember what colour they used to be because they were covered with posters, and photos he had downloaded off the internet and printed. Where *was* his printer? Where was the computer table - and his desktop PC come to that? There was nothing of his in here. Even his black duvet cover with the roaring flames had been replaced by something beige with pink decoration – and what had they done with all his books that had been piled up the walls? He hears his mother coming upstairs.

"I forgot to mention, I redecorated your room."

"Yes ... it looks like a hotel room ..."

She smiles, "I'm glad you like it. All your stuff's in the loft. I didn't throw anything out – well – not much, anyway. I rolled your posters up into a big tube. I don't expect you'll want them now – your interests have changed. But I kept them just in case."

"Thanks ..."

"But whilst you're here I'll get you to have a look through it all and see what we can chuck out. Now then, sausages and chips?"

"That sounds great."

"A few frozen peas?"

"Lovely."

Dominic's father returns from the Club with the congeniality of a man who has sunk his Friday night four-pint quota in a shorter time than usual. He greets his son with a friendly nod then switches on the television and settles into his usual armchair.

"Do you want your usual?" asks Dominic's mother.

"Aye, if you're doing some. Fancy some cheese on toast, son?"

"Not for me thanks, I've just had my ... usual"

"So ... You've packed in the course you've been paying to study all this time ..."

"Yes." Dominic knew this conversation would have to be had, and he knew that explaining his reasons to his father would not be easy. He takes a deep breath. "You see, I went into NLP with the idea that it was a therapy for people with low confidence, or low self-esteem, or learning difficulties ... you know, to help people who were disadvantaged. But the emphasis seemed to be on improving the confidence of people who were already achieving ... making people in the business world more assertive so they can win promotion and earn a better salary –"

"Nothing wrong with earning a better salary," his mother chips in unhelpfully.

Dominic goes on with the explanation he has prepared. "But then I got interested in Buddhism – particularly Zen," his father *tutts* and rolls his eyes but Dominic ploughs on, "And I found great peace in the idea that everything is as it should be – in its right place at the right time in the scheme of things ... which seemed to challenge some of the concepts of NLP ..."

His father yawns and looks at the newspaper. "There's some football on in a minute." He tracks down the remote control and switches channels. "I said you should train to be a plumber, or summat useful."

"He could train to be a plumber now," says his mother. "They're always advertising courses in the paper."

"Have you any idea how much those courses cost, Mum? Besides, I can't say I fancy spending the rest of my life fixing toilets."

"That's a shame," says his father. "The flusher on ours is not too good these days."

"So I noticed this morning," says his mother pointedly, and his father chuckles.

"Sorry about your room, son. I told your mother she should've asked you first – but there was a sale on so she'd already bought the paper and stuff."

"Well, all those weird pictures on the walls gave little Miranda nightmares when she was here last – and it's nice to have a proper guest room," says his mother defensively. *Little Miranda* is his sister's precocious five-year-old who gets dumped on his parents' whenever his sister and brother-in-law fancy a weekend to themselves. Frankly, Dominic is sick of hearing about *Little Miranda* and all her various achievements.

"She's doing tap dancing now, as well as ballet, you know. Doing very well too."

"Great."

"Oh, and they're building a new development called Poppy Fields on that little patch of land next to the Village Hall. *Thirty-two* houses and flats on that little bit of land! They've put the footings down already and it looks like they're building multi-storey rabbit hutches – but I expect it will be nice when it's finished. They call them *starter homes*. The cheapest is a *studio flat* - I suppose that's open plan with no bedrooms – all right for single people I suppose."

"And they want a *hundred grand* for them," his father points out.

Dominic tries to remain calm whilst feeling as though he is suppressing a scream from deep inside. In a voice as steady as he can manage, he says "And I expect they want a fifteen percent deposit. And what would the building society lend me? Three times my salary … which happens to be non-existent at the moment. And of course there's my student loan to be paid back which would be set against the amount I could borrow … in the event that I could actually borrow *any amount at all …*"

"Never mind, love. Something'll crop up, and until then this will always be your home, you know that."

"Thanks. If you don't mind I'll go up to *the guest room* and read in bed for a while. Good night." Dominic leaves the room.

"Now look what you've done," says his mother.

"What! Me?" says his father. "How d'you make *that* out?"

Dominic closes the bedroom door. He finds one of *Little Miranda's* teddy bears in his bed and hurls it across the room, where it hits a bowl of pot pourri, spilling it all over the dressing table and carpet.

15

Bring back Dom

Beatrice listens again to the message her mother has left on her mobile: "Hello Darling, it's Mummy. If you're still coming over for dinner this evening, I wonder if you'd be so kind as to fetch me a box of Crunchy Nut Cornflakes from ... from *somewhere*. Please be sure to bring *flakes* and not *clusters*. Thank you Darling. See you later!" Her mother's voice sounds artificially bright and cheerful, like it often does when she is upset about something. Beatrice phones her back. "Hi Mum, it's me. You want me to get you some *Crunchy Nut Cornflakes*?"

"Oh, hello Darling. Thank you for getting back to me. It's *for your brother*. The supermarket had run out, and I'm afraid he caused a bit of a scene ..." Judith's voice falters.

"Mum? Look I'll go and find some now and then come straight over. Geoff's got one of his internet dates tonight so he's gone off to prepare himself. He more or less told me to have the afternoon off."

"Well, if you're sure it will be all right ..."

Beatrice hears Serge's voice in the background, "Don't cry Mom." His voice sounds unusually thick and heavy.

"Mum? I'll be there as soon as I can. *Flakes* right? *Not* clusters."

When Beatrice arrives at her parents' home, her mother is calmly preparing vegetables for the evening meal with half a glass of red wine on the worktop. Serge is sitting at the kitchen table gazing into space. Beatrice puts a box of cereal on the table in front of him and he looks at it blankly, the huge fuss that had blown up earlier seemingly forgotten. She slides her arms briefly around his shoulders and kisses his golden hair but today he is unresponsive. "Don't you *dare* say you want

Weetabix in the morning," she chides and helps herself to some orange juice from the fridge. "Fancy some juice?"

"Tea, I does," Serge responds.

"Damn, I should have known better than to ask." She puts the kettle on. "So, what happened at the supermarket?"

Judith sighs. "I wandered up and down the cereal aisle and couldn't find the Crunchy Nut Cornflakes so I told him they must have run out, so would he like to choose something else. But he wouldn't stop looking for them – thought they might be behind some of the other boxes and started lifting them all off the shelves to look behind. So, he was lifting them down faster than I could put them back up and the manager came along and asked if we *needed any help.* Serge told him he could make a start at the other end and tell his *bloody mother* to stop putting them back." Beatrice giggles and Judith sees the funny side too. "Anyway, he said he'd go and see if there were any more in the back, and Serge insisted on following him ... They had to get the security officers involved in the end, and I have to say, they handled it pretty well. But then someone called his name. I thought it must be someone we knew – but then others began to join in – and they were taking photos of him with their mobile phones, and running up to have their photos taken with him and the security guards – it was *terrible*! By the time we got to the car I was shaking so much I was quite incapable of going elsewhere to look for the cereal ..." Her voice wavers. She takes a sip of wine and declares, "I don't think I like him being famous! If only Dominic were still with us. Such a nice young man and he did have a *way* with Serge, and he didn't seem to be fazed by noisy crowds. I suppose that's part of being young – but yet there's something a little *old fashioned* about him too. And we've got this wretched court case coming up soon – I'm *dreading* it!"

"You *could* see if Dominic's available to support Serge on the day of the court case. Get him down here the night before. There's enough guest rooms in this place to start a hotel."

"That might be a good idea, Darling. You like him too, don't you?"

"Yeah, he's okay I guess... and *Serge* seemed to like him. Give him a call."

"I'd sooner email him. Phone calls tend to put one on the spot, whereas emails give one chance to think of a polite excuse. And I'd better suggest it to your father first."

"Suggest what?" asks Alistaire making them both jump by suddenly arriving in the kitchen.

"Hello Darling! Beatrice suggested we ask Dominic to come along to Serge's hearing. You know how *good* he was with Serge."

"*Marvellous*, I'd say. The last time Dominic took him out for the day Serge ended up in a derelict building with some nutcase with a sawn-off shotgun."

"Oh, Alistaire! That could have happened to *anyone*."

Alistaire raises his eyebrows at Serge who is carefully tracing his finger around the wood-grain patterns on the kitchen table. "Well ... yes, I know it could."

When Dominic checks his email he is delighted to find a message from Judith - lurking amongst all the adverts for Viagra and penis enlargements:

Dear Dominic,

I do hope you well and you are enjoying being back home.

Alistaire and I were wondering if you might be available to attend Serge's compensation hearing - the date of which has been confirmed as 20th October. Of course we understand if you are otherwise committed on that date, and we are most grateful for your submission of the diary detailing your time with Serge that you were so conscientious to upkeep. Regina, his case manager, is confident that this alone will provide evidence that a financial award to employ a support worker in the future is justified.

If you are disposed to join us for this occasion (which I must confess I am absolutely dreading) I suggest that you travel down the evening before. We have a guest room which is nice and quiet, over-looking the orchard. Of course we would pay you for your time and travelling expenses, and I am sure Alistaire would agree to double your previous rate since this is a one-off event.

Please let me know whether or not you can make it.

Kindest regards,
Judith

The next morning, on his way to the office, Leo stops at the news agent's to pick up his copy of The Times but a picture on the front of one of the tabloids halts him in his tracks.

Two hours later when he arrives at the office, Alistaire greets him with a sarcastic "Glad you could make it."

"Have you seen this?" Leo unrolls a newspaper and puts it on the desk in front of his father.

Alistaire takes it in. "'Struth! I hope your mother hasn't seen this – she's started walking to the paper shop with Serge in the morning to give him a bit of an airing. Most days, lately, that's their only outing. Seeing this, I can begin to appreciate why."

"Don't worry, I got there first and bought them all. Mrs O'Grady said Mum hadn't been in yet and assured me she wouldn't mention it to her. She likes Mum – doesn't everyone? Anyway, they're in the back of the car. I'll call at the recycling centre on the way home and dump them."

"Front page headlines, eh? Talk about a slow news day! Hasn't anything more interesting happened in the world since yesterday morning than your mother going out to buy breakfast cereal?"

"No. Not according to three national newspapers."

Alistaire puts on his glasses to read the small print beneath the headline *Crunchy Nutter Serge*. 'Serge Freeman, the male talent who inspired Justin Beaver's prolific creations that have stormed the men's designer fashion world went one step further this morning to substantiate rumours that his mind is not as fit as his physique. Wearing saggy jogging bottoms and a tee-shirt with what appeared to be tea stains down the front; he was seen out shopping today with his girlfriend who looked ill at ease in the limelight and old enough to be his mother - in a shapeless, floral patterned cotton dress. Appearing tense and tearful under the intense public scrutiny she should have known she would attract, she declined to be interviewed. An on-scene security officer confirmed that Mr Freeman's prima donna antics were triggered by his favourite breakfast cereal being temporarily out of stock.'

"*Poor Judith.*" Alistaire strokes her little shoulder on the picture then remembers Leo is watching and examines his finger as if checking the print fixing quality. "I think I might pop home at lunch time and make sure everything's in order."

Judith greets him with a forced smile. He notices for the first time how pale and tired she is looking. A television is blaring loudly from somewhere in the house and he follows the noise to find Serge fast asleep on the sofa in front of a cartoon channel. He switches off the television. "That's better; I can hear him snoring now!" He sweeps back the golden curls to rest a palm on his son's forehead.

Judith has followed him and is standing in the doorway. "I'm afraid I gave him Diazepam," she says, guiltily. "I planted it in a slice of chocolate cake." Alistaire raises his eyebrows and she explains; "We went to the paper shop as usual and he thought he saw Leo's car coming towards us. It must have been the same sort of car – I didn't notice really. I told him it couldn't be Leo because he would be at the office. But he *wouldn't* have it, so I said *very well*, if it *were* Leo he must have called to see us for some reason, and he would be at home when we got back. *Of course* he wasn't here because it *wasn't* Leo he saw - but *would he have it?* No! And he went on, and on *and on!*" Judith begins to weep quietly and Alistaire puts his arms around her and holds her against his chest. "I *do* miss having Dominic to take him out for the day . or just to spend the day here with him." She pushes Alistaire away in order to blow her nose. "I remember how worried I was that first day they went off together, but then I got used to it, and it's only *now* that I realise how much I benefitted from that bit of freedom."

"Then we'll find him another 'Buddy'. It'll be fine, I promise you! Has Dominic replied to your email?"

"Not when I checked first thing this morning. I'll have another look now."

Finally the PC boots up and allows Judith access to her email. Her face lights up, "Yes – he's replied! Now then, let's see what he says ..."

Hi Judith,

Thank you for your email. I have checked my diary and yes I am available on the 20th October. In fact there are not many days when I'm not available! Despite the glowing reference you were kind enough to provide there is very little work in this area at the moment. I shall apply to help with the Christmas post if nothing comes up within the next week or two. Thanks also for your offer of a sleepover - that would be great.

It was a surprise to see your picture in the paper this morning. I cut out the article to keep. I hope you weren't offended by their description of you - in a way it was a compliment, because the reporters thought you were Serge's girlfriend and therefore they felt obliged to criticise - whereas if they had known you were his mother they would have said flattering things, if you know what I mean. Anyway, if you don't mind me saying, I think you looked as lovely and elegant as you always do.

Look forward to seeing you on 19th October.

Yours,
Dominic

16

Hearing Serge

Ralph recognises the scrunch of Dominic's car tyres on the gravel outside; stands up, stretches and trots to the door with his tail wagging. Serge follows with a delighted lopsided grin. As Dominic ascends the steps to the front door, Serge waits in the doorway, shifting impatiently from one foot to the other; arms outstretched to receive him. Dominic laughs and blinks back unexpected tears as Serge takes him in a bear hug whilst Ralph jumps up behind Serge and clasps his front paws over his shoulders, panting excitedly in both their faces.

"Blimey, I hope that's the dog's breath and not yours," says Dominic.

"Dog breff thattiz. Serge cleans *his* teeth." Serge stretches back his lips hideously to reveal a perfect set of brilliant white teeth.

"Wow, I wish I had teeth like that!"

Judith appears in the hallway. "Serge, let Dominic come in! Hello Dominic!" She greets him with a kiss on the cheek and genuine affection that leaves him glowing. "I'm *so* glad you could make it. *Serge, stop pulling your face around, please!* Ralph, you're far too big to be leaping around like that – *goodness me!*"

Dominic catches a vase as the small table it was standing crashes down on the parquet then follows Judith to the refuge of the kitchen with Serge hopping on one foot behind him. Dominic takes his usual place at the kitchen table and is overwhelmed by a sense of being more at home here than in his parents' house. Serge sits beside him but leans across into his space still grinning joyfully and flushed with exhilaration, and Alistaire, who has come to see what all the fuss is about, stands transfixed in the kitchen doorway – never having seen Serge so attentive to anyone other person – except the dog, maybe, but then Ralph was not actually a person – he only *thought* he was... Finally he steps forward and shakes Dominic's hand.

"Thank you for coming. You are clearly most welcome! We'll have a little chat about tomorrow's itinerary later, once you've settled in."

Judith shows Dominic to his room, which is "in an original wing of the house so the walls are extremely thick, which makes it very sound proof, you see. The poor plumber had a devil of a job fitting the ensuite; I think he dreaded hearing my voice on the phone, wondering what on earth could be leaking this time ..."

Dominic takes in the sloping white ceilings and walls with thick black beams he would have to mind his head on - and a double bed with ivory damask pillow cases and sheets and a crimson satin bedspread – and original polished floorboards showing around the edges of a huge woven rug - and the window seat with views over the rear orchard to a beautiful sunset way beyond on the distant horizon.

"You do like it, don't you? Otherwise I'll show you the other spare rooms and you can take your pick – but this is *my* favourite."

"Judith, it's beautiful! I've never seen such a lovely room."

"Oh *good!* And this is the ensuite!"

"Wow!" says Dominic as Judith opens what appears to be a fitted wardrobe to reveal a shower, toilet and wash basin.

"Bog blocker, that is!" says Serge who has just tracked them down.

"Oh, erm ... the water pressure is a little low in this part of the house," explains Judith. "*Please* don't be so *rude*, Serge."

"I'm sure it will be fine!" enthuses Dominic. *I'll break it up with my bare hand if I have to.*

"Come on Serge, let's leave Dominic to make himself at home whilst we go and prepare supper." Judith looks over her shoulder at Dominic, "I think Alistaire would like a word with you - *about tomorrow* - he'll be in his study if you just pop in there when you're ready."

Dominic has a quick and exhilarating shower – the water temperature becoming almost too hot to bear before plunging down to what feels like zero degrees. He tries out the toilet flusher and finds the handle is loose – presumably from being pedalled up and down in an effort to shift anything stubborn or any quantity of paper. *No problem at all - but worth being aware of…*

Dominic is hungry and decides it must be time to 'pop in' to Alistaire's study before supper. Half way down the stairs he is met by a distinctive smell of hydrogen sulphide and hesitates. "*Stink bomb*," says Serge from the kitchen, in his usual carrying voice.

"No, Serge," says Judith, softly but clearly. "*Hard boiled eggs*."

Thank goodness for that! Dominic finds that the door to Alistaire's study is ajar, knocks gently and looks in cautiously.

"Come in, Dominic, sit down."

Dominic does as he is bid. Alistaire is one of those people who do not feel obliged to put others at ease by making conversation just for the sake of it. He stares at Dominic over spectacles that rest on the end of his nose. His eyes lack warmth and his mouth is unsmiling – a straight line across his face. He frowns suddenly and twitches his nose – his spectacles wobbling precariously. Dominic reddens. "I think we've got hard boiled eggs for supper."

"Oh. Thank heavens for that! Now then. About tomorrow. The hearing is at two o'clock. It will be an informal affair - and there is no need for you to sit through the entire hearing. His case manager, Regina, will be there, and you have kindly submitted your work diary, which provides evidence of how Serge's life could be enriched by the employment of a full time ... *Buddy* ... odd term, but one must move with the times ... Anyway - I think it would support our case if Serge attended the opening, and then, when he starts to make a nuisance of himself, you could take him to the park or something. It's only a short walk from the courtrooms – I'll show you it on the way

– they've got a putting green or '*crazy golf*' as they call it these days, and a lake with ducks and rowing boats – although I suggest you steer him away from the rowing boats ... Or, if it's raining, there's a cinema nearby. And I realise you have a long drive home, so you're very welcome to stay tomorrow night. That's if you haven't had enough of us by then." Alistaire's eyes lose their coldness with a knowing twinkle and Dominic likes him suddenly.

"Thanks very much, Mr Freeman. I've got nothing to rush back for. In fact -"

"Good." Alistaire clears his throat. "So, back to tomorrow. Hmm – I mean *moving forward* to tomorrow... I decided it would be better if Judith did not come along since you will be there to support Serge. It will give her chance to sort out a few things here, at home, and, although I wouldn't say this in front of Judith, frankly, we will get along better without her. Her anxiety transmits to him, you see. I think it stems from the endless hospital appointments we had to attend when he was a child – the appointments we *still* attend, albeit with less frequency. We would always come away with Judith in tears, which, naturally, would upset Serge. So nowadays, if we have any formal appointment to attend as family, he tends to get agitated." Alistaire raises his eyebrows, questioning whether Dominic is still with him.

"I understand completely, I've spent the last two years studying such patterns of behaviour and the various methods of conquering them. For example -"

"*Good.* Serge associates *your* presence with going out to have fun. We could have done with your company a couple of weeks ago when we attended the trial of *Paddy* with the sawn-off shotgun - what's his name - Patrick Hardman. Serge has apparently promised him some kind of future employment, according to a custody officer who contacted us, so we thought we should take a look."

"*Smallman*," Dominic corrects him. "It's association again, you see – Hardman seems a more appropriate name for someone walking the streets with a sawn-off shotgun."

Alistaire blinks at Dominic a few times over the top of his glasses and says, "*Smallman*."

Dominic resolves to keep his mouth shut in future unless Alistaire asks him to speak.

Alistaire resumes; "I was interested to know how *Smallman* came about this sawn-off shotgun, and it turned out that it had been left under his bed in the stable lads' quarters at the racing stables where he worked. He hadn't thought too much about it – believing he was taking over responsibility from the previous lad to guard those race horses he was in charge of. Then, when he was made redundant and asked to clear out all his belongings, he took it with him, again without thinking much about it." Alistaire hesitates, then smiles. "We were proud of Serge, the day of the trial. He was quiet and calm so we allowed him to take the stand, and he was able to confirm that at no time had he felt frightened or threatened by Paddy, and that Paddy had been '*sad*'. And then," Alistaire rolls his eyes, "he told everybody present that Paddy was going to look after Franchesca's ponies... When, finally, the judge passed sentence, Paddy became emotional. Not *angry*, you understand, just tearful. And that upset Serge, which, in turn upset Judith. And then when Serge had forgotten about it and calmed down, he saw his mother in tears and started again. So we will be better off without her tomorrow ..."

Judith puts her head round the door at that particular moment, frowns at her husband then says brightly, "*Supper's ready*" and scurries back to the kitchen where she has prepared a buffet so as not to make Dominic feel daunted by sticking a plate of food in front of him when she is not entirely sure of his preferences.

"Great! I could eat a scabby donkey," says Dominic.

"Knowing Judith, that's probably about the only thing that is not on the table," says Alistaire, and stands up, gesturing that Dominic should precede him to the kitchen.

Judith and Serge both appear to be clutching the same plate, in the early stages of a restrained tug of war; "Give me the plate, Serge and I'll fill it with the things I know you like."

"Ungry Serge. After six now."

"*Yes, I know!* ... Let's put your favourite things on the plate."

"*Serge do it imself.*"

"Very well then. But *please* don't open up all the sandwiches to see what's inside them. *And you don't need to put your fingers all over everything!* Just pick up whatever you are going to eat and put it on your plate."

Next morning is The Hearing. Dominic wakes up thinking that he did not get to sleep last night but knows he must have because of the worrying and complicated memories of dreams of unsolved problems that are still disturbing him. He has Crunchy Nut Cornflakes for breakfast – the same as Serge. In fact, if Serge had requested horse manure for breakfast Dominic would probably have gone along with it – such is his desire to stay in this home, with these people, where there is the potential for him feel useful and needed – along with an ensuite room and wireless internet access. Dominic has come equipped with a fortnight's supply of underwear and shirts, in the hope they might ask him to stay. If anyone queries the amount of luggage he has brought for one night he will tell them he is going to stay with friends from college. The truth is, there are none. Well, of course he has 'friends' – albeit on Face Book – but none he would wish to meet face to face.

Dominic is expecting the courtroom to be gothic and theatrical, and is pleasantly surprised to find it modern and well-lit – not dissimilar to one of his college lecture rooms. Serge sits down on the first chair he encounters – the one closest to the exit. Dominic looks to Alistaire for direction and sits down next to Serge. Alistaire drove them in the Mercedes; Dominic next to Serge on the back seat, conversing with Alistaire eye to eye via the driver's mirror. Alistaire explained that Serge might need to confirm that he was, in fact, Serge Freeman, but other than that, since the weather was fine, they were free to wander off to the park or wherever. Alistaire would phone Dominic when it was time to go home.

Regina, the case manager is already there. Alistaire glances at Serge and lowers his voice as he points her out to Dominic, but nonetheless, Serge pipes up "Allo Vagina!"

Regina looks back at Serge with eyes that to Dominic look far too huge for her very small head that rests on a petite body wearing a smart, small suit. Serge buries his head suddenly and uncharacteristically in Dominic's neck. "*Too scary!*"

"It's all right, Bud," says Dominic quietly, and steers Serge's head round to face the small gathering of professionals.

A man with a kind, patient, smiling face is looking at Serge, trying to capture his attention. Dominic urges Serge to look at him. "Are you *Serge Ambrose Freeman*?" asks the man with the kind, patient, smiling face.

"Oi don't *fink* so," replies Serge.

Alistaire, who is sitting adjacent, leans forward, "We rarely use his middle name. He is not familiar with it."

The man with the kind, patient, smiling face tries again; "Are you Serge Freeman?"

"Aye, Serge, that's me!"

"Thank you, Serge. Well done."

A man with a huge purple birthmark like a map of Great Britain across his face begins to read documents relating to the various tests that have been carried out on Serge's brain over the years. Serge appears to be riveted by the man's words, displaying open mouthed attention. Dominic is aware that the source of fascination is the man's face and not his words – and prays that Serge does not pipe up about it.

"Boring, this," declares Serge, when the hearing has been in progress for a full seven minutes and the current speaker has neither a speech impediment nor any obvious physical disfigurement.

Alistaire raises his hand and suggests that this might be an appropriate time for Serge to leave, accompanied by Dominic, his support worker, who has *lots of interesting activities* planned for Serge this afternoon. Dominic smiles and nods obligingly, and exchanges a high five with Serge as they step out into the street.

The rain has held off so they walk to the park and play repetitive rounds of 'crazy golf'. Serge is surprisingly good at the game so they complete the course in no time. It costs one pound fifty per person per round, and Dominic keeps the tickets to return to Alistaire along with whatever is left of the generous 'entertainment allowance' he has been allocated. His mobile phone vibrates in his pocket. Alistaire has just left the courtroom and is on his way to meet them. "The traffic is awful, very stop-start, so just wait by the park gates and get ready to jump in the car as it crawls past."

"Okay, Mr Freeman." Dominic turns to Serge. "That was your Dad – we've got to go now and wait by the park gates."

Serge is not one for standing around waiting for anything and draws attention to himself by smiling and waving at passing vehicles. Dominic is surprised and slightly disturbed to discover that Serge is so well recognised and, judging by the comments, wolf-whistles and gestures of excitement from the open car windows, his celebrity status is spreading like a forest fire.

Suddenly Serge's posture changes completely – his head droops and his arms hang limply by his sides.

"What's up Bud?" asks Dominic.

"Serge don't wanna go to prison."

"What? I don't understand what you're talking about."

Serge kicks some gravel on to the road. "Serge just don't wanna go to prison. That's all."

Dominic works it out. "Is this something to do with Paddy? Because he went to court?"

"Paddy went to prison and ee wassan very 'appy 'bout it. Serge don't wanna go there ... Bad place!"

"Serge, that was completely different! People who do bad things go to court, and then, sometimes, they go to prison. But people who have done nothing wrong often go to court as well ... sometimes because something bad has happened to them ... which might have been someone else's fault. And they *don't* go to prison. And sometimes they get some compensation money or something out of it ... that's if the judge decides that someone else did something wrong ..." he tails off, lamely.

"But *Paddy* hadn't dun nuthin wrong. Paddy just gorra bit upset – like Serge does sometimes. And *ee* went to prison."

"In the eyes of the law he *had* done wrong, Serge. People can't be allowed to walk the streets taking hostages with sawn-off shotguns!"

Alistaire arrives and toots his horn briefly, keeping his place in the queue of traffic, noticing his son's unhappy demeanour and raising his eyebrows questioningly. Dominic shoves Serge into the back of the car; scrambles in after him, and registers Alistaire's enquiring expression in the rear view mirror.

"Serge thinks that because he's been to court he is now going to jail – because that's what happened to Paddy."

Alistaire rolls his eyes as it clicks into place. "*Serge!*"

"Yes Dad."

"This court case was for your benefit. The intent was to secure you the compensation you deserve ... to provide for your future security when your mother and I are no longer around to take care of you."

Serge becomes alarmed anew and rocks back and forth, finger nails digging into the car seat. "*Where's you and Mom goin' then?*"

Dominic sees that Alistaire is floundering and puts a hand on Serge's shoulder. "It's okay, Serge. Your Dad's talking about *years* from now – when he and your Mom are *really old ...*"

"Serge is 'ungry. McDonald's. I does. Big Mac and large fries and regular coke. *Meal deal.*"

Alistaire's swings the Mercedes off the main road and into a retail park. He hands Dominic a twenty pound note to spend on burgers and a business card of a taxi firm. “This is the taxi company we use. When you are done here just give them a ring and ask them to charge it to my account. The account number, should they ask for it, is on the back.” Alistaire casts a look of abhorrence at the heaving, neon-lit fast food cafe and accelerates away – joining the traffic that is now flowing normally.

“Nutherwun I does,” says Serge, after demolishing his burger in four bites. “Dom ‘aving nuther?”

“Well ... it seems a bit greedy, but they *do* go down quickly. I might have a coffee as well.”

“Milk shake, I does. Strawberry pleez.”

The taxi delivers them home and although Judith bestows her usual warm greeting, Dominic detects a hint of tension in her demeanour as the three of them take their usual places at the kitchen table. “How did the hearing go?” he asks. “Has Alistaire mentioned it?”

“Oh, yes, it seems it went very well. Alistaire and I are *so* grateful for your assistance in today’s proceedings.”

How formal. What’s wrong? “Really? Oh, good. But it was my pleasure ...”

“In fact – ” Judith’s voice has become anxious and squeaky, and she blurts out, “we were hoping you might stay on here for a while ...” She hesitates but hurries on when Dominic opens his mouth to speak. “That’s if you have nothing planned for the next few days ... only ... I couldn’t help noticing you’d brought rather a lot of clothes for just a couple of nights – so you’ve most likely stopped off here *en route* to some other engagement.”

“I just brought a few extra things with the intention of visiting friends from last year’s course.”

Judith lowers her eyes, disappointedly.

“Urm … no I didn’t. That was the excuse I had prepared to explain why I had brought so much stuff here.” Dominic beams happily at Judith. “I came prepared in the hope ... well

... just in case you might ask me to stay here for a few days – as Serge's 'Buddy'. If it's okay with Alistaire, I'd love to stay."

"*Yes. Yes!*" Judith smiles delightedly – her previous tension welling up in her eyes. She lowers her voice. "Alistaire thought it better that I should put the idea to you without his presence. He feels that he intimidates you a little."

"*Oh, no, not at all,*" lies Dominic, his voice rising an octave.

"It's okay – everyone feels that way about Alistaire until they get to know him really well and see him for the great big softy he really is! Actually, Alistaire and Leo are in the study right now if you'd like to pop along for a chat."

Pop along. Chat. "Righteo, I'll *pop along* now."

Serge lowers his voice to a conspiratorial whisper. "*Don't sign anything, Dom.*"

Dominic taps politely on the study door that has been left ajar.

"Come in, sit down," says Alistaire, breezily. "I trust Judith told you what this is about?"

"Yes, Mr Freeman," says Dominic, suddenly nervous as if attending a job interview. Alistaire is sitting at his large desk with Leo to his right and a stack of documents in front of him. Dominic sits opposite the pair of them and wishes he hadn't had that second burger.

"Please call me Alistaire ... Now then. Thank you for your assistance today, Dominic. I am pleased to report that the judge was very sympathetic towards Serge's case, in fact, he deems it appropriate that Serge should be awarded compensation in the region of two hundred and fifty thousand pounds, to provide for his future financial security."

"That's *brilliant*," enthuses Dominic.

"Yes. However, Serge's brother Leo has been looking after Serge's affairs, and it seems that Serge's financial situation has changed ... overwhelmingly ... during the time that the compensation case has been in progress."

Dominic looks at Leo, who returns a cool, steady gaze. It is difficult to imagine Leo being overwhelmed by anything, ever.

Alistaire shuffles the documents on his desk, bringing a new one to the top of the pile. "What with Serge's modelling contract and the range of aftershave he launched, the designer suits, shoes, wallets, next year's calendar … and it seems we've got 'SErge' underwear coming out soon." Alistaire hesitates and raises his eyebrows at the thought, then looks at Dominic over the top of his reading glasses. "It seems my younger son is already worth his financial award several times over."

"Wow," obliges Dominic.

"Quite," says Alistaire. "So, in view of this, we will only be accepting a nominal portion of the compensation award, and this will be donated to a charity for disabled children from … erm … *less privileged* families. The important thing is that we *won the case*. And, of course, that Serge's future is financially secure," he adds hastily.

Leo opens his mouth for the first time. "Dominic must be wondering where he fits into this."

"Yes. Indeed. Well, Dominic … the thing is, Serge has surprised us all by expressing a wish to set up home with Franchesca – a young woman with learning difficulties. I believe you've met her?"

"Yes, on several occasions. They do seem besotted with each other."

Alistaire nods. "So, it only seems fair that Serge is allowed the opportunity to fulfil this desire. Of course, they are going to need a good degree of supervision and support … and this is where you come in."

"Well, I don't know about looking after Franchesca …"

"No, of course not. Depending on the course the relationship takes, a team of support workers may eventually be recruited. But you seemed the obvious starting point, primarily as a support worker for Serge, but also to assist with the recruitment process. That's if you are interested …"

"Yes please! I mean, yes, I *am* interested."

“Good. We will draw up a contract of employment. If you’re happy to stay here in the meantime, you could get started house hunting with Serge – take him round a few estate agents – it’ll be something to do, to get you both out and about. He seems to be set on a large place with stables and a paddock to keep ponies – or with land where stables could be built. And ...” he rolls his eyes, “he’s hell bent on having Patrick Smallman employed to look after the ponies. What’s more …” Alistaire studies the figures on the paper before him and shakes his head as if he can’t quite believe his eyes, “It would appear that he can easily afford all of this. Oh, and without wishing to sound rude, your car has just about had it. I suggest spending some of Serge’s money on a car, and insuring you to drive it. Let him help to choose it, but steer him in the direction of something sensible.”

“I’ll do my best! I think tinted windows would be a good idea, considering the attention he attracted waiting outside the park gates. And in McDonalds ...”

“Yes, good thinking. I wondered what was holding up the traffic on my way to meet you. It started moving quite normally once he was in the car. So, have you any questions, or any other observations?”

“None that I can think of right now.”

“Well, if you think of anything …”

“Thank you very much.” Dominic beams happily and Alistaire stands up and shakes his hand, indicating that the meeting is over. Dominic offers his hand to Leo, who responds with a firm handshake and a scrutinising stare. Dominic heads for the door – glad to escape, but Leo calls his name.

“Yes Leo?”

“If you’re looking after my brother, there’s one important thing that I ask of you …”

“Yes, of course. What is it?”

“Will you promise that you won’t let Serge and Franchesca go on ‘Britain’s Got Talent’ with that *knee-twitching to music* act that they do?”

“Urm … yes of course. I’ll do everything within my power to discourage it.” He reaches the door.

“Dominic.” This time it is Alistaire calling him back.

“Yes Alistaire?”

Alistaire has removed his reading glasses and his eyes are twinkling. “Leo was joking. It is not always obvious.”

17

Viewing Serge

Alistaire and Judith have studied a few brochures of properties on the market that are within the price range and geographical proximity to the family home that Leo has calculated to be most suitable for Serge. Today, Dominic is taking Serge for an initial viewing. Judith hands Dominic the brochures, "These five are all within a twenty minute drive from here. Alistaire and I still expect to help out as and when required."

"Thank goodness for that," says Dominic, and she returns his smile.

"Are you ready then Serge? Go to the toilet quick whilst I do your flask."

Alistaire follows them out to the new black Land Rover with tinted windows that has become the 'SErge' company car. Dominic enters the postal code of the first property into the sat nav. "I've arranged them in sequence of proximity to this place," says Alistaire, "closest first. Take your time. If you don't get round them all today you'll at least have something lined up for tomorrow. I'm sure Judith has briefed you, but the agreement for the two unoccupied properties is that you phone the estate agent if and when you get there, and they will come out to meet you. That gives you the opportunity to survey the grounds at leisure. As for those where the vendors have opted to conduct their own viewings, they have been informed of the circumstances and accept that they have a *tentative* appointment for a viewing."

"Yes Alistaire, I understand. Judith *did* explain, and er ... so did Leo."

"Just don't appear too keen on any off them. Make notes of the pros and cons, but don't let the estate agents influence you. Let them deliver their patter – but use your own judgement."

"And Serge's judgement? After all, it's his home we're looking for."

"Well ... yes ... quite. But – "

"If Serge is in the right frame of mind he does have a good sense of *vibes* about places." Dominic shuffles swiftly through the brochures. "If, by the time we get there, his attention is still focussed on house-hunting, then I think Serge will make his own choice about where to make his home." Dominic returns Alistaire's uneasy frown with a reassuring smile, and starts the Land Rover.

Alistaire retreats up the steps to the front door where Judith has been standing for some time, waiting to wave them off. She is starting to get cold and he puts his arm around her shoulders. "Dominic has gained confidence, hasn't he, since we took him on. We gave him responsibility and he appears to have run with it."

"Yes. I *do like* Dominic."

"I know you do." They wave off the Land Rover – although unable to see the occupants through the tinted windows. "Come on in ... we've got the place to ourselves, for a change."

As Dominic turns left at the end of the drive, Aunt Devina's car is just turning into the drive from the right. "Uh-Oh," says Serge. "Put yer fut down Dom!" Dominic smiles and waves and accelerates away.

After a couple of miles Dominic pulls into a lay-by.

"Wot's up Dom, need a pee?" asks Serge.

"No. I just wanted to check the instructions for our first appointment. Like who's meeting us, and whether the house is occupied – that sort of thing."

"Diddun evwewun tell you all that?"

"Well, yes. I suppose *everyone did.* But I was too busy trying to look as if I was listening to them all to make much sense of what they were all saying." Dominic consults the brochure on the top of the pile.

"Now then. Our first viewing is at 'Hardwicke Heights', currently owned by Rear Admiral and Mrs Hardwicke. Still in '*occupant possession'* but with '*vacant possession upon completion*'. The estate agent will meet us outside the main entrance to the property."

"Ow many entwances assit got, Dom?"

"Dunno Bud. We'll have to see."

"Wot does *vacant possess-fing* mean?"

"Nothing really. It just means if you buy the place they'll move *out* of it when you move *in*."

"Aw ... that's good of em. But if there's enuff room for all of us they don't av to ... so long as they're nice to Serge and Fwan. They don't av to move out."

"Yes they do, Serge. If they're selling the house they must move out ... Don't look like that. They wouldn't be selling the place if they didn't want to move out, would they?" The sat nav informs Dominic that he has arrived at his destination so he slows the Land Rover to a crawl and finally pulls in by some imposingly high wrought-iron gates, which are closed. A silver Porsche Carrera is parked a short distance beyond, and a woman in a large red dress begins her ascent from it. "This must be the estate agent."

Serge watches with interest as she reaches her full height. "Ay, that's 'er off the telly init? John at the Centre likes that wun. Reckons she looks like she gives a good blow job. What's a *blow job*, Dom?"

"Serge, *please promise* me you won't ask about that in front of this lady! I will explain it to you later. Okay?"

"Okay Dom. But issit 'er off the telly?"

Dominic assesses the voluptuous brunette as she approaches, taking in the smouldering eyes and the crimson velvet dress with matching lipstick emphasising lips already full and slightly parted as if in readiness to perform a good - "No Serge, she's *not* the one off the telly."

"Hello, I'm Gloria and I'm *so* pleased you could make it!"

"Hello Gloria," Dominic shakes her hand then retreats a couple of steps. Gloria is a very tall lady of proportionate width, with a loud voice. Dominic finds himself overwhelmed by her physical presence at close proximity. She turns her attention to Serge and her clear white skin flushes pink. "I am *so excited* to meet you in the flesh!" Serge glances down at himself as if checking he is fully dressed. "I expect you're *dying* to view the property. The vendors are currently occupant. They *are* expecting us. I suggest we leave the cars out here and walk through the grounds to the house." Gloria casts a puzzled glance at the flask that is resting in the crook of Serge's arm but doesn't ask. She presses the intercom button on the box on the gatepost and gushingly announces their arrival. The gates swing slowly open, and then begin to close behind them. Serge looks slightly alarmed.

"Stick summat in the gap, Dom. Quick, fore it shuts. *Doh* … too late!"

"Hah, hah, *hah*," says Gloria politely, thinking he is joking.

"Serge faut the 'ouse would be bigger than that."

"The *Gatehouse* - hah, hah, *hah* - is available by separate negotiation. If sold separately the access from here will be fenced off. There is a gate and footpath from the road. Two bedrooms I believe."

"Serge'll av that'n as well. Do for Fwan's Mom and Nan. Then she can go see 'em wivout cwossing the road."

Dominic taps Serge's arm and says quietly, "Don't forget what your Dad said about not sounding too keen." They follow the driveway as it curves around a huge oak tree and Hardwicke Heights stands magnificently before them.

Serge stands still and looks from Hardwicke House to the Gatehouse and back again. "Gloria …"

"Yes Serge?"

"Serge don't wanna sound too keen but ee's gonna buy the biggun *and* the little-un."

Dominic frowns. "Let's go and have a look at it first, shall we? Have you any idea why they're moving, Gloria?"

"They're down-sizing. They've lived here twenty-five years and the children have grown up and moved out, so they're rattling around rather."

The viewers are greeted at the front door by Admiral Hardwicke; a thick-set, broad shouldered man with twinkling blue eyes. He is bald with a dense white beard and a fringe of fuzzy white hair round the back of his head. Whilst Gloria makes an enthusiastic introduction, Serge lowers his voice and says to Dominic, "Is that him off the fish finger advert?"

"*No* Serge. There is a world outside your television, you know."

They are joined by Mrs Hardwicke, a small, elegant lady with a kind face and sculptured grey hair. She is dressed simply but expensively in a tweed skirt and cashmere jersey.

"Nice lady," says Serge.

"Oh, how kind!" Mrs Hardwicke glows with pleasure. "I say, I bought my son some of your aftershave. I wonder if you would be so kind as to sign your autograph on the box. I'm sure he'd be *thrilled*."

Serge has become accustomed to signing his autograph and is always very happy to do so, which can be frustrating for Dominic on occasions when time is of the essence. Serge takes the pen, checks with Dominic that he is holding it correctly, then with measured deliberation, inscribes 'SErge' on the box and shows it to Dominic for approval before returning it to a delighted Mrs Hardwicke.

Gloria's smile is by this time looking a little strained. "Now shall we have a look around the house, *hah – hah*?"

Serge surveys his immediate surroundings. The hallway in which they stand is oak panelled and smells pleasantly of furniture polish. It is similar to his Mom and Dad's hallway, but even bigger. A broad staircase with carved oaken banisters and a plush port wine coloured stair carpet sweeps in a gentle curve to the upstairs landing. "Nice, innit."

"Right then!" says the Admiral in a rousing tone to encourage everyone to leap into action; "We don't intend to follow you around the place, but if you have any questions I'll be in the study – last door on the left ... and my wife will be pottering around somewhere." Retreating to the study, he reiterates,

"Any questions at all, I'm just in there. Ask me anything!" In the doorway he hesitates, deliberating whether to leave the door wide open or just ajar. Settling for half-open, he sits down at his desk and is startled to find Serge in the doorway already. "My word, that was quick. Is it about the utility bills? I've prepared them as it happens – gas and electricity for the last three quarters and council tax demand for the year."

Serge shakes his head. "Wot's a blow job? That's all Serge wanted to ask."

Admiral Hardwicke is momentarily stunned then laughs aloud but regains his composure with admirable speed. "You're not joking, are you?"

"No. Dom said eed tell me later, but I faut you might know. Never mind." Serge hears Dominic calling his name and begins to retreat.

"Just a moment," says the Admiral. "What's seven plus five?"

"Serge dunno that one ..."

"Ah. Just as I suspected." The Admiral's eyes settle on the large colourful flask and he shakes his head and chuckles.

"But three hundred and twelve times one hundred and twenty three is thirty eight thousand, three hundred and seventy-six," says Serge with a wink. "*Just coming Dom!*"

18

Welcome Paddy

Serge and Franchesca are looking forward to moving into Hardwicke Heights early in the New Year. Franchesca's mother and grandmother are equally excited about moving into the Gate House at the entrance to Hardwicke Heights. Leo had been there when Pat Cunliffe and her ninety-year-old mother had gone to have a look at the curiously shaped bungalow, and had made some comment about them being ideal gate keepers. Dominic, thinking it was some sort of reference to dragons or Rotweilers, had laughed to share the joke but then turned it into a tickly cough when Leo had turned to him with raised eyebrows and a cold, blue stare. Dominic regrets that he does not understand Leo, but thinks he would look great in the form of a tall, marble statue, situated in a city centre shopping precinct. No, it would have to be placed in an indoor arcade; otherwise pigeons would shit on it, which would be wrong. There is something very ... *clean and hygienic* about Leo, and his clipped, cultivated tones make Dominic feel like a northern oaf.

Judith, meanwhile, is stressing over Christmas. She has so much shopping to do, and so few shopping days left and so many social functions to attend looking beautifully dressed and made up – with no excuse *not* to now that Serge is getting on so well with Dominic. Yet she really *must* invite Franchesca and her mother and grandmother round, in order to get to know them a little better.

Serge also, with a little encouragement from Dominic, has turned his mind to Christmas shopping. "Serge'll get Fran a flask with spots on it – don't you fink she's looking a bit spotty lately, Dom?"

"Hm ... a little bit perhaps. I expect it's just hormones. How old is Franchesca?"

“Fwee years younger than Serge.”
“Twenty-four then.” Dominic had thought she was about sixteen.
“Yeah, twenty-four ... not like er muvver.” Serge startles Dominic by suddenly throwing back his head and laughing raucously; “Sixteen sixty-four *she* is! *Hah, Hah, Hah!*”
“And who are you mimicking now then? John from the Centre?”
“Yeah ...”
“I thought so.” A pause as Serge struts around a little – presumably still mimicking John from the Centre. “And what about the rest of your Christmas shopping. How about your Mom and Dad?”
“Mom can av the flask wiv cherries and apples onnit; Dad the plain blue. Wot about Leo?”
“Urm ... I’d go for the tall unbreakable stainless steel model for Leo. But it has to be your choice. Are you sure they all want flasks?”
“Well, they liked the wuns Serge gorrem last year ...”
“Oh. Listen, Serge, if you bought everyone a flask last year, are you sure it’s a good idea to buy the same thing again this year?”
“Yer ... *Flasks*. For Cwismus.”

Alistaire is working from home and taking telephone calls in his study. He comes into the kitchen to find Judith, wearing a slightly perplexed expression. “That was Patrick Smallman’s probation officer on the phone, regarding Serge’s mention of possible employment to look after the ponies he’s talking about getting. Apparently Serge gave Patrick one of those business cards he carries around – and it had our number on the back. He was hoping we might be in a position to offer ‘*Paddy*’ a job.”
“But I thought he was sentenced for over a year,” says Judith.
“Yes. But apparently he’s ‘*not coping well*’ with prison life, whatever that means … and they have a system whereby

prisoners can be released '*on licence*'. It means they are still serving their sentence, with various rules to follow … but within the community instead of in prison. And if they break those rules they go straight back behind bars. But they need to be resident at an address approved by the probation officer."

"What did you tell him?"

"I told him we couldn't help at present."

"Poor Paddy. He didn't *cope* very well with his *trial*, bless him."

Alistaire rolls his eyes. "I rather suspect he doesn't *cope* very well with *very much*. Otherwise he wouldn't have got in such a mess in the first place."

"That's a little unfair, Dear. You heard how he'd been divorced and lost his job, which was also his home, and the ex-wife was being difficult over access to his son …"

"With good reason, for all *we* know."

"But if Serge is set on having him run his stables, don't you think it would be a good idea if we had him here between now and then, so we can get to know him?"

"*Here* doing *what*? Would you like me to buy him some horses to look after?"

"He could help with the garden. Archie only does one day a week now, which leaves a lot more work for Derrick. Derrick could supervise him."

Serge and Dominic arrive home from Christmas shopping, bearing carriers bags filled mainly with flasks. Judith greets them with news of the phone call.

"It does sound like a good way for us all to get to know Paddy," agrees Dominic.

"Wot sort of flask shall we get for Paddy, Dom?"

"Urm … a small rugged one."

"We could put him in the little magnolia room, just along the landing from Dominic. Dom can keep an eye on him then." Judith picks up the handset in the kitchen, dials one four seven one and makes a note of the number of the last caller.

Alistaire glares crossly at the three of them before retreating to his study. "I am *not* having a *convicted criminal* in this house!"

"Good morning. My name's Alistaire Freeman. I was hoping to speak to Patrick Smallman's probation officer. He phoned to speak to me yesterday afternoon, but I didn't make a note of his name."

"Andy Salter. That's me. This is my direct line. How can I help you?"

"Well, it might be the other way round. I discussed your phone call with my wife, and she … we agreed that it might be an idea to get to know Paddy if there's a chance that he might be living at my son's house. I'm not sure if you're aware, but my son and his … erm *partner* are what might be termed as *vulnerable within society*."

"Yes, Paddy did mention it. So, are you able to offer him employment and fixed accommodation?"

"Well, I'm not sure I like the term '*fixed*'. But yes, we have spare rooms and there's always work to be done in the garden."

"Ah, *live in groundsman*," says Andy, writing it down. "I hope you don't mind but I'll have to call and have a look at your place – so I can tick the box to say I've approved it, you understand?"

"Yes … I understand."

"And you must also understand that if Paddy is released on licence he will still be serving a prison sentence, and will therefore be tagged and on an overnight curfew between seven in the evening and seven in the morning. He will be monitored by our tagging company who will inform the Home Office if he breaks the curfew, and if that happens he'll go straight back to prison. Just so as you know what's what." Andy pauses and then softens his businesslike tone. "And I won't mention any of this to Paddy until it's all signed and sealed. He's fragile at the moment. Determined not to spend Christmas in prison at any cost. We're, urm, keeping an eye on him."

Alistaire reports back to Judith. "There's a probation officer coming to check up on us. Just a formality of course. And then Smallman will be delivered to us tagged, and grounded by an overnight curfew." He frowns and shakes his head. "I find this all so *unsavoury*."

"Oh, *Alistaire*." Judith takes the hand that hangs loosely by his side and squeezes it. "It's only terminology. Just think of him as someone who's had a bit of bad fortune recently ... someone who has found himself in difficult situations and hasn't handled them very well. *Do* let's give him a chance."

Andy Salter, the probation officer, is shown to the room that Judith has prepared for Paddy. "It's very nice," he says, "but not at all what he's used to. A small caravan at the bottom of the garden would be more his scene."

"Really?" says Judith. "Well ... I suppose –"

"No, Judith," says Alistaire. "We're not putting a caravan in the back garden that we'll have to get rid of again in a couple of months' time. And think how cold it would be at night, this time of year."

Andy gazes out of the bedroom window, down the length of the garden and across to the orchard. "You have a fair sized plot here. Please bear in mind that Paddy's left leg has been badly broken in the past and he limps rather badly."

"We've managed without him so far," says Alistaire. "As you can see, the grounds are in good order."

They leave Paddy's room and continue along the landing.

"Oh, and something I should mention, that Paddy has expressed a concern about, is that he doesn't like eating in front of people. He's worried you might take it personally – but if you wouldn't mind, he'd prefer to take his meals to his room, or else eat in the garden if the weather's fine. He's never been properly socialised, you see, and he has this little phobia about inadvertently ... urm ...*gobbing* on someone."

"Charming," says Alistaire. "As it happens, we don't have many dinner parties – but you can assure him we won't set a place and his company will not be missed."

Andy stops abruptly and turns to Alistaire. "You *are* committed to this, aren't you, Mr Freeman? Paddy wept when I had to tell him you were unable to offer him employment just yet but then wept even harder when I went back and told him that you'd had a re-think."

Alistaire looks at him sharply. "I thought you weren't going to mention anything to him until it was *all signed and sealed*."

Unnerved by such steely eye contact, Andy lowers his gaze to the power sockets, as if to make a superficial assessment of the safety of the electrical wiring. "Yes, I did say that. But when I looked in later that day, he was so *down* that I ended up telling him you'd phoned me back." Andy straightens to his full height, juts out his chin and looks up to return Alistaire's stare. "So, I would hate to have to go back and tell him you'd changed your mind again ... He would be distraught."

"I see," says Alistaire. "Well, yes, we *are* committed. He *will* be made welcome here."

Judith makes a mental note to put a box of tissues on Paddy's bedside table.

When Paddy is duly delivered, tagged and on a curfew, to the Freeman residence, Judith is at first surprised by how little and thin he is, but then she remembers he used to be a jockey and is therefore entitled to resemble a prune. She also notices that he has acquired a nervous twitch. When he speaks to her his eyes at first stare but then blink rapidly, like a small animal that has been startled by a bright light – the spasm ending in one full hard blink. He also has a stammer, but she cannot be certain whether it was there before the prison sentence or if it is newly acquired. Andy, the probation officer is at his side and Alistaire is surprised to feel slightly irked that he is showing Paddy around the place as if he owns it. After all, it is not a task that Alistaire himself was particularly keen to carry out – especially not with Serge hopping excitedly in tow. "Come on Paddy. Come up an' see yer room. Got yer own shower and a bog that flushes proper ..."

Judith, in the kitchen, is preparing coq au vin and is wondering how large or small a portion to put on Paddy's plate that he is to take upstairs. Ralph, who has been gazing hopefully at the chopping board, hears people descending the stairs and saunters out to the hallway to meet them. Judith, with the realisation that Ralph is probably heavier and taller (on two legs) than Paddy, washes her hands quickly and hurries after him to find Paddy's face transformed with delight as he takes the dog's huge head between his hands and kisses him between the eyes. "Now, you're what I call a dog – so you are," he says, without a hint of a twitch or a stammer. Ralph reciprocates by licking the anxious salt from his forehead.

Serge tugs Paddy's sleeve. "Come on Paddy. Me and Ralphie will show yer the garden."

Andy stays in the kitchen with Judith and watches them make their way down the garden – Ralph breaking into a springy trot. "Well, he's certainly hit it off with Serge and the dog … or is it a pony? Perhaps that's why they've hit it off so well."

"Hah, hah," says Judith politely, accustomed to the horse and donkey comments that Ralph's size invariably provokes. "Now, I know you said he'd prefer to eat in his room, but are you *sure* about that? I don't want him to feel excluded or unwelcome. I'm doing coq au vin for dinner. What size portion would you recommend?"

"Sorry?" Andy's eyes turn away from the window and settle on the casserole dish. "Oh. Whilst we were upstairs Serge asked Paddy what he wanted for tea and he said he'd really like a banana sandwich. He noticed you had a large bunch ripening on the table."

"A banana sandwich!"

"Yes, if that's okay. Bananas were about all he would eat in prison. Stress, you see, affects his appetite."

"Well," says Judith disappointedly. "One likes to make a little more effort - especially on his first day. But *of course*, if that's what he fancies. I wonder if he prefers white bread or wholemeal … and whether to mash or slice the bananas? My Gran used to sprinkle sugar on them – but it's not considered healthy these days. I'll ask when he comes back in."

"I shouldn't bother asking ... he'll only get flustered if you make him choose. He's so very anxious to please – and also very grateful to you for … erm, *rescuing* him. Just make it like you would for Serge. Bananas are quite nutritious, you know."

Serge, Paddy and Ralph return, bright and glowing, from their tour of the grounds and Judith smiles brightly; "I've done you some banana sandwiches, Paddy. Andy told me that's what you fancied." Paddy hangs his head and mutters something about not wishing to be any trouble whatsoever to anybody - *to be sure.*

Serge examines the china plate heaped with small triangular sandwiches beneath cling film. "Can Serge av nana samwidges for tea as well – instead of that cock fing?"

Judith sighs, "Oh, I suppose so." She puts the casserole dish in the oven and says to Andy, "If you'd like to stay for dinner it looks as if there's going to be plenty. It might help Paddy settle in if you stay for an hour or two."

"That's very kind of you but he seems fine to me – very much at ease with your son and the dog. I'll just remind him of a few rules, and then I'll be off. Thank you so much for having him. Any questions or problems, don't hesitate to get in touch."

Leo calls in on his way home from the office. "You look tired, darling," says Judith, noting his dark shadows and general pallor.

"I'm fine." He sits at the kitchen table, droops forward onto his elbows and loosens his tie. "Something smells good."

"It's coq au vin. *Do* stay and have some ... although I suppose Bridget might have something in the oven."

"If only she had … No, as it happens she's going out for a meal with friends from work, so I'd love to stay."

"Going out *again*? What's the occasion *this* time?"

"*Another* of her colleagues is leaving to have a baby." He hesitates. "Bridget has seen a doctor who says there's no reason why she shouldn't conceive. So now she wants me to go and be tested …"

"Oh, *Leo*," she rubs the tense muscles in his neck and he tolerates it with a frown. She resists the urge to kiss the nape of his neck. Poor Leo. Was it because he had a younger brother with a disability that he had grown up so undemonstrative? Had he missed out on hugs because Serge had been such a demanding child? She has a sudden memory of Leo as a boy; intelligent and serious, quietly doing his homework whilst Serge threw a tantrum on the hearthrug – screaming and kicking anything or anyone within range - until he was finally exhausted. Then he would be all cuddles, clinging to her like a leach, and Leo would take himself off to bed and prepare his school bag for the next morning. Such a good boy. For Beatrice, it was different ... the middle child; the only daughter, the apple of her Daddy's eye. A pretty little girl, popular at school, confident and slightly precocious, she was always making Serge laugh with her song and dance routines. Her eyes fill up. "I'm sure everything's fine. I imagine you're just *trying too hard*."

"Mmm." Leo is not entirely comfortable with the idea of his mother imagining him *trying* on any level. "It's certainly beginning to seem like a chore. I'm starting to feel like a laboratory technician. What makes it worse is that Bridget wanted us to start a family as soon as we were married. Like you and Dad did. But I calculated that, financially, we'd be better off waiting until we were thirty. It still seemed young enough; plenty of time, and I thought we'd have more equity in the house and a good start on the school fees if we waited three years. I remember how excited she was on her thirtieth birthday – as if her life was about to begin. Only it didn't happen."

Judith recalls the joint thirtieth birthday party they'd had, eighteen months ago. Leo and Bridget had appeared so happy and ... *in love*. The poor girl had no doubt been convinced she would be a mother by now. "Never mind," she says, inadequately. "Eighteen months is no time at all – it doesn't mean there's anything *wrong*. The Christmas break will do you both the world of good. Crack open a bottle of your favourite tipple; relax ... and who knows?"

"I wonder if she'll allow me to have a Christmas drink… Anyway, enough about that. Has your resident criminal arrived yet?"

"Yes, he's upstairs with Serge and Dominic. It sounds as if they're having fun up there."

"I might go along and see what they're up to. I keep hearing Serge guffaw like a maniac. I'm intrigued."

"They're playing Snap. At least Serge and Paddy are. Dom's reading a book."

"*Snap?*"

"You know. Picture cards, some of which are the same, and the first player to shout 'Snap' wins the cards."

"I *do* know what *Snap* is …"

Judith lowers her voice confidentially, "Paddy's door was ajar so I told Serge to knock and go in. Paddy was sitting on the bed playing Snap and he shoved the cards under his pillow and looked startled and guilty. Serge said to him '*Is that a porn mag?*' I sometimes wonder how on earth Serge learns about these things."

"I'd put my money on *that John* he sometimes sees at the Centre on a Wednesday."

"Yes, I think we all would, so the odds wouldn't be very high. Anyway, Paddy was mortified at the suggestion and declared that he would never bring such a thing into this home. Isn't that nice? And then he got the cards out from under the pillow.

It was one of the few things Paddy brought with him - a pack of Snap cards. He normally plays Snap by himself - *yes, I know* - so he's happy to have someone who genuinely wants to play the game with him. And you can hear what a good time they're having!"

Judith opens the kitchen door and they both listen to the sound of Serge's delighted laughter.

"You know, Mum. Sometimes I *envy* my brother."

19

Shortly before Christmas

Dominic and Serge take Paddy to Hardwicke Heights to see the paddock and stables. The Hardwickes are spending December in their apartment in Marbella so the house is locked up, but Paddy is not interested in seeing the interior. He is adamant that he will live in the stables with the ponies; "Oi'll guard dohs ponies night an' day ..."

Hopefully not with a sawn-off shot gun, thinks Dominic. "I don't think the stables have been used for a while; they're rather run down. There's electricity but no heating or plumbing."

Paddy's eyes sparkle with delight as he enters the stable block and examines the condition of the individual stalls. "Perfect. All it needs is a splash of white wash – and maybe a little woodworm treatment on these doors – lest we get a kicker."

They walk round the perimeter of the paddock, slowly, owing to Paddy's limp, checking the fencing. Paddy's brow furrows at the leaves of various plants amidst the grass. "Oi think that's buttercups. We need ter get rid of de buttercup plants – de flowers are poisonous ter horses, an' de fence will need patchin' up a bit. But other than dat it's perfect. This place has a *really good smell about it,* so it has."

"Serge can't smell nothin – he just finks it's a bit *futtin cold* hanging round 'ere so can we go to McDonald's now pleez? Ple-eez ..."

Paddy chuckles and takes a last satisfied look around the paddock and, from old habit, checks the bolt on the door of the stable block as they pass, even though there is nothing more lively within than woodworm, two rusty old lawn mowers and a huge iron roller.

It is dark by the time they get to McDonalds, which makes it easier for them to cross the car park without people asking

Serge to pose for photos or sign autographs. Dominic spots a corner table and ushers Paddy into the corner seat whilst coaxing Serge into the seat with his back to the restaurant. Such is Serge's fame that it is difficult to go anywhere now without him being recognised and attracting a crowd. Dominic goes to buy the burgers; returning with a loaded tray. He winks at Paddy, "I got double for Serge, hoping it might save me going back and queuing again." Paddy stares at him and blinks rapidly a few times, ending with one full hard blink. After what Judith had said about Paddy preferring to eat alone, Dominic feels somehow flattered to observe, with his peripheral vision, Paddy unselfconsciously tucking in.

Just as they're about to leave, Serge says, "Nuvver wun, I does. Ungry Serge. Nana milk shake wivvit. *Plee*-eze" Dominic rolls his eyes and counts to ten (as opposed to saying a mantra, like he might have done a few weeks ago). Paddy appears to have fallen asleep in the corner. "Would you like anything else, Paddy?"

Paddy blinks, yawns and stretches, like a hamster whose bedroom roof has been lifted off in the middle of the day; then shakes his head and shuts his eyes again.

Judith has been having a baking session. Tomorrow, Franchesca and her mother and grandmother will be visiting. Dominic has texted to say they are having tea at McDonald's, and Alistaire has a Rotary Club dinner this evening, so she is taking the opportunity to bake quiches, scones and fairy cakes in advance and to start the first layer of a huge trifle. Whilst she knows that the cakes and scones would be better if made tomorrow morning, she finds it difficult to drop the habit of doing things in advance, even though she now has Dominic's help with looking after Serge. She must ask Dominic what he is doing for Christmas. Surely he will want to spend a few days with his family ...

She hears the heavy scrunch of the Land Rover on the gravel, and is surprised when Serge arrives in the kitchen alone and asks, “Is it seven o’clock yet, Mom?”

“Hello Darling,” she says, and looks at the clock. “It will be in five minutes, why? Oh, my goodness, the curfew!”

“Paddy’s shittin’ imself. Finks ‘e’s goin’ back to jail ... Serge wishes ‘e hadn’t wanted anuvver burger now.”

“Well, everything’s all right, it’s not seven yet, but you were cutting it fine, it has to be said. Where *is* Paddy?”

“Ee gone all funny and Dom tryin’ to get ‘im to come in.”

“Oh dear. Will you be good and sit still here for a minute whilst I go and have a look?”

Serge sits at the kitchen table and places his flask in front of him. The special one that Justin gave him, with the colourful diamond pattern.

Paddy, in the back of the Land Rover, looks terrified and is taking huge deep breaths. His arms are trembling and his knuckles are white as he clutches the back of the passenger seat. Dominic, ashen faced, is struggling to maintain a demeanour to assure everyone that all is well.

“He’s having a panic attack”, says Judith. “It’s happened to me now and again, in the past.” She climbs in and sits next to Paddy.

“Oh, I see!” Dominic consults his mental encyclopaedia of the books he has studied; “Think of a pendulum, slowly swinging from left to right ...” Judith shakes her head at him and he stops. “I’m so sorry we were nearly late,” he says. “I completely forgot that the road works were starting today on the by-pass. We were queuing for ages – then it was all stop-start.”

“Never mind,” says Judith, in a very calm voice that is new to Dominic. “You were home in time, and if you *had* been delayed beyond seven o’clock, we’ve got a phone number ... I would have phoned and explained. Dominic, would you like to pop indoors and keep an eye on Serge? We’ll be with you in a minute ...”

"Er, yes, okay. Thanks, Judith! Urm ... should I fetch a paper bag or something?" Judith shakes her head again, this time with an amused smile, and waves him away.

Whilst Paddy trembles and takes huge gulping breaths like a drowning man whose face is occasionally bobbing above the water, Judith tells him, mundanely, about her day; "So I thought I'd do a bit of baking. Quiches are always good for a gathering because you can re-heat them at the last minute and of course they're nice and easy to eat." She goes on to explain, in detail, how she always manages to circumvent a soggy pastry base. "And I've made some fairy cakes as well ... that's when you slice off the hard surface and make it into wings ... I might do the wings tomorrow and whip up some fresh cream." Paddy has stopped shaking but looks like a man who has been washed ashore by a tidal wave. Judith goes on; "Franchesca and her mother and grandmother are coming over tomorrow ... It would be nice for you to meet Pat and, erm, *Nan*, if you're feeling up to it, since they'll be living at Hardwicke Heights, just down the drive from you. My daughter, Beatrice is hoping to come along as well. Do you feel better now, Patrick?"

"Well, yes oi do, thank you," says Paddy, after a huge pause. After another huge pause he adds, "Oi taut we wus gonna be late back. Oi taut oi was goin back to jail. *It smelled like the devil*, that place, so it did."

"I expect it was a problem with the drains," says Judith. "I'm afraid we get that here occasionally, in the summer. There are a couple of wash basins in rooms on the west side that always seem to me to have a slight *odour* when you run the water, no matter how much bleach I put down them."

"Your place smells *good*, so it does."

"We don't have the problem on the east side where your room is. Shall we go indoors now and see what the others are up to?"

Paddy sits at the kitchen table, still looking pale and miserable but his hands are steady and he is breathing normally.

"All right?" asks Dominic and Paddy nods and winks – or it might have been a twitch.

"*Serge*, those cakes were meant for *tomorrow*. I haven't even put the *wings* on them yet."

"Serge don't need wings on 'is cakes."

Judith smiles indulgently. "Oh go on, have another then. Dominic, Paddy, please help yourselves. I'll make some more in the morning ... Perhaps I should put bits of cherry and green leaves on the top to look like holly. That would be a little more seasonal."

"Fran'll like that. And a trifle. Lurvely!"

The next day, Serge and Dominic go to the local train station to meet Franchesca, her mother Pat and ninety year old grandmother. The deaf old lady sits in the front shouting remarks at Dominic who bellows obligingly back at her, and Franchesca sits in the back between Serge and her mother. Franchesca is wearing a scarlet cape edged with white synthetic fur, and a headband with reindeer antlers sits lopsidedly on her head.

Paddy is in the front garden when they get back, using a leaf blower to blow leaves from one place to another. He stops and shakes hands solemnly with everyone, Dominic and Serge included. Beatrice is in the kitchen with her mother, whipping up cream for the trifle. She shrieks in protest as Serge exclaims, "Beatie!" and envelops her in a bear hug; sending flecks of cream across the kitchen window.

The women talk and laugh with loud high-pitched voices, as is the tendency of women who don't know each other very well but are thrust together as a group. Serge asks Dominic; "Don't you think Fran looks a bit of a spacker wiv that reindeer fing on 'er head?"

Dominic frowns and puts a finger to his lips. "No, I think she looks *very festive*," then adds, "I expect it was her mother who put that on her head."

Alistaire puts in a polite appearance when the buffet is served; eats a slice of quiche and a couple of sandwiches and then excuses himself and retreats to his study as he has some work to complete. The conversation, which had all but died when he showed his face begins to pick up again and soon accelerates to its previous raucous volume. Only Paddy, who has joined them at Judith's gentle request, is quiet; attempting nervous conversation with Beatrice, his eyes blinking rapidly as he tussles with the small ham sandwich on his plate. Judith makes a mental note to put something on a tray for him to have in his room later, and rescues him by asking Beatrice what she has been doing at work recently.

Beatrice pulls a face; "Very little as it happens. Geoff is away all the time. He's got this girlfriend in *Thailand?*"

"Yes, you did mention her. I take it they're still getting on well."

Beatrice rolls her eyes; "He's like over there more than he is here?"

"But he's still paying your wages, isn't he?"

"Oh yeah. But how long will it be before he decides to stay out there?"

"You'll be fine, Darling. Just be glad for Geoff that he seems to have finally found who he was looking for."

"Dom. *Dom!* Stop letchin' at my sister and pass us the rest of that pie fing!"

Dominic turns bright red and passes the quiche across the table.

"Young love is a wonderful thing, isn't it?" says Pat. "I mean, just look at these two now, how happy they are!" All eyes turn to see Serge break off a lump of quiche and stuff it into Franchesca's mouth, which is ringed with cream from the bowl of trifle she is still working through. All eyes turn away again. "And you don't have to worry about Family Planning cos we've got that sorted, *haven't we Mum!"*

Judith's eyes widen and her neck turns pink. Dominic, horrified at the prospect of such subject matter being aired at this particular tea party watches in morbid fascination as the colour travels up her face. "Well ..." Judith takes a deep breath, realising that the assembled company, apart from Serge and Franchesca, and possibly Paddy who is gazing at the kitchen window, are waiting to hear what she has to say on the subject. Alistaire has picked this particular moment to return to the kitchen for his mobile phone and appears to be rooted in a state of suspended animation. "Well ..." Judith starts again, but ends rather lamely, "It had crossed my mind that it was something we ought to consider, but I had no real feeling for, erm, whether or not the relationship was likely to develop in that particular direction ..."

"*Our Fran's had a Marian fitted!*" bellows Franchesca's grandmother.

"A *what*?" asks Judith.

"You mean a Mirena?" suggests Beatrice helpfully.

Alistaire recovers from his catalepsy and scurries back to the study.

"Yes, I expect you're right," says Pat. "*Mirena, Mum! Not Marian!*" She winks at Judith. "Her sister was called Marian, that's where *that* came from. Our Fran squawked a bit having it put in, bless 'er, but it's solved a few problems, *hasn't it Mum!*"

"Aye. *Terrible flooding*, she had. *Terrible!* But that's a thing of the past now, isn't it Pat! These days, you'd hardly know she was *on*. And it's killing two birds with one stone if them two's gonna start *having it off!*" There is a short silence. "I said –"

"Yes, I think we all heard you, Mum!"

Paddy puts his hand over his mouth to stifle a sound that is somewhere between clearing his throat and retching. He stands up abruptly. "Would yer excuse me - there's a few wee jobs outside I need to do before it gets dark."

Dominic and Beatrice meet each other's gaze and begin to giggle uncontrollably. Dominic makes a swift exit, as if to help Paddy in the garden and Beatrice immediately follows him. They find Paddy in a garden shed, oiling a lawn mower in the weak light of an old oil lantern. He smiles apologetically, “I'm sorry but dat wus 'ardly a conversation for the tea table, wus it now?” Dominic and Beatrice begin to laugh again and Paddy joins in, his face wrinkling like old leather. “Now yer understand why oi prefer to live with de ‘orses!”

20

Christmas

The day before Christmas Eve, Judith and Serge wave goodbye to the tinted windows of the Land Rover as Dominic drives up north to spend two nights at his parents' home. He will be returning on Christmas Day and has assured Judith he will be back early evening. Dominic did not want to go. Judith did not want him to go either – indeed she still has some presents to wrap and lots of cooking to do and the table decoration to complete ... and wonders how she managed last Christmas without Dominic's help – but yet it was she who persuaded him that his parents would want him home for Christmas. "I'll feel guilty if you don't go. Your parents might blame me for keeping you from them. Perhaps you feel obliged to stay here in case I can't cope with Serge without you? Surely you want to exchange gifts with your family?"

"Judith! No one will *blame* you for *anything*. Mum and Dad are as grateful as I am for all you have done for me. I don't fit in *there* any more and my old room has been taken over by my sister's girl. If they're all going to Mum's for Christmas I'll only be in the way. As for Christmas gifts I bought theirs online and they've already been delivered. But I expect they might have a few things for me under the Christmas tree."

"Dominic, *please* phone your mother and talk to her about it."

It turns out that Dominic's sister and her family are going to his parents' house for Christmas dinner and will be staying for a couple of nights. Dominic ends up agreeing to have dinner with them and then drive back down south in the afternoon, which will leave the guest room vacated for *Little Miranda* who is so excited already but wants to be in her own bed on Christmas morning *so as not to confuse Santa Claus*. "Hah, hah, isn't that sweet?"

"I hope I don't get snowed in," says Dominic to Judith.

"You'll be all right in the Land Rover," says Judith. "And it should be nice and quiet on the roads on Christmas Day … although it seems a shame for you to have to drive."

"It suits me fine. I tend to find Christmas Day a bit claustrophobic."

"Yes. I *do* understand what you mean. I think I might feel the same if I didn't have all the food to worry about."

Now, the Land Rover has turned out of the drive and the throb of the diesel engine has faded away up the road. Serge stops waving and stands dejectedly, hands hanging by his sides. "How many sleeps until Dom comes back?"

"Only two," replies Judith in her best soothing voice. "Come along and help me wrap up Dominic and Paddy's Christmas presents."

For Dominic there is a selection of books from his Amazon Wish List and for Paddy some warm outdoor clothes from one of those stores that sell animal feed, horse tackle, riding gear and expensive wellington boots. Judith wraps the quilted waistcoat, the thick boot-socks and the waxed jacket in separate parcels and takes the sturdy walking boots out of the box to admire them whilst Serge decides which sheet of wrapping paper to use next. Although Paddy chose these clothes himself and tried them on, it will still be a surprise. He had come from prison with little more than the clothes he stood in and has been wearing Alistaire's old Barbour jacket for gardening, which is several sizes too big for him. Dominic had taken Serge and Paddy along to the store and they had made a game of trying on the clothes. Pretending to be texting, Dominic had made notes on his mobile of the styles and sizes that Paddy had preferred and had taken Judith along later to buy them. "There's a playful side to Paddy that you haven't seen," Dominic told her. "He did a little act in front of the mirror wearing these things – he had me and Serge in stitches."

Judith hopes Paddy won't be embarrassed by how much she has spent, but she couldn't resist buying *all* the things that

Dominic picked out as Paddy's choices – especially when she heard that trying these boots on was the first time in his life that Paddy had worn new shoes, "*that weren't already the shape of someone else's feet.*"

Poor Paddy … he had taken it quite well when Andy the probation officer told him he would not be allowed to see his son Tommy at Christmas. Over-hearing Paddy asking how he could send "a wee bit of cash to the lad's ma to buy him a Christmas present," and knowing how little he could possibly have saved from the meagre wages they had been advised to pay for his gardening duties, Judith introduced an impromptu Christmas bonus for all the gardeners and cleaning staff, and told Paddy, "Once you move to Hardwicke Heights with Serge you will have a contract of employment and a proper salary," to which he replied that he would be eternally grateful for everything they had already done for him, "Oi can't believe oi don't owe yer any rent or nothin'."

It was as if his life had always been a challenge and he couldn't quite accept that anyone wanted to make it easier.

On Christmas Day, Beatrice arrives mid-morning to help Judith prepare the dinner and pours them both a small sherry. "Happy Christmas Mum!"

"You look *beautiful* darling," says Judith, kissing her daughter's glowing cheek. Beatrice does not normally make such an effort with her appearance if there is only her family to appreciate it.

"And Dominic isn't *here*?" Beatrice seems slightly miffed by his absence but nonetheless sets about transferring the contents of her handbag into the new Gucci handbag (with matching kid-leather gloves) that she chose as her Christmas present from her parents. "Thanks, Mum, it's gorgeous!"

"Well, *you* chose it dear, so you *ought* to like it."

"I did think maybe I should have gone for a 'SErge' one. But it seems a bit *twee* when he's my brother."

“I got a little black ‘SErge’ one for Bridget. I *do* hope she likes it.”

“Oh? You know she’s not his *biggest* fan.”

“Well, it’s not as if his picture’s on it – there’s just a small gold-plated ‘SErge’ logo.”

Serge hops excitedly into the kitchen and wraps an arm around his sister. “Beatie! Beatie!” His other arm is cradling a brand new flask with bright red glitter-effect plastic and a white cup on top.

“Happy Christmas! Careful – you’ll ruin my makeup! So, when *is* Dominic coming back?”

“Yeah … when’s Dom coming back Mom?”

“Some time this evening, thank goodness.” Judith tells Beatrice, “I’m so used to him keeping an eye on Serge that I forget – and then suddenly panic, wondering what he’s up to. Fortunately, Paddy’s very good at keeping him entertained.”

“Serge ‘elped Paddy make the bird table.”

“Oh, yes, *do look*,” says Judith, and points out of the kitchen window at a sturdy new bird table with a pitched roof and coconut shells and bags of nuts hanging from the corners. “Paddy made it from some spare wood that Derrick said he could use as it had been in one of the sheds for ages. He also made a wooden rack for Serge to keep all his flasks in.”

“Varnished it too, dinny Mom?”

“Didn’t he just!” Judith lowers her voice. “It was supposed to be a surprise but he was varnishing it in his room one evening and your Dad smelt the varnish out on the landing and thought he was glue-sniffing. Poor Paddy almost died of fright when confronted about it.”

Beatrice giggles. “What happened?”

“Well, your Dad knocked on the door and Paddy hid the rack and the varnish; opened the door then just stood there speechless with fear and doing that *eye-blinking* thing, whilst Alistaire demanded to know what he was doing. The longer Alistaire stood there glowering in the doorway, waiting for an answer, the more stressed Paddy became – trying to speak but he just kept stammering then finally burst into tears – at which point Alistaire backed out onto the landing and sent *me* in to sort it out." Judith rolls her eyes. "And then of course, when he showed us what he was doing, we felt *absolutely awful*. Your Dad went off for a while and then came back with an apology and a better brush for him to use for the varnish."

"Good old Dad," says Beatrice.

Serge adds, "Paddy cwied again this morning when 'e opened his Cwismus pwesents and put 'is new boots an' stuff on. But that was because 'e was pleased. Cwies a lot does Paddy. Sometimes when e's 'appy and sometimes when e's sad."

"I shall set a place at the dining table for Paddy – at the end, next to Serge. I hope he will join us, but he might be a little over-awed, so don't make a fuss if he takes a tray to his room instead."

"Paddy's scared 'e might gob on someone," explains Serge, helpfully. "Dunno why 'e's scared of that. *ATISHOO*!"

"Serge! Please use a tissue when you sneeze!" Judith grabs the antibacterial spray and sanitises the work surface.

"*Great*. It is okay if I sit up the opposite end of the table from the pair of them?"

Leo and Bridget arrive with an atmosphere between them that is almost tangible. Bridget looks stunning in a vampish style that is bound to provoke comments from Serge. She has long dark hair that falls in luxuriant waves around the flawless olive complexion of her face – a face that would be so much prettier were it not for the petulant expression she always seems to be wearing these days. "An expression is about all she *does* wear," Alistaire had once remarked, and today is no exception. Despite the cold weather, Bridget is wearing a low cut scarlet top, *almost* held together by a black leather cord that is straining to contain her large firm breasts; and a leather mini-skirt, so short that it would surely be possible to see the tops of her black fishnet stockings if she bent over. Only her calves look cosy as her black stiletto boots cling like a second skin almost up to knee level. Judith nudges Alistaire and he closes his mouth, levels his gaze and wishes her a Happy Christmas. Leo, kissing his mother's cheek and shaking his father's hand, seems unaware of his wife's visual impact.

By dinner time, Judith and Beatrice are looking warm and rosy from the kitchen and the sherry. Judith had waited until Paddy had quaffed the glass of port she'd put in his hand before reminding him that she had set him a place at the table next to Serge, and she is delighted when he sidles in apologetically to join them – just as everyone else is finishing their melon balls. She fills his wine glass with red wine until it overflows; runs down the stem and seeps into the white tablecloth. Alistaire, arriving from the kitchen with a huge oval plate bearing the turkey surrounded by chipolatas and stuffing balls, steps in and pours an inch of wine in Serge's glass and tops it up with lemonade, then asks everyone else, "Red or white?" Leo, who is driving because Bridget refuses to stay the night, has mineral water. "Leg or breast?" asks Alistaire next, in the same flat tone, and Paddy almost chokes on his wine when Serge gawps openly at his sister-in-law's chest then lifts the table cloth, looks beneath and says, "*Both please, since she's offering!*"

There is a short, aghast silence. Paddy, whose wine glass is already empty, is the first to speak. "Dat's a really nice family portrait dat yer gave Serge for Christmas. T'will look lovely above der fireplace in 'is new home, so it will."

Everyone except Serge and Bridget turns their attention to the large framed studio photo that stands on the floor, leaning against the wall. Judith had insisted that they couldn't only give Serge yet another flask for Christmas, even though that was all he said he wanted. Even now, whilst most other eyes are on the photograph, Serge is re-examining the finer details of his new flask.

Beatrice, who looks as lovely on the photo as she does today, says what a shame it is that Serge was being so awkward on the day of the appointment at the studio. "I saw on the internet that my little brother is like *the most photographed guy in the UK right now?*"

Judith agrees, "Yes, it's not one of the *best* photos I've seen of Serge, but they did a very good job of editing out Dominic's hand." She explains to Paddy, "Serge kept wandering out of the shot just as the photographer was about to click the shutter. *That* was the *best* photo except Dom's arm was coming in from the side as if he'd just propelled Serge back into the scene."

Paddy giggles, his face creasing into a myriad lines, as he looks again at the photo. "Now yer mention it dat's *just* 'ow it looks!" Leo's hand is on Serge's shoulder and at first glance it appears to be a gesture of affection – but a closer look reveals the whitening around the knuckles of a grip that is a little too firm. Paddy glances down the table to where Leo is sitting now, with a similar but lighter hold on his wife's arm, as if to deter her from storming out. Bridget is knocking back red wine even faster than Paddy, but as he gets nice and merry, she becomes increasingly morose.

Finally, Judith and Beatrice clear away the dinner plates and Alistaire carries in the Christmas pudding. Judith is relieved that the meal was a success and happy that everyone seems to have done it justice. Alistaire pours brandy over the pudding and sets it alight making Serge whoop with excitement. He begins to rock back and forth and Paddy murmurs soothingly, "Steady boy, *steady* … we don't want a magic table cloth act, so we don't …"

Serge notices that Bridget's Christmas cracker remains unpulled. "Cracker, Bridge! Cracker! Pull it wiv Serge. *Go on, plee-ez*!"

Bridget responds with a belligerent frown and takes a gulp of the dessert wine that Alistaire has just poured. Leo sends a subtle *no more, she's had enough* signal to his father.

Beatrice, who is sitting next to her sister-in-law and has had enough of her self-indulgent sulks, says brightly, "Go on Bridget, pull the cracker! It doesn't require much effort;

you've only like got to hold the one end whilst my brother pulls the other?"

Leo sighs, unhappily.

Beatrice picks up the cracker and waves it at Serge, "Come on, *I'll* pull it with you!" Serge gets up from his place at the table and stands behind Leo and Bridget to pull the cracker. Bridget, startled out of her brooding by the noise of the cracker, whirls round angrily with perfect timing for the small plastic novelty that is flying through the air to fall down the crevice of her considerable cleavage.

"Serge gerrit, *Serge gerrit!*" Serge thrusts forward his hand to retrieve it.

"*No*," says Leo, sternly, and grabs Serge's wrist.

"*Will you piss off!*" yells Bridget, and attempts to fling the wine from her glass at Serge's face. It misses him and goes all over Leo.

Beatrice mops his shirt and jacket with her napkin and says cheerfully, "At least she'd moved on to the white!"

Bridget stands up with the intention of stomping off and slamming the door, but she lurches sideways and sits down again. Leo puts his arm around her and steers her across the room. Judith hurries to open the door and looks anxiously at Leo. "We'll just go up to my old room for a while, Mum. I think Bridget could do with a lie down … she hasn't been sleeping well these last few days."

And neither have you by the look of it. Judith notices again his pale, drawn face and the grey-purple shadows beneath his eyes.

There is an awkward silence after their exit, which is broken by Serge; "Bridge pissed, she is. *Futtin legless!*"

Alistaire, livid but dangerously silent, suddenly flips, and yells at Serge, "*GO TO YOUR ROOM!*" with such vehemence that Serge emits a loud wail and runs away, with Ralph prancing after him. Alistaire rests his head in his hands for a moment, then demands, "*Where the hell did that dog come from*? I hope Serge and Patrick have not been feeding him under the table – otherwise he'll have me up all night!" He lowers the volume of his voice a little. “At least I now know where that dreadful smell came from – I thought it was strangely familiar.”

Paddy stands up suddenly. “Mr Freeman, indeed I ‘*ave* been feedin’ the dog a wee bit o’ turkey. I wassun aware he had such a sensitive stomach – but I assure you I will listen out for ‘im tonight an’ will attend to him as nature necessitates and will clear any mess from the garden in the morning!”

Beatrice giggles helplessly and Paddy sits down again.

Judith says quietly to Beatrice, “*Don’t laugh*, Darling.”

Beatrice pours herself some more sweet white wine and cuts another small slice of Christmas pudding. “This is gorgeous! No-one else having any?”

Paddy takes courage again, although Judith notices his hands are shaking quite badly. Noticing that she has noticed, he clasps his hands behind his back and manages to control his stammer, “Thanks so much, Mrs Freeman for a truly grand dinner. Truly grateful, so I am, but if yer don't mind I'll pass on de puddin'. If yer don’t mind, I might go an’ find the lad and see if ‘e fancies a game o’ Snap wiv me new cards ... if dat’s all the same with you ...”

Alistaire gives him a piercing stare. “Very well, Patrick. I’ll leave the key in the back door if you will kindly see to the dog tonight … if it er … becomes necessary. But please remember you are tagged. Just let him out in the garden to do his *business*. Don’t go walking him up the road or anything.”

Her father’s inflexion on the word ‘business’ triggers another fit of uncontrollable giggles from Beatrice. Alistaire frowns with irritation and Paddy’s eyes blink rapidly with anxiety.

“No problem, Mr Freeman. Thank you – goodnight.” Paddy escapes.

Serge is sitting on the edge of his bed, rocking back and forth, his eyes wide and fearful. Paddy taps on the open door, goes in, perches next to him and takes the new pack of Snap cards from his pocket. The cards are a Christmas present from Dominic and have a farm animal theme; a change from the cards he normally plays with that have pictures of nurses, doctors, firemen and so on. "They're brand new so we'll need ter give dem a really good shuffle before we use dem. Would you like ter do it?"

"Serge do it!" Before beginning to shuffle the cards, Serge examines them all. "Four cows … four pigs … four ducks … four sheeps … four gooses … four 'orses. Dom tried to get you some cards that was all 'orses but couldn't find any, so you 'ad these … but at least there's no futtin people."

Paddy throws back his head and laughs. "Dees ones is just fine!"

Leo returns to the dining room and pours himself some coffee. "She's fast asleep," he says, tiredly, declining the offer of Christmas pudding.

"Maybe she'll wake up in a better mood?" says Beatrice, slurring her words slightly. She puts an arm around Leo's shoulders to draw him close, leans against him and takes a photo on her mobile. "Aw, look Mum! Leo looks exactly like Serge sometimes looks when he's having a bad day."

Judith takes the mobile phone and studies the photo of Beatrice and Leo. She is happy and glowing; he looks weary and dejected, almost as if he is about to burst into tears. His façade of steely cold control has dropped, and he does indeed have the look of Serge in one of his moments of extreme sorrow, like the occasion when he dropped his old blue flask and the inside of it shattered.

Beatrice pours herself a brandy and strokes her brother's arm. "Come and watch telly with me? There's bound to be some boring old film we can fall asleep in front of."

A couple of hours later, Leo yawns and stretches and drags himself upstairs to check on his wife. She is still asleep and does not stir when he sweeps back her hair and kisses her forehead. She looks like the Sleeping Beauty. He hopes she won't wake up feeling bad. He puts a glass of water on the bedside table. "Wake up soon, and then we can go home," he whispers, and heads off back downstairs. Judith is in Serge's doorway with a tray bearing a pot of tea and Christmas pudding and mince pies and Christmas cake and cream and brandy butter and rum sauce. Serge and Paddy have completed two hours of solid Snap-playing and are now relaxing on Serge's bed. Paddy jumps to attention and clears a space for Judith to put down the tray. She indicates discreetly the large tumbler of Irish whiskey and the mug of coffee that is not for Serge and Paddy winks and grins and whisks them off the tray. "Thanks so much, Mrs Freeman, you're too kind to everyone, you'll wear yerself out."

Leo goes to the kitchen and sits at the table where Judith soon joins him. "Oh dear, look at the state of your shirt! I should have sorted out one of Serge's for you to wear ... I'll go and do that now."

"Leave it Mum, it's fine. It's dry now - but the smell of it's making me fancy a glass of something. Port I think. As soon as Bridget wakes up we'll be off. I'm sorry she went over the top like that. She hasn't drunk alcohol for ages, because she was trying to conceive – that's why it went straight to her head."

"What do you mean; she *was* trying to conceive … she hasn't given up, has she?"

Leo lowers his eyes and wishes all the kitchen appliances would stop making such a noise. The kettle is on; the percolator is bubbling and belching, and the dishwasher is performing its final rinse.

"I wasn't going to tell you until after Christmas ..."

"Tell me what? *What is it Leo?*" asks Judith with great concern.

"Well … I went for some tests." Leo studies the wood-grain of the kitchen table ... for quite some time. "It seems that the problem is with me." Finally, he comes out with it. "The results proved that I have a very low sperm count."

Judith frowns and says, "Sorry, you have a what?" and switches off the kettle, which was getting louder as it approached boiling point, just as the dishwasher cycle ends and

Leo declares loud and clear above all the noise – which has suddenly stopped; "*I'm firing blanks, Mum!*"

Dominic, who has just walked in through the back door, was about to say, "Happy Christmas Everyone!" Instead he attempts to retreat unnoticed but fails and says cheerfully, "I'll just pop and see what Serge is up to and I'll catch up with you later ..." and walks past Leo and out through the kitchen door to the hallway.

"Oh Leo, is there *no possibility at all*? Low doesn't mean nonexistent, does it?"

"Well ... there *is* a small chance. More so if we relax and forget about it for a while. But Bridget doesn't seem able to do that ... I suggested we book a skiing holiday but she's not interested." He sighs, sadly. "I just don't see how we can go on, living month by disappointing month like this ..."

"But Bridget married *you* – for the lovely man that you *are*. She didn't marry a *reproductive system!*"

"Well ... I guess babies were part of the deal."

Serge bounces around his room in excitement when he realises Dominic is back. (Dominic had walked along the landing shouting, "*Hello,Serge, I'm back!*")

Paddy steps out onto the landing and gravely shakes Dominic's hand. "Tis good to have yer back, so it is!"

"Why? What's been going on?"

"Oh, nothin' serious, but his Dad just got a bit angry with him. Twas the sister-in-law's fault, so it was."

"Ah, Bridget. Never met her but I've heard that Serge is inclined to make himself unpopular with her."

"Beggin' yer pardon but 'tis 'ardly surprisin' she provokes a bit of reaction if she comes 'ere dressed like a high class whore."

Dominic laughs. "I'm just going to unpack my stuff and I'll be with you in a minute." He opens the door of his own room, still smiling, happy to be back. His face drops. Beatrice is curled up on his bed, apparently asleep, but she must be only dosing as she sits up and yawns and stretches gracefully as he walks in ... and then she smiles rather beautifully. The smoky makeup around her blue eyes is smudging and her wavy blonde hair is beginning to tumble down – silky tendrils curling around her face. Dominic, whispers "Happy Christmas," and hugs her gently, kissing her cheek, and his heart leaps with joy when she holds on to his arms to prolong the embrace. He hopes her affection is genuine and she is not simply pissed ...

Serge and Paddy have followed Dominic into his room. "Bejesus, look what Santa brought *you*!" exclaims Paddy. His cheeks are flushed and his voice a little louder than usual.

"Open your *real* pressie, Dom!" says Serge.

"Just give me a minute, I'm bustin'." Dominic nips into the ensuite, and then puts his head round the door shyly. "Could you lot sing a Christmas carol or something?"

Paddy pipes up with '*Once in Royal David's City*' and the others join in, loud and tunelessly. The din drives Bridget grumpily downstairs to find Leo.

"That's better," sighs Dominic reappearing.

"Open it now, open it now," demands Serge. The gift tag reads, 'Happy Christmas Dominic, with love, thanks and best wishes from all the Freeman family,' and Dominic opens the parcel to find all the books that were on his Amazon wish list.

For a moment he is speechless as he scans and recognises the titles. "Oh, *wow*!"

"Beatie found Dom's wish list when she went snooping on the net," says Serge, helpfully.

"I wasn't snooping," says Beatrice. "Didn't you notice they'd all been bought off your wish list? I didn't think it would be such a surprise."

"No, I didn't notice. My family don't do internet shopping, and I didn't think anyone knew about the wish list. I only keep it as my little catalogue of books I might treat myself to over the coming year … Wow … Thank you so much. I must go down and thank your parents!"

They all troop downstairs just as Leo and Bridget are in the hallway saying goodbye to Judith and Alistaire. Bridget bends over to pick up her bag.

"Corr*! Do that again, will yer Bridge*?" shouts Serge from half way up the stairs.

Bridget glares at him, her face ugly with contempt; "*Drop dead*, you retard!" She turns on Leo, "It's just as well you *can't* have kids with *that* in the gene pool!"

There is a horrified silence as no-one moves or breathes for a few seconds, and then Bridget leaves through the front door, dragging Leo out behind her.

"*Poor Leo!*" says Judith, and begins to weep.

Alistaire steers her into his study; "What the hell was *that* about?" Judith explains about the test results, and Alistaire says, "Fancy Leo telling you about *that* on Christmas Day! The clumsy oaf. And Serge is *brain damaged.* We proved it in court. Nothing to do with *genes*."

Dominic leads the troop to the kitchen, "I'm surprised at Leo for driving, he reeked of booze when I walked past him earlier."

"That was Bridget's booze," says Beatrice. "Talking of which, you must be ready for a drink?"

Dominic opts for whiskey, and Paddy joins him, *just to be sociable.* Beatrice pours a generous measure for Serge and tops it up with lemonade. "It'll help him sleep," she says, winking at Dominic, "but *don't tell Dad*."

Judith joins them and starts making turkey sandwiches. Her eyes are red but she seems to cheer up when Dominic hugs her and thanks her for the books. "It was Beatrice's idea," says Judith. "She's obviously on your wavelength."

Beatrice is organising the pickles and chutney and pretends she didn't hear, but Dominic can see in his peripheral vision that she is watching him all the time. It makes him feel excited and slightly edgy. "Are you staying here tonight?" he asks casually.

"Yeah, in my old room … Have some more whiskey?"

"Go on then - but just a small one. I'd better not have too much."

"Yeah, I'd better ease off it myself ..."

Dominic fears he may be misreading the signs, but can't help feeling he is on a promise. Must have a quick shower before bed – just in case. He starts to wonder about the use-by date on his condoms then remembers that tea-table conversation about the Marian or Mirena or whatever it was ...

"Pickled gherkin?" asks Beatrice, holding a large turgid specimen in front of his face.

"Erm ... No thanks!"

She fixes him with her eyes and licks the vinegar that is running down the sides then sucks the end. Dominic's jaw drops. She inserts the gherkin into her mouth, gently gliding her teeth half way down the length of it. Then she bites through it, crisply.

"Ouch!"

An hour later, Serge is falling asleep. His head keeps drooping until it almost touches the table, and then his neck suddenly jerks it back up again – but his eyes are still closed.

"Come on, mate, let's get you to bed, shall we?" says Dominic.

"Tired Serge ..."

"Yes, *I know*. Come on ... let's go and clean your teeth. I'll carry your new flask."

"More Cwismus tomorrow ..."

"That's right. We can get up in the morning and do it all over again."

"Heaven help us," says Alistaire, with an upward roll of his eyes. "*Good night Serge*. Looks like he's helped himself to some of that whiskey ..."

Dominic says, "If you'll all excuse me, once Serge is settled I think I'll have a shower and then read some of my new books in bed."

Serge is asleep almost before he lands in bed. Dominic tucks in the new red and white flask next to him and strokes the golden curls back off his forehead. He feels guilty now for not confiscating that whiskey and lemonade Beatrice gave him. Judith had told him they didn't often allow Serge alcohol as it tended to make him drowsy when combined with his daily medication. "Night-night, God bless, sweet dreams," he murmurs, and leaves Serge's room.

Dominic showers; meticulously. He picks the tickets off a pair of the new boxer shorts he had for Christmas, puts them on and checks his appearance in the full-length mirror, frowning at the beginnings of moobs. *Must take up running again in the New Year.* He is standing beneath a light and can see his head shining pinkly through his thin hair. *Not yet twenty-one and I'm turning into my father.* He gets into bed and tries to read one of his new books but is unable to concentrate. He dims down the lamp. Would Beatrice come to his room tonight, or was she just playing him along? She made a point of telling him she was in her old room – but he couldn't possibly go waltzing in there. For a start, Alistaire would kill him if he caught him entering his daughter's room ... and what if he had misread the signs and was kidding himself? Why would a gorgeous girl like Beatrice be interested in him? But then Sabrina had been attracted to him – and she had been, fitness-wise, of a similar calibre to Beatrice … but without such a sweet, kind heart. As the middle child between Leo and Serge, Beatrice must be about twenty-nine. For some reason, the idea of an older woman excites him, especially a woman as gorgeous as Beatrice. *But why is she interested in me? Or is it just a game she's playing?*

Eventually he switches off the lamp and settles down to go to sleep. He hears a distant sound and strains his ears to listen, but it is only Ralph, whining in the kitchen. It is by now half past one - Boxing Day morning and everyone in this house has surely had enough of Christmas Day. *She won't come now – she's probably fallen asleep herself … she seemed a bit pissed...* However, he resists the urge to start playing with himself just yet … give her another few minutes.

He hears a small creak on the landing and immediately becomes alert and stops breathing in order to listen exclusively.

Perhaps it is just Judith going to check on Serge, as she sometimes does…

His door opens, making him jump even though he was half expecting her, and a small figure sways towards his bed – only visible as a vague silhouette in the subtle glow that emanates from the footlights on the landing. Not knowing how to respond, he pretends to be sleeping quietly. She stands over his bed, smelling strongly of whiskey, hesitates for a moment but then appeals with a deep, throaty Irish accent, "Dominic! Oim so sorry ter disturb yer but yer gotta help me open der back door. The dog needs ter go out in der garden but oi can't seem ter open der door an' everyone's gone ter bed."

"Ah, yes," says Dominic, trying to sound in control whilst his heart pounds and a sensation of weakness tingles outwards along his limbs ... "It's not just you, Paddy; I've had problems with that door myself. Once you've opened all the bolts and turned the key round twice, you've got to push the handle down to *position one,* and then lift it up to *position two* ... and then back down, and the door should fall open quite easily..."

"Then would yer kindly come an' give me a hand, as a matter of some urgency, before der dog shits all over der kitchen floor!"

Fully grasping the *urgency*, Dominic pulls on his towelling robe and hurries down to the kitchen with Paddy limping along behind. By the time Paddy reaches the kitchen, the back door is open and Ralph is out in the garden. Dominic demonstrates to Paddy how the door works and then they both gaze out into the darkness.

"Oi think 'e should 'ave finished by now," says Paddy.

"Perhaps we could coax him back in with a bit of turkey," suggests Dominic.

“No, no … dat was what caused der problem in der first place. Twas my fault for feedin’ ‘im me dinner under der table.” Paddy sets off down the steps to the garden.

“Mind you don’t tread in anything!” says Dominic.

“Oh ah,” says Paddy. He retreats back up the steps and is almost knocked over by Ralph who pushes past and settles back on his bed with a heavy sigh. Paddy strokes his huge head tenderly, thanks Dominic for his help, and the two of them head back off upstairs.

Dominic cannot help pausing on his way past Beatrice’s room, but there is no light beneath the door and he can hear no sound whatsoever. She must be asleep. He checks on Serge and finds him sleeping peacefully, cuddling the hard plastic flask against his chest. Back in his own room, he hangs his robe on the hook on the door, feels his way across to the bed in the dark, and gets in quickly, wondering how long it will take for his feet to warm up.

“*Aaaaaaagh!*”

“*Hush!*” Beatrice clamps her hand over his mouth and giggles.

“*Ker-iste!* You nearly gave me a heart attack.”

She rests her head on his chest, where his heart is pounding dramatically for the second time within half an hour. He strokes her silky hair and tries to calm down.

“What you need is a little something to help you relax,” she says, playfully, and slides her head downwards from his chest.

He gasps. “*Oh Bri.* I mean Bea!” She laughs it off and carries on … but Dominic knows women well enough to be certain that he will be reminded of this clanger on some future occasion.

21

Moving and Shaking

The purchase of Hardwicke Heights is complete and Serge is gradually moving in. Judith has equipped his new bedroom with lots of his favourite things, including a range of flasks and some of his favourite picture books, and it is a huge relief to her when Serge sleeps in his new home for the first night and does not change his mind about moving.

"Can Serge keep 'is old room 'ere like Beatie and Leo did?"

"Of course you can. We have plenty of other rooms to rattle around in and we *like* to preserve our memories."

Leo's old room is still as he had left it. As a student at Oxford he had often been home during holidays, but had never stayed the night since he and Bridget had got married and moved into their own home. Leo has not only handled the conveyancing of Hardwicke Heights; he has also assisted with every aspect of this move with his customary efficiency, but everyone can see a difference in him. At the office, the dynamic steely resolve that always defied anyone to question his judgment has diminished; there is a change in both his mental and physical attitude that riles Alistaire.

"He languishes around the office like a – like a flaccid penis!"

"Oh, *Alistaire*," protests Judith, frowning with distaste.

"Well, it's true. It's that bloody wife of his – she's *emasculated* him."

Dominic, however, sees the change in Leo as an improvement; a self-effacing openness making him far more approachable than he used to be.

"Do you get on all right with my sister," Leo had asked him, casually, and when Dominic had turned bright red and begun to stammer, Leo had hurried on to explain his reason for asking. In the past, Leo would have stood like a brick wall, waiting for an answer. “Beatrice’s boss, Geoff, is getting married to his Thai girlfriend, and is going to live in Thailand. So he no longer requires Beatrice’s personal assistance. I wondered how you might feel about having her on board for the time being to help run Serge’s place. I wanted to ask *you* before mentioning it to Beatrice. Your role with Serge is too important to risk introducing someone who might rock the boat. But once Franchesca is in place, it might be useful to have a woman on the scene. I know her mother will be around, but I should imagine you’d prefer to keep *her* involvement in daily activities to a minimum. So that’s why I’m asking.”

Dominic smiles and nods enthusiastically. “I think that would be a brilliant idea! I had been wondering how I’d manage taking them out as a couple without female backup, and I must admit I worried it might prove necessary to take her mother along every time.”

“Good. I’ll suggest it to Beatrice.”

Paddy is busy white-washing the stables whilst passing on racing tips to the builders Judith has sent in to convert a section of the stable block into a bedroom, bathroom and combined kitchen-living room. He had made it clear that he wanted to live in the stables and not in the *big house* but was also anxious that there should be no fuss or expense on account of this preference. He has, however, grown accustomed to hot running water and soap since joining the Freeman family, and cannot believe his luck at this turn of events. Judith, who has a penchant for interior design, has told Paddy that she has ordered him a bed with one of those guest beds that pulls out from underneath, so that all will be in place when his son is allowed to come to visit him. Paddy blinks his eyes rapidly at the suggestion of Tommy coming to stay; his face breaking into a huge craggy smile that rapidly fades to doubt as he briefly explores the obstacles that might lie in the way of such a plan. “Yer so very kind, Mrs Freeman. Yer think of everything, so you do.”

Dominic has chosen the bedroom directly opposite to Serge's as opposed to the one that adjoins it. He is arranging some of his books on a shelf whilst Serge sits on the bed and turns the pages, looking for pictures.

"Dom ... Do-*om* ..."

"Yes Serge?"

"Dom ... 'ave you futted my sister?"

"Erm ..." Dominic had wondered how much longer they could get away with it before Serge caught on. "*Yes*, Serge."

"Oh. Well I know Beatie likes you, so that's orright." There is a short silence that Dominic does not attempt to fill. Serge resumes, "It's funny to fink about it though!"

"Then *please don't.* I'd rather you *didn't* think about it," says Dominic.

"Serge is gonna futt Fwan soon. Got any tips for Serge? *Go-on*, Dom, tell Serge."

"Okay, I'm *thinking.* Well then, here's my advice. You know what to do, right? You know how the bits fit together?"

"Yer ... John from the Centre swapped a porn movie for some daft badge that Beatie brought from one of 'er trips abroad. Serge saw what they did. Except it wassan Fwan that was getting futted. It was sum shag piece wot looked like she was just doing it for the camera. I don't fink she even liked the man that was futtin 'er."

There is a pause whilst Dominic assimilates this and formulates his response.

"Right ... *okay* ... well, the only advice I can come up with is that you take it *really gently* the first time – because it might seem very strange to Fran, and a bit scary. So just be very careful. Treat her as if she's ... as if she's your *favourite flask.* Just be gentle until she gets used to it, and then take it from there ..."

"Fanks Dom. Serge'll do that. *Did* once try to futt one of me flasks but it was too narrow and Fwank got stuck in it. Had to wait for 'im to go down."

Judith returns from the post office on a Tuesday afternoon to find Leo's car parked in the drive. Instinctively, she checks her mobile and finds a text from Alistaire that simply says 'Leo phoned in sick today.' Most unusual for their workaholic son.

She finds him sitting at the kitchen table, in jeans and tee-shirt, red-eyed and unshaven ... "What's wrong, Darling? Dad says you phoned in sick today."

"Oh, I'm fine," says Leo, automatically. "There's just something I came to tell you about ... but now that I'm here I don't quite know what to say ..."

"Whatever is it, Leo, please just tell me."

"Well, there's been a turn of events that has rather taken my mind off ... everything. I didn't go into work today because I wouldn't have been able to concentrate. So I asked for my appointments to be cancelled." Judith waits, pensively, as Leo looks down at his hands and flexes his long tensile fingers as if physically grasping for the words to tell her. "You see, when I got home yesterday evening, Bridget told me she is expecting a baby."

"Oh, Leo, that's marvellous news!" Judith advances with outstretched arms but Leo ducks from her embrace; dives down the kitchen steps and out through the side gate. Judith, bewildered, stands in the doorway and watches him go.

Such is Dominic's karma that he happens to turn up on an errand just as Leo appears in the front driveway. "Hi Leo, the stables are finished now. I just called to collect the kettle, microwave and toaster that your Mum saved for Paddy's kitchen. We're having a barbecue in the paddock this evening if you fancy joining us ... Leo, are you okay?"

Leo leans against his car, swallowing and blinking, his right hand resting on his chest. Just for a moment Dominic thinks he is having a heart attack and tries to recall his first aid training – then Leo exhales with a deep sigh and says, "I'm fine, thanks, but I'll give the barbecue a miss. Would you ... would you please tell Mum ... You see, I just told her ..."

Dominic looks up towards the house and sees Judith's figure watching from a window. He waves, and she waves back.

Leo gets in the car, starts it and lowers the window. His normally steady hands are trembling. "Please tell Mum not to celebrate. Tell her I will phone later to explain." He drives away.

Dominic passes on the message to Judith, and adds. "He was clearly upset about something."

"Oh dear, what on earth could be the matter? Maybe they've had a scan and there's something wrong. Perhaps they've found out they're expecting a baby like Serge. That would be a double whammy for Leo if Serge's problem turned out to be genetic after all, when they've won their blessed case by proving it isn't. But of course, whatever the baby turns out like it will be loved, and we'll all help out. This time we'll be better prepared, having been through it already with Serge, and we'll know what to expect."

When Leo finally phones, his voice is level and calm. Judith recognises it as the detached tone he uses when dictating a letter into his computer. "No Mum," he says, "as far as I know the baby is okay, but it's early days yet. The problem is ..."

"Oh, come on Leo, out with it!" Judith is becoming impatient.

"Mum, the baby's not mine."

"The baby's not *what*?"

"Not *mine*. I am not the father."

After a dumbfounded silence, Judith asks, "Well who on earth *is*?"

Leo sighs. "Some guy called Matt. He's the brother of one of Bridget's work colleagues. She met him at the New Year's Eve party, and she's been, erm, seeing him since then."

"Oh, *Leo*. So what are you going to *do*?"

"She erm ... she wants me to move out, so that he can move in to support her during the pregnancy. It seems he's looking forward to being a father, and he has asked her to marry him – just as soon as her divorce ... I mean *our* divorce can be finalised. And they would like to be married, *Bridget and Matt*, before the baby comes along." He stops but there is no response. "Are you still there, Mum?"

"Yes Darling ..." Her voice sounds tearful. "It's just a lot to take in ..."

"Yes, I know."

"So when did Bridget tell you all this news?"

"Yesterday evening ... although yesterday seems like a different life time."

"Where are you now?"

"Parked in a lay-by about three miles from home. From yesterday's home, that is. You see, I was hoping you wouldn't mind if ... Is it okay if I have my old room back for a week or two?"

"Of course it is! *For as long as you want*," sobs Judith. "I'll go and make your bed up *right now*."

"Thank you. I'm just going home now to collect my things. Bridget has packed them for me."

He says it as if Bridget has bestowed on him a huge kindness.

"Mum?"

"I'm here, Leo. Just go and pick up your belongings and we'll see you soon."

Leo lets himself into his marital home. His travel bag and three large black bin liners are positioned in the hallway. Bridget is perched on the sofa, looking insolent, defiant and as beautiful as ever. "I've put everything in the hallway," she says.

"So I see. Is my shaving stuff somewhere in there?"

"I expect so."

"I'll go upstairs and have a look. I know where I keep everything." He goes upstairs and opens his wardrobe and cupboards. Admittedly, she has done a pretty thorough job of clearing him out of her life. He looks around the bedroom for one last time, remembering how he and Bridget had enjoyed choosing the colours and decorating it together when they had first moved in. He picks up her pillow and holds it to his face, breathing in the smell of her hair – the close, connected smell of coming home when she nestles her head beneath his chin. Without knowing why, he extracts a couple of her long dark hairs from her hair brush on the dressing table and winds them around his finger, beneath his wedding ring, then places back the pillow and goes round to his own side of the bed to check his bedside cabinet.

He hears the front door opening and closing, followed by a half-hearted protest from his wife, and then someone – well, Matt, of course, coming up the stairs. Matt walks into the bedroom. He is about Leo's height, but of a more robust, stocky build. His brown hair is close-cropped, making his face look big, and he wears an annoying smirk that looks like a permanent expression as opposed to one he has put on for this particular occasion.

Leo is still kneeling by the side of the bed, checking the drawers where he keeps his batteries and chargers, aftershave and a wallet containing prints of some of his favourite photos. The drawer is empty. "Get out of my bedroom, please," requests Leo, with his customary polite delivery.

"*My* bedroom as from tonight, mate," says Matt with strong East End accent and a mocking smile. "Bridge packed all your stuff up, so how come it's taking you so long to clear off?"

Leo, still kneeling by the side of the bed, looks up at Matt; white-faced with anger, loathing and lack of sleep.

"Go on, sling yer hook," says Matt, cheerfully.

Leo flies at him, grabbing his shoulders and forcing him back against the wall – the pent up tension of the last twenty-four hours unleashed on Matt like a spring-trap being deployed. Matt's head and shoulders connect with the wall with a satisfying thud, and he shouts out in fear, bringing Bridget hurrying up the stairs.

"I thought his brother was the mad one," Matt attempts to quip, but his bravado is subdued by the dangerous blue glint in Leo's eyes. Leo, still holding Matt's shoulders with a vice-like grip, can feel the man's fear trembling into his palms.

Bridget suddenly ducks under Leo's arm and turns to face him - filling the narrow gap between the two men, leaning back against Matt with her face just a few inches from her husband's - her hands clasped protectively across her pelvis.

Leo releases his grasp and takes a step back. "Don't hurt him, Leo," she begs. "This is going to be difficult enough as it is. Don't make it worse for yourself."

"Go back downstairs, Bridget," demands Leo, gazing steadily into her deep brown eyes. She looks back at him, sullenly, but her lower lip is trembling. "*Go on.*" She moves as if to obey, but Matt wraps his arms around her and holds her close against him.

"You *coward!*" says Leo, in disbelief. "Using *my wife* as a shield to protect yourself!"

"Coward, eh? At least I'm a proper man – the *full package*, like! Now you just fuck off out of here. Your *wife* doesn't want you any more. Understand? Go on, sling yer hook!"

Leo looks past Bridget at Matt with a look that could kill and Bridget begins to weep - gulping noisily with distress. "*Please! Just go*," she sobs.

Leo, understanding how tired and stressed she is feeling, and suddenly fearful for the well-being of the baby that she has longed for all this time, turns away abruptly, goes downstairs, puts his bags in the car and closes the door quietly behind him.

"*Hah hah*, that told *him!*" says Matt. "And *he* called *me* a *coward!*"

22

Tears and Horses

Judith wakes up at three o'clock on Sunday morning and realises she has forgotten to take the leg of lamb out of the freezer for Sunday dinner. She goes quietly downstairs to put it out to thaw. The night is unseasonably warm for April, so it should be defrosted in time. Going back up to bed she hears a small sound and pauses at the top of the stairs to listen, then walks softly along the landing and stands outside Leo's room. She can hear him sobbing quietly. Tears spring to her own eyes. There is no light from beneath the door and she knows he would be mortified if she went in to comfort him. It breaks her heart.

At a more respectable hour in the morning, Judith returns to the kitchen to prepare the vegetables before going to church. Passing Serge's room, she glances as always through the open door and stops abruptly – seeing Serge sitting on the edge of his bed engrossed in a hardback book of illustrated fairy tales, his long lean legs and large bony feet stretching endlessly across the floor. Then Leo looks up from the book and says, "This is one of his favourites. I'm surprised he didn't take it with him."

"My God, I thought you *were* him!" says Judith.

"No, he's the good looking one with the attractive personality", he quips. "You know, I can remember reading these stories to him. Strange to think it was more than twenty years ago."

"That *is* still one of his favourite books. I think he wanted to leave a few things in place here to reserve his room."

"Ah, that's always a good plan, because you simply never know ... I must say it's not the same here without him."

“I know. I miss him dreadfully. All this time I’ve been thinking I can’t do this and that because I’ve got Serge to look after, but now he’s gone I don’t feel like doing any of those things although I could do them now. At least I’ve got *you* back … whatever *the circumstances*.”

Leo refrains from dwelling on *the circumstances*. “You and Dad should go away on holiday. It’s ages since you’ve been away, other than the odd night here and there. Serge is in good hands with Dominic and Beatrice – and I’ll be around if they need me. Talk to Dad about it.”

“Maybe ... Anyway, what have you got planned for today?”

“Nothing really ... I thought I might just go along to the office and sort a few things out.”

“Oh, *not* on a *Sunday*, Leo. Have the day off.”

“And do what?”

“Well, I don’t know. What do you normally do on a Sunday?”

He shrugs his shoulders. “We had a routine of sorts; a very flexible routine, but there was always something to do.” He stands up and looks out of the window. “It’s not like I can mow the lawn – it already looks like bowling green.”

“I expect Dad will be going to play golf this afternoon. Why don’t you tag along?”

“Mum, if I ever show signs of developing an interest in golf, please shoot me. I suppose I could take the dog for a walk ...”

Alistaire shouts from downstairs, “Just going out with the dog!”

Leo smiles. “Maybe not. It seems everything here is covered.”

“How about joining a gym?” Judith’s eyes travel up and down her son’s body with admiration and pride. This is the beautiful, intelligent son she was blessed with – and she hasn’t seen him in his underpants since he was about nine.

“I really don’t have the enthusiasm to join *anything* at the moment.” Suddenly realising he is chatting to his mother wearing nothing but his blue striped boxer shorts, he feels self-conscious. "I'll go and have a shower and get dressed, and take it from there."

"If I'm not here, I've gone to church. I don't suppose you fancy coming along ...?"

"No thanks. But you can say one for me."

"I very much intend to ..."

At Hardwicke Heights, Dominic, sitting at the kitchen table is reading out adverts from some horsey magazine to Paddy, Serge and Franchesca, all of whom are unable to read but are very keen to acquire their first pony.

"Look for something dat says fourteen hands, cob type and bomb-proof," says Paddy.

"Bomb-proof?" Serge looks alarmed.

"T'is just a term, Serge. It means it'll be nice an' safe for der young lady to ride, without it shying from everything dat moves."

"Oh. So wot's that cob fing?"

"It just means dat der pony is nice and big for its height – all der better to carry der young lady's weight, like."

"Yer saying she's fat?"

"No, no, no ... Oi just think she'd be better suited with a short stout pony than a tall thin one."

Dominic steps in. "Here's one; 'Cob type gelding, bomb-proof, good to shoe, box, catch etc.' Not too far from here either – it's same dialling code."

"Wot's a gelding?" asks Serge.

"T'is a castrated male, like. Most male 'orses are – unless yer intend to breed from dem."

Franchesca pauses from threading brightly coloured plastic beads on to a nylon thread to whisper something in Serge's ear.

"Fran says she wants a *girl* 'orse first," says Serge. "An' she'll 'ave wun of them gelding fings next time we goes 'orse shopping."

"Fair enough," says Paddy. "Can yer see anything similar that's a *mare,* Dom?"

Dominic scans the adverts again. "Here's one. She's knocking on a bit, though, aged thirteen. And there's some complication about an inseparable stable mate." He pauses to read the full advert to himself. "What's 'TB'? Nothing to do with tuberculosis, I hope!"

"No, dat means Thoroughbred. *Go on*, what else does it tell yer?"

"Okay. It seems if we buy this mare, they are throwing in her stable mate free of charge – to a good home. The stable mate is an ex-racehorse - sixteen hands high - that can no longer race owing to an injury that has left her chronically lame." Dominic frowns. "It says she *requires experienced handling* ... I don't like the sound of that."

Paddy's eyes are twinkling. "Oh, oi think it might be worth a look ..."

"Fran wants to know wot colour the girl-pony is," says Serge.

Dominic re-reads the advert. "Grey, it says here."

"Fran wanted one that was black or white or brown."

Paddy says, "Grey often means sort o' white, so it does. I *do* think we should take a look."

The appointment is made and Dominic, Beatrice, Serge and Franchesca pile into the Land Rover to go to see the pony and the ex-racehorse. The property they arrive at is similar in size and style to Hardwicke Heights, and Mr and Mrs Hersey, the middle aged couple who greet them, explain that they are planning to move to a lower maintenance property. Re-homing the horses is their first step towards this, as the pony belongs to their daughter but she has lost interest in riding.

Franchesca is delighted with Storm, who has a long white mane and tail, freshly washed for this viewing; beautiful dark eyes with black eye lashes, and a darker colouring around her nose and fetlocks. She has a wide back and plump white flanks.

“Got arse and eyes like yours, Fran,” compliments Serge.

Paddy, confident now that he is on his own territory, runs his hands up and down her legs, claps his hands behind her; pulls a white handkerchief suddenly from his pocket and waves it near her face, and then asks Mr Hersey to trot her around a little so he can see her action. The pony is approved by all, and Paddy is allowed to turn his attention to the tall chestnut mare that has been watching them suspiciously and keeping her distance in the paddock. She flares her nostrils and tosses her head, appearing weightless as she dances nervously on long spindly legs. Only when fear gets the better of her and she turns and trots away is it obvious that she is lame; her head bobbing each time her off-fore meets the ground. *Same bad leg as mine.* “So, what’s her story?” he asks.

Mr Hersey explains that the mare belonged to some friends who owned racing stables.

“She was a promising flat racer as a three year old – that’s if they could get her in the starting stalls - but then she had a bad fall. The leg wasn’t actually broken, and the vet believed she would heal in her own time. But that was four years ago, and she’s no better now. We brought her here as a companion for Storm. Everyone thought she would have a speedier recovery in this calm environment. Back at the racing stables, you see, even in a separate paddock, if the other horses were chasing around it would make her a bit frantic. And well, Storm here, as you can see, is so calm – giving Snowy the best chance of rest and recovery. But it hasn’t happened.”

Mrs Hersey takes up the story. “When we decided it was time for them to be re-homed, I phoned Janice at the racing stables, explained that we were selling Storm, and asked if they’d come and collect Snowy. They phoned me back and they said ... they said that she was no *use* to them. Owing to her temperament, they would not breed from her, and so ... if we sent her back to the racing stables they would ... they would send her to the abattoir.”

“Where’s that?” asks Serge.

Paddy takes a deep breath. "It's der place where they shoot der knackered 'orses," he says, his voice husky with emotion.

Beatrice decides the atmosphere needs a lift and declares brightly, "She's a red-head but they called her Snowy?"

"That's right; she's got red hair and a fiery temperament to match! Her racing name was 'Northwind's April Snowdrift' because she was born in the April of that year we had a sudden out of season snowfall - and her mother was called Northwind something or other. Maybe that's why she's so resilient to the cold weather – coming out of the womb into a world of snow. She's been with us more than three years, but we've never managed to get her into one of our loose boxes, not even the one next to Storm." Mrs Hersey looks round at the stable block and everyone follows her gaze. "She'll stand near the entrance to be close to Storm, but she won't go in there."

"So how are we ter get er back to Hardwicke Heights if yer can't box 'er?" Paddy asks and is aware of a slight frown from Dominic for sounding overly keen.

"Well, that's the funny thing." Mrs Hersey points to an old brown lorry with 'Horses' written on the back. "She'll go in the transporter so long as Storm goes in first."

"Mrs Hersey, would yer mind awfully if I went and 'ad a look in yer stables?" asks Paddy.

"Not at all, feel free," she replies, a little surprised at this request.

Paddy limps across to the stable block and disappears inside. After a few minutes he emerges with a large leather head collar that has gone stiff from lack of use and has fixed itself in a *hanging-on-a-hook* position. "I hope yer don't mind, but I've taken der liberty of 'elping meself to a handful of pony nuts." He sets off across the paddock towards Snowy.

"Please do be careful, she's *very nervous*," says Mrs Hersey, nervously.

All eyes are on Paddy as he limps across to the far corner of the paddock where Snowy stands uneasily, weaving her neck from side to side.

"She'll bolt in a minute," says Mr Hersey. "I just hope she doesn't knock him down."

But she doesn't bolt. Paddy stops a few feet in front of her and, after a minute or two, pony nuts and curiosity get the better of her and she walks over to meet him.

"*Blow me*," says Mr Hersey.

Before she knows it, Snowy's nose is through the head collar and the strap is over her head and fastened. She tosses her head a little in surprise and protest, but a few soothing words and a couple of pony nuts from Paddy and she allows him to rest his lips in the soft velvety space between her nostrils and blows a steamy smell of warm grass into his face. He runs a gentle hand down her lame leg. "Well, der's nothin' too bad goin' on now, is der? Come along and meet yer new family." Paddy leads the mare back across the paddock to the assembled group, the pair of them limping in unison. He halts a sensible distance away from them; close enough for everyone to have a good look at her but not so close as to endanger them if they should cause her to take fright. "She's a real sweetheart," he beams, trying to encourage a deal to be done there and then, "and der pony is just what der young lady was looking for."

Dominic takes charge. "Thank you Paddy." He turns to Mr and Mrs Hersey. "As you can see, everyone seems very keen, but I think it best if we go home now and have a think about it."

"That's fine, we understand," says Mrs Hersey. "Would you like to come indoors first for a cup of tea or coffee?"

Dominic looks at his watch. "It's very kind of you to offer, but we have to get back."

Serge elaborates, "Fanks Mrs Horsey, but we've got to get home before seven o'clock because of Paddy's curfew. He's tagged – ain't yer Paddy. Go on, show 'em yer tag, Pad!"

Back at Hardwicke Heights and tucking into chips, scallops, fish cakes, mushy peas, curry sauce, battered sausages and fizzy pop that they picked up from the local chippy on the way home, Dominic, Beatrice, Paddy, Serge and Franchesca decide that it would be right for Storm and Snowy to join the household.

Dominic still has reservations about Snowy, but Paddy, tucking into a Pukka pie - eating nerves a thing of the past - reassures him she will be no trouble. "When I checked out doze stables der was a bad smell about dem, so there was. I dunno what happened there in der past, an' oim not so sure as I want to know – but Snowy could smell it too. Der *bomb proof* pony wasn't too bothered about it, but Snowy now – well she is a *sensitive*. She will be better here, so she will. And I bet you 'er leg'll mend an' all."

Whilst Dominic does not fully understand Paddy's *bad smells*, he has great respect for them. With everyone's agreement he phones the Herseys and offers the full asking price for Storm, and a good home for Snowy. The deal is agreed, subject to Mr and Mrs Hersey visiting Hardwicke Heights the next morning to verify the *good home* part of the deal.

"That's fair enough," Dominic reports back to the others. "You can understand them wanting to see where the horses are going."

Beatrice pipes up, "It's hardly surprising really, after Serge made Paddy show them his tag!" Everybody laughs, especially Paddy. He is sitting with his back to the window but swings round suddenly and looks out.

Dominic, sitting opposite Paddy, thought he saw a movement outside and opens the door to take a look, but only startles a few birds into flight. He gathers up the take-away cartons and takes them out to the bin.

Franchesca likes to spend an hour each evening with her mother and grandmother, so Beatrice walks with her down the driveway to the Gatehouse. The sky is very pink, prompting Beatrice to look back over her shoulder at the sunset. "Wow! Just look at that Fran, isn't it beautiful!"

"Yer ... it's beautiful, Beatie," murmurs Franchesca in her quiet, shy voice. Apart from Serge and Pat Cunliffe, Beatrice is the only one who ever hears her speak. She knocks on the door and gazes out to the road and is surprised to see a black Audi Q5 parked in the off-road area just before the gate. "Hey, that's Leo's car," she says.

Pat opens the door and assures Beatrice she will walk Fran back up to the Big House before it gets properly dark. "Thanks Pat. Have you seen my brother? That's his car."

"Yes Beatie, your *other* brother – the posh, miserable one. He went skulking past here about half an hour ago. I thought he'd be with you."

"No. Oh well, he must be around somewhere. I'll go and find him." Back at the house she tells Dominic that Leo's car is outside.

"Oh, poor Leo," says Dominic. "He must have seen us all through the kitchen window and ducked out. Let's have a walk down the garden and find him."

"I expect he's watching the sun setting," says Beatrice, and sure enough he is standing with his back to them, leaning against the new five bar gate that has just been put on the paddock to replace the old heavy sagging gate that had to be lifted or dragged.

Dominic and Beatrice hesitate, not wishing to intrude, but Serge speeds up; "Leo! Leo!" The others have no choice but to follow.

Leo backs away from the gate, wipes a sleeve across his face and mumbles something about hay fever.

"They said on the local news that the pollen count is very high today," says Dominic. "Come on Paddy, let's go and check the stables before the Herseys come tomorrow for the inspection."

Serge wraps his arms around Leo and hugs him tight. "Don't cry Leo. *We* all still loves yer."

23

Leo has Visitors

At the offices of 'Freeman & Freeman' another busy day is coming to a close. Michelle, the secretary, diverted the phones to the answering machine at five o'clock and has gone home. Alistaire's brother, Theo, left shortly after five and Alistaire is packing up too. "Not *more* updates," he grumbles and has to wait for his PC to shut down. He looks into the end office where Leo is still working. "I'm going home now. Are you just about done?"

"No, I think I'll carry on here a bit longer."

"Well don't be too long."

"Why not?" *It's not like there's anything to rush back for.*

"Your mother's worried about you. I wish you make a bit more effort to ... to ..."

"To pretend everything is fine? Is that what you want? Righteo, I'll bear it in mind. But Mum will only find something else to worry about – it's just the way she is. You ought to take her away for a holiday this summer."

"A holiday?"

"Yes. Just a suggestion. Everyone seems to have an opinion about what *I* ought or ought not to be doing, and I'm just as capable of imparting advice."

"Well, it's not a bad idea. It would take some planning with cases and such – but I'll think about it."

Alistaire goes out to the courtyard that provides staff and client parking. Apart from his Mercedes and Leo's Audi, the car park is empty except for an ageing Ford Fiesta. The window lowers and a young woman with dark curly hair calls out, "Mr Freeman!" Alistaire puts his laptop in the boot and goes to see what she wants.

"Is that Leo's car?" she asks, pointing to the Audi Q5.

"May I ask why you're interested in Leo's car?" asks Alistaire, suspicious by nature.

She smiles. "It's Leo I'm interested in, not the car. Only I figured if that was his car then he was likely to be here. I'm Sally Whittaker, an old friend of Beatrice's. I used to stay at your place sometimes on a Friday after a night out."

"Well, you do look familiar, but the place was always full of Beatrice's friends when she was at home." *Most of them noisy, giggly and irritating.* Alistaire had done his best to keep out of their way. He notices there is a young child on the back seat – a little boy. The child sees Alistaire peering through the glass at him and closes his eyes tightly. A memory flickers in Alistaire's mind. "Your son looks familiar too but I can't recall meeting him before now. I'll go and tell Leo you're waiting to see him. May I ask what it's regarding?"

Sally lowers her eyes; "I'd prefer to tell Leo ..."

Alistaire returns to the office suite, calling "It's only me!" as he ascends the stairs. "There's a woman in the car park wanting to see you. An old friend of Beatrice's, she says. There's a young child with her."

"Oh? I'll go down and see what she wants."

"If it's a divorce case, I suggest you hand it over to Theo. In fact, I think it would be a good idea if you transferred *all* your divorce cases over to Theo. We have discussed it, Theo and I, and we agree that divorce cases are not healthy for you at the moment. You can take on all his open conveyancing."

"Just let me get on with it."

"What?"

"I really don't give a damn what you all think I should or should not be doing."

Alistaire is affronted by his son's rudeness but is at the same time reassured by the determined set of his jaw, and glad to see a return of some sort of spirit. "Very well, do as you will." He turns and leaves, pausing in the courtyard to tell Sally that Leo will be down in a moment.

Leo waits until his father's car has finally disappeared through the stone archway and then goes down to see who's there. It is unusual for anyone to turn up to see him without first making an appointment. When she sees him approaching she gets out of the car and lifts the little boy from the back seat. Leo has time to weigh her up; five foot seven, average build, dark, naturally curly hair. Blue jeans and red jumper. Very little makeup and no evidence of any particular effort with her appearance; but an air of confidence – probably bred from having to stand up for herself. He reads 'single mum' and hazards a guess that this visit is something to do with an ex-partner wanting access to the child.

"You don't remember me then?" Sally manages to conceal her disappointment.

"No, sorry," he says, flatly.

"It there somewhere we can talk?"

"Yes – of course. Would you like to come up to the office?" In the foyer, he hesitates awkwardly. She is still carrying the child but he looks too heavy for her. "I'm afraid the lift has already been switched off. Would you like me to carry him up the stairs?"

"Oh, go on then," she says, and thrusts the little boy into his arms.

Sam clings excitedly to Leo as they ascend the stairs, and calls him 'Daddy'. Leo laughs at the irony.

Leo, still holding the boy against his chest with one arm, pulls a couple of chairs up close to his desk and gestures Sally to sit down before placing her son on the seat beside her. He steps back and smiles at the child, who meets his eyes briefly but then closes them tightly.

"How old is he?" asks Leo.

"Three and a half," replies Sally. "His name's Sam."

"How come he can't walk?"

"What? Of course he can walk! But he keeps running off so it's easier to carry him."

"Oh. He's exactly how my brother was at about that age – he used to do that same shy expression."

"Then I expect he's exactly like *you* were at that age too ... since you and Serge are so alike."

Leo looks at her sharply but she averts her eyes. "My father said you were a friend of my sister's." What did she want from him? As a single mum she would probably qualify for legal aid. Perhaps she just wanted preferential treatment – such as unarranged, out of hour's appointments, like this one.

"Ungy," says Sam.

"What did he say?"

"He said he's *hungry*. It's past his tea time."

"Oh. Well, I think we've got some biscuits somewhere ... Erm, would you like me to make some coffee?"

"Yes please, that would be great," says Sally.

Leo goes along the corridor to the kitchen and begins to rummage through the cupboard, looking dubiously at filter papers, coffee beans and sealed foil sachets. The kitchen is Michelle's domain. He finds a jar of instant coffee as Sally appears in the doorway. "Will this do?" he asks. "I'm afraid we're down to powdered milk as well."

"Instant and black will do fine," she replies.

Leo finds the biscuit tin. "They're mostly plain – although I guess that's better for Sam. Uncle Theo's had all chocolate ones."

"Just the job. Give Sam anything with chocolate and he'll melt it all over his hands and then daub it all over your desk and down your suit."

"Really?" Leo frowns, unimpressed.

"Yes, *really*. Tell you what, you go and keep an eye on him and I'll sort out the coffee. Have you any orange squash or anything for Sam?"

"Well, there is some, but if you look at the label it's full of e-numbers and artificial sweeteners – and the colour doesn't look too natural. I wouldn't give it to a child of mine. Won't he drink water?"

“No way. That orange stuff will be fine. You get back to your office before he wrecks it.”

Leo returns to his office to find Sam climbing up the front of a filing cabinet, using the drawer handles like rungs of a ladder. “Get down off there.” He lifts the child down and sits him back on the chair. Sam sticks out his tongue and then closes his eyes tightly and turns away. “Little monkey,” says Leo and the boy begins to swing his foot so that each swing results in him kicking the desk. Sally comes in with the coffee and biscuits and orange squash.

“Michelle keeps colouring books and crayons in the reception area for our younger visitors. Just bear with me a minute whilst I fetch them.”

When Leo returns, thirty seconds later, there are biscuit crumbs all over the pale beige carpet and a dark wet patch, which he hopes is orange squash. Sam snatches a red wax crayon and deftly draws a huge streak of lightning across Leo’s desk. “No,” says Leo firmly. “This is how you use the crayons.” He opens the colouring book, bypasses some pages of flower pictures then stops when he comes to a fire engine. “Ah, *now then*. Please may I borrow the red crayon?” Sam hands it over. “Thank you.” Sam watches transfixed as Leo starts to colour in the fire engine – all around the edges, within the lines. “Do you think you could colour-in this middle bit, without going outside these edges?” Sam nods solemnly and Leo gives him the crayon.

Sally watches Sam concentrating on the task. “At playgroup they’ve suggested he might have ADHD. Although I’m a teacher – or at least I was before I had Sam – I always taught the nine to twelve age-groups, so it’s normally been detected before they reach me. I’ve urm ... I’ve sometimes wondered if Sam might be autistic or something ...”

“Nonsense, he’s just very sharp and a little bit naughty. All he needs is direction from someone in a position of authority - a father figure - to teach him right from wrong. If you are a friend of Beatrice’s you will know we have a brother with learning difficulties?" Sally nods. "Well, in order to ascertain that Serge was in fact brain damaged as opposed to autistic or whatever, I did a good deal of reading about development and learning, and from this short meeting alone – I am convinced that Sam is a very normal child." He watches Sam colouring-in the fire engine. "Does he have much contact with his father, or a grandfather?"

"No. My parents live in Australia and I've gone out of my way, *until now*, to avoid contact with his father."

"I see." So *that* is the purpose of the visit – she wants something from Sam's father. Leo looks at the broken biscuits on the floor and the mess on his desk. "I think you'd better tell me all about it before he gets bored again. Is it something to do with him paying maintenance?"

"It might be. But it might be more than that."

He lowers his voice and says gently; "Well then?"

"I heard you were getting divorced. I wouldn't have come here otherwise."

Leo flinches as if she has slapped his face. "How did you hear about that?" His voice is almost a whisper; the hurt evident in his eyes.

"On Beatrice's Facebook."

"On *Facebook*! Don't say my sister has put it out on the World Wide Web!"

"No, no ... She just put something vague about it on her wall and then we got chatting."

"Did she tell you *why* Bridget wants a ... divorce?" The word seems to stick in his throat.

"No. For all I knew it was *you* that was leaving *her*. So, it's not like you've met someone else then?"

He shakes his head.

"In that case, I'll tell you my story."

He nods, encouraging her to get on with it.

"Okay then." Sally takes a sip of coffee, wondering where to begin. "You really don't remember me, do you?"

"No, I'm sorry."

"No change there then. You see ... four or five years ago, Beatrice and I were really good friends. We used to go out together most Friday nights, and share a taxi back to her parents' place. Saturday mornings, I'd watch TV with her younger brother, Serge. I loved him to bits and he was a really good laugh; but the main reason I'd hang around on a Saturday morning is that I had a massive crush on their elder brother. Only he never seemed to notice me. A cold, polite 'hello' was all I ever got from him." Sally looks at Leo afresh. His face looks thinner but it accentuates his fine bone structure. He looks back at her impassively, waiting for her to carry on, and a tugging feeling in the pit of her stomach tells her she still fancies him as much as ever. She looks away again and continues her story.

"I knew he was going out with Bridget, but when I heard they were *engaged* I was gutted. Looks wise, she was stunning - but such a *bitch*. I knew her from school. She was two years above me, so I didn't have all that much to do with her - but she was so mean to everyone. Most of us were scared of her. Beatrice said she wasn't *that bad* - so I guess she must have mellowed - but I couldn't help thinking of the way she was at school. People who didn't know Leo - people who had only seen the hard-faced side of him - thought they were a good match. But I knew him better than many, just from being his sister's friend, and from seeing how brilliant he was with his little brother. Then came his stag night. It was on a Friday, so I was keener than ever for a night out with Beatrice. A couple of the girls whose fellas were out on the stag do came with us too, and we had a brilliant time and we all got *well and truly bladdered*." Sally has been looking away from him, towards the window, as if picturing the scene on a screen. Now she turns to face him, and his eyes fix hers so she cannot look away. She takes a deep breath and continues. "Our taxi got us back to your parents' place only about ten minutes before you arrived home. We thought it was *hilarious* as we watched you wandering around outside and then you finally made it up the steps and into the hallway. Then you sat down in that funny old antique armchair and fell asleep. We were all messing about, tickling your face with our hair – that kind of thing. Then Beatrice said we had to get you upstairs to bed – otherwise *your Dad would be cross*. Well, you can picture it, can't you – four girls, practically legless trying to get one tall guy – even more pissed and much heavier than he looked – up a flight of stairs. We were all in hysterics and falling over each other, and then your Dad appeared on the landing looking really, really angry. But he was stood there in his paisley pyjamas." Sally pauses, her face creasing into a smile at the memory, but Leo's mouth is set in a straight line, and her smile quickly fades. "Your Dad's appearance seemed to perk you up – like you were *scared* of him – but then, of course, he was your *figure of authority*, who taught you how to behave so *properly*." She doesn't overly stress it but he acknowledges it with a twitch of his lips and upward glance before locking her in again.

"Anyway," she resumes, "you somehow pulled yourself together and got upstairs under your own steam, but your Dad was still stood there glowering ... so Beatrice went to her room, Susan and Kelly went to the room they were sharing, and I went to the room I always had at your place on a Friday night – just two doors away from yours. And everything went quiet."

Sam, bored now with crayoning, climbs onto his mother's lap and starts putting his fingers up her nose and in her ears. Leo opens a drawer and takes out a Newton's Cradle that someone once gave him as a gift and demonstrates how it works. Sam is delighted and puts it down on the carpet to play with it amongst the biscuit crumbs. Leo returns to his seat behind the desk and Sally continues her story.

"You were always so bloody self controlled!" she says, crossly, and he raises his eyebrows at her sudden anger. "I wasn't the only one who thought so. I wasn't the *only one* who wanted to see you get *pissed*!" Leo glances at Sam, wishing she would stop saying 'pissed' in front of him.

"So me and Susan and Kelly got two half-bottles of vodka and gave them to Susan and Kelly's fellas to lace your drinks." She pauses to allow him to react, but can only detect maybe a glimmer of amusement. She lowers her eyes; "I realise *now* what a stupid thing it was to do – I have grown up since then. It just seemed like a bit of fun at the time. But I felt so very guilty in the morning – listening to you puking your guts out. And then Serge wanted me to watch TV with him, but I made some excuse why I had to get home."

When she hasn't spoken for a full five seconds, Leo says, "It probably explains my loathing for vodka." He is watching Sam. "Sorry, but I realise I've just given him an age-inappropriate toy. Could we have him back up on his seat so we can supervise him properly?"

Sally rolls her eyes and hoists Sam; body writhing and arms flailing, back on to the chair beside her.

"Sorry about that, Sam," says Leo. "I expect you know that there are some toys that you are not yet old enough to play with?"

Sam nods.

"Good. That's why your Mummy and I would like you to sit here at the desk where we can see you. Now then, *watch this*." Leo sets the ball bearings clicking together in a formation that captivates even Sally. He watches the pair of them, still wondering why they are here.

"Anyway," says Sally. "I was trying to tell you ..."

"Yes, please go on."

"Well, there's me – half cut and wide awake; silence ringing in my ears after the music from the nightclub, and there's this guy I fancy like mad just two doors along the landing."

Leo smiles politely, acknowledging the compliment but growing bored now and wishing she'd hurry up and get to the point and then clear off.

Sally goes on; "I crept into your room ... kidding myself I was just going to check you were okay. It suddenly didn't seem so funny, you know, putting vodka in someone's beer. Your shoes and clothes were in a heap on the floor, and I tripped over them in the dark and fell onto the bed. You didn't stir, and I felt cold so I got under the duvet – just to be next to you." He is looking at her attentively now, finally drawn in to what she has to tell him. "I didn't think you'd be up to ... *anything,* in that state. But at the same time I knew you were marrying Bridget the following weekend – so this was my last chance to see what it would be like to lie next to you in bed. But of course, I couldn't just leave it at that ... and you *were* up for it – surprisingly – my God, you were *up for it!*" Leo's expression gives nothing away, but his pale face takes on a little colour, she is pleased to note. After a pause, whilst she glares at him and he looks back intently, she says in a softer tone, "Afterwards, I fell asleep next to you for a couple of hours and panicked when I woke up - but you were *well-unconscious*. I quickly nipped back to my own room - but I left something behind in your bed ... a pair of black lacy knickers. I couldn't find them and was afraid I'd wake you up if I went groping around under the sheets."

"So they were *yours*," says Leo. Whatever is going on in his mind is veiled behind his steady gaze.

She blushes. "You found them, then! What did you do with them?"

"Well, I had to dispose of them of course. I'd no idea who they belonged to. I did wonder if one of the chaps had put them there as a joke."

"So you didn't remember *anything* ...?" Her disappointment is clear.

"Well ... yes, I did. In fact I still do. But I convinced myself it was just an ... erm ... *erotic dream* and that the *lingerie* had been put there as a joke." He reads her doubtful expression. "Yes, I was kidding myself. But I honestly couldn't remember who'd been around that night. The place was always full of my sister's friends at the weekend. I could hear lots of people milling around the next day, but couldn't keep my head out of the toilet long enough to see what was going on."

“I told you how guilty I felt,” she says apologetically, then grins mischievously. “So, how did you dispose of my knickers?”

“Ah, yes. Well, I couldn’t put them in a rubbish bin at home. My mother had become passionate about recycling and always seemed to be sifting through the bins, examining the contents.” He shares a smile with Sally at the image of his elegant mother sifting through the rubbish bins. “So, I put them in a pocket of the suit I was going to wear to work on Monday - so I could pop out at lunch time and put them in a bin on the High Street. But Ralph sniffed them out, and there I was on Monday morning, listening to Mum going on about the latest charity she wanted some money out of the business for, and I noticed Ralph had the knickers on his bed, between his paws, with his chin resting on them.” Sally laughs out loud and Leo’s eyes respond with a twinkle. “He growled when I took them off him. I had to pretend I was pulling a piece of bramble out of his coat. But still, I got away with it and they did end up in a bin on the High Street.”

The smile lingers between them for a few seconds and then Sally says; “So, here’s the punch line, because I don’t think you’ve worked it out yet, have you?”

“Worked what out?”

“A few weeks after your stag night, I found out I was pregnant.” She looks down at Sam and says gently. “He’s yours, Leo.”

Leo breathes in sharply. He looks down at the desk and blinks a few times, trying to focus his vision. He looks at Sam and then stands abruptly, walks to the window and gazes down into the courtyard. Sally studies his broad shoulders and long slim back, accentuated by the well cut suit, and yearns for him to take her in his arms. Sam climbs down from his chair and stands on tiptoes next to Leo, not tall enough to see out of the window but wanting to know what he is looking at. Leo lifts him up. Sam puts an arm round Leo’s neck and watches a couple of pigeons pecking at the moss between the cobbles.

Sally had said Sam was three and a half, so the timing was right – and he certainly had the Freeman blue-eyed blond colouring as opposed to Sally's dark hair and brown eyes. But what's to say she hadn't slept with someone else soon after? He knows nothing about her. He wants to request a paternity test but is afraid she might be offended and go off in a huff, never to be seen again. Sam has seen enough of the pigeons but is fascinated with Leo's tie, which he is trying to undo. Leo turns round to face Sally. "Have you *really* no idea why Bridget wants a divorce?"

"No. I assumed you were leaving her because you were fed up of her being such a bitch."

Leo frowns. "I wish you'd stop calling her that."

"Sorry." She shrugs her shoulders. "Tell me then. Why does she want a divorce?"

"Because she was desperate to have a baby, and it turned out that I couldn't give her one because ... because I have a very low sperm count."

She sees what it costs him to tell her. "Well, *low* doesn't mean nonexistent, does it? Wasn't she prepared to give it some time?"

The stock response ... the same reaction as his mother's. "Apparently not. She found a *real* man and got pregnant immediately. Now she wants to marry him before the baby is born."

"*The bitch*. Sorry, but she never deserved you."

"Thank you ..." Leo, for once, cannot quite think what else to say.

"Listen," says Sally, after a moment's thought. "If you'd like to have a paternity test, then I have no problem with that. I give you my word there was no-one else I slept with around that time – but why should you accept that when all you see now is a girl who would spike someone's drink and then take advantage of him. And if you're going to start paying maintenance for Sam – which is one of the reasons I'm here - then it's only fair that you are *sure*."

Leo is surprised and touched by her acuity. "I also see a girl who had enough respect for my marriage to keep this a secret until she knew it was over – even though she disliked my wife. But yes ... I would appreciate a test - as soon as possible - before I become too attached." He puts Sam down but he clings around his knee and tries to see how far up he can pull a trouser leg. Leo battles on, "I know you must feel that I'm questioning your integrity by wanting to see proof – but in the light of what I've been told about my prospects of becoming a father, there would always be doubt in my mind. What if, for example, the following Friday night you'd gone out and someone had put something in your drink and *had their way* with you? You're shaking your head, but if you see it from my point of view it's a justifiable possibility."

"Fair enough, we'll arrange a test."

"Have you told anyone else I'm his father?"

"No. Well, I thought I'd given away the secret to your sister, but I realised later that I'd led her to believe *Serge* was his father. Serge came round to dig a car-parking space for me, and Beatrice came with him and said, the same as you did, that Sam looked exactly like Serge did at that age. Beatrice was all for telling your parents they had a grandson. It wasn't until after they'd left that it dawned on me that she thought I'd seduced Serge. Not that the thought hadn't crossed my mind – he'd make *beautiful* babies!"

Leo laughs. "You should see the letters he gets from women who want to have his babies. Serge can't read but my parents made it a policy that all his letters should be read out to him unless the content is offensive, so poor Dominic has to read them out loud. Some of these women are quite graphic in respect of how they would prefer to conceive."

"So, Dominic passes them on to you to read?"

Leo explains; "I think Dominic's concern is that people should understand where Serge's ideas have come from, in the event that Serge should reiterate the contents." He realises he is becoming loquacious and shuts up, recognising it as the result of his mind trying to process this potentially happy bombshell with Sally still there at his desk. He wishes she would go away now and give him some quiet time to think – but he is also afraid of letting her go off with Sam in case they never come back. He must at least memorise her car registration number in order to track her down if necessary.

"Listen, do you fancy buying us a pizza?" asks Sally and watches him struggling to identify with this random enquiry. "Only it's well past Sam's tea time and I noticed a pizza place on the High Street. Pizza is the one thing he really tucks into because it's finger food, you see."

Leo's mobile phone rings and he looks at it. "Sorry, it's my mother," he says, and takes the call. "Yes – yes, fine thanks. No, really, I'm okay. Please don't save me any dinner as I'm just off to the pizza place on the High Street with a friend who's dropped by ..."

"I take it that's a 'yes' then," says Sally when he ends the call. She stands up, "Come on, let's go." She picks Sam up but hands him over to Leo to carry down the stairs.

When they get to the bottom, Leo asks them to wait in the courtyard whilst he sets the alarm; then they walk beneath a stone archway and, awkwardly, along a narrow passageway to reach the High Street.

"Your Mum phoned because she was worried about you," says Sally.

"Yes. She is inclined to worry."

"Does she think you're gonna to jump in the river?"

"No, not the river ..."

She perceives it has crossed his mind and links her arm through his, as if to provide an anchor, and he realises she has a deeper understanding than he had credited her with.

"Well, you're not gonna do anything now, are you?" She looks down at Sam. "Not if we're going to do this *test* – which will prove he is yours – and then you've got no choice but to stick around and be his Daddy."

In the pizza place Sally picks up the menu and reads it out, glancing from Sam to Leo and ending with; "Or we could just order one big pizza to share – with salad and wedges."

"Yes let's do that," says Leo, not caring much about eating. The 'pizza to share' option sounds less of an obligation on his part to gratify anyone by clearing his plate.

"What would you like to drink?" she asks and begins to read out the drinks menu.

"Oh, just a mineral water," he cuts in, so she orders a mineral water for him and a large diet cola for herself and asks for a small empty glass so that her son can share her drink.

Leo is aroused. "Surely you are not going to give Sam *diet cola*?"

"What's wrong with *that*?" Her face has taken on a disagreeable, challenging look, now that she is out of his office and on mutual ground.

"Well, for a start, depending on the brand, it might contain caffeine, which he is far too young for - and artificial sweeteners - *aspartame* for goodness sake is potentially carcinogenic and has caused lymphomas in experiments with rats; from what I've read."

"Leo! We're not talking about *rat poison*. All kids drink this stuff! I never realised you were such a *nerd*." A huge pizza arrives on the table. "And Sam is *much bigger* than a rat."

"Nerd, nerd, *nerd* ..." chants Sam, repeatedly, liking the sound of this new word.

Sally circles a wedge of pizza around in the air, like an aeroplane, and when it is cool enough, lands the tip of it in Sam's mouth. Sam chuckles happily and pushes half the slice into his mouth in one go, tearing off the crust and dropping it on the table.

"So, what would *you* have ordered as a drink for your son?"

"Well, since you say he won't drink water, I'd have asked for fruit juice and then watered it down a little so as to reduce the acid."

"And do you imagine he would drink it?"

"Possibly *not* if he's become accustomed to diet cola."

"Leo! Until we get the result of this test you want done, you have no say whatsoever! Now, *shut up* and help us eat this pizza."

Leo sips his mineral water morosely then opens his mouth to pass comment but his words are stifled by a wedge of pizza propelled by Sam, aeroplane style, across the table and straight into his mouth; "Shut up Leo and eat Peter!"

24

Getting Results

Serge and Franchesca walk down to the stables to see Storm and Snowy; Dominic and Beatrice following some distance behind, hand in hand, exchanging secret kisses. Storm, the thick-set pony comes to meet them at the paddock gate and walks with them to the stables where Snowy is standing in her loose box, apparently asleep with her bottom lip relaxed and drooping.

"Shush ..." whispers Franchesca to the others and puts her fingers to her lips. "Paddy's mending Snowy's leg."

It is a scene they are all familiar with; Paddy sitting on an upside down bucket with his eyes closed and his hands clasped around Snowy's left fore leg, both of them apparently in a trance.

Serge is patient for all of thirty seconds before saying "Hello Snowy," and then hooking his fingers behind her hanging lip and waggling it three times; saying "Hello Serge," trying not to move his own lips.

Paddy finally gives in and stands up to greet them. "Would der young lady like to ride Storm around der paddock?"

"Yes, please," says Franchesca, shyly. Everyone has remarked on how her speech has improved of late. Her mother is delighted.

Paddy puts the bridle on Storm and gives her back and girth regions a few quick strokes with a body brush before putting on the saddle and politely averting his eyes from Franchesca's ample rear as she mounts the pony. He clips a leading rein to the bit ring.

"Serge do it," says Serge, and Paddy hands him the leading rein to walk them around the paddock.

“How’s Snowy’s leg?” asks Beatrice and leans over to have a look. Snowy tosses her head nervously a couple of times – but it is more out of habit than fear.

“Getting there,” says Paddy. “You’d hardly notice she was lame if yer weren’t looking out for it. She’s far less nervous too. There must’ve been something not right at der place she came from.”

Dominic is keen to hear more about the *hands on healing* that Paddy is apparently performing.

“I don’t know if der’s anything in it or not,” admits Paddy, “other than dat it is very relaxing for both me an’ der ‘orse. I think I told yer, Dominic, dat me Ma was a traveller. Well, we never had a doctor like, so me Ma used to sit with ‘er hands on us if der was anything hurting, and it did seem ter make it better. T’is possible it was simply a mother’s love dat made it seem right, but it always helped.”

Beatrice points out - rather tactlessly Dominic thinks - that perhaps Paddy’s own leg might benefit from some of this ‘*healing*’.

“I have tried it, to be sure – but yer right in observing dat it didn’t fix me own leg. Perhaps it might have been different if me mother ‘ad been around because my own hands, as yer say Miss, diddun work for me – same as none of the surgical operations did.” Paddy turns to Dominic. “Now dat Snowy’s so much better I was thinking of getting her a bridle. Would yer do me a favour and have a look in the small ads in the paper an’ see if yer can find us one?”

“Yes, of course Paddy. But couldn’t she just borrow Storm’s bridle for now?”

“Whilst I’m sure Storm wouldn’t mind if she borrowed it, you must ‘ave noticed that Snowy’s head is twice the length of Storm’s?”

“Oh yes, I never thought ... Are you going to ride her then? How about a saddle?”

“Yes, I am goin’ to ride her – bareback at first to see how she goes – an’ then we might get a saddle. Snowy and Storm get on so well dat when Snowy's up to it we could ride der two of 'em out together, outside der boundaries of der paddock. It would be a waste of money to buy new tack for her – der's always plenty to be had second hand, an' I'll pay for it out of me wages. Only I can't read der bloody ads."

"Would you like me to teach you to read, Paddy?"

"No, not really. Thanks all der same."

"Okay, I'll look at the newspaper ads and I'll check out the internet as well." Dominic decides to phone Leo, partly to ask if a bridle for Snowy can be claimed on expenses, but also to see if he has any advice about the advertising event that Serge is to attend tomorrow.

Leo sounds brighter than of late, and is interested to hear about Paddy's work on Snowy's bad leg. "I thought that horse was nothing more than a high maintenance companion for the pony. By all means put any expenses for equine sundries on the card – don't let Paddy pay for them, his wages don't amount to much, and I know he has a young son somewhere ... If you need cash for second hand tack, just draw it from a cash machine and get a receipt for the purchase - hand-written or whatever." Leo is at the office and consults the calendar on his PC. "I see it's the motor bike shoot tomorrow. Are you driving, or did you decide to take the train?"

"I'm driving. There's too much kit to take along on the train – flasks and books and, well, jigsaw puzzles are the latest thing. And then Fran might insist on coming too, at the last minute, in which case Beatrice will have to come along ..."

"Yes, I get the picture. Listen, Dominic. Just make it clear to the chaps who are filming this advert that Serge is only going to sit on the bike. He is *not* going to ride it. Otherwise with a bit of encouragement from them, he'll ride off and he won't be able to stop or turn around. There should be another man there wearing the same coloured leathers who does the action shots."

"Don't worry, Leo. I'll take care of him."

“Yes. Sorry, Dominic, I wasn’t questioning your capability. But this is quite a lucrative contract. There will be a couple of follow-up ads.”

Leo is up early on Sunday morning, pacing around his parents’ home not knowing what to do with himself. The results of the paternity test are due tomorrow afternoon and he cannot think of anything to fill the time between now and then.

“What on earth is the matter with you?” asks Judith when he is standing in her way in the kitchen for the fourth time in half an hour.

“Nothing,” he answers, and walks out into the back garden, only to return again five minutes later. He leans against the cutlery drawer, and when she shoos him out of the way to open it he moves over and stands in front of the fridge where she is about to go next.

“Why don’t you pop over to Hardwicke Heights and see you brother and sister.”

“Could do, I suppose.”

Leo has developed a habit of calling at the stables first to get the lie of the land from Paddy. He drives past the main entrance, half a mile down the lane and then up the track that leads straight to the stable block. Paddy is in the paddock with Snowy, holding her by the reins of her newly acquired bridle whilst she fidgets and turns in small circles and chomps at the bit. Paddy is pleased to see Leo. In the early days, Leo had seemed cold and aloof, arrogant even; but Paddy now knows it is a misleading hard exterior he presents.

“It’s Franchesca’s grandmother’s birthday and they’re having a bit of a do at der house. Everyone’s welcome, so they are.”

“Phew, just as well I called here first. Narrow escape.” Leo runs a hand down Snowy’s long face and she tosses her head. “Dominic told me you’d healed her leg.”

Paddy shrugs modestly. “Her leg is very much better, to be sure, but it may just be der fact that she is so much more relaxed here than at her old place. Der was something at dat place dat she disagreed with. This is a healing place."

"It certainly feels very peaceful here," Leo agrees.

"Leo, would yer do us a favour and give us a leg up. I could mount 'er from der fence but I can't get 'er to stand next to it."

"Erm, yes, of course – if she will stand still for five seconds. Hasn't she got a saddle?"

"Not yet, no. Just go forrit, Leo. Now!"

Leo propels Paddy up on to Snowy and stands back as she prances, bucks and rears with Paddy swinging precariously one way then the other, clinging to her mane to stay astride. Finally she settles down, trots in a circle and then slows to a walk.

Leo removes his hands from his face. "That was terrifying to watch – but well done! I don't know how you managed to stay on."

Paddy puffs out his cheeks and wipes the sweat from his face. "It's just been a while since she had anyone on her back, dat's all. A while since I've been on a 'orse, come to dat." He leans back and nudges her into a trot and then a gentle canter and after two circuits of the paddock, pulls her up next to Leo and slithers to the ground. His face is glowing with pleasure, as much from Leo's acknowledgement as from the ride. He runs his hand down her leg. "Seems all right, but dat's enough for today. Mustn't over do it."

"You really must get a saddle. Is there anywhere open today that sells them? I'll buy it. I'm at a loose end today and could do with a mission to accomplish."

"Well, Dom did find an advert in der paper that suited 'er measurements, like - but we haven't phoned 'em yet. He's had a lot going on these last few days. We'd have to try it on 'er yer see. So then if it didn't fit we'd have to take it back again."

"Where's the advert? I'll phone them now."

Paddy removes Snowy's bridle and rinses the bit under the tap over the water trough and hangs it on a hook in the stable block. "Come in," he beckons Leo to follow him along to his living area.

Leo surveys the drop-leaf dining table and chairs; the retro-style radio on top of the fridge-freezer; the armchair in the corner and the two-seater sofa along the wall. Two doors lead from this room to the bathroom and the bedroom. "You've made this place really cosy."

"Mrs Freeman and Beatrice chose der lot for me. I diddun have a clue."

Paddy finds the advert for the saddle and Leo makes a phone call and writes down the address. "Do you fancy a ride out, Paddy?"

Paddy quickly changes his clothes. "The trouble with bareback riding is yer get 'orse sweat all over yer backside."

Half a mile down the lane Leo slows the car to a crawl. "There's a bridle path just along here that I wanted to show you … I found it on the internet. Ah, here we are. Once Snowy's up and running this might be a good place to ride out – away from the traffic." He turns the Audi Q5 off the road and up the narrow track.

"I'm not so sure as yer supposed to drive cars up here," says Paddy with a worried frown, hanging on to the edge of the seat as they bounce along.

"Oh, where's your sense of adventure, Paddy? Although we will have to reverse out if it doesn't get any wider than this." Finally the path opens up into a clearing before winding away into a dark forest. Leo lowers the windows and cuts the engine. "What a lovely place. Just listen to the silence."

Paddy says obligingly, "It's der most peaceful place I've ever known, so it is."

They give the silence two minutes respect before Leo restarts the engine. "Oh well, best turn round and get back to the road before anything else comes along."

They drive through a village that Paddy recognises. "There's a pub by der river called der 'Horse and Jockey' that does good Guinness. Well, it used ter do, about ten years ago."

"We'll call in on the way home if you wish. Unless there's anything you want to get back for?"

"No, I got all day – so long as we're back before seven."

Leo sees a cash dispenser and stops on the yellow lines right next to it, leaving the hazards flashing as he uses two cards to withdraw the required amount of cash for the saddle.

The sat nav informs them they have reached their destination outside a large detached house with wrought iron gates. Paddy examines the saddle and declares it sound. "I think it should fit 'er all right, but we still 'ave ter try it."

They buy the saddle on the understanding that if it doesn't fit, Leo will return it the same evening for a full refund. "I'll phone you before seven and let you know either way," Leo assures the vendors.

They find the 'Horse and Jockey' on the way home and Paddy proclaims the Guinness to be as good as it was ten years ago and reminisces about the time he spent working at the nearby stables. Leo orders two Sunday roasts and another pint for Paddy. He sips mineral water and allows his mind to wander. Results day tomorrow – surely he must be Sam's father since Sally agreed to the test ...

"Boring you, am I?" asks Paddy with a twinkle in his eye.

"Sorry? No, no … not at all. I'm glad of your company and a day out. There's erm … I'm expecting some good news tomorrow, but I don't want to jinx it by talking about it. If the result is what I'm expecting then you'll hear it through the grapevine."

"Well, best of luck to yer then, let's drink to a happy result for whatever it is. Cheers!"

Leo passes Paddy a dessert menu then remembers he cannot read and reads his own menu out aloud.

"The one advantage of no longer being a jockey is dat yer don't 'ave ter watch yer weight," says Paddy, and opts for apple pie. He winks cheekily at the teenage waitress (with ample cleavage and short skirt) who serves it. There is something about being Leo's companion that makes him feel confident and self-assured.

Leo shakes his head and looks at Paddy. He appears younger and less prune-like than usual. "How old are you, Paddy?"

Paddy has to think about it. "Forty-eight. How old did yer think I was?"

"Anywhere between thirty and sixty."

"Well, yer got dat right then!"

Leo stands up. "I'm going to pay the bill. Would you like another pint for the road?"

"Not unless yer want ter stop every five minutes on der way back. But a whiskey coffee might go down nicely."

Leo returns with an Irish coffee for Paddy and an ordinary coffee for himself. He looks at his watch. Time is passing quite nicely ...

Lunch over, they go in search of the stables where Paddy used to work, and find they have been converted into semi-detached bungalows with integral garages. Paddy looks wistful for a moment, remembering the good times he had there. "Oh well. Even if I was still der I wouldn't be still der nigh, if yer know what I mean."

"I know what you mean," says Leo. "Never mind. Let's go home and try the saddle on Snowy."

The saddle fits fine. Whilst Leo makes the phone call to report that the deal is done, Paddy sets about preparing the loose boxes for Snowy and Storm. Leo thinks his limp looks a little more severe than usual. He follows Paddy around, wanting to help. "Go and fill up dem water buckets then, from the tap above der trough."

Leo does as he is told, and asks Paddy about his leg. "T'is maybe a little stiff from der riding this morning and then sitting in der car." He turns to face Leo; "But thank you so much, not just for der saddle but for a truly grand day out. Listen, I might finish the day with a wee drop of whiskey and some cheese on toast if you'd care to join me – and then I'll be off ter bed.

Although you may think it's a bit early for bed like... and I shouldn't be offering you whiskey when yer driving."

Leo shakes his head. "I've very much enjoyed today, Paddy, thank you, and since I've heard you're *up with the larks* it makes sense to retire early. As for the whiskey, alcohol doesn't do much for me – apart from the one occasion when it seemed to do the trick ... maybe. But that's tomorrow's story and I'm going now before I start to talk about it. Good night, Paddy."

They shake hands with awkward formality and Leo turns away.

"Good luck for tomorrow," Paddy calls after him. "Whatever it is dat's happening..."

Next morning at the office, Theo is filling Leo in on the details of some planning permission issue that a client wants to see him about. "Leo! You're not listening, are you?"

"Er ... no. Sorry."

Theo rolls his eyes. "Then just make sure you listen to *them* when they tell you the story. They're coming to see you this afternoon at four-thirty."

"I have to leave at four o'clock today. Could you or Dad see them?"

"No, they specifically asked for *you*."

"Then I hope they won't mind coming earlier this afternoon or else at four-thirty on any other day this week. I *did* put it on the calendar that I was leaving early." The calendar is in a shared folder on the network, but Theo hates computers and refuses to use it.

"Leo, this issue is very important to these clients. I think you should see them today, as arranged."

"As arranged by *you alone*." Leo's reaction raises Theo's eyebrows. Leo goes on in a level tone. "Uncle Theo, my appointment this afternoon is very important to me. I am *not* going to cancel it. I will ask Michelle to contact these people to re-arrange."

“Oh, you *will*, will you?” Theo enjoys a good argument and is trying to provoke one.

“Yes I will,” says Leo simply and delivers the cold impassive stare that gives nothing away and never fails to infuriate Theo.

Out in the reception area Michelle lowers her voice. “I *told* him it was on the calendar that you were leaving early today.”

“I knew you would have been aware.”

“Don’t worry, Leo, I’ll rearrange the appointment.” Michelle adores Leo and is excited that he is getting divorced. She is ten years his junior, and has a boyfriend her own age, but can’t help wondering if she might be in with a chance when he is single. Meanwhile, she fantasises about being his personal assistant - in every respect. She is about to say something else, but hesitates.

“Go on,” he says.

She lowers her eyes, “I probably shouldn’t tell you this, but everyone these days who phones here as a new client wants to see *you*. There’s just a few *old folks* who’ve known Theo and Alistaire for *centuries* and still want to see them. You have a reputation outside this place Leo, for being a *winner*. That’s why new clients want you to handle their case. Doesn’t that make you feel *good*?”

Leo considers it for a moment. “It’s both a blessing and a curse, Michelle.”

The paternity test proves that Leo is Sam’s father. Leo is elated and hugs Sally and then gathers up Sam for a group hug. Sally laughs happily and Sam copies her reaction and puts his arms round Leo’s neck and laughs in his face. Back in Leo’s car they observe the stationary traffic with no immediate desire to join the queue.

Leo turns to Sally, “What now, then?”

“I think we should put some more money in the metre and then go and get a burger. By that time the traffic might have eased off a bit.”

"A *burger*?" says Leo, then catches Sally's sideways look and hurries off to put some more money in the metre.

Leo obligingly eats the burger, without analysing it too obviously, which isn't difficult since he cannot take his eyes off his son. "Sally, would you mind awfully ... it's not too far out of the way back to your place ..."

"What isn't?"

"Well, I'd love to introduce Sam – and you of course – to my Mum and Dad. They know something's going on and I've been keeping it from them until we got the result."

"Well, yes ... I'm in no hurry to get back, and it would be good to get it out of the way whilst we're all so hyped up about it."

Sally sits next to Sam in the back of Leo's car. In the stop-start traffic, Leo talks to her via the rear-view mirror. "How about your Mum and Dad? Do they know who Sam's father is?"

"No. They moved out to Australia five years ago. They bought a big place just outside of Sidney. They'd really like me and Sam to move out there and join them. I was thinking about doing just that – but then I heard you were getting divorced ... Anyway, my folks are coming here in September, so you'll get to meet them *soon enough*."

Leo pulls a face at her in the mirror. "You make is sound like a threat."

Judith is watching anxiously from the window, wondering what is going on *now* with Leo, and is relieved to see his car turn into the driveway. "There's someone with him," she tells Alistaire, and he joins her at the window.

"That's the woman who turned up at the office asking for him. She had a young child with her – there you are, look." They watch as Leo lifts the little boy from the back seat and sets him down, still holding his hand. The woman gets out and joins them, taking the boy's other hand, so they walk to the house with the child between them.

Judith opens the door to greet them and recognises Sally from when she used to come and stay. "Hello, you're Sally, aren't you? Beatrice's old friend."

"Hey, *someone remembers* me," says Sally.

Leo is smiling, eyes down, with more colour in his face than usual. Judith touches his arm, "What is it, Leo. Tell me." His smile broadens and he laughs, happily. Sam, responding to the laughter, slips his hand from Sally's and reaches up to Leo. "Daddy! Daddy!"

Leo lifts him up and declares, "That's right, Mum, Dad, you have a grandson! This is Sam. He's my son."

Judith takes a moment to register and then bursts into happy tears, hugging everyone.

Alistaire looks perplexed. "How old is he?"

Leo says, "Erm ... three and a half."

Sally explains cheerfully, "I seduced Leo on his stag night when he was drunk. You must remember the *state* he was in, Mr Freeman?"

Leaving Alistaire to absorb this, they take Sam for a tour of the garden, Judith deliriously telling him the names of the flowers. Ralph comes to join them and Sam says "donkey" and tries to climb on his back. "No you don't," says Leo and lifts Sam up on to his shoulders. "And stop pulling my ears!"

Judith turns on the oven and takes quiches and all sorts out of the freezer, and prepares a salad. A buffet appears on the kitchen table as if by magic.

"Thanks Mrs Freeman, that's brilliant. It means Sam can just have his bath when we get home and go to bed at his usual time before he gets too ratty."

"Please call me Judith." She cannot take her eyes off Sam. "He looks exactly like Serge did at that age – except Serge had a slight squint."

"I think Beatrice thinks Serge is Sam's father. I guess you'd better put her right on that one," says Sally.

"And ask Beatrice to tell Paddy," says Leo, smiling at his mother's bewilderment.

When Sally decides it is time to leave, Leo fastens Sam in his seat in the back of his car. As Judith and Alistaire stand in the doorway waving, Sally says suddenly, "Run back and get your overnight kit and a shirt for tomorrow."

"What?"

"*Go on.*" She glances at Sam and lowers he voice. "I'm wearing black lacy knickers."

Acutely embarrassed as to what to say to his parents, Leo goes back up the steps to the front door, and they part to let him through. "Er ... Sally suggests I take an overnight bag ... in case ... erm ... in case it gets late." He hurries off upstairs and quickly returns with a travel bag and walks between them again and down the steps. "So, I might not be back tonight ... not too sure."

"Good luck," says Alistaire, and Judith giggles.

Sally baths Sam and Leo stands in the doorway watching as Sam chuckles and splashes the water at her.

"Would you like to read him a bed time story?" asks Sally.

"Yes, of course."

Sally, popping back and forth across the landing sorting out laundry, listens in amusement to Leo's refined tones reciting a story about a talking pig that wants to play football with a talking goat. The effort he puts into varying the voices of these unlikely characters makes her love him more and more ...

She finds him standing awkwardly on the landing with the book still open. "He's fast asleep. I stopped reading and he didn't notice. Maybe we should bookmark the previous page for tomorrow, I'm not sure at what point he drifted off."

"Come here," she takes the book and tosses it onto the blanket box on the landing; losing the page he had wanted to bookmark. He puts his arms around her and finds she is the same height as Bridget; the top of her head nestles in precisely the same place beneath his chin. But Sally's hair is not soft and silky like Bridget's, nor does it have the same delicate perfume. Sally's hair has a frizzy texture and a *chemical* scent that is not entirely pleasant. He feels a sudden pang of anxiety and says, "Maybe I should just go?"

"Go on then. *Just go*!" Sally feels hurt and pushes him away so he has no choice but to retreat to his car where the overnight bag is still stowed undecidedly in the boot.

She looks out of the window and sees he is still there – his car parked across hers that is parked on the space that Serge created for her. She races down the stairs and out through the door, slowing to a casual pace as she approaches his car. "What's up then, won't it start?"

"No. There's a sensor, you see, that prevents the engine from starting if it detects that driving away is the wrong thing to do."

"Well, get back indoors!" He still seems hesitant. She softens her voice. "Come on, Leo. Stay here tonight. It'll be okay."

25

Wedding Day

Serge and Franchesca are looking forward to their wedding this coming weekend. Judith has a friend who is an Interfaith Minister who is going to conduct the ceremony. It will not be a legal marriage as both Serge and Franchesca's families have agreed that to propose a legal wedding would open up all sorts of discussions regarding the couple's cognitive capabilities and the validity of a lawful union. The Interfaith blessing means that everyone can enjoy a wonderful party with the minimum of hassle.

Justin Beaver has designed the suits to be worn by Serge and his best man, Leo and by Dominic who is an usher. They are charcoal grey with dark red waistcoats and bow ties and worn with a white silk shirt. Justin is overcome with emotion when the two brothers try on their suits and stand side by side. "To think there is another – almost as divine as *The Serge*. But you are not so *buff,* I think they say. You look as if you spend your life behind a desk." Leo tolerates having his clothes pulled around by a small excited Italian. "I will have this taken in. You are a little too thin. You need more sunshine and exercise. But you and Serge together ... would you consider a photo-shoot alongside your brother to advertise these suits? They will be in *such* demand the week after the wedding."

Leo shakes his head. "I'm not very photogenic." As usual, Leo has negotiated photographic rights on Serge's behalf. Rather than do an exclusive deal with any one particular glossy magazine it worked out more profitable on this occasion to sell press passes for huge fees to three different magazines to allow their photographers to come along. The wedding is to take place in the grounds of Hardwicke Heights. Marquees have already been erected and portaloos delivered – all of which have been dutifully tested and approved by Serge. Leo is adamant that none of the photographers is to be allowed in the house unless the weather is so bad that everyone is driven indoors. "That way, we can always invite them back here for a tour of the house on a different occasion if Serge's appointments slacken off. As I understand it, fame can be a fickle friend."

Ivan Ardonne turns up to trim everyone's hair. He is accompanied by Sabrina who will also be taking photos at the weekend, but without having to pay a fee for some reason that Leo is prepared to overlook because everyone else seems happy with the arrangement. Dominic is pleased by the way Beatrice moves in close to him when Sabrina comes near, but she need not have worried since Sabrina is flashing a huge diamond engagement ring and is clearly besotted with Ivan.

Franchesca's wedding dress is a *secret*; a secret shared with her mother, her grandmother, Beatrice, Sabrina, and a host of other people who have been involved in its creation. It is in fact shared with anyone who is remotely interested. Beatrice is to be maid of honour and will supervise the two young bridesmaids who are Franchesca's nieces. As a consequence, Dominic is also in on the secret of Franchesca's wedding dress. Although he hasn't seen it, he has had it described in excruciating detail on account of the fact that Beatrice will have to wear a dress that in some way co-ordinates with Franchesca's. This, to Beatrice, is not an option. "It's okay for the little ones. They don't *mind* wearing *pantomime costumes*!"

"But you will look gorgeous wearing *anything*, Beatrice," he tries, but she is not appeased.

Wendy, the Interfaith Minister comes along to meet Serge and Franchesca. She is a very small lady, possibly in her sixties, who radiates warmth and affection. She strikes up an immediate rapport with Serge and Franchesca, asking them what they like best about being with each other, and somehow puts together a script that they both seem to understand and approve of.

"So, we're going to have a little rehearsal, in order that it will all seem *very familiar* to you tomorrow."

Leo stands next to Serge, facing Wendy at the altar that has been set up in the middle of the garden and waits whilst Franchesca is steered through the archway by her mother. When asked if there was a male relative to give Franchesca away, Pat Cunliffe had replied that there had never been any man prepared to take her on in the first place – never mind give her away. Wendy catches Leo glancing at his watch and gives him a reproving look that has him apologising. Her eyes twinkle, forgivingly. The poor man does look rather tired, and there is clearly somewhere else he would rather be.

Later that night when everyone is in bed and the house is quiet, Serge cuddles up close to Franchesca; "Yer know how we was practising today gettin' mawwied?"

"Yeah," says Franchesca.

"Well ... if yer fancied practising *being* mawwied, then Serge wouldn't mind that ..."

"Yeah," says Franchesca.

He puts his hands on her breasts and waits to see if she is going to scream and make a fuss like what happened when he did that to some girl at the Centre who had big tits and a low cut top. It had landed him in trouble, and again the next time when he saw her and shouted, "Shouldn't futtin' flash 'em if yer don't want ter share!"

Franchesca doesn't shout or squeal so he lifts off her tee-shirt. "Futtin' 'ell, Fwan. Them's massive!"

Franchesca giggles happily.

Serge puts his face between her breasts and says "Flubble-ubble-ubble!" and she lays back on the bed, looking shyly away but holding her breasts apart for him to do it again. Serge is happy to oblige. "Is it okay if Serge touches you just there?"

"Yeah."

"How about there?"

"Yeah."

“It diddun hurt then? Dom said Serge ‘ad to be careful not to ‘urt Fwan. Is that nice?”
“Yeah.”
“Close yer eyes Fwan. Now wot you see?”
“Fran see a sunflower ...”
“Ah, that’s nice, innit.” He moves his fingers. “Can yer still see it Fwan?”
“Yeah ...”
“And Serge still ain’t ‘urting yer?”
“No ... Fran okay ...”
“Still see sunflower?”
“Yeah ... Fran okay ... Oooh!”
“Hey, Fwan!”

Sally half opens her eyes in the early hours and finds Leo sitting up in bed chewing a Rennie. It is becoming a habit. “Got that pain again?” she mutters, sleepily.
“Mmm.”
She rests a warm hand at the top of his stomach. It makes him feel nauseas but he doesn’t like to reject the caring gesture. “You should see a doctor. It might be an ulcer ...”
“Mmm.”
She falls asleep again and, thankfully, the hand slides away.

Saturday dawns bright and sunny with an almost cloudless sky. Serge and Franchesca are in high spirits and particularly loud and vocal.
“Where the hell’s Leo?” demands Beatrice, irritably. “He promised he’d be here early to keep Serge out of the way whilst us girls get ready.”
“I’m here,” says Leo apologetically. “But I don’t think we’ll be going far this morning – there’s a huge mob of paparazzi outside the gates and crowds of people with banners. There are several huge cardboard cut-outs of Serge – the sort they have in

all the department stores. I thought there might have been at least one police car out there by now, since we're funding the policing for the event. Perhaps I'll just take Serge down to the stables and see how Paddy and the horses are doing."

"I told you you should have stayed here last night."

Leo has been staying at Sally's every weekend. He goes back to her place after work on Friday and they spend the weekend together, as a family. Sally and Sam will be coming along later, with Judith and Alistaire.

Paddy senses visitors and switches off his television and picks up Snowy's bridle in order to appear as if he were just in the process of cleaning it. He smiles at Serge, "Tis yer big day, then?"

"Yer – tis," says Serge.

"I hear you declined the invitation," says Leo.

Paddy nods. "Not my type o' thing, really ..."

Leo smiles. "Nor mine. If you change your mind just come and join us. Come as you are – it's a very informal gathering. There will be a number of friends from the Day Centre that Serge and Franchesca attend, accompanied by their support workers. Serge, Dominic and I are obliged to wear suits for the photographers, but-"

"Leo, if it's all der same ter you I'd prefer ter stay here and make sure dat der party doesn't extend itself dis far. I turned der 'orses out dis morning but brought dem back in again. Snowy could hear der noise of the cars tooting horns and people cheering and it was exciting 'er a bit, like. I was worried she might hurt 'er leg again. Anyway, was der something yer wanted?"

"Erm, well, we've been banished from the house whilst the girls are getting ready, and there's a crowd outside the gate, so we didn't quite know where to go."

"Well, come on in then."

They follow Paddy through the door to his living area. Leo doesn't like to intrude. "Shall we go and see the horses, Serge?"

“You go see ‘em, Leo. Serge wants to watch ‘orse racing on telly wiv Paddy.” Serge sits himself down on Paddy’s sofa. “Put telly on, Pad.”

Leo goes through the door that leads to the row of loose boxes. Snowy tosses her chestnut head nervously as he approaches. “It’s okay,” he assures her and runs his hand down her neck, surprised how she flinches at his touch, as if his fingers are hot needles on her skin. Storm leans over to say hello and Leo pats her sturdy neck, noticing her skin feels thicker and her hair more coarse than Snowy’s. He returns to Snowy and slowly traces his hand around her face and neck, feeling the veins, muscles and sinews, so close to the surface. A shaft of sunlight on her back highlights the vivid red hues of her fine chestnut coat. “You are a truly magnificent creature,” he murmurs, then makes a fuss of Storm so she does not feel left out. He returns to Serge and sits next to him on the sofa and watches the horse racing. Paddy points out things going on in the background that would otherwise have gone unnoticed, and remarks, with an expert eye, on the form of the horses as he observes their action. Leo, like Serge, is completely drawn in to this new world. A text message makes him jump. “That was from Dominic. He says it’s time we went to get ready.” He stands up and coaxes Serge from the sofa. “Thank you for having us Paddy.”

Franchesca’s dress is finally revealed as she walks down the aisle between the two blocks of linked chairs. She is wearing a mass of taffeta in bright orange and yellow, with what looks like an upside down yellow poppy on her head. Her mother is holding her left hand whilst her right hand clutches a huge single sunflower that she brandishes at people, giggling as they duck to avoid being bludgeoned by it. “Stop that Fran!” her mother says sharply.

“Dio Mio!” exclaims Justin Beaver and wipes away a tear of emotion. “How could such a costume be paraded beside my beautiful suits!”

Beatrice looks stunning in a close fitting silk dress. It is a very pale lemon colour with tiny embroidered sunflowers running up the seams. The two little bridesmaids are dressed one as a buttercup and the other as a dandelion.

Wendy the Interfaith Minister welcomes everybody and explains that Serge and Franchesca made up their own wedding vows during the little meeting they had yesterday. Leo takes Franchesca's ring from his pocket and hands it to Serge. It is a gold band engraved with tiny sunflowers. Serge puts it on her finger and, prompted quietly by Leo who reads from the piece of notepaper passed to him by Wendy, he says; "Fwanchesca, I promise I will try to fill your days with sunshine, and to fill your nights with sunflowers. I promise to comfort and encourage you and to be your best friend ever, and to love you all my life, with all my heart. And tonight Serge'll give Fwan a whole field full of sun flowers."

The congregation murmurs "Aw …"

Franchesca takes her turn, prompted by her mother; "I take you, Serge, to be my partner. I promise I will love you forever. I look forward to spending the rest of my life with you - my best friend - and I promise not to be cross if you bring a flask to bed. So long as it is only a small one."

"Go on, Serge, give 'er one!" shouts a deep male voice.

"Shurrup, John!" Serge bellows back.

The ceremony is short; the meal is a buffet, and there is no seating plan. Leo sees Sally in the distance; works his way through the crowd of guests, greets her with a kiss and picks Sam up for a cuddle. "It's good to see you both."

"You saw us this morning," Sally points out.

"It's good to see you *here,*" he qualifies. Someone calls him to pose with Serge for some more photos. Sally has made it clear that she does not want Sam to appear on any photos that are to be published in magazines or newspapers, and Sam makes a huge fuss when Leo tries to put him down; clinging round his neck and screaming.

"Why the hell didn't you get the photos out of the way and then come and see us *afterwards?*" says Sally crossly.

"Sorry ... I needed a cuddle."

Formal photos over, Leo takes Sam down the garden for a game of croquet, whilst Sally sits on a bench and sips champagne, watching them.

Serge walks past and stops to say hello to Sam.

"Do you fancy having a game with us, Serge?"

"No Leo. Serge is ungry ..."

Once the initial rush for the buffet has subsided, Leo and Sally find an empty table in the marquee. The tables have been arranged around the edges of the dance floor and there is a small stage at the opposite end from where the buffet has been placed. There is to be a disco later.

Sam starts to eat a plate of chips, using his fingers to stuff them into his mouth. Leo frowns, "He can't just have *chips*, for lunch."

"It's all he'll eat at the moment," says Sally, mildly.

"Try this, Sam," says Leo and pops a small piece of chicken into Sam's mouth, just as he opens it wide to push some more chips in. Sam spits it out at Leo, followed by a mush of chewed up chips. Leo gives him a stern telling off, picking the mess off his suit with a napkin and frowning at the oily patches it has made. "I didn't know you could be such a rude and naughty boy!"

Sam starts to cry, loudly, and Sally lifts him up on her lap. "Now look what you've done!" She glares at Leo and takes a large gulp of her gin and tonic. "I *told* you he only wanted *chips*!" She lowers her voice to a comforting tone, "Come on, Sam, eat some more chips and then you can have a big bowl of sherry trifle." She gives Leo a look that defies him to complain about the sherry in the trifle and tells him; "Just get yourself sorted out – never mind keep going on at me about what Sam should and shouldn't have. All I ever see *you* eat is *bloody Rennies*!" She drains her glass and a barman materialises with a refill.

Alistaire and Judith are circulating; floating on a few quick glasses of champagne. "Where's Leo?" asks Alistaire, and scans room. "I think, as *best man*, he should get up and say a few words ..."

"Oh, *don't* put him on the spot, Alistaire," says Judith. "We *all agreed* there would be no speeches."

"Yes, but it's all going *rather well*, isn't it? There he is, look. Just like old times, Leo looking grouchy with a sullen brunette at his side." Alistaire arrives beside Leo. "Don't you think you should make a speech?"

It is clear from Leo's expression that it is the last thing he thinks he should do. "I thought we said no speeches ... I haven't prepared anything."

"Well ... only if it didn't seem appropriate. Come on Leo! Since when did you need to *prepare?* Get the happy couple up on the stage."

Leo does as he is told and gets up on the stage and susses out how the microphone works. The noise diminishes rapidly as people notice that something is going on. Naturally, everyone is quiet and looking expectantly at Leo, whilst Serge and Franchesca are at the opposite end of the room, still picking at the buffet.

"Serge!" calls Leo through the microphone.

Serge jumps and shouts "Woht?" and everybody laughs.

"Would you and Franchesca come up this way, please?"

They leave the table but get distracted every inch of the way, so Leo starts without them. He begins by thanking various people; realising just after he has started that he is either going to offend people by not mentioning them or else be incredibly boring by mentioning *everyone*. "In your own time, Serge!" he says and there is a ripple of laughter as they take another two steps in his direction. Leo pays tribute to Serge as a brother who has brightened up his life over the years; "Serge has always had a way of pointing out the obvious at times when I have been thinking too much and clouding the issue." Dominic nods in agreement. Leo notices and gives thanks to Dominic not only for his work here today, on this happy occasion, but for the way he has so empathically integrated into the family; "Dominic's role is invaluable. We could never have imagined that he would respond so adeptly to the extreme variety of duties that his position has demanded." Dominic turns crimson and Beatrice gives him a hug.

Leo scans the floor. Where are they now? Some of the guests help out by sending them on towards the stage. Leo ploughs on, "If everyone could share Serge's uncomplicated outlook; his warmth; his strong sense of right and wrong and the pleasure that he takes from simply waking up each new morning, then the world would be a much happier place. His affection for Franchesca has never wavered since the day he fell for her – and anyone can see how happy they are together – not just today on this special occasion, but every day of the week when they are together. I firmly believe that this is a union that will survive the test of time."

Sally meets his eyes briefly then looks away.

Everyone cheers as Serge and Franchesca are propelled onto the stage and stand grinning beside Leo, who is wondering what else he can possibly say, now that they have finally arrived.

"Nice tits, Fran!" shouts John. "Hey Serge! Bet she gives good tit wank; hah, hah, hah!"

The young man who is in attendance as John's support worker looks horrified but Leo winks at him. "Thanks for that, John. Yes, I am sure the pair will spend many happy hours bouncing around together. Any other contributions? What makes Serge and Franchesca the happy couple that we see here today?"

"They both like loads of pizza and loads of chocolate!" shouts Franchesca's friend, Samantha.

"Yes, that's right, I've witnessed it," says Leo with a grimace that makes everyone laugh.

"They've got no expectations of each other – they just accept each other for who they are." That is from Judith.

"They just enjoy a good natter without having to disagree."

"Thank you, Pat."

Beatrice says, "They don't try to change or control each other. Neither of them thinks the other is wrong for doing things differently from the way they would do it."

Dominic backs her up, "Yes, they acknowledge their differences without challenging them so they don't end up arguing."

Leo looks at Sally, and stage-whispers "*Sorry*" then diverts his gaze before people follow it. "Yes … I'll go along with that. Any more?"

"Fran looks like a bit of a *goer*. Bet she gives a good beejay, *yay!*"

"Thanks again, John but we've already acknowledged that aspect of the relationship – which must mean we've come a full circle; so would you all please join me in a toast to the *happy couple*; Serge and Franchesca!"

"Serge and Franchesca!" says everyone. Leo realises he doesn't have a glass but it doesn't seem to matter. He kisses Franchesca on the cheek and shakes hands with Serge who engulfs him in a huge happy hug, and then wraps his arms around Franchesca, making everyone croon "Aw ..."

Leo takes a step down from the stage but Alistaire shouts, "toast the bridesmaids" so he backtracks and asks everyone to drink a toast to the bridesmaids; his beautiful sister Beatrice and ... erm?

Franchesca's mother shouts, "Paige and Ariadne!"

"Paige and Ariadne," repeats Leo into the microphone, wondering what has become of girls' names, and the two little bridesmaids stop doing handstands and gaze up at the stage in delight.

Alistaire, his taxi booked for midnight is already glowing. "See how he can think on his feet – he would be good at the Bar." He looks into his empty glass and finds it immediately refilled by a barman. "I meant as a barrister," he clarifies to Judith, but when Leo joins them Alistaire only remarks on is the state of his suit.

Leo explains simply, "My son spat out his dinner at me," and walks away.
"Why didn't you tell him *how well* he did?" asks Judith.
"Leo doesn't need *telling*," replies Alistaire. "He *knows* how proud I am of him."
Leo returns to his seat beside Sally who has drunk an unaccustomed amount of gin. Sam has over done the sherry trifle; is disturbed by his mother's weepiness and starts climbing up on Leo – dinner rage apparently forgotten. Leo gathers him up and he quickly falls asleep in his Daddy's strong arms.
"Do you think we could just *go*?" asks Sally.
Leo looks disappointed and then at his watch. "Well ... there's a disco and a barbecue later – don't you fancy it? Probably not since we've only just got lunch out of the way ..."
"Just take us home Leo, and then you can come back here and have a few drinks with your family."
He glances around, "Well … come on then, let's make a swift exit."

Bridget, under doctor's orders to rest owing to her blood pressure being a little high, is reclining on the bed watching TV and flipping between channels. Matt has gone to Birmingham again. On the six o'clock News she sees Leo leaving the wedding carrying a sleeping child. She hoists herself up, recognising the woman from somewhere. It looks as if Leo has got himself a ready made family. They both look pretty miserable so they *must* be together...

Back at Sally's place, Leo carefully lifts Sam out of his car seat without fully waking him.
"Just take him straight upstairs," says Sally. "I'll sort him out later."

Leo lowers him down and waits until his little arms, rigid at being released, have relaxed. The navy shorts he is wearing appear tight around the belly, so he removes them; frowning at the red pattern the elastic has made across his skin. He tries to remove the top, thinking the fabric a little coarse, but is defeated by Sam's unexpectedly large head to shoulder-breadth ratio. Sam has never *appeared* deformed – big heads must therefore be something common to young children that he has simply never noticed before.

Back downstairs, Sally has switched on the TV and is looking to see what's on.

"Fancy a cup of tea?" asks Leo.

"Hadn't you better get back to your brother's wedding?" she asks without looking away from the television.

"I doubt they'll be missing me. It's good to be away from the noise for a while ..."

"Don't forget to put your bag in the car – you're set up for the morning then."

"Don't you want me to come back here tonight?"

"Leo, you are the *best man* at your brother's wedding. Get back there and party! It'll do you good to loosen up a little."

"Well ... I'll be back in the morning. We could go to the safari park. There's a new white lion cub or something ..."

"For godsake stop suffocating me! Sometimes I wish I'd never *told* you about Sam. We've managed without you for most of his life – I'm sure we'll find something to do tomorrow!"

Leo goes back upstairs, kisses the sleeping Sam, collects his travel bag from Sally's bedroom and goes back down to the living room. "Well, I'll be off then," he says from the doorway.

She is watching television and doesn't look up from it. With a sigh he puts down the bag and plants a kiss on her head. She ignores him.

Back at Hardwicke Heights there is still a gathering of photographers outside the main gates. Leo drives quickly past; round the bend in the lane then checks in his rear view mirror that no-one is following and turns into the concealed entrance that leads up the track to the stables.

As always, he switches off the engine and waits for Paddy to appear. "Come on up to the barbecue Paddy. It smells like they've got it going already." Paddy looks dubious. "There's a free bar with loads of every sort of drink. Come and get drunk with me."

"Well, I've never been known ter turn down a free drink. Just give us a minute to 'av a quick wash and change."

Serge sees them approaching and comes running excitedly to meet them. He holds Leo tight in an ecstatic hug and says, "They told Serge you'd gone 'ome!" Leo is suddenly very glad he came back.

Paddy has sniffed out the bar tent. "What will yer have?" he asks Leo.

"Oh, anything – are you having whiskey? I'll have the same, please." He turns back to Serge. "Are you and Fran enjoying your day?"

"Yeah!"

"Well done. Just make sure you stick to the soft drinks tonight. Remember that field of sunflowers you promised Fran."

"Yeah … but Fwan wouldn't mind 'aving it tomorrow instead."

The DJ calls Serge and Franchesca to the dance floor to share the first dance and Judith dabs away tears as they shuffle around to Ronan Keating's 'When you say nothing at all.' Serge becomes suddenly self-conscious and calls Beatrice and Dominic to join them, and then "Mom! Dad!" Alistaire takes Judith's arm and leads her to the floor.

"Will you dance with me, Paddy?" asks Leo.

"Well erm … No."

"I was joking," says Leo.

"Thank der Lord for dat! I'll get us another drink."

Paddy wakes up next morning rather later than the larks with a dry mouth and a slight whiskey headache. Knocking back a pint of cold water he reflects that it had turned out to be a very enjoyable evening; well worth the mild hangover.

As he sets about the morning stable duties a strange noise stops him in his tracks. There it is again. A vibrating noise. He traces it to the loose box next to Snowy's where a suit jacket is hanging in the hayrack, with a mobile phone vibrating against something else in the pocket. Leo is fast asleep, wrapped in an old horse blanket he has laid on top of a pile of straw. Paddy laughs and fishes the phone out of the jacket pocket. The screen is illuminated with a photo of Sally and Sam. He tugs at the horse blanket and Leo tries to open his eyes; squinting against the daylight.

"I think dat was der missus on yer phone – but she's rung off now."

"Bridget!" Leo sits up suddenly.

"Urm no, I meant Sally."

The phone emits a series of beeps. "That means she's left me a message." He listens to the voicemail and lowers himself back down on to the horse blanket with a groan.

The message says: "Hi Leo. I'm sorry about yesterday. It was the gin made me *like that* and I feel different this morning. Sam keeps asking where you are and he'd love to go to the safari park and see the new white lion cub. It's forecast to be another fine sunny day. Call me when you get this message so we know when to expect you. See you later!"

26

All is not lost

Friday evening, a couple of weeks after the wedding, Leo tells Sally; "Mum and Dad have booked a fortnight's holiday in the Seychelles in September, the week after the schools go back, when it's less busy. They haven't been away for years, owing to Serge, so it's really great that they're finally sufficiently confident that he'll be okay that they can relax a little. Only it does mean I'll have to stay at their place to take care of Ralph. Derrick, the gardener, will be there during the day – but I'll have to be there overnight. So, if you fancy a change of scenery for a couple of weeks ...?"

"No," says Sally. "That's the same two weeks my parents will be coming over from Sidney – so it's quite handy that you won't be here, otherwise we'd all be a bit cramped."

"Oh." He thinks for a minute. "Well, your Mum and Dad could stay there too. There are loads of spare rooms. Mum dislikes having the house so unused, but yet she doesn't want to move from there. And I'll be at the office all day, so you'll have the place to yourselves."

"No. Thank you, it's a nice thought but I want to have Mum and Dad at my own place ..."

"Oh well. Fair enough, I can understand that."

"But you must come over for dinner one evening whilst they're here. They're looking forward to meeting Sam's Dad."

Leo's mobile phone vibrates in his pocket and his stomach muscles clench when he sees it is Bridget calling. "Sorry, do you mind if I take this call?" He goes out through the back door and into the garden. Bridget is chasing up the divorce and accusing him of delaying the proceedings. Sally stands by the open window, trying to listen. "Okay – well maybe I did misfile the forms ..." He walks further down the garden and lowers his voice. "All right, I'll fill them in this weekend and send them off on Monday … if you're still sure it's what you want ... but ... please, *please* don't rush into marrying Matt." He goes back indoors.

"Who was that?" demands Sally, sensing a change in his mood.

"Just someone chasing up a divorce. Sorry, I thought I'd switched the phone off. It's switched off now."

"Let's go to bed then."

"What, *now*?"

"Yeah, that way we get a good night's sleep – before Sam wakes up."

Leo humps and grinds and uses his fingers as she has taught him until she is done; then takes his turn and they roll apart and stare silently into the darkness.

Sally is the first to speak. "That was Bridget on the phone, wasn't it?"

"Mmm."

"What did she want?"

"She was chasing up the divorce."

"So you've been dragging your feet over it?"

"No. Well ... maybe."

Sally sits up and glares down at him. Moonlight is filtering through the thin curtains and he can see her eyes, wide and shining. "I can feel her between us the whole time. You're still wearing your bloody wedding ring, for godsake."

Leo sighs. "Maybe if you'd come along a few months down the line it might have been different. Yet I'm glad you didn't wait else that would have been another few months of not knowing about Sam. As for the ring, well, I'm used to it being there – it's something to twiddle between the thumb and little finger whilst I'm thinking. I would miss it."

Sally says, "I had this romantic idea of us being together as a family. But it's not going to work, is it? We disagree over everything. I think it's time we called it a day ..."

"What? Right now? Oh, *Sally* ..." He takes her hand. "It will be better once the divorce is over. You are wonderful,

Sally. You are open and honest and bold ... a woman of integrity. *Please* give me another chance. I'll try not to interfere so much – I know it annoys you. I promise to keep my opinions to myself in future ..."

She pulls her hand away; switches on the bedside lamp and waits until he has stopped blinking against its brightness and is sitting up and looking at her.

"I am not willing to wait for you to get over Bridget – I'm not convinced you *ever will* – and I think we're simply incompatible. And ..." She stops and looks down, wanting to be honest but knowing this will hurt him.

"And what?"

"Well ... I want another baby." Seeing he has taken it like a punch in the guts she hurries on, in a lighter tone; "Sam is at the age where it would be a good time for him to have a younger brother or sister ... and ...well ... they say lightning doesn't strike twice in the same place." He is hanging his head and wearing the exact expression that Sam wears when something insufferable has happened – like last Wednesday when he realised he'd left his toy fire engine on the bus. She resists the urge to put her arms around him and says, "I feel such a bitch for saying that – but I have to be honest with you. And I'm really glad that I've had this opportunity to get to know you. It has helped me to understand my son a little better – now that I can see where some of his *stubborn little ways* have come from and ..." She stops, realising she is now insulting him in her attempt to justify her decision to split with him.

He reaches out for her, now that she has stopped, but she turns away. "You'd better go now. Better now, than in the morning in front of Sam ..."

"But I told him we were going to –"

"Leo! Me and Sam have managed an outing without you plenty of times before now, and we will do again tomorrow."

"But I still want to see Sam at weekends – and, well, whenever possible ..."

"Oh, you *will*. Whilst I wish that I'd kept Sam a secret from you, I do trust you to look after him, to the extent that I could take advantage of you and have a night out with the girls now and again. Maybe get my own life back on track."

"*Back on track*? What do you mean by that?"

"Leo, just go now, *please*."

Judith, lying awake, hears Leo's car in the drive. The back door opens and closes as quietly as is possible but she doesn't hear him come upstairs. She looks out of the window to check that it *is* Leo's car parked outside then puts on her dressing gown and goes down to the kitchen. He has not switched on the light but there is a full moon casting a silver glow around the edges of everything. She can see his silhouette, sitting on the dog bed next to Ralph.

"Sorry, Mum, did I wake you?" he asks quietly, afraid of startling her.

"No ... no ... I'd only just gone up, then I heard your car. Is everything okay?"

"Yes, everything's fine. Just ... erm ... Sally and I, we've decided to call it a day ..."

"Oh, *Leo!* What went wrong?" When he doesn't immediately answer, she goes on, "I thought you two were quite well-suited, and I *always* liked Sally – a very *natural* girl, and intelligent too."

Leo sniffs and tries to steady his breathing. Every sound seems unnaturally loud in the dark, quiet kitchen. Ralph licks his face, making great slapping noises with his tongue as Leo holds him at arm's length, trying to fend him off. Eventually, he says, "I wasn't what she expected. But she's got me out of her system now, and can move on. It was my fault ..."

"Oh, Leo, I do wish you wouldn't always blame yourself ... We *will* still see Sam, won't we? You will be able to fetch him back here ..?"

"Yes, yes. I'll make sure of it. I think Sally will be glad to off-load him now and again, so there shouldn't be any problem."

"Well, it will be good for you to have him by yourself sometimes, without Sally."

Sally's idea of Leo having access turns out to be a case of her phoning him short notice when she needs a baby sitter or fancies a night out with her friends.

One Saturday morning, Alistaire is returning from the paper shop just as Leo is driving away.

"Where's *he* going? He was looking happy for change."

"He's gone to collect Sam," says Judith. "Sally just phoned and said there's a party tonight that she'd like to go to. Sam's staying here overnight."

"Then it's just as well he was moping around waiting for her call, and hadn't made any plans of his own. *What is it with Leo?* We've got clients queuing up for him to resolve their affairs because he's so good at it but yet he doesn't seem able to sort out his own life. The divorce could have been finalised by now if only he'd got on with it, and he could very easily have arranged regular access to Sam instead of hanging around here like a spare part and jumping when his phone rings."

Judith has been updating the family photographs that hang in frames on the wall in an alcove. She has replaced Leo and Bridget's wedding photo with a particularly good one of Leo that was taken at Serge's wedding. His eyes are bright and happy and his expression is of amusement and delight.

"That's the photo they printed in one of the glossies, isn't it?" asks Alistaire.

"Yes, he was playing croquet with Sam."

Sally had refused permission for any photographs of Sam to be published but Judith has copies of them all on a CD. She looks again at the enigmatic photo. One of the contracted magazines had featured it on their website, attracting hundreds of comments speculating over what Serge's brother might be looking at.

"Anyway, I'm going to make Sam some gingerbread pigs."

The gingerbread pigs are cooling on the rack as Leo walks up the driveway with Sam clutching his hand with one hand and a teddy bear with the other.

"First he wants to see where he's going to sleep tonight." Leo pulls a nervous face at his at his mother.

"I'm sure you will love it, Sam!" Judith responds enthusiastically, with a *fingers-crossed* gesture in the air.

Leo leads Sam upstairs and along the landing, which suddenly seems a huge distance for such small steps. "Here we are." Leo has taken a mattress from a spare room and put it on the floor beside his own bed and is grateful to find that his mother has made it up with sheets, pillow and duvet, so it looks quite cosy. "Put your teddy in there, and then *Teddy* knows where he's sleeping tonight."

"His name's *Leo*, not *Teddy*," Sam corrects him, and puts the bear in the bed.

"Really? Did you name him Leo?"

"No. Mummy did."

Leo laughs. "Yes, I can see he is quite an *old* teddy bear."

"Leo was Mummy's bear before I was even born ... what's funny?"

"Oh, I'm sorry Sam, let's just tuck him in and then you know where he is ..."

"Daddy?"

"Yes?"

"Where *you* sleep?"

"Right here." Leo lies on his bed to demonstrate and Sam gets into his own bed to try it out. "Is that okay for you?"

"Yes. Where Mummy sleep?"

"In her own bed, but you will see her tomorrow. Hey, have you ever had a ride on a pony?" Sam shakes his head. "Well, if you'd like to try it, Auntie Fran has a pony called Storm, and I'm sure she would let you have a ride on her if you'd like to?"

"Yeah!"

"Good, well, let's go downstairs and have one of Nanny's gingerbread pigs – she made them especially for you – and a glass of milk, and then we'll go and see the pony."

On this occasion, Leo lets himself in through the main gates of Hardwicke Heights, but finds only Beatrice and Franchesca at home, watching a film. At least Beatrice is watching the film, whilst Franchesca is looking at the wall three feet to the left of the television screen.

"Where's Serge?" asks Leo.

"Dom took him to an airport," says Beatrice with a frown that suggests he has turned up during a key scene in the film.

"An *airport*. Why?"

"Oh, no reason ... Serge couldn't get his head round the idea of Mum and Dad going away in an aeroplane *up in the sky* so Dom thought it would be a good idea to take him to see the planes taking off and landing. *Hi Sam …*"

"Oh. Good idea. Serge is rapidly gaining popularity across Europe and the USA. It would be good to get him used to the idea of flying. Anyway, we came to ask Auntie Fran a favour." Leo waves at Franchesca to attract her attention, "Fran, would it be okay for Sam to have a ride on Storm in the paddock?" She looks at Sam who is clutching Leo's hand and smiles and nods. "Do you fancy coming with us whilst Beatrice watches the film?" She smiles and nods again. "Come on then." Franchesca stands up and takes Leo's free hand, lowering her eyes shyly.

"Just make sure you walk her back up here when you're done," says Beatrice. "Don't let her go wandering off."

Snowy and Storm are grazing in the paddock. Paddy coaxes them back to their boxes with a handful of pony nuts and watches whilst Leo gives Storm's back a brisk brush and then puts on her saddle and bridle. "Is that all right, Paddy?"

“Just der job, lad. Der young lady has decided she’d like a black gelding now, as well as Storm, so if yer see anything male, black and bomb-proof in der newspaper yer could let us know?”

“Will do. Now then, who’s first?” Franchesca points at Sam so Leo lifts him up on Storm’s back. Sam’s eyes widen and he chuckles delightedly; Franchesca joining in. “Hold on tight just here,” says Leo and puts Sam’s hands on the pommel of the saddle. Leo holds the lead rein and they amble round the edge of the paddock.

“Again, again!” says Sam.

“Once more and then it’s Fran’s turn.”

When Leo tries to lower him to the ground, Sam clings tightly round his neck. “Did you enjoy the pony ride?” Sam nods happily.

Fran hoists herself up into the saddle and takes up the reins.

“Yer can unclip der lead rein, der young lady will be all right. Storm’ll take care of her,” says Paddy, but Fran, in Serge’s absence, has taken a shining to Leo and insists on him leading the pony around the paddock with Sam on his shoulders. After she has ridden the same number of circuits as Sam, Leo leans back against the paddock gate and lifts Sam down off his shoulders.

“That’ll do then,” says Paddy. “Snowy wants to come out her box now.” He looks at Leo with concern. “Look at der state of yer lad, yer look done in. Yer need ter get more exercise. Just move der wee boy and Franchesca to the other side of the fence whilst I let Snowy out.”

Snowy flares her nostrils, kicks up her heels and trots airily around the paddock before settling to graze.

“She’s looking great, Paddy,” says Leo. “I know that the folks who had her before dismissed the idea of trying to breed from her owing to her temperament – but how do you feel about that now? She’s calmed down nicely under your care.”

“Funnily enough I was thinking der same meself – but the stud fee for a racehorse can be anything from a couple of grand to a couple of *hundred* grand or *more* – depending on whether der stallion is proven and der results of the 'orses he has sired in the der past."

"I see. But we couldn't *race* her foal – it might get hurt, like Snowy did – or worse."

Paddy looks at him to see if he is joking and sees that he isn't. "Well, any old stallion would do if yer just want ter breed a pet. Or maybe we'll find a small black gelding with a free thoroughbred stallion thrown in."

Back home, Judith has cooked tea and Leo watches with surprise as Sam tucks into pasta twists with Napolitana sauce, grated cheese and salad.

"Look at that," he says in a low voice. "He'll eat proper food when Sally's not around."

"Yes. How about *you* following his good example?"

Later when he takes Sam upstairs for his bath, Judith asks if he needs any help. "No, it's okay, I've watched what Sally does often enough, and he's brought all his kit – even a plastic duck! We'll use the main bathroom if that's okay - there's more space."

One of Sam's finger nails, softened by the bath water has begun to peel across. Leo rummages through the contents of the bathroom cabinet to find some nail scissors. Safety conscious now he is a father, he frowns at the out-of-date sleeping pills prescribed to Judith four years ago and the medication that didn't suit Serge because it made him drowsy. And *Diazepam* ... what is *that* doing here? Why on earth didn't his mother dispose of such things?

He takes the book of illustrated fairy tales from Serge's room and enjoys reading some of his old favourites to Sam – just like he used to read to Serge, and Sam looks so much like him too, curled up beneath the duvet with his thumb in his mouth. Realising Sam is fast asleep; Leo wonders how long he has been reading to himself. He returns the book to Serge's room and pops downstairs to say goodnight.

"I shall read in bed for a while. I assured Sam I would be there all the time, so I wouldn't like him to wake up and find himself alone. Goodnight."

27

Now it seems that all is lost

Alistaire and Judith have gone away on holiday and are into their second week at the Seychelles, whilst Sally's parents have left their *fantastic* home on the outskirts of Sidney and are into their second week at Sally's place on the outskirts of London.

Leo is in the office browsing through his remaining schedule of appointments. A couple of his father's cases have been transferred over to him - both to do with trees that people are wanting to fell. One tree has grown too high and is blocking out the light from a client's house; the other tree is dripping sticky sap on the client's car that has to be parked beneath it. Leo rests his head in his hands for a moment and then begins some research about people's rights with regard to trees. He yawns, remembering with a sigh, that he has agreed to go and have dinner at Sally's this evening, to meet her parents. It will be good to see Sam mid-week, that always gives him a boost, but he could do without the rest of it.

Just when Michelle has phoned to let him know Mr and Mrs Crosier are here to see him about the elm tree, Leo's mobile phone rings.

"Bridget?"

"*Oh, Leo!*" Her voice is almost a wail.

"Bridget, whatever is the matter?"

"The baby's on her way. She's not due for another six weeks!"

"Don't worry – that's not *too* early, she'll be fine."

"Matt's up in Birmingham – I've left a message on his mobile but he hasn't got back to me … Could you ...?"

"I'm on my way now, Bridget. Just try to relax."

"Oh … please get here quickly!"

Leo hurries out to the reception and Mr and Mrs Crosier stand up to meet him.

"I'm terribly sorry but I have to go," he says. "Michelle, please ask if Theo could see Mr and Mrs Crosier – and would you re-arrange the rest of my appointments today for another day."

"Where are you going?" asks Michelle, but he has already disappeared down the first flight of stairs.

Leo makes the familiar journey to his old home in record time and finds Bridget scared and tearful. He puts his arms gently around her and she leans against him.

"How often are the contractions?" Leo hasn't a clue how often they're supposed to be or what the frequency might signify, but it makes him sound in control.

"I don't know – the waters haven't broken yet. I've been trying to pack my bag … I don't know if I've got everything, I can't think."

"Never mind that, if there's anything you need someone will fetch it for you." He picks up the bag and ushers her down the drive and into his car. He cannot help hoping that '*the waters'* aren't about to break all over the plush upholstery.

"I wanted to be married to Matt before the baby arrived – and I'm not even divorced from *you* yet."

"The decree absolute should come through any time now, but *please* don't rush into marrying Matt."

Leo weaves in and out of the traffic as if there is an emergency, whilst reassuring her that everything is fine and there is no hurry. They quickly make it to the hospital but finding somewhere to park is a different matter. After two circuits of the complex, with Bridget cursing and groaning, he gives up and abandons the car outside the building labelled Maternity Unit. She clambers out into his arms and he hoists her through the entrance. "I'll go back in a minute and find a parking space," he says.

"I don't give a shit where you park the fucking car!" she yells at him.

"No, I don't suppose you do," Leo acknowledges.

He waits with her until she is escorted away to be 'assessed' and once he has seen where they have taken her he slips away to move the car, unsure now whether he is supposed to go back to the office or what ...

"Leo! *Leo!*"

He retraces his steps. "I'm just going to move the car."

"*Fuck the-* . Well, please don't be long!"

Someone who might be a nurse, a doctor or surgeon or a cleaner - he cannot tell - advises him to drive round to the 'H' zone and maybe put a three-hour ticket on the car, but by the time he gets there someone is just about to put a parking ticket on his windscreen. "Sorry, mate," he says cheerfully. "I've already printed the ticket - I have to give you it now."

"But my wife is in labour and there was nowhere to park."

He holds the ticket out for Leo to take; "Then you've got more important things to worry about than a parking ticket. Take it, will yer mate - I can't just stuff it back up the machine - no more than you can do with the kid; *hah, hah, hah*! Anyway - if I were you I'd try the 'H' zone. It's a fair way off but there's normally a space or two. Oh, and good luck with the little'un!"

By the time Leo gets back to the room where he left her, Bridget has been moved and there is someone else in her place. "Oh, I'm *so* sorry," he says retreating swiftly and goes back to reception to find out where she has gone.

"Where the hell have *you* been?" she demands, when he finally tracks her down.

"Sorry, I got a bit lost ..."

A large Jamaican nurse or midwife, with a relaxed, happy face and a big toothy smile, pats the seat next to her, and Leo sits down on it. She reassures him. "Don't, worry. Everything is going fine. Hubby often gets a bit of abuse at this time – for putting her in this situation, you understand?"

"Mmm," says Leo. He notes her ample, motherly chest and imagines how comfortable it would be to rest his head upon. He says quietly, "The baby isn't due yet ..."

"Then the baby won't be very big – but that's all the better for getting it out, you understand?"

"Urm, yes. I can imagine." What a very kind nurse she is.

"Leo!"

"I'm here Bridget."

"Where?"

The kind nurse propels him along to the seat beside Bridget, and she grasps his arm.

Someone who is gazing up between her legs says, "Come on now, another good, hard push at the next contraction." Bridget inhales the gas and air mixture and digs her finger nails into Leo's forearm as the baby emerges; looking rather purple and slimy.

The kind nurse reads Leo's expression. "It's okay; they always look like that at first." She laughs. "You look like you was watching a horror movie!"

The baby is placed on Bridget's chest and the cord is cut. Leo sees it twist away like some huge parasitic worm.

"You need some fresh air?" The kind nurse thinks Leo looks about to keel over.

"Mmm ... sorry ..." He stands up, carefully.

"Leo! Where are you going?"

He slumps down again and the kind nurse tells him to put his head between his knees for a minute, resting a supportive arm across his shoulders as he does so. He sits up with a bit more colour in his face, "Thanks, it's gone away now."

The midwife lifts the baby off Bridget, wraps a small cotton sheet around her and puts her down on Leo's lap. "Dad can have her for a minute whilst we sort Mum out."

Leo puts a finger in the baby's palm and she grips it. He is transfixed. "Oh, Bridget, she's *amazing*. She's even got tiny little finger nails!"

"She *is* okay, isn't she? Not too early ..."

"She's *perfect* ... a perfect little replica of *you*. I have seen premature babies on the TV and internet, and they tend to look like biology-book diagrams of foetuses. But your little girl is

... just beautiful." His voice falters and he looks at Bridget who is smiling happily with tears rolling down her face. "She's as beautiful as you are," he whispers.

At that moment, the door flies open and Matt storms in. "What the fuck is *he* doing here?"

Leo passes the baby to the kind nurse at his side and stands up to leave.

"I thought you were Bridget's husband," the astonished midwife says to Leo.

"I am," says Leo, "but *he's* the baby's father."

The midwife raises her eyebrows. "Well, that's *different*."

Matt is still standing in the doorway and Leo walks past and out into the corridor without looking at him. Instead of going to see Bridget and the baby, Matt follows Leo into the corridor, flings him back against the wall and delivers him an unexpected punch in the ribs. Leo is stunned for a moment then reacts by swinging a punch at Matt's face – which he deflects with ease and twists Leo's arm into an elbow lock and punches his ribs again in the same place, then lets go of his arm and stands back and laughs as Leo leans against the wall, bent double and struggling to breathe.

"I thought you were hard last time we met. Remember? You were clearing your junk out and you shoved me against the wall?" Matt glances along the corridor and sees a couple of security officers doing their rounds ... coming his way. "Remember that, do you?"

Leo nods, clutching his ribs, winded and unable to speak.

"Yeah, but then Bridget told me you wouldn't even kill a spider. She reckons you catch them in a glass and put them outside. Something to do with lack of balls, I guess." He sees that Leo has risen to the taunt, weighs up the distance of the approaching security officers and, tapping his index finger on his face says, "Come on, Leo, put it here; show us your a man."

Leo swings at him and manages a glancing blow to Matt's jaw even though he ducks. Matt exclaims loudly and clutches his face, saying to the security officers, "Did you see that? Get this crack head out of here!" His nasty laughter follows Leo along the corridor as they escort him from the premises.

Leo eventually finds where he left his car and steps into its sanctuary. After a minute's peace he is startled by a noise and realises it is his mobile phone vibrating in the glove compartment. It is Sally calling.

"Hello Sally?"

"Where the hell are you Leo?"

He suddenly remembers he was supposed to be having dinner with Sally and her parents. "Oh, Sally, I'm so sorry – something happened and it completely slipped my mind."

"Yeah? Well, we've had dinner without you."

"I'm glad to hear it. I'd hate to think you were all sitting there waiting for me to turn up."

"What happened? I've phoned you loads of times, and I tried the office but they said you got called away. You *are* still coming aren't you?"

Leo sighs. "Couldn't we make it tomorrow evening? I don't mean for dinner – but just to call in and say Hello."

Sally hesitates then says, in a softer tone. "*Please* come tonight. There's something I have to tell -"

"Sally? It's breaking up – what did you say?"

"Please come tonight Leo. I told Sam you were coming. He'll be disappointed if you don't."

He looks at his watch. "It's going to be at least an hour – depending on the traffic – before I get there. Will Sam still be up?"

"Yes, if you promise me you'll get here."

They hang up and Leo wonders why she sounded so ... *emotionally charged.* Checking his phone he finds a barrage of missed calls and texts from her. He doesn't read them – if he takes too long she might put Sam to bed. There is also a missed call from Uncle Theo who has left a disgruntled voicemail message. Theo is supposed to be in court tomorrow but will have to cancel if Leo cannot make it to the office. "So *will* you be there or *not*? I need to *know*."

Leo sends him a quick text. "Yes I will be in the office tomorrow. Sorry about today."

He arrives at Sally's house, knocks on the door and waits for her to open it. She seems about to greet him with a hug but changes her mind at the last instant and it turns into an awkward arm-shake. She stumbles against him giggling and he gasps at the sudden pain from his ribs. "Sorry," she says. "Dad bought a case of this really good wine – and I got a bit nervous waiting for you to turn up, and ... Oh, you smell funny!"

"What sort of funny?" he asks with concern.

"A disinfectant smell – like hospitals or dentists or T.C.P. or something ..."

"Well, so long as it's just T.C.P. and not B.O."

"Maybe the one smell is masking the other ..." she starts to giggle again, but at least she is not cross with him for missing dinner. "Anyway, come and meet the parents, now that you've finally arrived."

"Sorry but I *must* go in here first." He opens the door of the downstairs cloakroom. "Just realised I haven't been all day." He looks back at her with a comical wide eyed grimace that sends her into hysterics and then shuts the door behind him. The sun has gone down now, but has been radiating steadily on the marbled glass window all day, making the small room very hot. He notices the hospital smell that Sally had mentioned and it makes him feel vaguely nauseas. He washes his hands and runs cold water over them - cupping it in his hands and splashing it over his face, then finds there is no towel and dabs his face on rolled-up shirt sleeves. His ribs have stiffened up during the car journey and when he lifts up his shirt to examine them he finds a vast purple-grey area of deep bruising. In the heat of the moment when it happened, it hadn't seemed to hurt enough to justify all this.

He steps out into the kitchen with his hands and face still wet and Sally throws him a small towel that has been used as an oven glove and smells of meat fat whilst Sam reaches up his arms for a hug. Leo puts the towel over the back of a kitchen chair and lifts Sam up, the tension of the afternoon waning for a few seconds at least as the little hands clasp round his neck.

"Pissing like a donkey!" declares Sam, and Leo raises his eyebrows at Sally's Dad. He is bald with a shiny, round, red face and is wearing a smug expression and khaki shorts with a large belly hanging over the top and a colourful Hawaiian shirt.

Leo says, "At this age, they do tend to copy what grown-ups say. They think it must be clever, especially if a parent or grandparent - someone whose judgment they respect - has said it." Sally's Dad smiles apologetically and Leo adds, forgivingly, "But, I will bear it in mind and try to make *less noise* next time."

"Oh, I shouldn't worry about *that*." Leo looks at him sharply and he lowers his eyes. The couple of seconds' silence is long enough to be awkward. "*Ah, hum*. Well ... anyway, at least we can see where Sam gets his looks from now."

"Actually, he looks more like my brother. We've got photos of Serge at this age, and they're identical."

"Your *brother*. Sally told us he was a spastic or something."

Leo weighs it up and decides he is simply ignorant rather than intentionally offensive. He says casually, "No, he doesn't have cerebral palsy; he has mild brain damage. His muscle tone is excellent and his co-ordination is good too."

"Oh. Me and Sally's Mum were over here when Sam was born. We thought he looked like his Uncle Tom – that's Sally's brother, back in Aus."

"Yes, Sally has mentioned him – I've seen photos."

"Of course, you weren't around when Sam was born, were you? You only crawled out of the woodwork a few months ago ..."

Leo tries to block from his mind the very recent image of Bridget's baby emerging into the world. "It's true that I wasn't there ..." He suddenly understands Sally's father's intrinsic hostility and wonders what Sally has told her parents about him. Presumably *not* that she seduced him on his stag night when he was off his head.

Sam wriggles to get down; thrusting his knees against Leo's bruised ribs. Leo gasps and lowers him to the floor. Sam goes out into the garden where his Mum and Nan are sitting drinking wine. Leo feels suddenly dizzy again and leans back against the fridge-freezer.

Sally's Dad looks him up and down. Sally had said he was a solicitor and with his expensive looking clothes and - if that's a *genuine* Rolex watch - he does, in a way, look the part. But he also looks frazzled. Maybe he just had a bad day. Not that it's going to get any better... "You fancy a beer? I'm gonna have another."

"No thanks – I'll just get some water if that's okay." He walks slowly to the kitchen sink and takes a glass from the draining board and rinses and fills it. "Erm, it might be just me, but it seems *really hot* in here. Is it okay if we go outside?"

Leo and Sally's Dad sit on the wooden bench beneath the kitchen window, looking down the garden to where Sally and her Mum are sitting at the table beneath a parasol – although it is beginning to get dark. Sam is driving his toy cars around the grass – mostly underneath the table and around the chair legs.

"Just watch out if you move your chair back," says Leo. "He's right underneath."

Sally glares at him. "*We do know!*"

Leo realises Sally's Dad has just said something to him. "Sorry? I was miles away ..."

"You were, were you, now there's a coincidence - *hah, hah, hah!"*

Leo notices Sally and her Mum are frowning at Sally's Dad, who says, "Hey, why don't you girls go and make him a sandwich or something, since he missed dinner."

"No, honestly, I'm fine," says Leo.

"I told you he never eats," says Sally.

Sally's Dad asks, "Is it a stressful job, being a solicitor? I mean, you look a bit *done in*, if you don't mind me saying."

"No, not really. It's a small, family practice and most of our cases tend to be fairly routine. We're all equipped to take care of any case that is presented to us."

"Pretty cushy, working with the family, then?"

"Well – it has its advantages and disadvantages."

"Sally told me you were a trained barrister."

"No, not quite. I completed the first twelve months' training."

"So what made you give it up?"

"I felt silly wearing a wig," replies Leo, with a weary smile. He hopes they can leave it at that, but no ... so Leo goes on, "After the first six months you are 'on your feet' as they put it, which means you get to defend petty criminals in court. But you don't get given the brief until the end of the day – and you might have to be in court the next morning on the other side of London. That means spending the evening preparing the defence. I had just got engaged around the time I was offered a pupillage, but then - a year later - Bridget threatened to break it off because I was spending so little time with her. So I gave it up and re-joined the family firm, so I could finish work at five in the afternoon and spend the evenings with her."

Sally's Dad drains his bottle of beer and belches. "Pity you didn't stick with the wig – the way things have turned out."

Leo doesn't answer. He is watching Sam picking soil out of the wheels of his toy car.

Sally's Dad changes the subject. "Nice car, you've got."

"Yes ... although it is a *company* car."

"So it would have to go back if you left the *family firm*."

"Yes, indeed."

"He's rather more *gorgeous* than I was expecting – the way you spoke about him," says Sally's Mum to Sally. "And hasn't he got a lovely voice?"

Sally shrugs her shoulders. "He comes from a rather *middle class* family. Went to private school. Did I tell you he wanted

Sam to go to a private school? He was going to commit to some sort of finance plan to fund it all - but I went ballistic! I mean ... how *insensitive is that* when he *knew* I was intending to go back and teach at the local state school ..."

"Oh, don't be so hard on him. He only wanted what was best for Sam. And would it have been such a bad thing?"

"Oh, *I don't know*. I didn't like the idea of it. But it's irrelevant now, isn't it?"

"Yes, that's true. So when are you going to tell him?"

"I'll have to pick the right moment. Not in front of Sam. Maybe you could take Sam indoors when I give you the cue. I'm going to have another glass of wine first ... how about you?"

"No, I've had enough. And you've been knocking it back a bit, haven't you?"

"Dutch courage I guess."

"Australian courage, more like. Still, I think you should tell him sooner rather than later."

Sally casts a glance at Leo and finds his is looking directly at her.

"What is it that you have to tell me?" he asks, bleakly.

Sally's mother stands up, looks at her husband and nods her head at the house.

"Come on Gramps, let's go and start getting this little man ready for bed."

"Come here, Leo."

He goes to her obediently and takes the seat that is still warm from her mother. "What is it, Sally? What's going on?"

"I don't want you to make a big deal out of this ..."

"Out of *what*?"

"I should never have told you about Sam – it was a big mistake …"

Leo grasps Sally's hands suddenly, forcing her to look at him. "Please! Just tell me."

"I'm going back to Australia with Mum and Dad. To live there I mean. To start afresh."

The silence between them is like the gap between a flash of lightning and the inevitable noise of the thunder to follow, which might be anything from a distant rumble to an almighty crash.

Eventually, he says, "Were you thinking of taking Sam?"

"*Of course* I'm taking Sam, *you idiot!"* she shouts at him, and her mother and father appear at the window with Sam standing on the windowsill between them. Sally lowers her voice. "Please don't make a fuss. You've only known of Sam's existence for a few months – so don't start acting like *your whole life depends on it*."

"Please don't go, Sally. *Please*! Give me another chance to give you ... to give you what you were hoping for that day when you came to see me at the office. I promise to be different. If you tell me what you were expecting then I will change my ways."

"No. Stop it! Stop making this *difficult*. Can't you just wish me well and get on with your own life?"

"No. *No, I can't*." On impulse, he says; "Let me come with you Sally. We could make a new start in Sidney as a family, and forget the past. *Please*, Sally!"

"No! It's not *me* you want – it's Sam. Because his existence proves to you that you're a *proper man!*"

Leo tries to take this in, and the few seconds he needs to absorb the idea is like an eternity. "Oh, no, Sally! You can't really think that of me? Surely you don't? I've had very many thoughts about you and about Sam – but *that* thought never, ever entered into it. But you're not serious about going to Australia, are you?"

"Yes I *am really, seriously going!*" Sally bursts into tears and her father appears in the garden, his attitude suddenly menacing.

"Go on now, sling your hook. You're upsetting my daughter."

Leo doesn't move and Sally's Dad advances, slowly and deliberately.

"Leave it, Dad. Please don't ..."

Leo stands up. "Just let me say goodnight to Sam." Sam is still standing on the windowsill, watching solemnly, with Sally's Mum by his side.

Sally's Dad shakes his head and stands in front of Leo like a stone wall. "I don't think that's a good idea. Just go through the side gate there. Here's your keys. Go on. *Now.*"

Leo arrives at his parents' home without remembering the journey; walks up the back steps and opens the door to the kitchen. Ralph is delighted to see him, but reproachful – leaning against his legs and turning his head to gaze at him with a reprimanding expression. Leo kneels down and cradles his big hairy head. "I'm sorry boy, you're already missing Mum and Dad, and now I've come back late. Only six more bed times and then they'll be home." Ralph pants anxiously in his face and he backs away. "Come on then, let's just have a quick walk as far as the dog-bin, then you can have your supper."

Watching Ralph wolfing down his food, Leo knows he should eat something himself but the thought of it makes his throat constrict. There is an opened bottle of red wine on the worktop. He pours some into a glass and takes a gulp, but it hits his stomach like acid and he throws it away, rinsing the glass and drinking some water. Maybe the wine has gone off.

Ralph settles on his bed with a sigh and Leo goes upstairs and runs a bath, trying to do something to relax – to slow down his thoughts and think logically; the way he normally thinks – but his mind is a turmoil of images and thoughts that make no sense. He has always been able to think straight and arrive at clear conclusions, but tonight he is defeated as chaotic snapshots race through his mind and he fails to formulate any acceptable plan of action. Unable to sleep, and having left his laptop at the office, he sets off for work ridiculously early. There is a fair bit of paperwork to catch up on, but it is mostly routine stuff, and he works through it rapidly and accurately without much thought.

Michelle turns up a little earlier than usual. "Theo asked me to phone and let him know if you were here," she explains, apologetically. "I'll just do that and then I'll make some coffee." She returns a few minutes later with the coffee and asks, "Is everything okay?" He smiles. *What a question.* "I mean, you don't look too good if you don't mind me saying so ... is Sam okay?"

"Sam? Yes, he's fine. I saw him earlier. Yesterday, I mean." He changes the subject. "What's that massive skip doing occupying four of our parking spaces?"

"Oh, it turned up here yesterday afternoon. Next door are refurbishing. They apologised about the skip and said we're welcome to use it if we've anything to get rid of. I thought about those two wonky chairs we've been keeping in the kitchen."

"Good thinking – I'll put them in the lift and stick them in it before the first clients turn up. What's Theo doing in court today? Anything interesting?"

"No, just some rich old fart who built a barn on his land some time ago without planning permission and it's blocking out someone's light *between the hours of ten-thirty and thirteen-thirty*. It's a *pity* for them, isn't it?"

He laughs. "I guess any problem is as big as its owner's reaction to it. Has Theo left you much to do? I just dictated a couple of letters that need typing, but I'll do them myself if you're busy."

"No, Theo's done nothing but complain about being deserted by everyone. Email me the files and I'll type them up." *Because I love the sound of your voice and I will save them on my MP3 player and listen to them for pleasure at home ...*

When Theo returns to the office, early in the afternoon, Michelle can tell by his demeanour that his case must have gone well. He frowns briefly at the huge yellow skip, and then she watches his portly figure swagger across the car park and, without being asked, makes him tea and takes it to his office, tapping politely on the open door before entering.

"Oh, thank you so much!" Theo looks her up and down. Whilst he can't fault her work, he does wish she wouldn't turn up looking as if she has forgotten to put something on. Or perhaps he is simply getting old. Maybe a pink pullover worn with opaque black tights is acceptable office attire these days ... but why does an intelligent girl like Michelle need to draw attention to herself *that* way? "Would you be a darling and pop and ask Leo to come and see me?" He puffs out his chest, self-importantly and Michelle rolls her eyes, wondering why he can't *pop* to Leo's office rather than creating the drama of her having to go and tell Leo the head honcho wants to see him. She glances back and is gratified to catch the old letch checking out her bum.

She stops abruptly in the doorway of Leo's office. He is asleep at the desk, head down on his arms, looking so very pale that just for a moment she thinks he has had a heart attack and died. She is on the verge of waking him but stops. He is always so professional in the office that he would be mortified to think she had caught him taking a nap - and his next client isn't due for another forty minutes. She returns to Theo's office. "He's asleep," she says awkwardly.

"He's a *what?*"

"A*sleep*. I think he was here pretty early this morning ..."

Theo struts crossly to Leo's office and Michelle follows him but keeps her distance. "*Leo!*" he bellows, and Leo sits upright with a start, and then says "Oh ..." and rests his face in his hands for a few moments, then lowers his hands and shivers.

"Are you ill?" asks Theo, shocked by his nephew's appearance. The whites of his eyes are red and the shadows beneath them are like deep bruises in his otherwise ashen face.

"Urm ... I don't *think* so," Leo replies, after a pause.

"Where did you go yesterday? What happened?"

Leo looks down at the desk. There is no way, right now, that he can talk about what happened yesterday.

Theo mistakes his silence for mutiny and the anger rises within him. "Walking out like that with no explanation is unforgivable! It was *you* that put the *holiday idea* in your father's head and assured him you would take care of things here. You've badly let us down, Leo. You can forget about becoming a partner as we clearly cannot rely on you. *I don't understand it.* You've dealt with hundreds of divorces over the past few years yet you're acting like you're the only person it's ever happened to. Just pull yourself together man!"

Theo enjoys a good argument and pauses here for Leo to retaliate, but Leo says nothing; still looking at the desk, noticing the wax crayon marks made by Sam on their first meeting. They are gradually fading. Each time the cleaner polishes his desk they are less easy to detect ... but he can still just about see them.

Theo sighs. His over-achieving nephew suddenly looks like a ten year old boy about to burst into tears. "Go home, Leo." Leo shakes his head. "Go on. I'll take over the rest of your appointments for today. I didn't book any for myself, not knowing how long I would be in court."

Eventually, Leo says, "I don't want to go home... I wouldn't know what to do there."

"Get some sleep, for a start. Go on Leo, *clear off!* You are no use to me in this state. I really don't want you here!"

For the second time in two days, Michelle watches Leo hurry away down the stairs without looking back. She sits down at her PC and puts on the headphones to type the letters he dictated this morning. His voice sounds detached, like it always does when he is speaking to a machine – but this time there is such weariness and sorrow in his tone that it moves her to tears. Theo appears at the top of the stairs and rolls his eyes. After his successful morning he could have done without coming back to all *this*.

Michelle takes off the headphones and dabs around her eyes with a tissue, worried she might have ruined her makeup. "He just seems so *sad*," she says by way of explanation.

Theo lowers himself into the seat opposite her desk and invokes his paternal persona – the one that Michelle feels he should have got out for Leo. "He'll be okay, he's just over-tired. I had a look at the alarm panel – he deactivated it at *ten past four* this morning. All he needs is a good night's sleep. It does appear, Michelle, that whilst Leo has gained an impeccable reputation for successfully resolving other folks' affairs; he is pretty darned rubbish at sorting out his own life."

Leo drives away from the office and heads for Sally's house. He needs to hear Sally say it again – that she is going to Australia. Yesterday had been a strange day for him – and maybe it had been for her too. Perhaps she just told her parents she was going back with them after sharing a glass or two of wine. Yet the back of his mind is nagging him that she has mentioned it before. It was during that initial euphoria when they got together after the results of the paternity test. There was not only the joy of knowing he was Sam's Dad ... knowing he had *known her before* – albeit he had little recollection – but it had allowed them to sidestep the coyness and cut straight to the chase – to the passion. It hadn't lasted long enough ... but somewhere within that brief window, she had mentioned *something about moving to Australia* ... but he had dismissed it.

He arrives at Sally's and sees her car on Serge's parking space. He parks across it and knocks at the door, already knowing there is no-one home. Then he remembers her parents have hired a people carrier for the fortnight, and looks through the front windows, then checks round the back – in the vague hope that Sally and Sam have stayed at home today. Everyone is out, so he moves his car to a space some way down the road, and then settles in the back garden to wait for them to return.

After some time – he has no idea how long – Leo hears Sam's voice and goes immediately to meet them to avoid the awkwardness of being discovered lurking in the back garden.

"Daddy!" Sam runs to meet him and Leo kneels down and hugs him tight. "Go see ponies?"

"No, not today. The ponies have gone to bed now."

"Sleep at Daddy's house tonight?"

Sally's Mum steps in boldly and hauls him away from Leo. "Come on, Sweetheart, let's run your bath."

"Daddy do it! Daddy do it!" wails Sam – but his grandmother calmly and skilfully distracts him and he goes along with her without too much fuss.

"Sally – please give me a minute," says Leo.

She frowns. "I assured Mum and Dad that you weren't the type to be a nuisance."

He hangs his head and she sighs and beckons him down the garden to the table where they sat together last night. Her father settles on the bench beneath the kitchen window, arms folded and ankles crossed; an ostentatiously bored expression on his face.

"Well, then?" she prompts him.

"Erm ... you told me you were going to Australia. I just wondered if ..." Had her parents somehow put the idea into her head? He glances briefly at her father, who notices, yawns and looks at his watch.

"We bought the plane tickets today. One way tickets to Sidney."

"Oh." There is a long pause. "So you really are going then?"

"How many more times do you need to hear it?"

"Sorry. When are you thinking of ... I mean when are you going?"

Sally's Dad butts in. "Don't tell him, Sal." He can picture it now - Leo standing on the runway in front of the plane.

"Soon. You know I rent this place. I have no ties. I *really am going,* Leo."

"Will you leave me a forwarding address, so I can keep in touch with Sam?"

"No... No, sorry but I *won't.* It is to be a fresh start you see. Leo ... I really don't think you *get it.* I want to turn back the clock - as if I never met you ... like it was just a few months ago when Sam's Dad was *my secret* – and no-one else, not even Sam, would ever know who he was."

"Am I really *that bad?*"

Sally doesn't reply.

Her father laughs.

Leo stands up. "Well ... thank you for being straight with me. I just needed to know for sure ... to be certain ..."

"She told you yesterday," her father points out.

"Leave it Dad," says Sally. "I'd drunk a load of your wine when I told him yesterday. That's why he needed to hear it again."

Leo turns to leave then hesitates and takes off his watch.

"Would you save this for Sam, for when he's older?" He puts it on the table in front of Sally. "It was a twenty-first birthday present from my parents. I'd like Sam to have it."

28

Leo is Resolved

Leo drives away from Sally's house feeling calm. Now that there is no doubt, he knows what he must do. He can think clearly again, the patterns of thought falling readily into place, just like they always have done. Over the last day or two, with all sorts of possibilities racing through his mind, he had felt that he was going mad, but now the chaos has subsided and his mind has the renewed speed and clarity of a computer's hard drive that has been wiped clean and had its operating system reinstalled.

The venue is all important. Of course it cannot be his parents' home – it would ruin the place for them forever. In fact he cannot allow himself to think any further about his parents' reaction, beyond not leaving anything for them to have to sort out – otherwise it might weaken his resolve. Of course, his parents still have each other and they will quickly get over this. They are different types, but they complement each other, and over the years the bond between them has grown stronger; it is such that they will get over *anything*. Leo had imagined his relationship with Bridget had similar footings - maybe it would have done if they'd had children ... had it not been for his laboratory-proven lack of fertility.

The ideal location presents itself effortlessly ...

He sees a small parking space near a shopping parade and slots into it adeptly to visit the Tesco Metro; the chemist next door, and then a kiosk that sells what he is looking for, followed by a well-stocked corner shop. Driving on a bit further, he stops at a petrol station – only buying a few litres rather than filling right up, and instead of paying at the pump he goes into the shop to make some more purchases. The small shops are all closed by this time – but just a couple more supermarkets or petrol stations and he will be done. He will not go anywhere he might be recognised.

Shopping mission completed, head down, skulking back to his car, Leo realises someone is speaking to him. Automatically polite, he stops. "Sorry?"

"I said, *any spare change, please*?"

Leo looks at the young man sitting beneath the shelter of the trolley park and does a quick mental stock-take of his recent purchases. The young man sees him hesitate and adds, "I wouldn't ask, only I haven't eaten in three days."

"Really? Well, I have finished shopping and yes I do have some spare change." Leo opens his wallet and hands over its generous contents.

The young man's eyes widen at the sight of twenty pound notes. "May God bless you, Sir!"

"Well, thank you ... but I honestly don't know what to expect."

Back at his parents' house, Ralph greets him with the normal ritual of wagging, bowing and strutting. Leo loops the broad leather collar around his neck, attaches the extending lead and heads off for a walk – managing for once to get away without having to speak to any of the neighbours. Back in the kitchen he puts a scoop of Ralph's veterinary prescription diet food into his bowl, then looks in the fridge to see what he can add to tempt him to eat it; finds some cheese, cuts off a slice and dices it very small then plants it beneath the unappetising kibbles. He goes upstairs and showers and puts on his old soft black jeans and a tee-shirt. He sits on the bed – shoulders aching, and examines his hoard. Two boxes of painkillers from every shop he called at plus a litre bottle of vodka. This time he won't be around for the hangover. He goes to the bathroom cabinet and retrieves his mother's out of date sleeping pills and whatever it was they prescribed a couple of years ago that didn't agree with Serge. He reads the label. 'Do not mix with alcohol'. He grins wryly and adds them to his stash - and Diazepam, just in its foil, ready to be popped.

Most of his possessions are still in the black bags that Bridget packed them in – and for this he thanks her – but thinking about Bridget induces the aching behind his eyes again and that choking sensation in his throat - diminishing his strength. He focuses on the task in hand and opens the one black bin liner that is half empty and throws in the rest of his clothes, his toothbrush and everything from the bathroom followed by aftershave and the various bits and pieces that have accumulated on his bedside table. He looks around the room for any further evidence of his recent existence and notices Sam's mattress is still on the floor beside his bed. He had grown so used to it being there that it was almost overlooked. He drags it back into the next room, where it came from, and then wanders from one room to the next, looking at the gardens from each window, remembering the games he had played with Serge and Beatrice ... the igloo they had built that year when the snow had lasted a fortnight and his school was closed because the boiler broke down. He goes into Beatrice's room where a few of her old favourite dolls and cuddly toys are assembled on a blanket box in the corner. One of the teddies had been his originally – he had called it 'Terry' for some reason. Serge's old bedroom holds the most memories. Serge has had a double bed in recent years, but there is still the single bed in the corner where Leo had spent many a night when Serge was unsettled and fearful of being alone in the dark. He hesitates outside his parents' room, but then opens the door and goes in. It smells of his mother's perfume - a comforting smell. He sits on the bed and tears burn behind his eyes, making them ache even harder. *Please forgive me Mum.*

She will be so upset when she comes back from her holiday and someone has to tell her what he has done. Perhaps he should write a letter and leave it here – addressed to his parents ... but that might make it worse. Besides, he hasn't a clue what to write. He reminds himself again that his Mum and Dad will be okay. They have each other. They will get over it. Mum has her 'Faith in God' ... whatever *that* means ... He takes a photo album from a shelf and sits on the floor, looking at the old family photos, amazed to see Serge, as a four year old, looking so much like Sam. *Must show this one to Sally.* He shakes his head, reminding himself that it will never happen, then closes the album and puts it back on the shelf.

It is half past midnight. He seems to have whiled away the last few hours in a dream state. Paddy always said he was *up with the larks*. What time in the morning do larks get up? He carries the black bags downstairs and loads them into the back of the car. Ralph, curled up on his bed, has one eye open and one ear cocked, as Leo goes back and forth, loading up his car. Finally, he gathers his stash of pills off the bed and scoops them into a carrier bag; locks them in the glove compartment and places the bottle of vodka in the passenger foot-well. Back in the kitchen he kneels beside Ralph's bed. "I'll leave you in peace for a while ... but we'll have an early start ... we're going to visit Paddy." Ralph's ears twitch at the sound of 'Paddy'. "Yes, I *know* you love Paddy, so don't you worry, Ralphie, everything will be okay."

At four o'clock in the morning, Leo starts to load Ralph's kit into his car; a sack of his food, the rest of the cheese, his bowls and leads, and then finally his bed – after some coaxing to get him off it. "Come on, Ralph. Just got to get *you* in there now."

Ralph puts his front feet in the car but stubbornly refuses to go any further – turning his head to look mournfully at Leo – troubled that his routine has been disrupted. Leo forgets his injured ribs and tries to lift the back end of the huge dog into the car, then gasps with pain and says harshly; "Why can't you do as you're told, just this once!" Ralph's tail goes between his legs and he clambers in then turns around to face Leo and looks at him unhappily with huge baleful eyes. Leo gets in the back to sit next to him for a moment and wraps his arms around his neck. "Sorry Ralph, the last thing in the world I wanted to do was to shout at you ... or should I say I didn't want that to be the last thing I did ..." Ralph seems to understand a little and licks the salty wetness from Leo's face and then settles down, bemused and surrounded by black bags. Leo hurries back indoors and scribbles a quick note to Derrick the gardener; 'Ralph is with Serge at Hardwicke Heights' and then locks the door and drives away.

His first stop is the office building where he enters the code in the keypad to open the wrought iron gates to the courtyard car park. The skip is still there, thank goodness. Trying not to make too much noise this early in the morning, he treads carefully up and down the steps, lowering the black bags down the side of it - Ralph watching anxiously and wondering what is going on. As an afterthought he switches off his mobile phone and throws it over the edge of the skip – feeling fleetingly guilty owing to his mother's dedication to recycling.

He gets back into the car and shivers suddenly – not sure whether it is owing to the cool morning air or a sudden fear of the unknown. He drives to Hardwicke Heights and goes past the main gates and further down the road then turns into the concealed entrance and drives along the track that leads to the stables. Five-forty ... probably too early even for Paddy to be up yet. He stops before the stables are in sight and switches off the engine. No sound of any larks. No sound of anything. He unlocks the glove compartment and extracts the bottle of vodka from beneath the passenger seat. The first couple of gulps send him into a coughing fit and he clutches his ribs and quickly downs some more in an attempt to dull the pain, enjoying its warm glow coursing through his veins. Ralph tries to climb over into the front seat but Leo does not allow it until the glove compartment is safely locked again.

He drives to the stables and parks outside the paddock gate, drapes an arm across Ralph's shoulders and watches the sun begin to rise. "Looks like it's going to be a nice day," he says, and then laughs at himself for saying so.

Paddy has just finished his porridge and taken his bowl to the kitchen sink. He thought he heard a vehicle stop and start – and now he can see the silhouette of Leo's car. He goes out into the paddock to take a closer look.

Leo appears to be enjoying a cuddle with his dark-haired passenger. It must be Sally ... but then, as they both get out of the car on the driver's side, the passenger materialises into Ralph.

"Sorry to turn up here at this time, Paddy." Leo speaks slowly and deliberately for the vodka has gone straight to his head and he is trying not to slur. "I'm going away for a while, so I've brought Ralph for Beatrice and Serge to look after until Mum and Dad get back. But I knew they wouldn't be up yet, so I was hoping you would have him here until a little later in the morning."

Paddy narrows his eyes at Leo. Something is amiss. Even in this dim light he appears unshaven and dishevelled - and his voice sounds strange. "Yes, he'll be alright here for a while - but where are you going?"

"Urm ... I'm not too sure yet." Leo takes the huge dog bed out of his car and sets off towards the stables, carrying it in front of him so he cannot see where he is going. His foot goes over the edge of the path, twisting painfully and he rolls over on the grass. Paddy lifts the dog bed off him and watches as he stands up, hobbles a couple of steps and then loses his balance and falls over again. Ralph thinks it is a game and wags his tail delightedly, standing over Leo and licking his face. Paddy frowns at the pair of them rolling around in the dewy grass and shakes his head, then carries the dog bed to his living quarters.

"Is there anything else of his in der car?" asks Paddy, still unable to work out what's going on but knowing something is badly wrong.

"His food and bowls ..."

Paddy goes to the car and takes out the bowls, the sack of dried food, the long lead and the short lead and then finds that the car is empty. Wherever Leo is planning on going, he is travelling light. He sees the neck of the vodka bottle protruding from beneath the passenger seat and pulls it out. A litre bottle only a quarter full. So that's it. He glances back at Leo who is still sitting on the grass, examining his ankle in the weak morning light. He tries the glove compartment and finds it is locked. Paddy takes the keys from the ignition, puts them in his pocket and carries the rest of the dog's kit back to the kitchen. Ralph has found his bed and is already settled on it. Paddy strokes his head and wonders what to do about Leo. He is back on his feet again. "Come on in and have a coffee or something ... Der dog's settled already, come and see."

Leo shakes his head. "No thanks, Paddy. I can't stay. Get Serge and Dom to carry his bed up to the house – it must be taking up most of your living room." He hobbles slowly to the car and Paddy goes back indoors and watches nervously from behind the blinds as Leo discovers the keys are missing and starts to search the surrounding area. He retraces his steps to the point where he had fallen over with the dog bed and hunts through the grass, then gives up and hobbles to Paddy's door and knocks.

"Sorry Paddy, please would you look in the dog's bed and see if I dropped my car keys in it ..." Leo has trouble speaking and is holding on to the door frame. The pupils of his eyes are like pin pricks.

"Yer can't drive anywhere, man, yer pissed! I can't believe you drove here in dat state."

"I didn't ... I didn't drive here – well I *did* drive here but ..."

"So, yer got 'ere first and den yer hit der bottle?" Paddy recalls hearing the engine stop for a while and then restart.

Leo nods slowly, not daring to move his head too fast.

"Then dis is where yer staying."

An expression of alarm crosses Leo's face. "*I have to go*, Paddy. Please help me find the keys, *I can't stay here.* I haven't got far to go, honestly ... only I've twisted my ankle and ... I can't stay *here* ... it would spoil it for everyone."

"But I can't let yer go. I know dat yer gonna *do* something. I can feel it from you like I felt it myself – that day when I was in der squat an' yer brother turned up – an' then again in the jail when me head was about to explode and I wanted to just bash it against the stone wall to make everything stop." Paddy is trembling at the memory of his own despair. "What's yer plan? If you're thinking of yer father's shotgun yer can forget *dat* – yer might find yer arms aren't long enough to turn it against yer head – and if you saw it off it just makes a big explosive *mess* – or so I've been told." Leo slowly shakes his head. Paddy goes on, "No – yer a tidy person. I expect you've got some pills or something dat will do der trick quietly." Leo looks at him and then averts his eyes so Paddy knows he is right.

The room begins to spin and Leo leans back against the cool stone wall, his ears ringing and his vision darkening. Paddy takes his arm and steers him to the kitchen table. "Sit down, lad, before yer fall down." He fills a glass with water and puts it on the table in front of him.

"Thank you," says Leo. He takes a gulp of the water and looks thoughtfully at the glass for a few seconds then stands up suddenly. "Please may I use –" He dives through the door to the bathroom. Paddy glances briefly at him on hands and knees with his head down the toilet and then closes the door against the violent retching noises.

Leo returns apologetically and sits back down at the table, clutching his belly and ribs.

"Feel better for dat?"

"No" he croaks. "There wasn't much to *go at* so it just *hurt*."

"Well - yer need a few pints and a kebab for a decent chunder, so yer do."

"Last time – with vodka – it didn't happen until the next morning. I thought I had a few hours yet."

"And der wasn't supposed to be a *few hours* – never mind a *next morning*, right?" Paddy points to his bedroom door. "Go on in there and sleep it off."

Leo stands up with renewed exigency. "No Paddy, it's very kind of you, but I must get away from here." He limps to the door at a fair pace, ricochets off the door frame and stumbles away down the path. Paddy watches, wondering how far he will get and whether or not to pursue him. He sees him rest at the paddock gate, leaning over it to support his weight, then he gets as far as the car and leans against that for a moment, checks briefly in case the keys have materialised back in the ignition then hobbles off down the track, away from the house.

Paddy limps as far as the gate to see how far he has got and is amazed to find him already out of sight ... then sees him lying motionless by the edge of the track. As he approaches he can see the perspiration glistening on his deathly white face. He appears to have fainted. Paddy shakes his shoulders, "Wake up Leo."

Leo hears his keys rattling. Sam must have taken them again – he was always fascinated with keys. *Give them back to Daddy or they might get lost.* He opens his eyes, "Paddy? You've got my keys in your pocket. Give them back."

Paddy turns and limps back towards the stables as fast as his bad leg will allow. *What the hell am I to do now? Lock him out?* Leo goes after him, making slow and unsteady progress. He sees Paddy enter the stable block and follows him, then sits down weakly on a bale of straw, gasping and holding his head in his hands. When he looks up, Paddy is standing before him, red in the face, brandishing a pitchfork. Leo is surprised for a moment then laughs out loud. "Paddy, you look like a little red devil!" The laughter transforms suddenly into tears of despair, and he lunges at Paddy, undeterred by the pitchfork. "Just give me the keys and I'll be gone!"

Paddy drops the pitchfork and runs down the row of empty loose boxes towards the two that are occupied by Snowy and Storm. Just before Snowy's box, a wheelbarrow leans upturned against the wall. Paddy hurries past it but pushes it down so it lands in Leo's path, then closes his eyes and covers his ears as a clatter of metal is followed by a sickening thud as Leo trips over it and crashes down on the concrete floor.

Snowy, terrified by the racket, rears and plunges, whilst Storm looks on with mild interest. Paddy's first priority is to calm the panicking mare and he leaps into her box with the agility that somehow comes to him easily under such circumstances.

Snowy begins to settle down and Paddy looks at Leo's motionless body, face down on the concrete. *Holy Mother, he's dead! I'll end up in jail for life – his father will see to it. Just when me tag's almost due to come off ...*

He opens the door of the loose box from the inside, stumbles out and lands beside Leo. "Wake up, man!" He starts to shake his shoulders again but thinks better of it since he is face down on concrete. He tries to roll him over and is surprised how heavy he is. *A dead weight.* He runs some cold water in a bucket and throws it over the back of his neck. Leo moans softly, but does not move. "You're alive! I thank der Lord for it! Tell yer what lad, sleep it off in der box next to Snowy, same as yer did after yer brother's wedding." Paddy spreads the horse blanket over the straw and pulls Leo's arms, trying to drag him on to it. "Come on, move yerself, will you."

Leo shuffles on to the blanket and rolls over on his back. Paddy pushes back the hair from his forehead to examine the bruise that is swelling as he watches. During his time as a jockey he has experienced and witnessed many a bump on the head and isn't overly concerned about this one.

"Oh, Paddy ... I've got the most awful headache. Ironic, really ... considering ... Please ...please don't let Beatrice or Serge in here. I don't want them to see ... I'm not supposed to be here ... I only meant to drop Ralph off and then go ... but I miscalculated ... got it all wrong, I'm so sorry ...."

Paddy rests his hands on Leo's head, around the bump. "Where were you trying to get to?"

"Just down that bridle path where we went ... the day we got Snowy's saddle. Only a mile or so. Very quiet. Should have waited until I got there but I didn't expect it all to hit so quickly ... and Ralph is such good company – it was good to have him there. I think it's because he doesn't speak ..."

"I know what yer mean, lad. It's why I like der company of der 'orses." So, Leo was going to drive to the end of the bridle path, as far as the woodland area and then swill down some pills with the remaining vodka. Paddy sits with his hands on Leo's head until he falls asleep.

Paddy looks at his watch. Six thirty-five. It would be a while yet before they were up and about at the big house. He checks on Ralph and finds him still settled on his bed, catching up with lost sleep, then feeds Snowy and Storm, turns them out in the paddock, mucks out their stables and scrubs the buckets. Seeing Leo is undisturbed by the various clattering noises he decides to have a look in the glove compartment, curious to see what he had intended to take, and thinking it might be best to remove and hide it before he wakes up. He goes to the car, looking back over his shoulder, half-expecting Leo to appear at any moment. He unlocks the glove compartment. Just as he thought – a carrier bag full of little cardboard pill boxes. Paddy cannot read but he recognises them as boxes of pain killers. He opens one box and looks inside, and then another, and another ... and with dreadful realisation he finds that all the pills have been popped through the foil. The boxes are empty. *How could I be so stupid!* Of course he had already taken them – that's why he was so desperate to get away from this place ... why he had ended up trying to walk to the bridle path: *I can't stay here ... it would spoil it for everyone. Please don't let Beatrice or Serge in here. I don't want them to see ...*

Paddy returns to the stables. "Leo! Wake up!" He runs some more cold water in the bucket and throws it in his face but this time there is no response. Not daring to feel for a pulse, Paddy runs up to the big house as fast as his bad leg will allow. Finding the back door is locked as he expected, he bangs on it then walks around outside shouting "Dominic!" at the upstairs windows, most of which are slightly open.

After what seems like an age, Dominic opens wide one of the large windows and frowns down at him, blinking against the sudden daylight. "Paddy! What's up?"

"It's Leo!" Paddy is panting, trying to get his breath back.

"It's *what*?"

"It's *Leo*. He's taken an overdose!"

"Leo's taken *what*?"

"Dominic – will yer just get yer arse down to der stables as quick as yer like – *Leo* has taken *an overdose*!"

"I'm just coming, Paddy."

Beatrice rolls over and stretches. "What's up?"

"I'm ever so sorry, but Paddy says Leo has taken an overdose. I'm just off down to the stables"

Beatrice sits up in bed. "*Leo* has taken *what*?"

29

Aftermath

The paramedics check Leo's pulse; find he still has one, and shine lights into his eyes. Beatrice, hugging herself, sobs noisily and keeps repeating, "How *could* he?"

Dominic wishes she would shut up. "Why don't you go back to the house, Bea? Serge and Fran will be up soon, and there's no-one with them."

"No! He's my brother! How *could* he?"

Paddy hands over the bag of empty pill boxes and shows them the vodka bottle. When Paddy is stressed, his Irish accent becomes particularly strong. On this occasion he is almost unintelligible.

Dominic translates; "I think he said that Leo vomited in the bathroom, and, whilst it sounded like a good old *heave-hoh,* he's not too sure if much came up because it was *dry-heaving* ... because urm ... because he *hadn't had ten pints and a kebab...* And, erm, he tripped over a wheelbarrow and banged his head. Is that about right, Paddy?"

Paddy nods, vigorously.

All of a sudden, Leo is being loaded into the back of an ambulance. "I'll go with him," says Dominic.

"No, *I'm* going with him," says Beatrice. "He's *my brother.*"

"I'll go," says Dominic. "You can get Fran's Mum to sort out breakfast for Serge and Fran and then come along later."

"No way!" says Beatrice.

One of the paramedics looks out from the back of the ambulance. "I can see you're all upset but we need to get him to hospital *now*. He's unconscious, so he won't know whether you're there or not, and since there's not much space in this vehicle, I suggest you let us take care of him and then come along together in your own time." He slams the door; the blue light is flashing already, and they watch the ambulance leave.

Serge arrives, barefoot and wearing only the tee-shirt and boxers that he sleeps in. "Wot's up, Beatie?" He puts his arms around her. "Cuddle Serge. *Summat wrong!*"

Beatrice bursts into tears again and sobs into his tee-shirt.

"Wot's up, Dom?"

Dominic sighs. "Leo's poorly. He's had to go to hospital."

Serge says, "*Leo will be fine*," in a voice that is an imitation of his father's, but his sister's anxiety transmits to him and he starts to shuffle from one foot to the other.

Beatrice wails, "*That's what everyone has always said about Leo – since as long as I can remember! He'll be fine! He*'s *not* bloody well *fine now, is he?*"

Paddy detects a whining sound that is not coming from a human and goes off to release Ralph from his living quarters. Ralph bounds excitedly around Serge and then lies down on the horse blanket where Leo had been sleeping and stuffs his nose in the well-worn trainers that Paddy had carefully unlaced and eased off Leo's feet for want of something to do whilst they were waiting for the ambulance.

Dominic says quietly to Paddy, "I noticed how swollen one of his ankles looked. I'm afraid it might be a sign of liver failure."

"No, Dom, tis a sign dat he hurt his ankle, so it is. He drank der vodka an' den wobbled off der path with der dog bed."

"Oh. That's good, I suppose ... Will you keep Ralph down here until we get back from the hospital? I'll go and get Fran's Mum to stay at the house with Fran and Serge – but I don't know if she's used to dogs."

"Aye, he's all right here, so he is."

Serge becomes agitated when Beatrice and Dominic try to go to the hospital without him. "We're going to have to take him with us," Dominic tells Beatrice. "Pat won't be able to handle him if he gets in a state when we've gone."

Serge is standing by the door, an old familiar green flask under his arm, ready to go.

"Shall I put a drop of tea in the flask for you?" asks Pat.

"Yes pleez! Nice laydee ..."

"Put your trousers on, Serge, you can't go like that," says Dominic, struggling to remain patient with everyone. "*Oh, you stay there*, I'll go and fetch them."

At the hospital they are told they must wait for news. "The doctor is with him at the moment, so if you'd like to take a seat in the waiting area he will come and have a word with you as soon as there's anything to tell."

Finally, a tired looking doctor emerges through the swing doors; scans the three of them and settles for Beatrice. "Mrs Freeman?"

"*Miss* Freeman – I'm Leo's sister."

He speaks rapidly, informing them that Leo's stomach has been pumped and he has been given an antidote for paracetamol poisoning. "There may be some permanent liver damage – it is too early yet to tell. It is a good thing he got here in time as the stomach contained a potentially lethal overdose."

Beatrice bursts into tears again and Dominic thanks the doctor who nods and hurries away to deal with the next emergency as a nurse comes through the swing doors.

"Can I see my brother?" asks Beatrice.

"He's in the recovery room at the moment. He's had his stomach pumped and isn't very happy about it. I think it would be better if you came back this evening, or tomorrow, when he's a bit more comfortable –"

"Please let me see him!" Beatrice pushes her way through the swing doors, not taking *no* for an answer. Serge goes after her, giving Dominic no choice but to follow.

The nurse calls after them. "You won't be welcome ..."

Leo is curled on his side in a foetal position, sobbing and retching into a metal bowl. He has been stripped to his boxers and is covered by a loose sheet.

"There are bumps and bruises all over him," says the nurse, looking questioningly at Dominic.

"I don't know – I wasn't there, but I gather he was stumbling around after drinking the vodka ... tripped over a wheelbarrow and wobbled off a path and hurt his ankle. I noticed it was very swollen."

"Yes, we'll x-ray it later. That's the least of his troubles at the moment."

Dominic and Serge wait in the doorway whilst Beatrice goes to Leo's bedside. Seeing him in such a wretched state she is unexpectedly overcome by anger. "Leo! How could you do this to us? To your *family! How could you!* Think of *Mum and Dad* coming back from their holiday and finding out."

He retches unproductively into the bowl; clutching his belly and ribs as he heaves.

"Stop doing that Leo! There's nothing left to come up!"

"Go away," he groans and hides beneath the sheet then re-emerges suddenly and vomits fresh blood into the bowl.

"Ugh! *That's disgusting!*"

"*Beatrice!*" Dominic is amazed at her behaviour.

The nurse asks her to leave.

Dominic steps in and takes Beatrice's arm. "Sorry Leo, it was a shock for her. Come on, Bea."

Outside the hospital, Beatrice says, "I feel so angry – I felt like hitting him!"

"I thought you were *going* to."

Serge is unusually quiet. Dominic knows that at some point he will ask what's wrong with Leo, and wonders what to tell him.

"Dom?"

"Yes, Serge."

"What time is it, Dom?"

"Half past ten."

"Serge is 'ungry. Didn't have no breakfast. McDonald's, can we? Plea-eez!"

The next day, Leo is taken to the endoscopy unit, where the cause of the internal bleeding is to be investigated.

Furious to discover he is still alive; exhausted and in pain from the persistent retching and vomiting, he is bad tempered, uncooperative and overwrought.

A nurse does her best to coax him to sit back, open his mouth, and swallow the camera. "Come on now, it's probably nothing serious but we should take a look."

"Do you really think I *care* whether or not it's *serious*? I'm not supposed to be here!" His voice is weak and croaky but loaded with wrath.

"It will only take a few minutes."

"A lethal injection would be even quicker."

"Have you any idea how many people there are in this hospital who would give anything for a healthy young body like yours?"

"Then give me the injection and they're welcome to any reusable components. I'm on the donor register." The argument makes no sense to Leo, reminding him of when his mother used to say, "Eat you cabbage – other children in the world are starving." *Then give it to them because I don't want it!*

Beatrice, Serge and Dominic turn up again at this point. Fortunately, a different nurse is on duty today, so Beatrice, quiet, pale-faced and red eyed, is sympathetically received.

"Perhaps you can talk some sense into your brother. We just want to slip a tiny camera down his throat to see what's going on."

Dominic and Serge sit in the waiting area whilst Beatrice follows the nurse through some swing doors. Leo is in a wheelchair, wearing blue-striped hospital pyjamas – his right foot heavily bandaged with white crepe. His legs are long and skinny with sharply protruding knees. He face is bruised and he glowers at Beatrice with blood-shot eyes. If it weren't for his fair hair that appears to be growing healthily, he would look about ninety. This time she fights back the tears and kneels beside the chair.

"I'm sorry about the way I carried on yesterday. I felt so ashamed afterwards." He averts his eyes from her. "And then Serge remembered he hadn't had his breakfast, so we had to go straight from here to *bloody McDonald's*." His stony face twitches and Beatrice knows him well enough to recognise it as a flicker of amusement. *Leo is still there.* "Yeah, serves me right, doesn't it ... or *karma* – as Dom would say. Anyway, there are other people here waiting to be examined and your time-slot is running out. So will you please just let the doctor get on with the job?"

Leo sighs, just wanting to sleep ... for ever. He starts to speak but nothing happens. He clears his throat and tries again; "I've already told them to get on and see to the *other people*."

Beatrice looks anxiously at the nurse. "Please, just give me a minute." She goes out to the waiting area and kneels down in front of Serge. Dominic looks at her with mild surprise, and waits.

"Serge, do you remember when you were little and you wouldn't take your medicine, Dad used to hold you on the chair whilst Mum spooned it down the back of your throat?"

Serge looks blank. "No."

"Yes you do. Like *this*." She takes his strong wrists in each of her hands, puts her body between his knees and squeezes her elbows so his legs are pinned against her sides. "Remember now?"

People walk past. A crude laugh. "*Me next, Babe!*" followed by, "Hey man! That guy looks exactly like *Serge*."

"*Yeah man*, like *Serge* would come somewhere like *this* for a *BJ*?"

Beatrice ignores them and keeps her eyes locked on Serge's.

"Yer, I wemember ... *Yeah man. Beejay ... bee-jay.*"

"Serge, do you think you could hold Leo like this whilst the doctor looks down his throat?"

"*Yeah man.*"

"*Good.* Come on then." She takes Serge's hand and beckons Dominic to follow and they all troop in just as Leo is throwing up into a bowl. Beatrice and Dominic stand awkwardly, not knowing where to look, whilst Serge appears at first fascinated but then anxious. Eventually, Leo leans back, perspiring, and the nurse takes the bowl from him.

Serge, by now, is alarmed, but it is not the vomiting that has caught his attention. "Why you in that wheelchair, Leo?" The only wheelchair users Serge has ever met are people who have never been able to walk or are never likely to walk again.

When Leo doesn't answer, Dominic says, "Leo's in a wheelchair because he hurt his foot." He points at the rather large and obvious bandage. "But don't worry, he'll be walking again in a few days."

Serge laughs, reassured. "Got pissed and fell over, did yer Leo?"

"Mmm," responds Leo, miserably, with one arm across his front and the other hand, white-knuckled, gripping the side of the chair.

"Come on, Serge," prompts Beatrice. "Remember what I asked you to do." She steers Serge to the front of Leo's chair and coaxes him into position. Serge kneels down, grasps his brother's wrists and effortlessly immobilises his arms and legs whilst Beatrice eases back his shoulders. She glances at the medics, "Go for it!"

"Keep swallowing," croons the nurse, and the procedure only takes a few minutes, like they had told him it would.

Alistaire had always disliked using physical force on his son, and would follow it up with a cuddle. Now Serge re-enacts that aspect of the ritual and Leo slumps forward and weeps on his shoulder. Serge murmurs "Good boy," in a voice that sounds surprisingly like Alistaire's and strokes his brother's back. Beatrice turns away and sobs on Dominic's shoulder and Dominic finds his own eyes are welling up. The nurse hands around the tissues.

"Hey, don't Serge get one?" says Serge and she offers him the box. He takes a tissue, folds it carefully into four and puts it in his pocket.

"Well," says the consultant, wondering if anyone is at all interested in his findings. They all shut up and look at him. He addresses Leo but glances at the rest of them, in the hope that at least one member of this family is of sound mind. "Ulcers," he says. "Quite well established by the look of them – but they have become aggravated by this recent ... *episode*. I suspect they've been troubling you for some time ... and if you haven't been sleeping or eating properly, that's why you've become so run down; emotionally as well as physically. But now we know what the problem is it shouldn't be too difficult to sort out."

"Thank you," says Leo, his natural politeness resurfacing although his eyes are closing.

The nurse turns to Beatrice and lowers her voice. "Well done. We need to put him on a drip now and get some fluids into him – he can't keep water down. Could you all stick around to make sure he behaves himself?"

"Of course we can."

Leo is submissive; the drip is fitted uneventfully, and he falls asleep.

"Is there anything else I can do?" asks Beatrice.

"If you have access to where he was living, you could bring in some of his clothes and stuff. You know, tee-shirts and underwear and whatever. Young men don't seem to wear pyjamas these days ... he'll be better with his own things."

"Yes, of course – I should have thought of that. We'll call round there now and collect them."

Derrick the gardener is riding up and down the garden, mowing the lawn. He cuts the engine when finally he notices them. "How's Ralph doing? Leo left me a note that he'd taken him to Serge's house. I haven't seen him since. Seems a bit odd, with your parents being away – I thought Leo would be here keeping an eye on the place."

"Ralph's fine," says Beatrice. "He's been with Paddy most of the time. He'll be back here as soon as Mum and Dad get home." She cannot bring herself to mention Leo and is already wondering how she is going to tell her parents.

Serge stays in the garden with Derrick whilst Beatrice and Dominic let themselves into the house and traipse upstairs to Leo's room. Beatrice looks around in anguish and pulls open the drawers and cupboard doors then goes into the ensuite shower room. "He's cleared out all his stuff. Everything is gone! So typical of Leo ... he didn't want anyone else to have to sort it out."

Dominic holds her tight. "Then it wasn't just a 'cry for help'. He really meant it."

30

Where do we go from here?

Serge constantly receives parcels of clothes from designers who hope he will be seen in public wearing their labels. Since they don't always guess his size correctly, Beatrice puts aside those that don't fit or don't appeal and gives them to her mother to donate to charity. She sorts out some of these that might do for Leo, and puts them in a bag along with an assortment of 'SErge' labelled boxer shorts.

At the hospital Beatrice is informed that Leo is much better and has been moved to a small ward. Although it is not visiting time, she is allowed to go and see him. She finds him sitting up in bed gazing into space and pulls up a chair and sits beside him.

"Oh, hi Beatrice," he says, eventually noticing she is there.

She had thought at first that he was deliberately ignoring her. She scans the other beds. The one next to Leo's is empty but the others are occupied by elderly gentlemen who are snoring. Another old man appears in the doorway with a Zimmer frame, pauses to cough chestily and then progresses slowly to the bed next to Leo's. Beatrice smiles and says "Hello," but it seems he is deaf and cannot see very well either.

"I should have brought you some books," says Beatrice. "I'll bring some next time. What would you like? There's a place here where you can buy newspapers. Shall I pop and get one?" The ward is hot and stuffy. The idea of an errand appeals to her.

"No thanks." He has no interest in what's going on in the world and is bitterly disappointed to be still part of it owing to the failure of his plan ...

"I brought you some clothes – they're just rejects of Serge's." She resists the urge to ask what he did with all his stuff and takes a pair of grey, narrow-legged jeans from the top of the bag. "I think these will look great on you. They're too small for Serge and they're button-fly, so no good on two counts. Dom was eyeing them up but they'd have to be a foot shorter and a foot wider to fit him."

"Thank you," says Leo, mechanically, without looking. "That's very kind of you." He wonders vaguely whether the skip has been taken away from the office. Not that he wants his things back as he would only have to get rid of them again at a later date. But now he has acquired some *more* stuff, which of course he is going to need for the time being, until this apathy lifts and he has the energy to formulate a new plan of action... His old, familiar clothes would have been preferable in the meantime.

"Stop being so *polite*, it's *me*, your *sister.* Have they said how long you'll be in here?" She glances around, knowing she couldn't possibly spend even one night in this place.

"No." He hasn't given it a thought.

"Is the food okay?"

"Yes, it's fine."

She doubts he has even tried it. "So, you're okay here?"

"Yes thanks ... fine."

"Oh well ... I suppose I'd better go. It's not visiting time yet, but they said I could have a few minutes."

He nods. "Thanks for coming."

"If there's anything you want, they've got my number. Ask them to give me a call." She hurries out gratefully into the fresh air.

Judith and Alistaire return from their holiday, suntanned and relaxed, and ask casually if anything happened whilst they were away. Beatrice had contemplated only telling them about the stomach ulcers but the whole story comes pouring out in full drama. They turn up at the hospital, bewildered; Judith already in tears. Alistaire's tan has paled to white-faced incredulity, and he demands to know where his son is and then storms along the corridors, following overhead signposts and flinging open swing doors with Judith trotting along behind. He hesitates in the doorway, thinking this must be the wrong ward. These are all old men – shrunken with skin stretched over sharp bones.

"Leo!" Judith hurries to his bedside, hugging his shoulders and dripping tears into his hair.

"Judith! Leave him alone and sit down there," commands Alistaire, and then his anger is unleashed, fuelled by shock and disbelief as he tells Leo how badly he has let them down after the privileged upbringing they have provided and the sacrifices they have made ... it is similar, albeit more eloquent, to Beatrice's initial reaction. Leo looks vacantly at his knees and saying nothing, which infuriates Alistaire into twisting the knife. "Look what you've done to your mother! I hope you're *pleased* with the results of your *pathetic, attention-seeking* antics. Frankly I'm *amazed* and *disgusted.* Come on, Judith, we're going home."

It is only later, when dinner is being served, that Leo is found to be tearful and shaking. The food fumes are making him nauseas and the kitchen staff alert the nurses. Glenda, a solid, middle-aged dependable type, who has taken a shine to this dour, fine-boned and rather posh young man, volunteers to take a look even though she is on her well-earned break. She takes his arm and coaxes him off the bed and he hobbles out of the ward and through a fire exit that leads to a narrow paved area where there is a wooden bench.

He inhales the fresher air. "Thank you."

"That's okay. I'm glad to see some emotion from you. It looked to me like you'd switched from reactive to clinical."

"Oh," says Leo. He hasn't a clue what she is talking about but is aware of being in a better space.

Glenda looks at her watch and then at his feet on the cold concrete, the right ankle still visibly swollen. He doesn't seem to have footwear of any kind. "I've got to go now. Will you be okay here for a bit?"

"Yes. Thank you. It's better out here."

She checks her pockets, finds a tissue and holds it up to the light unfolded to check that it hasn't been used before giving him it to blow his nose. The door is flung open and two porters step out and light up cigarettes.

"I hope you don't mind passive smoking," says Glenda. "Staff tend to pop out here for a quick ciggie. They're not supposed to but -"

Leo shakes his head, "I'm not at all health-conscious."

A few days later, when he is sitting in the same place, his mother returns alone, bearing a letter. Glenda happens to be on duty; immediately identifies Judith as Leo's mother and shows her where he is. Judith sits down next to him on the bench and has to nudge him to get his attention.

"Oh ... hi Mum." He casts her a glance and then looks away again.

Judith holds the letter in front of him. "Dad sorted through the mail, and this was amongst it. He said you would recognise the envelope the same as he did."

Leo looks at the envelope. It is the decree absolute. He has seen plenty of these but all they ever meant to him was another case nearing completion. This one is different ... it is the final nail in the coffin of his own marriage.

"Aren't you going to open it?" prompts Judith.

He takes the document from the envelope, checks it briefly and puts it back in.

"Would you like me to file it away somewhere safe?"

"Yes please." He hands it back to her.

"Dad thought it might help you to *move on* ... knowing it was all over now ..."

"I was expecting it. At least Bridget will be happy now."

"Dad also said that you had a speeding fine and a parking ticket - both dated the second Wednesday of our holiday - shortly before ... They were sent to the office, where your car is registered, of course. Dad said you must be careful now –

since that's another three points on your license. Leo ... Look at me, *please*."

He turns and looks at her. "Oh *Leo* ..." Her eyes fill up and he looks away again. She goes on, "The parking ticket was at the hospital local to your old house ... so we didn't think it could be anything to do with Sam ... but when we called at Sally's place with the presents we brought back for her and Sam, it looked empty and there was a 'To Let' sign outside. "What's been going on? *Please* tell me."

He sighs, and looks down at the paving stones. It sounds as though his parents have exhausted their joint investigative skills before asking. "Bridget phoned. She'd gone into labour early. Matt wasn't there. I took her to the hospital. She had the baby – a girl. Then Matt turned up. I was supposed to be at Sally's. When I got there she told me she was going to Australia with her parents to start a new life. She said I would never see Sam again." He stops and waits for her to say, "*Oh Leo*," but she doesn't say anything and he turns and sees the silent tears running down her face. "Don't, Mum." He puts an arm around her shoulders. "It doesn't matter now ..."

"What do you mean, *it doesn't matter ...*?"

As Judith is leaving she sees Glenda again. "Would you keep an eye on him for me? I just told him his divorce has been finalised. He seems so ... *devoid of emotion*. I don't understand it."

"He was very emotional after your previous visit," says Glenda accusingly.

"Oh dear, I'm sorry. I'm afraid his father is still angry ... and can't come to terms with ... with what Leo tried to do. Leo always seems to have sailed so *effortlessly* through life; a brilliant mind, top marks in exams and nothing was ever too much for him. He's the one everyone always turns to because he's so quick-thinking and competent ..."

"But then something tripped the switch," says Glenda. She looks again at Judith's kind, tired face and softens to her a little. "Don't worry, I'll watch him."

A few days later Dominic arrives at the hospital with Paddy. It is pouring with rain so they go to the ward to look for Leo. "He's in the day room," says the ward sister, and directs them to it. "The doctor told him this morning he can go home any time after tomorrow, and carry on his treatment as an outpatient. I thought he'd have been pleased but he seems quite glum about it."

In the day room, a television is blaring with an old man in a wheelchair asleep in front of it. Leo is sitting by the window, watching the rain. He stands up when they come in and looks positively pleased to see them. He is wearing the new grey jeans and a white tee-shirt that Beatrice brought in but has nothing on his feet. His hair has not been cut for a while and is beginning to flop around his pale face. He looks so delicate and vulnerable that Dominic can hardly believe this is the same man whose strong presence used to so intimidate him when he first began working with Serge.

Leo's voice is weak and they can't hear what he says. He frowns at the television and makes an effort to shout. "I tried turning it down but he woke up and said he couldn't hear it, so I turned it up again and he went back to sleep. Are you okay Paddy?" He thinks Paddy looks rather anxious and sweaty.

"Don't like these places. Dey gives me der willies."

"I noticed a cafe area in the foyer, near the main entrance," says Leo. "We could go along there; it's a bit less ... hospitalish."

"Good idea," says Dominic.

The nurse with the medication trolley appears in the doorway just as they are about to walk out. "Pills first please, Leo," she says and hands him a cup of water and a shallow dish of assorted pills and capsules.

"Are they all yours?" asks Dominic. "No wonder you've no appetite for food if you've got to munch through that lot."

Leo is having trouble swallowing the pills, some of which are quite large. He re-fills the water cup and has another go.

Paddy, anxious to get out of this place, becomes impatient. "It's a pity yer weren't as feckin' reticent about taking pills a couple of weeks ago," he says, and makes Leo laugh just as he is about to swallow. The water goes down the wrong way sending him into a painful fit of coughing and he sits down, weakly.

"You go on; I'll catch up with you in a minute."

"No, we'll wait," says Paddy.

By the time they have walked along the corridors to the cafe, Leo is exhausted. The bandage has gone from his ankle but he is still limping and his right foot is shaded grey, purple and yellow. "I never realised I was so unfit," he says as they sit down at a table in a corner.

"It'll soon come back," says Dominic. "Those jeans look great on you, by the way. Beatrice said they would. You need a belt though, until you fatten up a bit. I'll sort one out. Serge has got hundreds. In fact he's got more belts than anything. I suppose there's more scope for guessing the right size of a belt. There are some black tee-shirts as well. Serge doesn't like wearing black."

Leo shrugs his shoulders. "Thanks."

"Anyway, what would you like, a coffee or something?"

"Nothing for me thanks. I'd get them for you, only I don't have any cash."

Dominic goes off to buy the coffee and feels suddenly angry with Alistaire and Judith for being so wrapped up with how *they feel* about what Leo has done that they didn't even think to give him a few quid for sundries ... and a pair of slippers wouldn't have gone amiss.

When Leo is left alone with Paddy, he says, "I'm very sorry for putting you through what must have been quite an ordeal. I honestly only intended to drop Ralph off with you and then go."

"I know yer did, lad, an' yer kept telling me so at the time. I'm just glad it worked out differently."

"But ... I know you've been down ... twice in the last few months ... when Serge first met you, and then again in the prison. You were the *last* person I should have involved. It must have resurrected many bad memories for you."

Dominic returns with two coffees. "Are you sure you don't want anything, Leo?"

Leo has observed the queue lengthening significantly since Dominic joined it. He winks at Paddy. "Well, maybe I will have one after all ..."

Paddy shouts after him, "Dominic! He's joking!"

"Sit down, Dom," says Leo.

Dominic does as he's told. "It's good to have you back, Leo. Erm ... talking of which, the *ward guard dog* told us you're going home soon."

Leo's face clouds. "They need the bed."

Paddy says, "But surely you don't want ter stay in *dis place*?"

"No, you're right ... but *here* – you never really sleep so you don't forget and then have to re-remember. I really *can't* go back to my parents' place. I can't face Dad ... and Mum keeps crying ..."

"Where yer going then?" asks Paddy, bluntly.

"I quite fancy going away for a long walk. Back-packing. I've done it before, some years ago. A small tent if it's raining, otherwise you sleep beneath the stars."

Dominic looks concerned. "But you're not fit, Leo. It took all of your strength to get from the day room to here, and your foot's obviously still painful. You'd die of exposure an hour after the temperature went below body heat ..."

"Ah, yes. Good point." Leo grins, as of old, displaying his even white teeth.

Dominic thinks; *He has already formulated his next plan of action.* He looks hard at Leo. He's going to walk away into the horizon and die of hypothermia, like some tribal elder whose life has run its course.

Leo lowers his eyes. Damn. He had always found Dominic a bit slow on the uptake and didn't expect him to pick up that thought. Yet again, his judgement has failed him.

Dominic stands up. "I just got a text from Beatrice. I'll pop outside and give her a call - make sure everything's okay."

Leo stands up, "Please don't!"

"Why not?" asks Dominic.

Leo scans his surroundings, as if expecting the *men in white coats* to appear at any moment and take him away. "She didn't text you – you just made that up. Were you going to get me *sectioned*?"

"*No.*" Dominic sits down again. "Okay, she *didn't text me*, and maybe I have questioned the wisdom of simply *sending you home* ... but -" The cafe has suddenly become very rowdy. "Shall we go and sit in the Land Rover? It's parked quite close and it will be easier to talk."

Carrying the coffee mugs they walk across the car park; Dominic and Paddy skirting around the puddles and Leo, barefoot, hitching up his jeans and wading through them. Dominic gets in the driver's seat and Leo and Paddy sit together in the back, Leo swinging his feet to dry them off a little before tucking them in and shutting the door. He twiddles his wedding ring ... and then the hospital identity band on his wrist and waits for Dominic to say something.

"I was going to phone Beatrice because I wanted to ask you to come and stay with us at Hardwicke Heights but I thought it was only fair to mention it to her first, in case she's got enough on with your celebrity brother and his missus. I *know* she'll be fine with it, but we, urm, get along better if I consult her first about everything. It makes her feel ... *important*."

"Oh ... I see. Well it was a *very kind thought*, and I know how ungrateful this will sound, but I'm not sure I could tolerate Serge and Fran *going on* all the time with Beatrice shrilling over the top of them. If I do have any remaining sanity, *that* would extort it."

Dominic smiles, "I can understand that, but I would have thought both your Mum and Dad's place and Hardwicke Heights are big enough for you to find a peaceful space ... You need to rest and get your strength back before you take a hike."

"But outdoors you don't get the *empty bed*, the *silent room* and the white ceilings bearing down ... The night sky is better."

"I got a suggestion," says Paddy. "I don't know how much yer remember about what happened der last time yer were at der stables, and maybe yer don't wish ter go back there ... but der loose box next to Snowy's is still free. Twould be like halfway house to camping."

Leo's face lights up. "The stables are the most peaceful place I've ever slept ..."

"But you've only ever slept there when you've been blind drunk or else concussed, stoned *and* blind drunk."

"That's true." His smile fades. "Paddy, I don't remember very clearly what happened. Did I erm ... did I *hurt* you?"

"No, lad, yer didn't. What *do* you remember?"

"I can only recall it as one of those dreams where you're trying to go somewhere but you're wading through treacle in thick fog."

Paddy nods, understanding.

"I was trying to get to the bridle path just down the lane but my legs wouldn't work and I'd lost my car keys. I thought Sam must have picked them up – but then Sam turned into *you* ... and I remember chasing you through the stables – determined to get them back. But it goes blank after that. I don't know what happened next – and I was afraid I might have ... *mugged* you to get the keys ... One of the nurses said I looked as if I'd been fighting."

"No, lad. I shoved a wheelbarrow in yer way and yer went flying over it and smacked yer head on der concrete floor and got knocked out."

Leo laughs, "Oh, well *that's* all right then!"

"Snowy didn't think so, she nearly went through der roof. Anyway, if yer coming back ter der stables, which I *hope* you are, you must promise me there'll be no more *antics*. Much as I like yer company, I don't want ter have ter watch yer like a babbie."

"I promise, Paddy. Best behaviour. You have my word."

They walk back to the ward and are greeted with a frown. "*There* you are! I was about to send out a search party."

Dominic blinks away an image of Leo limping barefoot along the M25 and explains to the nurse that they had been making arrangements for Leo's home-coming, and agrees to come back for him the day after tomorrow.

"Make it the afternoon," says the nurse, "otherwise you might have to wait whilst they sort out his prescription."

When Dominic and Paddy say goodbye, Leo thanks them effusively. "I promise not to cramp your style, Paddy. You won't even know I'm there."

"We'll see you the day after tomorrow, in the afternoon," re-affirms Dominic. *Poor Leo, he seems so grateful ...*

"Thank you! Oh, do either of you know where my shoes are? I'm sure I was wearing some."

Paddy turns back and winks. "Your shoes are with yer car keys. You'll have them the day after tomorrow."

31

A place to heal

The evening before Leo is due to leave hospital, Alistaire and Judith visit the stables at Hardwicke Heights with some of his camping equipment that had been stored in their loft. "We didn't bring his tent," said Judith. "I was afraid it might encourage him to go camping."

Paddy looks at the camping stove, cooking utensils and sleeping bag. "I was going to put der guest bed in his loose box – you know, der one that slides beneath my bed. But he wouldn't have it. Said I had ter save it as new for Tommy – for when he comes ter visit. Anyway, let's stick dis lot in der stables and he can do what he likes with it."

Alistaire and Judith follow him, curious to see why this place so appeals to Leo.

"I just gave 'em their feed," says Paddy.

Alistaire and Judith are not used to horses, but feel that this must mean something – most likely that they have picked a bad time to intrude and they are disturbing the horses. Storm's head is firmly in the bucket as they walk past and they do not notice her. "*Oh, sorry*," says Judith when Snowy, clearly alarmed, tosses her head and some sort of fodder flies from her mouth. She brushes flaked maize from her hair whilst Alistaire extracts a grain of something that has gone down her back.

Alistaire and Judith deposit Leo's kit in the appointed space beside the somewhat fearsome mare - who is now snorting and rolling her eyes - then retreat to their vehicle. "Oh, and there's this little bench-seat that Derrick made for him. Would that go in the corner of his stable?" Next, Judith hoists a shopping bag from the back, "And I brought these ... I did some baking today – there's a fruit cake and some quiches and scones and Cornish pasties. There's also a bottle of whiskey, as a little *thank you* from me for ... *having* him. I don't know much about whiskey, but they told me it was a good one."

Alistaire looks disapproving. "Please don't let Leo have any of that. It seems he's damaged his liver ... the *idiot*." He opens the car door.

"Mr Freeman!" Alistaire's final word was so loaded with contempt that Paddy is obliged to say his piece. This is a confrontation he has rehearsed in his mind several times over, so he is confident of the delivery but terrified of the consequences.

"Yes, Patrick?"

"Mr Freeman, do you mind if I speak openly to you?"

"Of course I don't. It's the way I prefer to be spoken to. Come on, man, get it off your chest."

Paddy takes a deep breath and tries to steady his nerves. "Mr Freeman ... Almost a year ago when I was in prison, in suicidal despair, you stepped in and saved me from der brink. Now I see you thinking ... like depression is some sort of weakness dat yer cannot tolerate in yer own family. If you can show der *compassion* dat yer did for me - a stranger - and a convicted criminal at dat, *how come yer can't do der same for yer own beloved son*?"

Alistaire stares at him without moving or speaking. Paddy can hear his heart thumping in his ears. "Have you finished?" demands Alistaire, after what seems to Paddy like ages.

"Yes, Sir. And if yer feel yer must ask me ter leave for being so outspoken then I'll ... then ... then I very much hope yer don't ... Please ..."

Alistaire shakes his head. "We *need* you here, Patrick." He gets in his car frowning discontentedly. Judith gives Paddy a subtle but reassuring smile of approval that Alistaire does not see, and gets in the passenger seat.

Leo spends his first day sitting outside the stable block, watching Snowy and Storm eating grass in the paddock. The weather is nicely warm and settled for the end of September but coming from a hot hospital, being so thin and hardly daring to eat, he feels cold, and sits on his rolled up sleeping bag with the horse blanket draped over his shoulders - the weight of it making them ache after a few hours.

"Why don't yer sit on der 'orse blanket and wrap the duvet around yer? It's lighter but just as warm."

"Sorry? Oh, yes. Thanks, Paddy I didn't think of that."

Paddy is slightly manic to begin with; feeling he should be seen to be doing the whole time, mostly on account of speaking his mind to Alistaire and still fearful of some delayed repercussion. Once he realises that Leo has no interest in his activities and appears to be in some kind of a dream world inside his head, he relaxes and carries on as normal. On the second evening he licks his finger and holds it in the air whilst watching the clouds and asks Leo, "Do yer fancy helping me make a camp fire?"

It seems a long time before Leo notices someone is speaking to him, but finally his heavy-lidded eyes turn their attention to Paddy.

Paddy gesticulates with mock Semaphore; "Earth ter Leo – come in Leo!"

Leo smiles. "Sorry?"

"I said *will yer help me make der camp fire?*"

Paddy watches approvingly as Leo comes to life to get the fire going, knowing that there is something innate in man about the challenge of lighting a camp fire that will always ignite enthusiasm. "Dat's it – bit more paper under dat bit. Der yer go!"

Leo, crouched in front of the rising fire; glances up at Paddy for approval.

"Well done lad!"

Dominic and Beatrice become aware of the fire and come to see what is going on, with Serge and Franchesca following behind. Franchesca, knowing Leo has been poorly puts her arms round him for a cuddle and gives him a small blue teddy bear. Beatrice explains that Fran wants the bear to sleep in the stable with Leo, to guard him.

"Oh ... thank you, Fran, how very kind," says Leo, deeply touched.

Paddy is glad they have all turned up on account of the vast amount of food that Judith brought along that is occupying his kitchen. "Serge, come and give me a hand carrying dis lot out."

Beatrice says, "Dom, pop back up to the house would you, and fetch a couple of bottles of wine and some beer. Oh, and bring some of those cardboard plates that were left over from the wedding."

Dominic returns in time to prevent Serge from eating an entire quiche before they've had the chance to cut it up. Meanwhile, Beatrice is trying to force Leo to eat a slice of fruit cake because their mother had baked it *especially for him*, because it had *always been his favourite.*

"Maybe it was, some years ago," says Leo. "But I don't feel it would go down too well right now."

"Oh *go on* Leo, if you don't eat anything else you should at least have some of *this*." She holds the cardboard plate in his face until he finally takes it and examines it doubtfully.

"I'll save it for tomorrow ..."

"It's all in your *mind,* Leo," says Beatrice, refilling her wine glass and pouring a small measure for Fran and Serge. "It's all in his mind, *isn't it*, Dom?"

"What is?" asks Dominic, but the fire is suddenly burning particularly well, and Beatrice's rapt attention has been drawn to it. Dominic pops the top off his beer and takes a swig, then says guiltily, "Sorry, Leo, do you mind us drinking? I just remembered you're not allowed to."

"Not at all. I was never much of a drinker anyway - apart from the odd occasion."

Paddy says, "And it was a *very* odd occasion, to be sure, as I remember it!"

They all laugh. Dominic turns to Paddy. "What do you prefer, beer or wine?"

"Neither really," says Paddy, "if by *beer* yer mean dat *fizzy lager* stuff. However, der's a nice bottle of single malt dat I was supposed to be hiding from Leo ... so if he doesn't mind?" Leo shakes his head. "Then I'll check dat der 'orses are all right with der fire and I'll fill up me own glass."

Paddy returns with his tumbler of whiskey and glowers at Beatrice when he finds she is still trying to make Leo eat the fruit cake. "You've got to start eating again Leo," she says. "I remember the last time I had a bug – well, okay, a *really bad hangover* – I had to force myself to eat, and after the first few bites I realised I was *starving*." She sees Paddy frowning at her. "I *know* my brother, Paddy. If he got a bug when he was a kid he could hold out for days without eating. Mum used to be frantic. I guess he has a *puking phobia* thing?"

"Well, I doubt *anybody enjoys* chucking up," says Paddy.

They all watch whilst Leo eats the cake to shut her up and then he is allowed to retreat within and watch the flames, enjoying their company but allowing the conversation to drift over him - and now that he has eaten the cake they seem happy enough to leave him alone.

Later, when the fire has died down, the night sky is still bright, owing to a beautiful full moon. Paddy does his final check on the horses and finds Leo perched on Derrick's low bench, bent double and rocking back and forth with a bucket in front of his feet.

"Oh," says Paddy. "Feckin fruit cake giving yer jip?" He sits next to Leo on the bench for a moment and looks down at his curled-up toes but the bench isn't big enough for two and he feels awkward sitting so close. He stands up again. "Well, I dare say yer don't want me ter stay here and watch?" Leo shakes his head and sweat runs down from his temples and drips off his hair. "Can I get yer anything?"

"No thanks."

“Well, yer know where I am. Just holler if yer want anything.”

Leo nods, gritting his teeth, looking very much as if he is trying not to holler right now.

Paddy leaves him to it, not expecting to sleep for worrying about him, but the whiskey works its magic and it is not until much later that he wakes up with a start and hears the outside tap running. He steps from the bedroom to the living area and listens at the open kitchen window to the sound of a bucket being swilled out, teeth being cleaned with water hitting the bucket, and then the bucket being swilled out again. He hears Snowy’s hooves fidgeting on the stable floor, followed by Leo’s voice, weak and tired, softly reassuring her, and the sound of the bolt going across the stable door ... then all is quiet and he goes back to bed.

In the morning when he goes to feed the horses Leo is sleeping peacefully but curled on his side with his knees tucked up. Paddy takes advantage and studies him for a moment, taking in the pallor of his face and not much liking the bluish tinge to his lips and the bruised look around his eyes. He moves on and starts preparing the buckets of feed, trying not to make a noise but Storm becomes impatient; pawing the ground and rattling her stable door.

“Sorry, lad, I tried not to wake you,” says Paddy, once the horses’ heads are firmly in the buckets. “How yer feeling?”

Leo looks at him with half-opened bloodshot eyes. “Okay now thanks ...”

“Der fruitcake took its time coming up, diddun it?”

“Mmm ... I must have disturbed you, since you noticed. Sorry. What time *was* it?”

“Ten past three. Any blood came up with it?”

“Mmm ... What time is it now?”

“Five past six. When these two have finished their grub I’ll turn ‘em out and we’ll leave you in peace. Go back ter sleep.”

Leo drifts off again almost immediately and Paddy grins mischievously as he pops the little blue teddy bear beside him so it is the first thing he will see when he opens his eyes.

Some hours later Beatrice appears with a notebook and pencil and a slightly anxious expression. Paddy stands up to greet her. "Is Leo all right? I thought he'd have been up for a shower by now."

Leo has opted to use the facilities at Hardwicke House whenever possible, in the hope that Paddy will put up with him staying at the stables for longer if his living accommodation is not invaded too often.

"He had a bad night ... but he's better now." Paddy nods towards the stables and follows some distance behind her.

Leo, sitting on his bench with the unzipped sleeping bag wrapped around his shoulders, reassures his sister that he is fine.

"You don't *look* fine," says Beatrice.

"Yer should've seen him last night," says Paddy, "after you made him eat that fruit cake."

"I never *made* him eat it," says Beatrice. "Which reminds me ..." she flourishes her notepad. "I'm doing an internet grocery order this afternoon, so what do you want?"

"Just my usual list, please," says Paddy, "but without any tea or coffee dis time – and I don't need no ketchup or nuthin'."

Leo starts to look stressed as Beatrice tries to make him place an order and he has no idea what to ask for.

"Get 'im some tins o' soup," says Paddy. "He can heat dem on der camp fire. And some baking potatoes an' a role of tin foil – they'll go in der fire. He's more likely ter eat what he's cooked himself on der fire. And get some soft white bread and a packet of butter and some instant porridge – yer know – not der coarse stuff dat I get but a smooth one."

"I know, the stuff that looks like baby food."

"Well, I diddun like ter say ... an' get some milk and honey maybe."

"What sort of soup do you want?" asks Beatrice, scribbling quickly on her notepad.

"Anything ..." says Leo.

"Don't get tomato," says Paddy, "or if it comes back up again he won't know if ders blood in it or not."

"Urgh!" says Beatrice.

"I'll give you my debit card," says Leo.

"Don't worry for now; I'll open up a tab for you."

"Okay. Next time you see Mum, ask her for my cheque book. It's in the drawer where they keep the passports and car documents."

"Oh, and Pat asked me to get your laundry bag."

Paddy goes off to fetch it whilst Beatrice explains to Leo. "Fran's Mum has taken on laundry duties – she does the ironing as well. It's great. She reckons it *gives her a role* as well as a chance to spend some time with Fran ... and Fran loves watching the clothes go round in the machines. If you hear shrieking coming from the laundry it's only that she's spotted something she recognises whirling past."

Paddy returns with the laundry bag and Beatrice sets off back to the house. "Wait a minute," says Leo. "I'll walk up with you and have a shower – create some more washing." He stands up slowly, not quite managing to straighten up. "Have I got any clean clothes that you know of?"

"Yes, I noticed your black jeans and some tee-shirts had made it through the system. Pat doesn't know whose is what, so she puts all the clean stuff in the airing cupboard and you have to reclaim it from there - unless you want to sew name tags on your knickers."

They walk slowly up the long path to the house. "Do you need any shaving stuff?"

"I don't know. Do you think I do?"

She runs a finger through the beginnings of a beard. "It rather suits you. It makes your cheeks look a little less hollow – and it kind of goes with the shaggy hair. I never realised your hair was so thick – you always kept it so short. It looks okay. I'll order you a trimmer off the internet – then you can go for the *designer stubble* look. That *will* suit you."

The camp fire becomes an evening ritual if the weather is right; and it is something both Paddy and Leo look forward to, whilst the novelty soon wears off for the rest of the household. The paddock is sufficiently remote that no-one will be bothered by the smoke and it provides them with a comforting medium ... sometimes they talk and sometimes they don't, and they never ask each other questions. One evening, Leo tries to describe to Paddy the despair he feels if he allows himself to believe he will never seeing Sam again. Paddy listens solemnly, watching the flames and nodding with understanding. Leo hesitates, then says casually, "I expect you miss Tommy ..."

"I don't want him ter see me tagged – I'd be ashamed." Paddy displays the ankle bracelet that Leo had forgotten about. "This comes off in just over four weeks – and then I'm a free man. Dat's when I'd like ter see Tommy." He hangs his head for a moment, "Only I don't know how ter go about it ... on account of his mother."

"Well, in the first instance you send her a polite letter, clearly stating your case; telling her how much you miss Sam – sorry, I mean *Tommy,* and that you believe he would enjoy coming here for weekend visits, and maybe some weekdays during the school holidays. You would be able to teach him to ride in a safe environment and allow the bond that you have already established with your son to develop – since it is important, at Tom's age, to –"

"*Leo.* Yer *know* I can't write. And so does my *ex*."

"We'll write the letter together. We only have to explain that your solicitor is helping you to write the letter – that should give it some leverage for a start. And if a polite letter doesn't suffice then I'll represent you in court - if it comes to it ... but I doubt it will. And I *always* win." Paddy detects a hardening of the eyes; a cold blue glint; a set of the jaw. It is a glimpse of the former, confident Leo, who used to intimidate him without even trying. When he looks again, it has gone; his eyes are down, thoughts concealed behind long eyelashes ... maybe it was just a reflection from the fire, flickering in his eyes. "We'll write the letter tomorrow, if you feel like it" says Leo. "We can put it aside until your tag comes off – at least then it's ready to go." He coaxes a foil-wrapped potato from the fire with a knife and prods it. "Look at *that*, done to *perfection* this time." He extracts another and sends it quickly in Paddy's direction.

"You passed me dat like it was a hot potato; *hah, hah*," says Paddy.

Paddy seems unusually pensive and withdrawn in the morning. Leo leaves him to it, just as Paddy has always respected Leo's space when an introspective mood comes over him - and gets on with painting the perimeter fence of the paddock. It is a project he has taken on since his strength has started to return and he feels the need to do something, and Paddy suggested it would be a good job to do before the winter. Leo had impressed everyone by quickly working out how much paint he would need, taking into account the paint's expected coverage per square metre and calculating the surface area of the eight foot planks and five foot posts, and estimating the number of fence sections required to surround a two point five acre paddock. Now he is doing a thorough job of painting the fence whilst checking its stability and pausing to hammer in a nail where necessary.

Paddy approaches him huffily. "I thought yer was going ter help me write dat letter today."

"Yes, of course," says Leo. He rests the paint brush on the upturned lid of the paint pot and stands up. "I wasn't sure if you wanted to. I know I got a bit carried away with the idea, because I was thinking about Sam. It's his fourth birthday next week and I can't even send him a card. I thought maybe I was projecting my own stuff on you, when your feelings – and the surrounding situation are quite different from mine. I thought perhaps I was interfering."

"Well ... maybe there's times when yer *need* someone to *interfere* ..."

Leo puts the lid on the paint. "Come on, let's go and ask Beatrice if we can use her laptop."

Beatrice is sitting at the kitchen table watching television with Fran and texting on her mobile at the same time. Dominic has taken Serge to Poole Harbour for a photo-shoot on a boat. "Of course you can," she says. "It's already on in the front room. Oh, just let me come and log out of Facebook." She walks down the hallway with them.

Facebook is something of a mystery to Leo. "Is Sally ...?"

She shakes her head. "Her account is still deactivated and none of my friends have a contact for her. Mum even phoned the letting agency she was renting her house off – but they had no forwarding address. Not that they'd have given it out – but they might have been willing to pass on a message to her. Anyway, I'll leave you to it."

Leo opens up a new document, and types in the address. "What date is your tag due to be removed?"

Paddy answers without hesitation.

"That's the date I'll put on the letter. Sorry, but you'll have to remind me of her name."

"Whose name?"

"Your ex-wife; the person we are writing to."

"*Oh*. That'll be Gina."

"Do you spell that G-i-n-a?"

"How the feck do I know?"

Leo types it and shows it to him. "Does that look familiar?"

Paddy squints at the combination of letters, trying to equate the pattern with what he's seen on birthday cards and such, in the past. "I think dat's about right."

Leo types the names Tom, Tommy and Thomas. Paddy recognises all three and they agree on Tom for the context of this letter.

"Would you like to learn to read?" Leo asks, casually.

"No, I don't think so. Dominic already offered ter teach me, so he did, but I got along without it dis far, and ... well I don't like ter be made ter feel so *thick*."

"Did the kids at school call you *thick*?"

"Aye. Not dat I went ter school very often, me Ma was a *Traveller*, and she did her best to teach me herself, but it was all just a jumble o' letters."

"You're certainly not *thick* – your mind is very shrewd. I suspect you're dyslexic. Imagine how much more confidence you might have if you could perceive yourself as *dyslexic* rather than *thick*. There are tests you could take, you know?"

"Dat's all very well but shall we just get on with dis letter for now?"

"Yes – of course ... *Dear Gina*," Leo starts by explaining to Gina that this letter is expressing Patrick's own sentiments that have been put into written word by a friend who is a solicitor. He says the words out loud as he is types. He stops and turns to Paddy. "So, what level of access are you going to request?"

Paddy shrugs his shoulders. "I dunno."

"Okay. How would you like it to be?" Paddy looks baffled. "Alternate weekends for example? Or maybe just a day visit at first and then take it from there?"

"Get Tommy here for a day and he'll want ter be back for a weekend and den for a week."

"Good, yes, Tom is of an age where he can weigh things up for himself. So, what would you like to say to Gina?"

"Nothing. I never want ter speak ter der feckin bitch again."

Leo laughs.

"Leo man, would yer just get on an' write der bloody letter. I'll tell yer if there's anything in it that I diddun want ter say."

"Okay." Leo types vigorously with two fingers - dictating the words as he types them. Paddy listens and studies the carpet, with the occasional nod and grunt of agreement. Leo's voice falters then stops and Paddy looks up to see tears drifting down his cheeks.

"Oh. Sorry, lad. This is your letter to Sally about Sam – der letter yer would like ter send. Let's leave it now since it's upsetting you."

"No ... please let's carry on ... it's ... it's therapeutic."

Paddy fetches a box of tissues from the dining table and places it on the desk. "Otherwise you'll short-circuit yer sister's computer."

"Thanks Paddy. I'm sorry for making you feel awkward."

"I don't feel *awkward*. I doubt there's much yer could do in front of me now that would make me feel *awkward*. Just finish der letter whilst yer on a roll an' den read it ter me when yer done. And make sure yer spell *Tom* and not *Sam*. And my ex is called *Gina*, not *Sally*. Okay?"

"Okay." Leo carries on typing, pausing now and again to grab another tissue, and when he is done he casts a glance back over it before reading it out to Paddy. Anticipating Paddy's approval, he looks round when he has finished and there is no comment, and then passes him the tissues. "Is there anything you want me to change or take out?"

Paddy shakes his head. "But she'll know them's not my words."

"But does it express how you *feel*? That's the important thing." He glances back over what he has written. He has tried to keep it simple and direct.

"Yes – it expresses perfectly how I feel. I just diddun know like ... I just diddun think dat anyone else would understand ..."

Beatrice comes breezing in and stops abruptly. "Oh, sorry."

"It's, okay, we're just indulging in a bit of therapy," says Leo. He prints off two copies of the letter – one to send and one to file, helps himself to a couple of envelopes and glances at the letter his sister is holding.

"Oh yes," she says. "That last cheque you gave me bounced."

"Oh? I'm *sorry*. I'll just have a look at my bank account ... that's if I can remember how to log on." He tries unsuccessfully a couple of times. "One more failed attempt and I disable my access." He thinks for a minute and tries again. "Ah, there we go." He looks at his online statement. "Oh."

"What?" asks Bridget, looking over his shoulder.

"It seems I've been paying Bridget and Matt's utility bills and council tax. Bridget took over the mortgage, so I assumed they would take on the bills at the same time ... maybe they did, but the direct debits are still going out for some reason. And I didn't get paid for September. Never mind. There's a couple of grand in a savings account I can transfer in."

"Is that all you've got? A *couple of grand*?"

"Yes. I only finished paying off my student loan last year."

"I thought solicitors were well paid?"

"I work for Dad and Theo, remember. They're behind the times. They'll soon realise that if they decide to recruit a replacement for me."

"But you must be entitled to sick pay?"

"I don't know. I haven't got an employment contract ... it didn't seem necessary working for Dad."

"Have you sent in a sick note?"

"I haven't got one of those either."

"Didn't you get a doctor's appointment or a date for a hospital visit? What about all that medication you came home with?"

"I took all that ..."

"Well maybe you should *still* be taking at least *some* of it? You might need a repeat prescription? And I thought you were supposed to be having counselling or something?"

She is starting to get on Leo's nerves. "Do you have to speak so loud so close to my ear? I don't need doctors or medication and as for *counselling* ... I'm okay now." He transfers the savings into his current account. "I could put the House Account details in here and set up a transfer but I need a card reader for that and I don't think I have it now." He clicks around a little and reads the details. "Okay, I can order a new one and it will be posted to my *home address.* Where's that? Ah, that's Bridget and Matt's address. *Change Address.*"

"Don't bother with all that – cheques will do so long as they don't bounce. It's not like you're here *long term*? Is it?"

"No, I suppose not ..." He realises Paddy is looking at him with interest. *Paddy wants to know how much longer I'm going to be here.*

Beatrice breaks the silence. "Unless you've actually *turned into a horse*, you're going to find it very cold in those stables in the winter."

Leo knows she is right. Since the beginning of this month, October, he has been waking up early in the morning, feeling cold.

"Of course you can always have a room here ..."

He shakes his head, suddenly remembering when he and Bridget were newly married and had just moved into their own home and then Bridget's twenty year old niece had needed somewhere to stay for a week or two, which had turned into three months, in the spare bedroom that adjoined theirs. Knowing she was just the other side of the thin wall had inhibited them, and whilst they had assured her that it was *fine,* they had been delighted to finally wave her off.

"Leo?"

"Sorry?"

"Didn't Dad say anything to you about going back to work when he was here the other day?"

"I haven't seen Dad since the day he stormed into the hospital and had a massive rant about how ashamed he was ..."

"Oh? He dropped in here after golf on Sunday. I thought he'd come to see *you* but felt like he had to call in here first?"

"Well no, he didn't." Leo has had enough. He stands up and walks out. "I'm going to do a bit more of that fence."

Paddy catches up with him. "No, yer not, it's dark already and it's starting ter rain, so there'll be no camp fire tonight."

“Oh, yes, I see what you mean. I’ll help you do the stables, and then I’ll have an early night.”

“I’ll be doing a corned beef hash and yer very welcome to join me – and watch a bit of telly maybe.”

“It’s good of you to offer, but I’ll leave you in peace.”

Paddy reaches up and grabs Leo’s bony shoulders and shakes him hard. “It’s only half past feckin five Leo. Sometimes I feel like giving you a *good hard shake*!”

“You just *did*.”

“So, you can sort out der horses whilst I start der tea – and you’ll come along when you’re done?”

“Yes, okay. Thank you.” He gives Paddy the letters and envelopes. “I’ll write the address on the envelope and then it’s ready to go.”

Leo joins Paddy in the kitchen with forced cheerfulness that Paddy sees straight through. “Something smells good,” he says and sits down at the table. The kitchen is warm and cosy with the television, low volume, in the background.

“Aye, it’ll be ready in under an hour. So, it *did* get yer down – writing dat letter.”

“No ... no, it’s not that.”

“What den. Der money?” That had been a surprise to Paddy who had assumed that Leo was minted on account of his profession, his accent, the smart suits he used to wear, the new Audi and his habitual generosity.

“Indirectly,” Leo replies. “It’s just ... having to think about the *future*. The good thing about being ill is that you hope either to die quietly in the night or else to feel better in the morning – and you don’t think much beyond that. I don’t know whether or not my Dad and Uncle want me back at the office – but I *can’t abide* the thought of going back there. It feels like a memory of a previous life. I’d like to do something different – something practical – but my wood-working skills won’t earn enough to pay the rent on the smallest, cheapest flat – and how depressing is the thought of moving into one of those places. And when Tommy starts coming here you’re not going to want me lurking around the stables." He stops. "Sorry Paddy, I'm done whinging."

Paddy is leaning against the kitchen unit, looking at the floor, shaking his head. "Leo, man, how many *more* times. You are welcome here and you have a *right* ter be here. I never had me own place – we lived in a caravan an' den I always worked in stables an' shared with de other lads. I'm not *used* to me own space. I know I was a bit funny like, when I first came out of prison and went ter yer Ma and Dad's – but dat was just nerves, an' fear of saying der wrong thing because I thought you was all so *grand.* And I discovered just de other day dat the sofa here folds out into a bed – so we only need ter move der table across here each night and yer sorted. So cheer up now. Yer don't have to go anywhere. I enjoy your company. Okay?"

Leo nods, looking away from Paddy and at the television, afraid he is going to start blubbering again. The remote control is on the table and he picks it up and begins channel-flipping to see if there is anything worth watching.

"Hey, I was watching that!"

"Oh, sorry," says Leo and channel-flips back again. "Is that what you were watching?"

Paddy rolls his eyes. "I wasn't watching anything, yer bloody fool. Put what yer want on."

32

Please come back

Judith answers the phone.

"Hi Judith, it's Bridget. Is Leo there, please?"

"*Bridget?*" Judith is taken aback. "No, he's not here. What do you want from him?"

Bridget hesitates, deterred by the hostility in Judith's voice. Her mother-in-law had always been so very kind and such a soft touch. "I phoned the office and the girl who answers the phone said he was having some time off, and she didn't know when he'd be back. Is he ... is he okay? Only we had a couple of appointment cards in the post for him for *hospital* appointments."

"Oh, when are they?" Judith has her pen at the ready to note down the dates and times.

"One was two weeks ago, and the other was about a week before that."

"And you didn't think to send them *here*?"

"Well ... no. He's always so organised I thought they would be on his calendar. Anyway, you just said he wasn't there – so it's just as well I didn't bother sending them on. But you know where he is, don't you? What's wrong with him? Why the hospital appointments?"

Judith hesitates. "He tried to – he took an - he had stomach ulcers ... but he's on the mend."

"Oh, nasty! Poor Leo. But you won't tell me where he is?"

"No. You've done him enough damage ..."

"Judith ... *please...*" Bridget sounds suddenly tearful, which is unusual for her.

"Is your baby all right?"

"Yes, she's fine. Look, if you won't tell me where he is, will you at least give him a message from me?"

"Only if it's a *positive*, message ... he's ... erm, he's a little bit *fragile* at the moment."

"Just tell him - Please, Judith, tell him that ..."

Judith's contempt for Bridget is overcome by her habitual compassion for anyone who is in distress and she switches to a more gentle tone. "What is it? Tell me, and I'll pass it on to him ... unless of course I feel it would be harmful."

"Just tell him that Matt has left. He's gone back to his ex-girlfriend in Birmingham. Matt is a *good man*, Judith, I swear he is ... but he couldn't cope with ... leaking breast milk and baby-sick and nappies and all that. So he went back to *her* ... So ... I just thought if Leo was still ... *available* ... then he might be willing to try again ... with a ready made family...? I just want him to *come home*."

After a pause, Judith says, "All right, I will tell him. But if you hurt my son again, I don't think I could ever forgive you. Have you thought this through, Bridget? Your divorce has only recently been finalised. I *know* he still has feelings for you, but you must *cherish* his feelings."

"I will, I *promise* I will ..."

Judith drives to Hardwicke Heights with a heavy heart, wondering if she is doing the right thing but not really feeling that there is any other option. She bypasses the house and heads straight to the stables. Someone is cantering the chestnut mare around the paddock with Paddy barking instructions; "Get 'er to do a figure o' eight and make 'er change legs properly!" Leo sees his mother's car and turns his head, "Concentrate lad! Don't be so easily distracted! Good afternoon, Mrs Freeman."

"Hello Paddy. I didn't know Leo could ride ..."

"He's a natural, so he is. Probably on account of not caring too much if he breaks his neck." Paddy chuckles but sees that Judith doesn't find it funny. "Sorry, Mrs Freeman. Bring 'er in now, Leo!"

Leo pulls Snowy up by the gate and slides down off her back. "Hi Mum!" Paddy takes the reins and leads Snowy back to the stables. "Oh, thanks, Paddy."

Judith looks up at his happy, invigorated face and pushes the windswept hair away from his eyes. "You're looking so much better," she says. His greyish pallor has been replaced by a healthier outdoor look ... unless it could be a sign of jaundice.

"I *feel* much better," he assures her. "How are you?"

"I'm fine."

"And Dad?"

"He's fine too." She sees the question is still on his face and adds, "Grumpy as ever."

"He hasn't forgiven me then."

"He'll come round in his own time."

"What's wrong Mum? You look worried ... Not bad news, I hope?"

"*I* hope it's not *bad news* as well."

Paddy rejoins them. "Would yer like a cup o' tea, Mrs Freeman?"

"No thank you, Paddy. I'll call and see Beatrice before I go, and we'll catch up with everything. I just came to tell Leo that -" She turns to Leo. "I had a phone call from Bridget this morning. Matt has left her ... gone back to his former girlfriend and, well, I hope it's not just a case of *tit for tat*, but she wants you to go back to her."

Leo blinks rapidly a few times, taking this in and then springs into action. "I'll go now. Paddy, do you know where my keys are?"

"Leo! At least have a shower and put a clean shirt on ... and that pullover has seen better days ... What will she think if you turn up smelling of horses?"

Leo hurries to the house for a shower and retrieves his clean jeans and a tee-shirt from the laundry. He contemplates shaving but settles for the *designer stubble* look that Beatrice thinks suits him.

In the living room, Beatrice is watching a film whilst Serge and Franchesca are sitting at the table doing a jigsaw puzzle.
"Hey, Serge, have you a pullover I could borrow? I've got a date and mine smells of horses."
"Yeah, 'elp yerself."
Leo glances at the puzzle. "That bit's in the wrong place, there's the edge of a roof look - and you've put it in the lawn." He picks it out and puts it in the correct place and swaps a few other pieces around; throws some more into place and soon there are only two pieces left. He gives one each to Serge and Franchesca. "Go on, you finish it."
Beatrice rolls her eyes. "Thanks Leo, that would have kept them busy all afternoon. Now I'll have to find something else for them to do."
"Well before you do that, would you sort out a long-sleeved top I can borrow? I don't like to go rummaging around in their room."
"Any particular colour?" she asks.
He glances at the bright red fleece Franchesca is wearing and the bright blue fleece Serge is wearing; "Preferably something that's not a primary colour."
"Well, come with me and see what there is."
He follows her upstairs and rifles through the bright colours. "Oh dear, yellow it is then. Actually, I think I'll leave it – it's not all that cold."
"Let me see – his black stuff will be at the back. He doesn't like black and never wears it unless they ask him to for a photo-shoot. Black *does* suit him though." She pulls out a black zip-up jumper. "Try this." She looks him up and down. "That looks good. You've got a date, then? You're actually *going out*? Anyone I know?"
"Mum will be here soon – it'll give you something to talk about - and I'd better get back to the stables now and rescue Mum and Paddy from each other ..."
He returns to the stables to find his mother watching horse racing with Paddy and showing a polite interest in his critique

of the form of the horses. She looks him up and down. "That's better. *Very* handsome."

"Thank you. Paddy, where are my car keys?"

Paddy grins mischievously, rattling the keys in his pocket and Leo pretends to pounce on him to retrieve them.

"Private joke, Mrs Freeman," says Paddy to a bemused Judith.

Leo kisses his mother and makes as if to kiss Paddy who responds, "Gerron with yer." Judith and Paddy share a smile as they watch him go off with a spring in his step.

"Go careful and good luck!" shouts Paddy. "Tis der first time he's left this place since he came here from der hospital, so it is. His sister and Dominic tried ter take him out but he wouldn't 'ave it. I thought he was gettin' a bit what's a name?"

"Agoraphobic?"

"Dat's der one."

"I do hope I did the right thing, telling him Bridget phoned."

"You did der right thing, Mrs Freeman. It would have wrong to do any different, so it would. He must go and sort it out for himself."

Bridget has been watching out for Leo ever since she made the phone call to Judith. She greets him with open arms and nestles her face against his neck, unable at first to look him in the eye. He inhales the scent of her hair - something he had thought he would never again experience - and drips hot tears down on her head. She looks up in surprise. She has never known him to shed a tear; didn't think he was capable. She runs a finger down his face, following the course of a tear - over the cheek bone and into the hollow ... he feels so thin but it gives him an … immediacy. As she leans against his chest she can feel his heart beating as if it is connected with hers - even though the pregnancy has left her with all this extra cladding. She feels a tugging sensation deep inside; a re-awakening of something she hasn't felt since her positive pregnancy test, and the heat rises rapidly upwards to her neck. She pulls away from him abruptly.

"Well, let's not stand here in the hallway," she says briskly, and he follows her to the sitting room and sits next to her awkwardly on the familiar sofa ... feeling like a visitor.

"You look so *different*," she says. "And you're so *skinny* and I'm so *fat!*"

"Mmm. But it's only temporary. We will mutually realign." Leo cringes at his own words – at his inadequacy in these situations. He remembers Sam's little voice repeating '*Nerd*'. Happily, Bridget has bypassed his response and is now delivering him the speech she has rehearsed about herself and Matt ...

"All he wanted, you see, was *sex*. And all I wanted, *as you well know*, was to have a *baby*. But then I wasn't interested in sex once I knew I was expecting – it was the last thing I wanted. But that was all he wanted me for ... for sex and for the way I dressed and for his self-image having me on his arm, looking *sexy*. But when you've just had a baby it's the last thing on your mind ... you really don't feel *sexy* at all. But he was so selfish and demanding ..."

Leo has been yearning to take her to bed since the moment they made contact, and hopes it is not too obvious. He fidgets, adjusting his pullover and tugging it down at the front.

"What's the matter? You've gone all pink. Take your top off if you're too hot."

He shakes his head and she goes on; "So, I made a bit of a fool of myself by getting some of my pre-pregnancy clothes out of the wardrobe - and managed to find something that would still fasten. But he said it simply didn't look *sexy* anymore and he said I would have to find a different style. That was all he cared about, you see. Just *sex*. *Leo*, whatever is *the matter*?" She puts her hand on his forehead.

"Oh ... Oh, Bridget ..." it is almost a groan. Her hand travels down to his chest and she is worried by how hard his heart is thumping. "I'm so sorry, but we're all the same, us men.

Here's you saying it's all *he* wanted but you keep on saying *the word* and it's all I've been able to think about since I stepped through the front door."

"*Really?* Oh! Well, in that case *come on, quick*, let's go to bed before the baby wakes up – she's due for a feed. Come on!"

She takes his hand and leads him to the bedroom with a sense of urgency. "Wow, you *are* pleased to see me!"

Noticing some differences he says, "You must tell me if I'm hurting you."

"You won't hurt me – it's more the case that I might not notice there's anyone there!"

"That'll improve ... Oh ... you are still *so amazing* ..."

"Don't touch my nipples else you'll drown in milk."

"I can think of worse ways to go ..."

She knows how close he is and begs him not to shoot just yet. He shuffles down the bed and uses first his fingers and then his lips and tongue, looking up at her from beneath his floppy hair - his gorgeous blue eyes intense – the pupils dilated. It takes her back to their first time together – and she recalls the excitement that surrounded it ...

Afterwards he rests on his elbows with his face between her huge breasts and reassures her how wonderful she still is. She sees his eyes shifting from one to the other and explains, "It's because they're full of milk. Matt said I was *no good* since having her. He said it was like waving a stick in a mountain crevice. I told him if he was as *well hung as Leo* he wouldn't have had a problem."

"*Oh, you never did.*" Leo is slightly shocked but mindlessly flattered.

She nods her head. "He hurt his right hand. Broke a small bone in it. He told me he did it breaking your ribs. The day Eve was born ... he took one quick look at *his daughter* and then hurried off to 'A and E' to get his *hand* x-rayed. Did he really break your ribs?"

"No, they were just bruised."

She can see that he wants the subject changed. "So, who taught you the good *finger-work*?"

"What?" He laughs and tries to avert his eyes but in his current position he is a blinkered horse and is forced to look back at her. He grins but says nothing.

"Well, someone showed you what to do, and it wasn't me ..."

He shuffles back and reaches down for the tissues but comes up with a toilet roll. "I see we've gone down market," he quips, and whilst that makes her smile, he doesn't get away without having to explain.

Slowly, choosing his words carefully, he tells her about Sally and Sam.

"The *bitch*!" says Bridget when he has finished.

He laughs again, attempting to diffuse her contempt, "Sally spoke similarly highly of *you*."

"I saw you and her and the kid on the telly, leaving Serge's wedding. I *thought* I recognised her. You looked like you were leaving a *funeral* rather than a *wedding*."

The baby begins to cry and Leo silently thanks her for such good timing. Bridget fetches her in and Leo, sitting next to her in the bed, watches with fascination whilst she feeds her.

"Do you think you could love someone else's child?" Bridget asks casually.

"I remember very clearly how I felt when she was born. I even forgot that she wasn't mine until Matt turned up. It helps that she's a girl and she looks like a miniature version of you ... although I guess it might all depend on how far *Matt* wants to be involved in her upbringing."

"He's gone back to his girlfriend in Birmingham. That's where he was the day Eve was born. He's not really interested in his daughter."

"Then I'm sure it will be fine. And it means we can have some fun together – like old times – without worrying about trying to make a baby."

"Oh, but we'll have to think about contraception – that's if you're *sure* Sam is yours? The last thing I want right now is *another baby*."

Leo sighs and puts his arm around her. "Isn't there always *something*?"

33

Terms and Conditions Apply

The *second honeymoon* lasts four and a half days. Leo is sitting at the desk fiddling with the computer, trying to make it run a little faster when Bridget says, "Have you got any money in the bank? We're behind with the mortgage payments."

"Er ... not very much. I did have about two thousand three hundred but transferred it into my current account. It appeared I was still paying all the utility bills for this place and I'd gone overdrawn. I remember transferring the mortgage over to you, and I had assumed you and Matt would take over the utilities at the same time. How far in arrears are you – I mean *we*?"

"Just a month or so. Well, since you left, really. You know most of my salary went on the monthly payments for my car, and Matt didn't see why *he* should pay anything towards the mortgage whilst I was still married to *you*, and *you* were dragging your feet over the divorce ... and as you know I hadn't been in my job long enough to qualify for full maternity benefits."

There is a short pause during which Leo absorbs this state of affairs. When he says nothing, she throws in; "Of course my car has gone back. Which is a shame really – there weren't all that many payments left on it."

"Yes, that *is* a shame," says Leo. "Dad and Uncle Theo are unlikely to extend the lease on my car if I'm no longer working for them."

"What do you mean, *no longer working for them*? You're *well* now – you told me so. You're going back to work soon, *aren't you*?"

He sighs. "I just wish ... I'd really like to ... do something different."

"What *sort of* different?"

"I'd like to work with horses. I miss the smell of the stables." His eyes light up with hopeful enthusiasm. "You like horses as well, don't you? Didn't you tell me you used to go riding?"

"Leo, *horses* are what you do for a hobby. Not to pay the *mortgage*."

He looks away, back at the computer screen. "Yes, of course ... I can understand security being important to you now, owing to the baby ... it's only natural. My skiing stuff is in the loft – we could sell that. And I suppose we could sell my Grandfather's antique violin, if it comes to it."

"I already sold it all." He is surprised for a moment and then attempts to veil the hurt. "How much did you get for the violin?"

"A hundred and seventy five pounds."

After a pause whilst he takes this in, he says mildly, "It was worth *far more* than that."

"Well *I* didn't know," she says defensively, "You went off and left it here."

Leo replays their parting scene in his mind, "Imagine if I'd left and then reappeared from the garage with the step ladders to check out the contents of the loft." She forces a laugh, pretending to see the funny side. He goes on, "It's a shame we have no equity in the house. I was surprised at the valuation of this place. Whilst I'm aware that house prices have gone down, one of the last jobs I did was conveyancing in this area, and the value was roughly the same on a two-bedroomed house with a smaller garden. Perhaps that new estate being so close has brought the price down."

"Look, maybe we *could* remortgage if we have to. The estate agent who valued this place for the settlement was a mate of Matt's so he deliberately undervalued it for us so we wouldn't have to pay you anything. I'm sorry."

"Oh. Well, thank you."

"But we could make an appointment at the building society *now* – and get them to remortgage and put it back in our joint names, like it was before."

"If you're happy to share the *debt* with me ..."

She bursts out suddenly, "Your parents are *loaded* and they're always giving handouts to charity. What about their own family? Doesn't charity begin at home?"

Leo hangs his head in dismay. Is this the only reason she asked him to come back ... to pay the mortgage? "My parents donate to selected charities that help people to help themselves. They don't give *handouts.* It's all about sustainability and enabling." He can't help but reflect that being dead would have had its advantages ... and Bridget would have had a good payout on the life insurance – unless there was a clause in the small print about suicide that he glossed over – never imagining it could ever be relevant.

She moves closer and massages his shoulders. "You're *so tense*. All that matters is that we're back together ..."

He looks up at her and is convinced she is looking at his wrist and wondering where the Rolex is. He holds her gaze for a moment and she looks away, guiltily. At least she has the grace not to ask where it went. "So, when *are* you going back to work?"

He doesn't answer for a moment; the computer has started popping up boxes and he is busy clicking Yes, No and Okay.

She opens her mouth to ask him again and he says, "*I don't know*. Okay?"

"No, it's *not okay*. I need to *know*. Will you switch that bloody thing off and talk to me?"

He sighs, shuts down the computer and swivels round to face her. "I haven't spoken to Dad or Theo since ... since I let them down. I was supposed to take care of things at the office whilst Mum and Dad went away on holiday for the first time in years, and, well, I *didn't*. When Dad came back from the Seychelles he went ballistic and I haven't seen him since."

"But you've never let *anyone* down. Apart from when you let *me* down on your *stag night*. You say you *haven't seen him since.* Have you made any attempt to get in touch with your Dad or Theo, to apologise and put things right?"

"Well, no, I suppose not."
"Why don't you go to the office *now* and see them?"
"*Now*?" He looks horrified.
"Well, there's nothing to be gained by putting it off."
He sighs. "I'll go tomorrow."

After a sleepless night, Leo decides to go to the office early in the morning to catch his Dad and Theo before their appointments begin.

"You're not going like *that,* are you?" says Bridget. He is wearing the same black jeans and pullover that he turned up in. "Put a suit on. Where *are* your suits? Isn't it time you brought all your stuff back if you're here to stay?"

"It all ended up in a skip," says Leo, heading for the front door.

"In *where*?"

"A skip."

He closes the door on her questions and makes the familiar journey to the office. Knowing that the code to open the gates to the car park is changed regularly, he parks in the *Pay and Display* just off the High Street and scurries along to the office building, using his key for the front entrance. The alarm code will still be the same as he is the only one who knows how to change it. He walks up the stairs and stands in the empty reception area. Had the office suite always smelt of old fashioned furniture polish? He walks along the passage to the last office, which was his own, opens the door and steps in. It is still his office – they haven't converted it into anything else, or dumped any junk in there – but yet it feels like it was his office in a previous life time. He looks at the desk and traces a finger where Sam's red crayon marks had endured for so long. They have gone now. The cleaners have finally eradicated all evidence that Sam was ever there. He goes to the window that looks down onto the courtyard car park and pulls up the blinds.

It has started to rain again, and he watches the droplets run down the window.

Michelle arrives and steps out of her car wearing ankle boots, opaque black tights and a very short black skirt. He watches her walk across the car park and thinks it would be a good idea to go back to the reception area to meet her. She might feel nervous to discover that the alarm has been deactivated whilst the car park is empty. He finds, however, that he is unable to move away from the window. Maybe she will just think no-one remembered to set it yesterday evening.

When Michelle finds that the alarm has been deactivated, she hesitates for just an instant then knows that Leo is back and bounds up the three flights of stairs, accelerating as she goes. She scans the reception area but there is no sign of him so she bolts into the Ladies to redo her makeup, wishing she had worn the new top she bought at the weekend, then walks confidently to his office, as if to pull up the blinds, like she has done every morning since he hasn't been around.

She stops in the doorway; startled, thinking she was wrong and there is an intruder – not recognising the tall thin man with shaggy hair who is seemingly absorbed in watching the raindrops running down the windows. He turns to face her, smiling coyly. "Hi Michelle."

She gasps. His unmistakeable voice; the cutting twinkle of blue eyes and a flash of white teeth. "Leo!" On impulse, she rushes over and hugs him tight for an instant before leaning back to properly take in the new look. "You look so ... so *different*!"

He laughs. "I *feel* a bit *different*."

"Leo ... you're shaking ..."

"Mmm ... I haven't been out much lately but didn't expect it to be like *this*." He looks down at his hands and realises he is still clinging on to her. "Oh, sorry." He releases his grasp and stands awkwardly whilst she checks him out.

"When are you coming back? It's rubbish here without you."

“Well, that was the purpose of this visit ... but I can’t see it now.” He hears a car enter the courtyard and looks out of the window. “Oh no, it’s Uncle Theo!” There is a note of panic in his voice.

Michelle laughs, “Hey, you look like a horse about to bolt.”

“Do you like horses?”

“Yeah, love ‘em!”

“Me too. Does Theo still use the lift?”

“Always.”

He flees from the room, giving her shoulder an affectionate pat as he leaves. Not taking any chances, he hesitates on the landing until he can hear the lift ascending, then runs down the stairs, two at a time, and splashes through the puddles in the High Street; back to the car and then home.

Michelle bursts into tears. She had loved Leo for his nerves of steel – the infallible self-assurance that people who did not know him sometimes mistook for arrogance. But now he is altered ... his expression, his whole demeanour – everything about him appears so *vulnerable*. And today she loves him *more than ever ...*

Bridget meets him in the hallway. “That was quick. What did they say?”

“I didn’t see them.”

“What? Why not? Were they both out or something? When *are* you going to see them?”

“*Leave it*, will you.” He hurries past her, to the kitchen and out through the back door into the garden, but the cold wind and rain drive him back indoors. She is in the kitchen now and he is cornered. He leans back against the wall and hangs his head.

“What is it, Leo? What’s the matter?”

“I don’t know,” he says miserably.

“Oh, come here,” she draws him against her. He sinks into her ample warmth. “We’ll manage somehow.”

Later, in the afternoon when Leo is staring glumly at the television and Bridget is just about to feed the baby, a car pulls up outside. Leo cranes his neck to see who is blocking his car in the drive. "*Oh no*, it's *Dad.* And *Theo* is with him!"

Leo opens the front door and his father looks him up and down but manages to conceal his surprise at what appears to be a *new image*. "Come in," says Leo when they stand on the doorstep, waiting to be invited.

"We didn't phone first because we thought you'd put us off," says Alistaire. They follow him to the living room where he switches off the television. Bridget is standing there holding the baby. Alistaire and Theo acknowledge her politely and Alistaire gives the baby his perfunctory approval and adds, "She looks like you."

"Well, she's not gonna look like *Leo*, is she?" retorts Bridget.

"That was unnecessary," says Alistaire.

"Please sit down," says Leo, and Alistaire and Theo sit side by side on the sofa, looking awkward. The baby begins to grizzle. "Bridget, I thought Eve was due for a feed. Why not take her upstairs?"

"I want to hear what they've got to say."

Alistaire reacts to her petulant tone. "And I would prefer to speak to my son in private, if you don't mind. Whilst I would be glad to think you wanted to back him up him for once ... I am not convinced."

"*Dad, please ...*"

"It's okay," frowns Bridget, "I don't think I want to listen to this after all - you can tell me about it later ... that's if it's *worth hearing*." She goes upstairs.

"Would you like some coffee or something?" asks Leo.

"No. Sit down and listen," demands Alistaire. Leo sits in the armchair and stares at the floor.

After a short silence, Theo clears his throat. Leo understands he is calling him in, and musters some attention.

"Leo, I know I was hard on you and I apologise," says Theo.

Leo shakes his head. "There's no need. You're not a mind reader, and I know I let you down."

"Your father and I agreed that we would need to recruit a replacement for you. We're having to turn new clients away."

"Oh." Another silence whilst Leo studies the pattern on the rug. "So, do you want me to look at some CV's or something?"

Alistaire *tuts* impatiently. "No, you *fool.* We want *you* to come back!"

"Oh."

Theo picks it up again. "Michelle gave us a bit of a *dressing down* this morning."

"Really?"

"Yes. She started by demanding a pay rise ... and showed us some adverts for jobs that she was thinking of applying for."

"*Good girl!*" Leo laughs suddenly and then looks solemn again. "Please don't let her go. She is so good with the clients; she is everything to everyone, whatever they are carrying."

Theo reflects for a moment then nods in agreement. "And then she went on to show us the salary we would have to pay to recruit a replacement for *you*, and, well, frankly, we have to admit that we would have to pay an awful lot more to recruit a ... a *stranger* with your experience and qualifications."

Alistaire takes over. "Michelle told us a few *home truths* this morning. Whilst Theo and I had thought we were coping without you, it would appear that we were managing so well because most of the clients want to see *the young* Mr Freeman."

Theo goes on, "Michelle also mentioned that you called at the office this morning – but you, erm ... *ran away* when I turned up."

Leo smiles apologetically. "I went along with the intention of asking if I could come back to work. But ... but ..."

"Yes, yes, she told us. So, we had a bit of a think." Theo turns to Alistaire. "You can put it to him."

Leo shifts his gaze from Theo to Alistaire, who clears his throat. "Whilst you must understand, for the reasons just cited, that our ultimate aim is to have you back in the office *dealing with the clients*, we wondered how you might feel about working from home to begin with – taking much of the paperwork off our hands, with your previous salary reinstated. We would expect you to visit the office to collect and deliver any non-electronic communication; and – as soon as you feel able – we would like you to return to work at the office – maybe one day a week at first, then two, and so on, but without seeing clients until you are ready – but bearing in mind, of course, that this is the ultimate aim. And, when you *are* ready to receive clients, we will review your salary to put in line with what it would cost us to recruit a replacement. At which point ... I hope you might consider having a hair-cut."

Alistaire has finished but Leo does not reply immediately. "Well?" says Alistaire, deeming that the silence has lasted long enough.

"Well ... I'm not sure about having my hair cut."

Alistaire smiles, satisfied that the deal is done. "Good. Then we'll sort out some work for you in the morning. Call and collect it tomorrow, any time after midday."

Leo turns up at one o'clock, on the basis that the work should be ready for him by that time and it is unlikely he will meet any clients in the reception area. No-one is there, not even Michelle. He can hear the kettle coming to the boil in the kitchen and can picture her sitting at the table with her lunchbox. He sits on one of the small black leather sofas in the waiting area, and imagines he is a client who has made an appointment to see himself as he used to be and feels suddenly nostalgic about being that person that he no longer is.

Michelle returns to her desk but does not notice him. She takes a small mirror from her handbag and Leo wonders, not for the first time, why women have to open their mouths to apply mascara ... but then there's not much that the women he has known *can* do without *opening their mouths* ... Feeling like a voyeur, sitting there saying nothing, he stands up and walks over to her desk.

"*Shit!* Where the hell did *you* spring from? I nearly poked my eye out!"

"Sorry." He grins wickedly and she laughs.

"Yesterday I thought you looked like an artist or a poet. Do that smile again – it makes you look like a baddy in a film!"

He smiles again, this time narrowing his eyes a little.

"That's it, you've got it!" But his nerves do not escape her and she knows he won't hang around for long. "I'll go and tell Alistaire you're here."

She returns quickly and is relieved to find him still standing by her desk. "Pull up a chair." He sits opposite her and begins to jiggle his feet, then realises he is doing it and stops. "I split up with Darren," says Michelle. "Did you know?"

"No, I didn't." Bearing in mind the fuss he made over his own break-up he is careful not to trivialise this news. "I'm really sorry to hear that. Are you okay?"

"Yes ... better than him I think – but he'll get over it. It was my decision, you see. That does make a difference."

"Yes, I suppose it must ..."

"He wanted us to get a place together. We both live with our parents, so there's not always anywhere to go, like?"

Leo nods. She sees him look askance towards Alistaire's office, wishing he would hurry up.

"They're sorting out a mobile phone for you. It's Theo's old one. He's just upgraded but he hasn't a clue how to use it. He'd be better off keeping the old one and giving you the new one. Anyway ... I was telling you ... it brought it to a head, you see. Because there's no way I could make the commitment of getting a place with Darren ... we were only gonna rent like – but it still would have been a hassle to break up – so I thought rather now than later."

"Very wise," says Leo. "Look, I'll just go and tell them I don't need a mobile. The landline will do."

"Not for Alistaire, it won't. He doesn't want to risk having to speak to you ex-wife in case he says something he might regret. Anyway, the *reason* I couldn't make the commitment with Darren is because there's *someone else* I love."

"Well, I *really hope* it works out for you ... and him."

"But he doesn't *know* I love him. How do I *tell* him?"

"What? Oh, erm ... my sister reckons Facebook is good for flirting."

"I don't think he's on Facebook."

"Sensible man. Try texting him, maybe?"

Alistaire appears with a pile of documents and a mobile phone. "Theo was going to keep his old number but it was too much hassle so he gave up. He said he wasn't bothered as there are a few contacts who have this number that he is happy to lose, albeit you're about to inherit them. You can always block their numbers if they become a nuisance."

Leo is already on his way to the exit with the pile of documents and the mobile phone.

"Don't you want me to talk you through those?"

"No, I'll work it out. If I get stuck I'll phone you." He waves the phone in the air and it rings. He answers it, "No, sorry, this is Leo. I think you were after Theo. No, I'm *Leo*. Can I give Theo a message from you?" He rolls his eyes at Alistaire and Michelle and begins to retreat down the stairs. "No, I'm his nephew, Leo. *Theo* is my uncle – this used to be his phone."

Michelle looks at Alistaire and they both laugh. "He's gonna have some fun with that."

34

The Final Chapter

Saturday morning, three weeks before Christmas, Leo meets Paddy at the stables and they drive to a housing estate in South London to collect Tommy – to take him back to Hardwicke Heights for the day.

"Dis is putting you out," says Paddy. "Yer must have something better to do with der weekend."

"No, it's doing me a favour," replies Leo. "Matt is visiting our house to see the baby, so I'm glad to have something to do."

"How's it goin' den? You an' yer ex-missus?"

"Well, thanks for putting it like that ... it's a bit *up and down* as it happens."

"*In and out* as well, I should hope?" Paddy's face folds in a huge wink.

"Well, yes, at first. But then it dropped off."

"Bejesus – yer must've been going at it some for that ter happen!" Paddy is gratified when Leo laughs like a school boy.

They drive past a block of garages and Leo reads snatches of obscene graffiti. "They, erm, don't hold back on expressing themselves around here, do they?"

"We're nearly der now."

"I guessed we must be." Paddy had described in some detail the area where Tommy and his mother were living.

They pull up outside Gina's house and Paddy gets out. "Will yer come to the door with me?" he asks Leo. "Dat way Gina's less likely ter give me any shit."

Leo reflects on how fearlessly Paddy has handled a temperamental mare weighing more than a thousand pounds and how fearful he looks now at the prospect of confronting

Gina. He follows Paddy and stands a couple of paces behind him at the door.

Tommy rushes out and hugs his father. Gina looks at Paddy with contempt and then transfers her attention to Leo. "Who the hell are you?"

"Leo Freeman. I'm Paddy's solicitor who helped him to write the letter."

She looks him up and down. "You don't *look* much like a solicitor."

"That's because I need a haircut and a suit. We'll have Tommy back here by eight-thirty. Okay?"

"Okay. It'll give *me* a break from the little toe-rag."

"Then everyone's a winner," says Leo, and bestows on her a big happy smile as they depart.

Back at the stables, Tommy runs off to see the ponies whilst Paddy eyeballs Leo frantically to catch his attention.

"What's up?" asks Leo.

"Would yer mind introducing him to der ponies whilst I get rid of me porn?"

"Whilst you do *what*?"

"I was just about ter show me boy der little bed beneath me own bed – and then I remembered it's where I keep me old porn mags – along with dat pack of Snap cards I used ter pretend I was playing with."

"*Paddy!*"

"Just go talk ter him about der 'orses would yer!"

The first pony they come to is Flint, the new *bomb-proof* black gelding that has only been there a week. The box between Flint and Snowy, where Leo had been sleeping is still unoccupied. Leo looks at it thoughtfully as he rubs Flint's ears and tickles his chin. "I guess your Dad will move Flint next to Snowy once they've got used to each other." He explains what a state Snowy was in when she first came to them. "She had been traumatised by something and she had a bad leg and she was so nervous and crotchety that no-one could get near her, except your Dad. But she's fine now, thanks to him. She'll never be as docile as the two ponies, but there's nothing wrong with showing a bit of spirit. I believe your Dad healed her ..."

"You like my Dad, don't you?"

Paddy is on his way to join them but ducks out of sight to listen.

"Yes, I do," replies Leo.

"You're not like his usual mates. Me Mam says Dad's no good because he went to jail."

"*Good people* end up in jail sometimes, Tommy. The law is a strange thing."

"Do you just like my Dad because he healed that horse?"

"No, I like him for a good many reasons ..."

"Such as?"

Leo looks down at Tommy, wondering why he has got his teeth into this. "Such as ... he's kind-hearted, intuitive and ... you see this empty box, next to Snowy's? I came here in a similar state to Snowy, and slept here for a while. And I believe your Dad healed *me* in just the same way as he healed Snowy."

Paddy clears his throat conspicuously as he walks along the stable block to join them and rests a hand on Tommy's shoulder, just as Leo's mobile text alert sounds. Leo reads the message and raises his eyebrows then glances guiltily at Paddy as if afraid he can read his thoughts.

Paddy laughs. "Is dat der missus saying what she's gonna do with yer later?"

"No, no ... This is a second-hand phone and whilst the previous owner's contacts have been deleted, it appears that some of them still have this number. And I keep getting these ... *messages* from someone."

"Block der number then, if you don't want ter read the messages."

"Well, it's kind of intriguing ..."

"Hah, and there's you looking daggers at me over a couple of old mags. Yer can tell me what it says later."

"I couldn't possibly read *this one* out loud – not even *later*." He puts the phone back in his pocket.
"Maybe I'll get Dom to teach me ter read after all."
"I don't imagine he'd start you off with words like *those*." Leo had occasionally wondered if his Uncle Theo had any kind of sex life. He had married young and divorced after a short time with no memorable fuss, and there had been no mention of anyone else since.

Beatrice and Dominic have prepared a buffet lunch in honour of Tommy's first visit.
Serge greets Tommy enthusiastically. "You come play Tomb Raider with Serge?"
"Not today, Serge," says Leo, battling to escape from Franchesca's hugs. "Maybe another time, if Tommy is here for the whole weekend and his Dad's got nothing else planned."
"Yeah," says Tommy. "Next time I'm gonna sleep at the stables. There's another bed under Dad's that was put there for me and it's brand new and has *never been used*."
Leo gives in and allows Franchesca to cuddle him and stroke his hair. "Did that little teddy find his way back to you?" She nods. "That's good. I'm sorry I didn't fetch him back myself – I left here in rather a hurry."
"Not *too* much of a hurry, I hope," says Paddy, knowingly. "I'll see dat there's always a spare loose box in der block, lest yer need it."

The following Friday, Leo is in the office when Michelle comes in with the coffee to find him sneezing repeatedly. He has lined the waste paper basket beside his desk with a polythene bag that is already half-full of used tissues.
"Oh, bless you," she says.
"Thanks, but *please* keep out of here today – I don't want you to catch my lurgy for Christmas."

“Oh, I *never* catch colds – haven’t had one for ages.” She puts the coffee on the desk and sits opposite him. He turns away from her to sneeze again. “How come you caught it? You never go anywhere except here.”

“The baby started with it on Monday. She probably picked it up at the Doctors’ surgery when Bridget took her in last Friday. Bridget’s okay though.”

“Well, the baby’s got no immunity yet - so that’s to be expected - and you’re still run down, so that’s why *you* caught it. Although your clothes are starting to fit you better,” she says appreciatively, then adds; “Are you still getting on okay with Bridget?”

He sighs and it turns into an unexpected sneeze. “Oh, *sorry*, that’s *gross*.” He wipes the desk with some tissues. “I don’t really know how we’re getting on. It’s all quite civil, but she’s overly keen to know which days I’m coming *here.* It seems that Matt wants to see more of his daughter ... and ... well, he’s got my Achilles heel there - so I can’t say no. Especially if he’s making the effort to drive down from Birmingham to spend an hour or two with the baby.” He pauses to sneeze and blows his nose again. “I would have worked from home today, rather than coming here spreading *this* around, but Matt had arranged to visit. And then Bridget nearly had a fit when I suggested I might work from home - so I can’t help *wondering* ... but it might just be that she’s tired and irritable because the baby isn’t sleeping well with her cold.” He has another sneezing session and looks into the box of tissues to see what’s left. “Anyway, enough of all that, how’s *your* life? I expect you’ll be out partying tonight ... since it’s Friday and so close to Christmas.”

Her face clouds. “Well, it *ought* to be a *brilliant* weekend. Mum and Dad are going off to Dad’s work’s Christmas do, which is at a hotel in Bournemouth and they’re making a weekend of it – which means I’ve got the place to myself, which is rare. I’ll probably invite a friend to come round ... There are a couple of parties on – but I found out that Darren’s got a new girlfriend – and I don't want to bump into the two of them."

"Ah, yes, I can imagine that would be awkward. Didn't you did mention there was someone else you were interested in? Any developments there?"

"Well ... I've tried texting, like you suggested, but he doesn't reply." Her eyes fill up and she looks away.

"Oh, *Michelle*, you will soon meet someone else – you are *wonderful* – I really hope that whoever you end up *deserves you.*"

"*Leo, that's exactly how I feel about you!*" But he is sneezing violently, backing away so as not to shower her with germs, and he doesn't hear. She waits until he has disposed of another bundle of tissues then says, "Why don't you go back there now and catch them at it?"

"*Sorry?*"

"Bridget and Matt. They're probably having a shag *right now.* Imagine if you went back there and caught them *at it!"*

"I'm not so sure that I *want* to catch them '*at it'*. But if Dad and Theo go off early this afternoon, like they often do on a Friday, I might just go and wait outside for Matt ... I'd like to hear *his* account of what's going on. I had envisaged bringing Eve up as my own daughter, but if her *real* daddy is going to keep dropping in all the time that could prove difficult."

"Alistaire and Theo will be off just after twelve. It's the golf-club Christmas lunch today. Go for it!"

The Friday afternoon traffic is particularly slow as commuters battle to escape from the City but Leo arrives home just after five and tucks the Q5 in behind a new Golf he does not recognise, which is parked beneath a street light a few doors away from his house. Maybe Matt has already left, and this is some neighbours' friends doing the Christmas rounds. He scans the interior of the car and spies a collection of little biros – the sort they have in betting or catalogue shops. Bridget had said Matt owned a chain of betting shops, so this is quite likely to be his car – plus it has fancy wheels and a noisy-looking exhaust.

Leo gets back into his own car, shivering violently. They had said on the radio that the temperature would go down to minus eight tonight, and it feels like it has done so already. Half an hour later he sees Matt approaching, gets out of the car and steps into position beneath the street light, right beside Matt's car.

Matt slows down, not recognising him. *Some waster who's lost money in one of my shops – but how did he track me down here?* "What the hell do you want?"

"I just wanted to talk to you. About Bridget."

"Oh, it's *you.*" It is the deep, intelligent voice that he recognises – not his appearance. "Would you like me to break your ribs *properly,* this time?" He looks meanly at Leo and points a finger down at the hard looking boots he is wearing.

Leo gives the boots a cursory glance. "I'd very much prefer that you didn't. Nice boots, however. They make you look tough." Matt is wearing a leather jacket that looks thick, heavy and new. "And they match your jacket."

"You're taking the piss."

"Yes. Sorry, it wasn't my intention ... Like I said; I just want to talk to you about Bridget."

Matt does not approach him, but glances around nervously, as if expecting a gang of Leo's mates to jump out at any moment from behind the car and the garden walls. "Hey, you're shaking. *Scared*, are you?"

"No, I'm just *really cold.*" Leo hasn't got round to buying a coat yet, and an icy wind is blowing through his pullover. "Could we sit in the car, where it's a bit warmer?" He presses a button on his key fob and the lights of his car flash invitingly.

"No," says Matt. "*My* car."

They get in the Golf and Matt picks up a can of de-icer, takes off the lid and puts his finger on the nozzle. "Now, put your hands together in front of you and keep them there. Any sudden move and I'll squirt this in your eyes, okay?"

Leo looks at the can and looks at Matt and doesn't dare to move much more than his eyebrows. He clasps his hands together and says, "I feel a sneeze coming on. I don't suppose you have any tissues?"

"No I fucking haven't!"

"Oh. There are some in my car – do you mind if I go and –" Hands still clasped together, Leo turns away to sneeze and then sniffs vigorously but is unable to prevent his nose from dripping down his pullover. Seeing Matt's revulsion he looks down and sees a small packet of tissues tucked in the passenger door – the sort Bridget takes everywhere since having the baby. They are next to a pair of fluffy mittens that he recognises.

"There is a packet of tissues here. Next to Bridget's mittens."

"Use those then. If there's one thing I can't stand, it's *snot.*"

"Well, this isn't exactly *snot* – it's just at that preliminary watery stage ..."

"Oh, *please* ... The baby's got a bloody cold as well. No sudden movements, now!"

Leo takes the tissues from the packet whilst glancing nervously at the de-icer. The mobile phone beeps loudly in his pocket, startling them both. Leo turns away with his eyes tightly closed. "That was not a sudden movement, it was a text message. *Please* don't squirt."

"Are you *always* this annoying?"

"Very probably."

"No wonder Bridget can't live with you."

"Is that what she told you?" Leo turns back to face Matt with eyes that are laden with hurt.

"She told me you'd *gone round the twist.* Now, put your hands back in front of you, like they were."

Leo sneezes unexpectedly and automatically raises the tissues to his nose, then realises he has moved his hands and remains in horrified suspense with eyes tightly closed. When finally he dares to look, he finds Matt is laughing at him.

Leo sees the funny side and laughs at himself. "You know, a loaded gun wouldn't bother me one bit ... but *de-icer!* Ugh!"

"Who was that text from? Bridget?"

"I don't know."

Matt rolls his eyes. "Well have a look."

Leo takes some time to read the message and Matt watches his reaction with interest. Eventually he says, "No. It's not from Bridget."

"Show us then."

Leo shows him the unknown number in the Received list, but not the content of the message.

"When did you speak to her last?"

"This morning, before I went to the office. Why?"

"I just reckoned she must have texted you. I thought that's why you were waiting here."

"No. I came here hoping to meet you because I have a feeling that Bridget is not being straight with me about ... about *you*."

"How do you mean?"

"Well ... are you currently living somewhere in Birmingham with your former girlfriend?"

"Urm, no. I'm living in the flat above the Newbury shop. I did go back to Mandy for about a week. Bridget was so wrapped up with the baby it seemed like there was no point me sticking around. But then she got her interest back ..."

"Oh. So, you're not just visiting Bridget to have contact with your daughter?"

"Eh? You're joking, aren't you, at *three months old* there's fuck-all point. All they do is swallow milk and then puke it back up again. And today it was just *snot* ... It'll be different when she's older, I hope." He hesitates. "Did you *really think* I was coming down from Birmingham so often just to see *the baby*?"

"Yes."

"And Bridget really hasn't contacted you today? Not since you left the house this morning?"

"No. Why? What's happened? Are they okay?"

"Yeah, but she was texting someone."

"She's made friends with women at *Mums and Tots*. They exchange news. What *is* the news, Matt? I do wish you'd tell me."

Can of de-icer poised at the ready, Matt tells him. "We're going to Lapland for a fortnight over Christmas. Me and Bridget are going to get married. The *real Father Christmas* is doing the service for us on Christmas Eve."

Leo laughs - picturing a wedding scene with Bridget pushing a pram down the aisle for Eve to meet Father Christmas. He had thought Serge and Fran's ceremony was *different*, but this one sounds like pure comedy... His smile quickly fades. Matt is deadly serious. "We collected her engagement ring from the jewellers today. It's similar to the one you gave her that she no longer wears; only the diamond is three times the size."

Leo's heart seems to be pounding in his ears. He realises he has forgotten to breathe and leans back, struggling to stay calm.

"Well, that's shut you up," says Matt, awkwardly, wishing now that he hadn't mentioned the ring. There had been no need to gloat. "Anyway, you'd best go and hear it from Bridget. I *told* her to tell you a couple of weeks ago."

"Come with me, will you?"

"What?"

"I want to hear the same story from the two of you together. If I go back to her alone she will tell me something different – I *know* she will."

"You calling *my fiancée* a *liar*?"

Leo sighs, sneezes several times, blows his nose and says; "Bridget tends to say or do whatever's easiest at the time ... and then she justifies her actions in her own mind and is pretty good at explaining them later, in a way that makes them seem reasonable."

Matt isn't quite sure he follows this, but gets out of the car. Still not trusting Leo, who seems a bit clever, he says, "Go on then, lead the way."

Bridget is expecting Leo back any time now and thinks it would be best to say nothing about the engagement or the trip to Lapland. She has planned to wait until she is at the airport, next Thursday, and then send him a text message to explain her future plans ... or maybe it would be better to leave him a note – there is only so much you can say in a text – and she will have to make it clear that he must be gone from the house by the time they get back in the New Year. This decided; she is dismayed to see both Matt and Leo approaching the front door.

"Where's your ring gone?" asks Matt, instantly.

"I thought you were on your way back to ..." she glances at Leo and then back at Matt.

"Birmingham?" Leo suggests.

"*Newbury*," she concedes, looking at Matt. "And I knew Leo was due back ..."

"So, when *were* you going to tell him? It is still *on*, isn't it?"

"*Of course it's still on!*"

"I'll be in the kitchen," says Leo. "Please come and tell me what's what when you've worked it out between yourselves."

He goes into the kitchen and blows his nose on a piece kitchen roll, deposits it in the pedal bin, then sits at the table and waits. After a few minutes they join him. Matt is looking down at the laminate flooring, whilst Bridget is wearing a large diamond solitaire ring and what Michelle would have described as an *arsey expression.*

"What Matt told you is true," she says. "We're getting married on Christmas Eve, and we're coming back here in the New Year."

"So, when *were* you going to tell me? Or did you fancy a ménage à trois?"

"I would have told you, in my own time!"

"How much time did you need? Have you any idea how close to Christmas Eve we already are?" Leo stands up. "I'll go and collect my things from upstairs and then I'll be gone ... again."

"Wait there, I'll go," says Bridget. "You'll wake Eve."

Leo sits down again, looking dazed, and Matt stands in the doorway like an awkward sentinel. The baby starts to cry and Leo looks up forlornly whilst Matt rolls his eyes and looks irritated.

"She's normally very easy," says Leo. "It's having a cold that's unsettled her and made her slightly grizzly. She's all blocked up, you see, and not feeding properly because in order to *suck* for any length of time, she needs to be able to breathe through her nose ... and ... well, she *can't* at the moment."

Bridget comes downstairs with the baby; hands her wordlessly to Matt and then goes off back upstairs. Matt holds her away from his jacket on account of her nose badly needing wiping and she screams and paddles the air, then sees Leo and reaches out for him.

Leo stands up to take her and Matt hesitates for just a moment before handing her over. Leo holds her against his chest and the noise stops instantly. He takes her to the kitchen sink and wipes her nose and face with moistened kitchen roll before patting it dry with another piece and then makes her smile by blowing his own nose loudly. He turns to face Matt and leans back against the kitchen sink.

"She likes to be held upright, like this – and if she's recently been fed it's a good idea to put a towel over your shoulder." The baby starts tugging at the front of his pullover. In his most tender voice he murmurs, "No, I'm sorry, I can't help you there - you'll have to wait for Mummy," then turns his attention back to Matt. "There's this little thing that she does ... as a signal that she's ready to go back down in her cot. She turns her head sideways and rubs her ear against you. If you wait until she does that she'll be fine. Try putting her down too early and she'll just scream."

Matt realises that Leo is conducting a hand-over ... showing him how to look after the baby, for *her* sake, because he cares about her and doesn't want her to miss him. It makes him feel like a proper git.

Bridget comes downstairs with a plastic carrier bag and stops abruptly when she sees Leo holding the baby. She glares at Matt, puts the bag down on the kitchen table, glances at the back door then hurries over and snatches her from Leo and steps back to stand beside Matt. The baby's eyes widen with surprise at this rough handling and her lower lip wobbles.

Leo turns away and blows his nose. *She really does think I'm mad. She thought I was going to run off with the baby.*

"Your things are on the table," says Bridget. "I picked your clothes out of the washing basket and put them in a separate bag inside."

"Thank you."

"Look, you don't have to go *tonight*," says Matt, and Bridget glares at him again.

Leo picks up the bag off the table. They realise they are blocking his way and step apart. He walks between them and through the front door without looking back.

"Where's all his stuff then?" asks Matt. "Is that *it*?"

"Yes, that's all he brought back here. He told me everything ended up in a skip. He wasn't on speaking terms with his father – but he didn't seem to want to tell me about it. I reckon him and his dad had some kind of bust up and his dad chucked all his things out of their mansion."

"But they've made it up now, haven't they? Do you reckon he'll go back to his folks tonight?"

"You sound like you care!"

Matt shrugs his shoulders. "Well, he seemed *okay*. The way you talked about him I thought he was a *right twat*."

"I had to make out he was – else you'd have been dead jealous about him being here."

"You sure you picked the right guy? His car hasn't gone past yet and there's no room to turn round. Shall I go and call him back?"

"Don't be stupid – it's *you* I want." Her voice wobbles. "He tried too hard to please me. The more I demanded, the more he gave ... and that just made me behave really badly sometimes –

just to see how far I could go. He brought out the worst in me somehow, whereas you bring out the best." The tears roll down her cheeks. "Are there any tissues left, or did he use them all?"

Matt goes to the kitchen. "Will kitchen roll do? There's only two bits left on this one – but he's put a new one out ready."

"See what I mean? He thinks of everything. He's turned me into a bit of a slob."

Matt returns to the front window. "I'm going to see what he's doing. Probably slashing my car tyres or something."

"Just leave it, Matt. He wouldn't do a thing like that."

"Well, that's what I'd do, if the glove was on the other foot."

Bridget laughs. It's good to be with someone who occasionally sounds a bit stupid. It makes her feel more in control. Leo always made her feel a bit thick – not deliberately – it was just the way they were ...

Still not taking any chances, Matt takes a small but sharply pointed kitchen knife from the cutlery drawer and puts it in his pocket, then walks down the street to his car. Leo's car is still parked behind with the engine running and Matt realises that the windscreen is iced over. He taps on the window on the driver's side and Leo tries to lower it but it is frozen shut, so he opens the door instead – the interior light revealing him snivelling into a bundle of tissues.

"What's up?" asks Leo. "Don't tell me she's changed her mind again."

"No, mate. Your problem is you're *too nice* for her. With women like Bridget – the wilful, demanding type, you've got to play it a bit *mean* to keep them interested."

Leo considers this. "Thanks for the tip – but if there were to be anyone else in my life – it would have to be someone who enjoyed being treated well."

Matt runs a finger over the windscreen and finds the wipers are stuck solid to the glass. He goes to his own car and returns with the can of de-icer. "Shut the door then. Nasty stuff this, if it gets in your eyes."

Leo laughs and shuts the door.

Matt taps the window again after a few squirts, and Leo opens the door. "You should be okay now, the wipers have loosened off."

"Thanks, I'll be off then. Good luck."

"Yeah, and you."

Away from the familiar neighbourhood, Leo has no idea which way to go. Back to Paddy? His old room at Mum and Dad's place is the obvious choice but he can't face going back there right now and having to explain yet another failure. He drives through a High Street without noticing the huge display of Christmas lights. He is in unfamiliar territory now - even though he is less than thirty miles from the area where he has spent most of his life.

He sees a signpost for a *Thames picnic area*, drives in, turns off the headlights and switches off the engine. At first he can see nothing but blackness – but then he sees the River, just a silvery thread to begin with but it seems to expand as his eyes adjust. He walks down to the waters' edge and finds there is a well-established riverside path, separated from the riverbank by a post and rail fence. Looking to the left he is mesmerised for a few seconds by the reflection of coloured flashing Christmas lights gyrating on the fast-flowing water. Looking to the right he sees only darkness. He turns right.

On account of it being so cold he covers a good distance quite rapidly before stopping and looking down into the freezing black water. Last time, the Thames had not been an appealing choice - but the water had been so much warmer then. Tonight, it should be fairly quick - surely it would - and it is conveniently here, in front of him. He feels chilled through already - so it shouldn't take long - and there is no scope to mess it up. His previous attempt had been so carefully planned – but the plan had failed. This time there is no plan.

He hears voices and steps back off the path and stands amongst the frosty bushes. A little dog on an extending lead rushes to say hello but gets dragged away by the couple who are walking him. Leo sees the man glance over his shoulder to make sure they are not being followed, and then they are out of sight.

He steps over the fence and stands on the edge looking down into the horrid freezing blackness of the Thames, feeling the force of its flow pulling him closer. He leans forward. Suddenly, the monkey that lurks in his mind jumps out in front of him and he wonders how poor David Walliams coped with diarrhoea in a wet suit during his epic swim of this filthy watercourse – then the mobile phone in his pocket beeps with a message and he steps back from the edge to read it. This is not as graphic as the previous messages; it is simply revolting; 'Want u so much. Don't care what sort of nasty lurgy I might catch off u.'

Uncle Theo. Leo has had enough – it had been funny and intriguing at first – but now he will block the number. Better still he will plunge the mobile into the water – as far down as he can sink it – and then jump in after it and follow it down to the depths where the water turns to mud. He raises it above his head to achieve the maximum downward thrust but slips on the ice and falls to his knees – the phone flying from his hand and almost slithering over the edge. He remains kneeling on the ice and clasps together his painfully cold hands, and sobs in despair ...

"Oh, Lord. If you really *do* exist – as my mother believes you do – then *please* don't let me ruin her Christmas."

A few moments pass and he watches the reflection of the silver moon shimmering on the black water and begins to feel less distraught. The phone startles him by beeping again and he snatches it away from the river's edge lest the vibration should carry it over. His hands are so cold that it takes some time to press the right buttons to display the message. He wipes a sleeve across his face and reads it: 'Catch ur cold I mean :>) xxx'

Leo shakes his head, struggling to make sense of this in his current state of anguish. He checks again to make sure this latest text is from the same number as the previous dirty messages. Whoever is sending these messages knows that he has a cold – but who knows about it other than Bridget and Matt? He selects the option to call the number.

"Leo!" It is almost a squeal.

"Who are you?" asks Leo.

"It's *me* of course. It's *Michelle*."

"Michelle!"

"Yes! Leo?"

"Yes ... *Michelle*?"

"What's that funny noise that sounds like ... like teeth chattering?"

"That's urm ... that's probably my teeth chattering. *Michelle* ... is it really *you*?"

"Yes, of course it's me. Where are you?"

"I parked the car somewhere and ... went for a walk."

"Leo! It's *minus eight* out there. Go back to your car *right now* and get the heater going – and then call me back."

He returns to the car to find the windscreen has iced over again already. He starts the engine, opens a new box of tissues and calls her number.

She answers immediately. "Warmer now?"

"I don't think I'll ever be warm again ..."

"Did you catch them *at it*, then ... Bridget and Matt?"

"As good as. They erm ... they're getting married on Christmas Eve."

"Oh, wow! Does that mean you're free tonight?"

"*Free*... How do mean?"

"Free to come and spend the night with me!" He doesn't answer, so she goes on; "I *love* you Leo – I always *have* done. Please give me a chance … I know I can make you happy."

When he still doesn't answer, her heart sinks. He simply doesn't fancy her but doesn't know what to say to let her down gently. She listens to the muffled sound of sniffing and nose blowing. “Leo? Are you still there?”

“Yes,” he says huskily and she realises he is fighting back tears. She hears a shuddering sigh, and when he is able to speak again, he says, “Michelle, you are so young and beautiful. Don’t waste your time on a miserable, screwed up wretch like me. I’m *damaged goods* and you deserve the best.”

“You *are* the best, Leo. You’re the reason I split with Darren so you must at least give us a chance. You’re not *permanently* damaged. I’ll *love* you better if only you’ll let me.”

“Oh, *Michelle* ...” He moves the phone away to blow his nose, then says hesitantly, “But … all those messages ... the content ... I’m struggling to equate – ”

“Leo! Please don’t try to *equate*. Just come and spend the night with me. Please? Have you got a sat nav?”

“Yes, there’s one in the glove compartment.”

“Get it out then.” She listens to some clattering and clunking. “Got it? Good.” She gives him a postal code to enter.

“According to this I’m just forty-seven minutes away.”

“Leo?”

“Yes?”

“Don’t be worried by my text messages. I just didn’t know how to get your attention – and I was inspired by this *dirty book* a friend gave me as a joke. *Please* come. Mum and Dad have had this huge corner bath put in that’s big enough for two. I thought we might start off with a deep hot bath in candlelight with ylang-ylang and take it from there. Does that sound okay?”

“Yes ... it sounds lovely ... only ...”

“Only what ...?”

“Well – not *all* the ideas in the texts sounded too bad – I’ll just have to re-read any that I haven’t deleted in a new context.”

“Sorry? What’s the *new context*?”

“The context of *you and me*, as opposed to Uncle Theo and some ... some *woman*.”

“Oh wow! There’s me trying to get some sort of response from you … and you thought the messages were meant for Theo - from one of those dodgy contacts he was glad to ditch!”
“Indeed … and there are certain things that you don’t like to imagine your old Uncle doing ...” She giggles down the phone and makes him smile. “But, I have to say, the hot tub sounds wonderful.”
“Then I’ll see you in about forty-seven minutes ... Don’t worry, Leo … everything will be okay. Forget the past – it only exists in your mind. Just *get* here!”